Love
the Wine
You're
With

ALSO BY KIM GRUENENFELDER

Keep Calm and Carry a Big Drink

There's Cake in My Future

Misery Loves Cabernet

A Total Waste of Makeup

Love
the Wine
You're
With

Kim Gruenenfelder

ST. MARTIN'S GRIFFIN

NEW YORK

LOVE THE WINE YOU'RE WITH. Copyright © 2017 by Kim Gruenenfelder. All rights reserved. Printed in the United States of America. For information, address St. Martin's Press, 175 Fifth Avenue, New York, N.Y. 10010.

www.stmartins.com

The Library of Congress Cataloging-in-Publication Data is available upon request.

ISBN 978-1-250-06674-9 (trade paperback)
ISBN 978-1-4668-7463-3 (e-book)

Our books may be purchased in bulk for promotional, educational, or business use. Please contact your local bookseller or the Macmillan Corporate and Premium Sales Department at 1-800-221-7945, extension 5442, or by e-mail at Macmillan SpecialMarkets@macmillan.com.

First Edition: June 2017

10 9 8 7 6 5 4 3 2 1

To Alex, Brian, and Dad

Acknowledgments

First off, I need to thank my fans for buying this book, even though it took me forever to write it. When my father died in July 2013, I was beyond heartbroken, and never thought I could write again. He was (and is) the voice in my head. The hole in my heart will never be completely filled. But I did write again, and I thank you all for your patience and support.

Next, I need to thank some ladies who, when I said I wasn't sure I could ever write again, just weren't having it. To Kim Whalen, my agent, and Jennifer Weis, my editor: thank you for standing by me and not letting me quit. Even though I tried. Twice. (Frankly, I'd have fired my ass a long time ago.) You both had way more faith in me and my work than I had in myself, and I cannot put into words how life changing that turned out to be.

Finally, thank you to my friends and family who helped me get through losing the first man in my life: Brian Smith, Alex Gruenenfelder, Patrick Bishop, Quinn Cummings, Cormac Funge, Lila Funge, Jeff Greco, Jeff Greenstein, Brian Gordon, Dorothy Kozak, Blake Masters, Missy Masters, Laurie Lehman, Marcelline Love, Nancy Redd, Carolyn Townsend, and (again) Kim Whalen: You took care of me in the weeks and months afterward in quiet and profound ways: making me tea, forcing me to eat, driving me places, singing "Oh Danny Boy," taking long walks with me, immediately picking up the phone in the middle of the night when I accidentally called, and coming to his funeral. I treasure you to a degree that would make your eyes roll. You made me feel loved and cared for at a time when I had absolutely nothing to give, and if weren't for you, I would not have moved on to write this book (or done very much else for that matter). At the time, most of you had already lost a parent: which is, to quote Missy, "The shittiest club in the world to be a part of." I will never be able to repay you—I will try like hell to pay it forward.

And as always, thank you, Jenn, Haley, Declan, Maibre, Rob, Carol, and Janis, and to all of my wonderful extended family and in-laws.

Oh! One more "Thank you!" to Brittany Ann Albaugh, for my wonderful title.

Love
the Wine
You're
With

Prologue

HOLLY

It is early evening, and I am at our dining room table with Jessie and Nat, pouring a flight of wines for us to taste. Nat has a pad of paper in front of her (how retro!) and has just crossed off another suggestion from her list. "Okay, Holly's idea, 'Once Upon a Wine,' is out, as is 'The Vintage Point.'" Nat looks over at Jessie as she continues, "You also killed my idea, 'Que Syrah, Syrah.'"

"Because we're not serving only one type of wine," Jessie pipes up defensively.

"Which is the same reason you didn't like 'Don't Get Me a Cab,'" Nat says as she crosses out another line on her page.

"No, I just found that one to be a passive-aggressive snipe about my taste in wine."

"I don't think it was passive . . ." I think aloud.

Nat continues reading from the elimination round. "Holly made a face at 'Wined-up Dolls.' And 'It's Ireland Somewhere' doesn't even make sense—they don't make wine in Ireland. Next."

My face lights up. "How about 'Corkscrewed'?"

"We are not putting the word 'screwed' in the name of our bar," Jessie tells me firmly.

"Why not? People will want to go there either because they already feel that way . . ."

"Too dark . . ." Nat says, shaking her head.

"Or they want to get—"

Jessie shuts me down with, "I'll give you a thousand dollars not to finish that thought."

I shrug, finish pouring a Meritage from the Central Coast of California, then watch quietly as Nat and Jessie take a minute to stare into space with writer's block.

Some days the Muse not only refuses to visit, she texts you to say she went to Cabo for the week.

" 'Pinot envy'?" I ask.

Nat winces. She absentmindedly runs her fingers through her shiny, dark brunette pixie cut as she stares off into space, thinking.

Jessie eventually snaps her fingers. "Oh. How about 'A Clean, Well-Lighted Place'?"

"You want to name the bar after a short story about the inevitability of death?" Nat asks, mildly horrified. "Why don't we just call it 'We're All Gonna Die. Everybody Drink'?"

Jessie's eyes widen. "Wait. That's what that story's about?"

"Yeah. Remember, the old man sits in a corner by himself getting drunk, and the young waiter with the hot wife waiting for him at home just wants to call it a night, and the middle-aged guy is all pensive because he knows he'll be the old man one day."

Jessie looks crestfallen. "Crap. How depressing. See, this is why we shouldn't read the classics at sixteen. No one should take AP English until they're thirty. How about 'Grapes of Wrath'?"

Nat narrows her eyes at her. "Honestly, would you ever go into a bar with the word 'wrath' in its name?"

"I would before I'd go to one with 'screwed' in its name," Jessie counters. " 'Grape Expectations'?"

"Do you want to know what that book's about?" Nat asks in an almost threatening tone.

"I'm gonna say no. 'Waiting for Merlot'?"

"I am seriously going to make you take an English class."

A bit later . . .

"'Something Fabulous'?" I throw out.

Nat juts her chin back and forth quickly, debating. "It's, like, it's good, but not great. I'll date that name, but I won't marry it."

"Oh! 'Nice Stems'?" Jessie suggests.

Nat begins doodling a flower on her pad. "We're a wine bar, not a florist. 'Hollywood and Wine'?"

"We're in Echo Park, not Hollywood," I point out.

And we're back to thinking.

And a while after that . . .

"'Eternally Grapeful'?" Jessie suggests. "'Who's Drinking Gilbert Grape'? 'Dinner Is Poured,' 'Wine Girls,' 'Wine Notes,' 'Quit Your Whining,' 'Winenot'? Snickers!"

"Snickers?" Nat repeats. "You want to name our place after a candy bar?"

"No, I'm getting snickers from both of you," Jessie snaps. "If I were to name the bar after a candy, obviously it would be 3 Musketeers."

Nat opens her mouth, but Jessie shuts her down before she can speak. "And don't tell me what that's really about, because no, I've never read it, and the only thing I know is, 'All for Wine and Wine for All.' And if you tell me they all die at the end, I'm just going to get upset and have to eat some Snickers."

Nat shakes her head. "Seriously. Next time you get the urge to watch Bravo, promise me you'll crack a book instead. The line is—"

"Wait," I tell Nat. "I think Jessie just came up with our name."

"I did?!" Jessie blurts out happily, her face glowing. "Oh, yay! Good for me! Which one was it? It wasn't the Gilbert Grape one, was it? Because actually I hate that one."

"'All for Wine, and Wine for All.' No matter who you are, and what you like, we will find a wine for everyone."

And, with that, we finally had our name.

Now all we needed to do was get the sign made, get it out on social media, finish redoing the ladies' room, move in the rest of the furniture, teach those two how to use a cash register, and pick some wines for opening night.

Three months earlier . . .

Chapter One

9:58 A.M.

Man, I love my job!

Not very many people can go to work every day feeling like this is exactly where they are supposed to be. As a kid growing up in San Diego, I had always dreamed of being a TV writer. And now, at thirty-two, I am the head writer for one of the top-rated game shows of the season. I even won an Emmy last year.

How many people can say they are excited to get out of bed in the morning? On tape days, I don't even hit the snooze button once.

I am standing at the judges' table on the set of the game show *Million Dollar Genius!* feeling fantastic in my new purple cashmere sweater. (At the beginning of a tape day, most people on the crew wear a sweater or a jacket, because the lights have not heated the place up yet, so the set is beyond freezing. I've been on sets in August watching a two-hundred-pound cameraman shiver in a wool peacoat.) I'm sipping a large vanilla cappuccino made especially for me by the craft services guy (who also made me my favorite bacon-and-cheese burrito earlier; gotta love tape days—Free food!) and am going over a few questions with our host, Cordelia Mumford, a beautiful former CNN reporter who accidentally got into game show hosting, and my producer, Marc Winslow, a handsome Brit who accidentally got into game show producing.

The contestants are still squired away in a soundproof greenroom in back, but we keep our voices low so that the audience can't hear us as we hunch over the table, poring over our scripts.

"Okay, we switched out the six-hundred-thousand-dollar question in this game so that we didn't have Kafka as the answer twice in the same week," I whisper to Cordelia. "Here's the new question." I point to a pink paper square that has been glue-sticked onto her white script, which she silently reads.

"As long as the answer is never Kardashian, I'm a happy camper," Cordelia quietly jokes.

I chuckle, then continue. "And by the way, for the million, it's the South Sea Bubble, not the South Seas Bubble. If they say 'Seas,' we're going to have to rule them wrong."

"Frankly, I think if they know the name of a market bubble from another country three hundred years ago, they deserve a million dollars," Cordelia tells me.

"That's because you're not from England," Marc, who's from London, politely tells her in his perfectly lilting English accent.

"No. That's because I spent my college days getting drunk and under an assortment of frat boys and football players. Far better use of one's time," Cordelia counters playfully.

"Yet here you are, the maven of American trivia," Marc says, rather flirtatiously.

"I know. Life's weird," Cordelia says, lightly folding her script in half and pulling away from our table. "Did I tell you that I got invited to the White House?"

"That's awesome," I say, surprised. "I didn't even know you were a fan of the president."

She leans in to me to cheerfully confide, "I'm so not. Plus, I was in the middle of a transcontinental move that year and couldn't even figure out where my polling place was." Then she walks to the middle of the stage and breaks into a huge smile as she booms to the audience, "Thank you guys so much for coming! We are going to have a great time today! Isn't our warm-up guy Jerry amazing?!"

Marc and I take our seats as judges while the contestant coordinator escorts the first three contestants to the stage. Cordelia walks to her podium, then stands patiently as the makeup artist presses her face with a powder puff and does "last looks," which is exactly what it sounds like—the last look the makeup person gives before Cordelia is ready for the camera.

I forget about work for a second to clear my mind, look around the room, and savor the moment.

There is no better feeling than being on a set right before a show begins. When all of the hard work is done: the writing, the rewriting, the arguing with your nerd staff about whether or not the average American knows the difference between the national debt and the national deficit, or explaining that Jean Patou was a French *parfumeuse,* not the inventor of pâté à choux pastry.

That moment when you get to just bask in the glow of a happy audience, a crew filled with people who worked their butts off to get to where they are, and that rare feeling of being exactly where you're supposed to be, working on something you'll want to be remembered for at your funeral.

Okay, that last point may be a bit dark. Let's just say rest home. I'll be proud of *Million Dollar Genius!* at my rest home.

I smile at Marc next to me, and rolling begins. The first assistant

director announces to the crew, "And we're on in . . . !" He puts up
his left hand and fans out his five fingers, "Five!" then ticks back one
finger at a time, "four . . . three!" and then he goes silent as he folds
down his ring finger for two. Then one. Then he points his index
finger toward the host.

"Welcome to *Million Dollar Genius!*" Jerry Winters, our show's an-
nouncer, belts out in his smooth baritone voice as Marc slips me a
sheet of paper. I open it with a serious look on my face, and read:

*You look so bewitching in that sweater. It makes your olive skin
glow. It's taking all of my self-control not to slide my hands under
it right now. And that red lipstick? I want traces of it smeared all
over my body from your kisses.*

I try to suppress a smile as I earnestly scribble a note back:

*Well, the only way your suit would look better is if it were beside
you in a heap on the floor.*

I fold the note and pass it back to him. Marc opens it to read. No
smile, just a stern note back:

*Meet me at the top level, northwest corner of parking lot two at
lunch.*

Oh, yeah. There might be one downside to my job. Small detail.
Hardly worth mentioning, really. I'm kind of, maybe, sleeping with
my boss.

Chapter Two

HOLLY

8:00 A.M.

I want to quit my job.

Actually, that's not true. I love my job—when I'm actually working. I'm an actress, and there is nothing more fun than being paid to spend the day flying around the set in a harness, or being outfitted by a costume designer in a seven-thousand-dollar sequined dress, or looking across a table at a love-struck George Clooney, who asks you to pass the salt.

But today my job is to get a job. Which sucks. Always, always, always. I wish I could be like that actor who said every audition is an opportunity, however short, to practice your craft. I'm thirty-two years old and have been working for fourteen years. I'm done. I'm ready to (a) start fielding offers or (b) win the lottery and retire.

I start today's round of auditions at six (fucking) A.M., because audition #1 is at eight A.M., but in Santa Monica, a city west of Los Angeles. I live with my roommate, Natasha, in Silverlake, which is a good hour from Santa Monica even in the best of traffic conditions.

Add drizzling rain, the usual frazzled commuters, and two lane closures for road work, and one must leave the house two hours early.

As if that weren't bad enough, it's for a commercial for a pharmaceutical where I have to look like a scientist, and where I've been told to "dress the part."

You tell me how not to look like an ass when you show up to a job interview in a white lab coat. (The same lab coat you've worn to at least twelve auditions, and one very weird second date.)

I don't know why the trend lately, but I'm half Asian, half Caucasian, and I seem to be getting audition after audition for "scientist" and "doctor."

Okay, I totally know why the trend. And the stereotype totally pisses me off. Although I suppose one advantage of being in my thirties is I'm now the smart scientist type. Once, in my twenties, a director gave me the most back-handed compliment when he said, "With your straight, black, 'shampoo commercial' hair, and porcelain"—(read: half-white)—"skin, you're like an approachable geisha."

Yeah, as opposed to all of those stand-offish geishas.

Anyway, a little before eight, I make my way to the ad agency, which is on the third floor of a mirrored building that looks like all of the other mirrored buildings in the area. I sign in at the reception area to let them know I'm there and try to pretend that I don't see twelve other Asian women, all dressed in lab coats, silently rehearsing their lines.

The receptionist hands me the sides, which is what we call the pages with the actor's lines on them. On the top of the first page is a word: XKLGGENZS. Judging from the rest of the script, I'm guessing that's the name of the drug they're selling. I resist the urge to ask to buy a vowel.

I sit down on a white pleather sofa and read through the script.

The first page is for a younger actress, who will play Sarah, my afflicted patient. What she is afflicted with, the script will not say.

My part, on page 2, starts out innocuously enough:

INT. LAB—DAY

JULIA, a handsome woman, older, approachable, tells us in her authoritative voice . . .

JULIA

But now, we women have options.

Then page 3 scares the shit out of me. Because over a shot of four beautiful young women laughing over cocktails (Sarah and her friends), I (the phony doctor) have a voice-over to warn consumers:

JULIA

(v.o.)

*Side effects include drowsiness, short-term memory loss,
decreased libido, stroke, depressed mood, dry mouth,
tinnitus, and death. Pregnant women should not take
Xklggenzs. If you have thoughts of suicide, please stop
using Xklggenzs and consult your doctor immediately.*

EXT. BEACH—MORNING

A glowing Sarah runs up to the camera to confide . . .

SARAH

It's time for a new start. It's time for Xklggenzs.

I quickly look up tinnitus on my phone: ringing in the ears. Seriously?

"Holly Graham." A curly-haired guy in a navy blue suit calls out, clipboard in hand.

I raise my hand and tell him cheerfully, "That's me." I gather up my things and make my way into the casting room, whispering to him as we walk in, "How do I pronounce . . . ?"

"x-KEL-ggenzs."

"x-KEL-ggenzs," I repeat.

"No, the second g is silent," he tells me, then raises his voice to announce to a roomful of executives, "This is Holly Graham. She'll be reading for the part of Julia."

I quickly survey the room to see who I'm playing to. In front of the floor-to-ceiling windows is a super-long table with twelve people seated to face me. Shades of Da Vinci's *The Last Supper*. In the center of the table, substituting for Jesus, is a video camera. While one of the execs stands up to run the camera, the man farthest to my left (I assume he's the casting director) says to me, "Can you state your name?"

"Holly Graham."

"Great. Now, Holly, can you read the side effects for me as quickly as possible?"

"Sure," I say, giving him a huge *I'm-a-team-player* smile. "Side effects include drowsiness, short-term memory loss, decreased libido—"

"Let me stop you right there," he says, putting up his palm. "You gotta go faster than that. I'm understanding every word you're saying."

"Absolutely. Thanks for the note," I say cheerfully. Then I begin again, rapid-firing it; "Side effects include drowsiness, short-term memory loss, decreased libido, stroke, depressed mood, dry mouth, tinnitus, and death. Pregnant women should not take Xklggenzs. If you have thoughts of suicide, please stop using Xklggenzs and consult your doctor immediately."

"Oh, my God. You sound sooooo bummed out when you say that," the executive the second from my right tells me. "Can you sound a bit more upbeat?"

As I talk about thoughts of suicide? I think to myself. Then I tell him, "Absolutely," and run through it again.

"Okay, now you're sounding too happy," the one woman executive in the room tells me. "How about something a little more authoritarian?"

This went on for five more read-throughs. If I'm supposed to be grateful to the universe for giving me this free opportunity to pursue my passion, I'd like to remind the universe that my passions also include ice cream and pretty much anything to do with Hawaii, France, or Ryan Gosling.

10:00 A.M.

I want to quit my job.

I should have been a dental hygienist. You never have to audition to clean out people's mouths.

Audition #2 of the day is a callback, meaning I have already auditioned for the casting director, and either she wants to see me again, or I get to audition for the director. After a snail's crawl commute down the 405 freeway to get from Santa Monica to the Valley, I make my way to soundstage three of the CBS Studios lot, where I see a line of stunningly beautiful women waiting patiently. Most of them are wearing shiny neon spandex from the 1980s.

Uh-oh. Before I get in the line, I quickly text my agent, Karen:

Hey—question about the NCI: Boise callback. Why is everyone in spandex?

I wait for Karen to text back.

Didn't I tell you to wear spandex?

No, I'm pretty sure I would have remembered that.

Hold on . . .

I wait about fifty feet away from the line of actresses while (I assume) Karen talks to her assistant. My friend Audra (who is also mixed-race Asian and Caucasian, so we frequently end up at the same auditions) spots me.

I put out the palms of my hands and lift my shoulders to mutely signal, *What the fuck?* She responds by shaking her head, then pretending to hang herself.

I love her.

My phone pings that I have a new text. Karen.

Apparently they want you to look like Jane Fonda.

They want an Asian-looking Jane Fonda? Would that be before or after she was in Hanoi?

Very funny. Why did you put "Hip-Hop Dance" under special skills on your resume?

**Because I'm desperate for a job. But
Jane Fonda taught aerobics in the 80s,
not hip-hop in the 90s.**

Pretty sure they don't know that.

Swell. I quickly head to a ladies' room to change into some (circa 2010s, very unshiny) yoga pants, then Google the term "Fly Girls" to get a crash course in hip-hop from the 1990s. The Fly Girls were a group of dancing girls choreographed by Rosie Perez and featured on the show *In Living Color.* Jennifer Lopez got her start dancing with them. On my phone, I check out a picture of her from that time—she looks nothing like Jennifer Lopez. Welcome to Hollywood.

Twenty minutes later, I clumsily manage the Cabbage Patch and the Running Man, then nearly break my neck while attempting a move with my leg that the choreographer should just call the Broken Clavicle. This is followed up by a dance that should be renamed, Learning to Ski at the Age of Fifty.

Needless to say, I don't think I got the part.

12:00 NOON

If I quit my job to become an Uber driver, would the amount of driving for work actually go down?

Audition #3 is on the Paramount lot in Hollywood, a short enough drive that I have time to hit Arby's, change out of yoga pants and into blue jeans in their ladies' room, then wolf down a large roast beef sandwich, potato cakes, and Diet Coke. All in less than five minutes. On my way out, I drive through for a ham and cheese with

Horsey Sauce, silently promising myself to hit the gym before seeing Nat and Jessie tonight.

Twenty minutes later, I am signing in at the next production front office, where I am handed my sides. Normally, sides look like this:

NORMAN
Can we speak to Mr. Huang?

RECEPTIONIST
I'll see if he's in.

Only for this audition, I am given a blank sheet of paper—except for one blue line drawn horizontally across the sheet.

I flip the sheet over, thinking the casting director's assistant must have handed me the sides upside down.

Nope, nothing but white on the other side.

I smile pleasantly at the receptionist. "I'm sorry, you just handed me a blank sheet of paper."

"Oh, did I?" she responds politely, looking over at the paper. Then she shakes her head. "No, that's right. You're Blue."

I can feel my lips scrunching toward my left ear, trying to figure this out, when my name is called. "Holly Graham."

"Here!" I pipe up nervously, then follow a puffy middle-aged woman with fried bleached blonde hair and long acrylic nails into a room where three men in suits sit at a table across from me.

"Okay, Holly is coming in as Blue," Bleachie announces to the men before taking her seat at the side of the table.

They all wait for me expectantly.

I stand in the middle of the room and stare back at them.

The man in the center seat of the table beams a cheerful smile at me. "Whenever you're ready. Just have fun with it."

"Okay," I say awkwardly, trying to study the blue line.

Crap.

I look up at the main guy and say, "If I could just maybe get a little direction here. If there were to be words on my script, what might they sound like?"

He laughs, and the other men laugh with him, half a second too late. "You are a riot. Karen said we'd love you. The whole point of our show is that it's unscripted. So say whatever Blue would say."

I nod, making sure to look him in the eye so that he can see that I'm totally getting where he's coming from. "And who am I in this script?"

"You're Blue," he answers with a flourish.

"Well, thank you for not making me calculus."

Polite laughs on their parts.

I try again. "What I meant is . . ." *How the hell else can I ask this?* "How do you see Blue?"

He nods, furrowing his brow as he ponders my deep question. "That is a good question." Then he turns to the man on his left. "Dave, how do you see Blue?"

"Well, obviously, she's female," Dave answers, then motions toward me, "And extremely hot."

Oh, yay me.

Then Dave shrugs. "I would say just play with it. Really make it your own."

Believe it or not, the audition went downhill from there.

12:45 P.M.

I think I'm never getting a job again.

The good news: My next audition is at 1:20 on the Paramount

lot, so I don't have to drive. I grab a cup of coffee at the commissary and go through my e-mails to learn that Xklggenzs has already passed on me, but am I interested in auditioning for a medical marijuana commercial? I e-mail back to ask if they want me to be pro or con? Not that it matters—I'll probably go in anyway. Sigh.

I waste some time texting Jessie.

Tell me again why it's bad to be an accountant?

**Pick one: Spreadsheet. Monotony. Nude
hosiery. Sensible shoes. (I can't find the emoji
for Munch's Scream.) Oh! And having to sleep with Kevin.**

I realize that I have accidentally texted my roommate, Nat, a game show writer, not our friend Jessie, the accountant. I point out to Nat . . .

I have to wear nude hosiery sometimes.

> **Yes, and your reward for that is you get to kiss a
> One Direction member as part of your day job.
> By the way, did you eat the rest of the Cheetos?**

**I did, and I'd do it again. Yesterday was brutal.
Today is worse. Plus, it paired well with the
double-chocolate Milanos you hid behind the
canned string beans.**

I hear a *ping* from my phone, alerting me to a text from Jessie.

> **Tell me again why it's bad to be an actress?**

1:10 P.M.

I walk in to my audition ten minutes early to have Marion, an assistant whom I know fairly well, look up at me from her desk and do a double take. I turn to get a gander at the room full of actresses I'll be competing against: They're all drag queens. I smile at Marion, silently wave good-bye, and see myself out.

"You're coming to bingo Monday, right, baby?" I hear from the waiting room on my way out.

"Wouldn't miss it, Roxy," I yell back to one of the ladies. "Just promise me you'll tell me I-29 at least once."

Six more hours until I'm sitting at the bar of Wine O'Clock with my friends, sipping on something from somewhere weird, and not having to pretend to be something I'm not.

Chapter Three

JESSICA (JESSIE)

8:00 A.M.

I want to quit my job.

Don't get me wrong: Staring at the Sexiest Man Alive (according to *People* magazine, not me) is not the worst way to spend a morning. It's just, you know, when he opens his mouth that we have a problem.

"So I'm a little unclear here . . ." I begin carefully. "You spent a hundred thousand dollars on a pair of shoes . . ."

"Two pairs of shoes," Justin Hayes corrects me, then proudly flashes me his big laser-whitened smile. "Pretty fiscally responsible of me, huh?"

I want to say, "They're shoes," in the driest way possible, but I decide to keep my job for at least two more minutes. "It's just that I'm wondering how such a purchase fits in with your goal to cut your expenses by thirty percent this year?"

Justin pulls out his phone and begins ignoring me to read his screen. "You should look happier, Jess. Clearly I've cut my expenses by fifty percent. I just told you, I got two pairs of shoes for the price of one."

I silently breathe in a cleansing breath, then continue. "Fair enough. Can we maybe agree not to spend any more money on shoes this year?"

He looks up from his phone. "When I win an eBay auction, that doesn't actually mean I won something, right?"

I'm afraid to ask. So instead I answer, "No. It means you were the highest bidder, and you now have to pay for whatever it is you bought."

Justin scrunches his lips so close that they disappear. "Hm." He shrugs, then pockets his iPhone. "So we'll have something to talk about next month. Do you have cookies?"

I give him a tight smile. "Sure." Then I press the intercom. "Jacquie, can you bring some cookies in for Mr. Hayes?"

"Are they vegan?" Justin asks me.

I push the intercom button again, wondering in that split second where my life went. "Jacquie can you bring us some vegan cookies?"

"What the hell are vegan cookies?" Jacquie asks through the intercom, not realizing she's on speaker.

Seriously, how can you live in Los Angeles and not know what a vegan cookie is?

"They're cookies without butter," I tell her. "Or eggs."

"Why would anyone eat cookies without butter?" she asks.

Justin knocks my hand out of the way so he can push the button. "Jacquie, honey, I made a mistake. I'm not vegan this week, I'm gluten free."

"So you want gluten-free cookies?" Jacquie asks.

"Yes."

"Then I amend my question: Why would anyone eat cookies without gluten?"

"I'm so sorry," I tell Justin. "She's new here and a little green."

"She's smoking hot. Do you think she'd go out with me?"

"Doesn't your wife frown on you dating?" I ask him.

He shrugs. "Not as much as you'd think."

Jacquie, 19 and a size 0, strides in and places a bag of (not gluten-free) Milano cookies on my desk. "These are the only cookies in the kitchen right now. Are Starburst gluten free?" she asks Justin, who turns to me for an answer (like I have any idea).

"Do you have a pot brownie?" Justin asks her.

Jacquie's face lights up. "In my purse! Let me go get it."

As she walks out, I return to my lecture. "Okay, so you can't live without super-nice shoes. What red-blooded American man doesn't feel that way? What if we got rid of your plane? You could be saving . . ."

"I can't give up my plane. Then I'd have to go through the regular airport."

"So?"

"So my wife might not exactly frown on my dating, but she does frown on TMZ taking pictures of me and my mistress coming back from Bora Bora. One-hundred-mile rule and all that."

"You have a mistress?" Jacquie says as she glides back in and hands him the brownie. "That's a shame. I thought you were hot."

Justin is unfazed by the rejection, turning away from me to check out Jacquie's backside as she returns to her desk. After she disappears, he turns back to me. "So, what other cuts can I make to my budget? Let's keep this ball rolling."

"Well, You own five vacation houses, each of which requires money for upkeep, insurance, etc. How do you feel about selling two of them?"

"Which two?" he asks me.

"Which ones are you not using as much?"

He looks up to think. "And by 'as much' you mean . . ."

"At all," I instantaneously rephrase. "Which ones are you not us-ing *at all*?"

Justin furrows his brow. "Okay, I'm definitely using the Miami house . . ."

"You don't own a Miami house . . ."

"Oh. Well, that's disappointing. Do I own one in Prague? I feel like I should own one in Prague."

"No."

"Should I buy one in Prague?"

"Please don't. Why don't we go over the five houses, and you can pick two to sell. Now the house in Bora Bora . . ."

Justin nearly spits out his brownie. "Wait! I have a house there? Damn! I have been wasting a LOT of money renting overwater bungalows. I mean, don't get me wrong, women LOVE overwater bungalows." He flashes me his sexiest smile. "If you know what I mean."

I nod wearily and try to smile back. "You leave little to the imag-ination."

Jacquie reappears. "I found gluten-free ham. Would that work?"

Justin turns to her. "Want to go to my house in Bora Bora before I sell it?"

While she makes a show of considering it, all I can think is, *This is going to be a long fucking day.*

9:00 A.M.

I want to quit my job.

"Time is of the essence here," Chad, my trust fund baby client (and yes, his name really is Chad), tells me in irritation. "I only have nine hundred and sixty thousand to last me until the end of the year. So what can I cut? Are there any charities I can get rid of?"

Dear Karma: Seriously—how can you explain this guy?

I look down at his list of bills, printed out in front of me. The guy gets several million dollars a year from his family, and yet he still can't afford to buy a house. I take a deep breath, and begin, "As you don't actually donate to any charities, Mr. Connors, I'm afraid eliminating that line from the budget doesn't do you much good. However, as I told you over the phone"—(when he called me at one in the morning during a bender in Vegas)—"If we're going to cut expenses, I think we should start with your cars . . ."

"Babe, I'm not taking the bus."

"I'm not suggesting that. But maybe you don't need *seven* cars."

"Oh, come on. None of them are that expensive. Why, I'm pretty sure I have a Prius in there."

His girlfriend's car, I'm betting.

"Fair enough," I say, suppressing a sigh. "What's a hyperbaric oxygen chamber?"

"How the fuck would I know?"

"I thought since you bought two of them last month . . ."

"Then obviously I need them," he says with a tone of disdain. Then he quickly reverses course. "I'm sorry, baby. I'm sure the girlfriend bought them as part of her healing regimen. She's got a private yoga instructor now too. Trying to be all Zen after I gave her a gift last month that was not graciously received."

"Did you give her flowers? Because you guys are spending an awful lot on—"

"I gave her something from Vegas. A little surprise I picked up that she was not happy with."

"Oh. Well, can she return it? Because the money—"

"It was a disease. I have this booty call in Vegas, and apparently she sees other dudes when I'm not in town."

I make a note on the list of bills. "Which would explain the ten-thousand-dollar cash withdrawal in Henderson . . ."

"She's worth it. Do you know what the girlfriend experience is?"

I look up. "She makes you miss football on Sunday to go anti-quing?"

"You're funny, Jess. Oh . . . but you should be proud of me here . . . she's totally comping me the next time I'm in town because of that . . . uh . . . gift she gave me."

"Clearly, she's a woman of character," I tell him as I scroll down more expenses. Then I ask. "Back to the flowers. You and your girl-friend are having four bouquets delivered twice a week from the most expensive florist in Beverly Hills."

Now Chad looks irritated. "Yeah?"

Deep breaths, Jessie. "Okay, well, for example, one of the bouquets, the peonies, cost six hundred and twenty-seven dollars. Now, if you could go for only having flowers delivered once a week . . ."

"Oh, please. These are minor changes. You might as well tell me not to go to Starbucks for a Venti Mocha. Give me a big item to cross off the list."

"Big item! You got it! You spent one hundred and twenty thou-sand dollars last month on 'entertainment.' If you could bring that down to even forty thousand a month . . ."

Chad pulls out his phone, pressing a button as he stands up to let himself out. "You know what? I'm late to a thing. You'll figure it out." As he walks out without so much as a good-bye, I hear him tell the person on the other end of the phone, "Linda. Send my ac-countant Jessica some peonies."

10:00 A.M.

I want to firebomb my building.

On the other side of my desk now sits Methuselah and his trophy wife, Tiffani, who's dressed like a sex doll, and dots her *i*'s with hearts. (I'm not being a bitch; her official signature has hearts on it. Okay, I am being a bitch—but how can I not be? Seriously!)

"So I understand why you paid for a reverse vasectomy," I tell Methus . . . Mr. Kennedy.

"He needed it so we could have children," Tiffani practically spits out at me.

"Of course. And mazel tov, by the way. I'm sure you'll make an amazing mother."

And he'll make an amazing great grandfather. Nope, need this job.

"Now what I'm unclear on is why you're still spending money every month on maintenance for sperm you froze in the 1990s."

Mr. Kennedy's eyes nearly pop out at me as Tiffani asks me, "What does that mean? Maintenance on sperm he froze?"

I nervously look over at Mr. Kennedy. He pleads with me with his eyes. I take a deep breath and tell her, "My mistake. It's just a medical expense."

"Daddy Issues" turns to her husband. "This is why we need a man accountant. She doesn't understand what a medical expense is."

"Mrs. Kennedy, I assure you that any accountant in the city will tell you that Juvederm and Botox injections are not medical expenses . . ."

"But I need them for my job."

"Oh. Are you working?"

"Yes. I'm his wife. I have to look good for his client dinners."

Methuselah closes his eyes, lowers his chin, and appears to drift off to sleep.

11:00 A.M.

I wonder if it's too late to get into hooking? Nah. I'd still have to deal with the Chads and the Methuselahs of the world.

My next client comes in with a full-on crew: including a director of photography (DP), lighting guy, gaffer, and two hair and makeup people.

Oh, and a director. Who, as the gaffer and DP set up lights around my office, tells me, "So the feeling here is *aspirational*. I need you to let the audience know how rich Gretchen is without actually saying it."

Did I mention that my client is a reality star known mostly for a sex tape she made before marrying a sitcom star? Or maybe she made the sex tape with a famous sitcom star and then married her husband? Or her dad defended a famous murd . . . Well, anyway, only in L.A. could an accountant come back from a secret donut and two-minute coffee break to a lighting crew and a guy putting black tape on her carpet and showing her her mark.

"But she's not rich. She declared bankruptcy last year," I point out to the director. Then I turn to Gretchen and say gently, "You do know you're not rich, right?"

Before she can say anything, the director says, "Love it! So just talk to Gretchen like you would any other client who's wasting money. Maybe give her a lecture, so our viewers can feel superior, yet make it clear this is how she lives, so they can want to be like her."

I think I can manage that.

Is it too early to start drinking?

Chapter Four

JESSIE

I'm going to guess we're not really having a fight over the color beige.

"I hate beige," my boyfriend, Kevin, whispers to me, so as not to be heard by our real estate agent. We are staring at the beige Formica counters in what will soon be our new kitchen. In what will, in just a few weeks, be our new home.

Okay, I will admit, the counters are a special kind of "Yikes!" No doubt from the back of a van "closeout special" from 1986. I'm surprised it doesn't come with a Nagel poster at no extra charge. But that's no reason not to buy a house.

"And I hate orange," I whisper back, making sure I keep my voice calm and soothing, "with the fire of a thousand suns, which is ironic, since they would be orange. And all of the tiles in the guest bathroom are orange. But I don't care. Because we can replace these counters and rip out those tiles. Haven't you ever seen HGTV? Entire shows are made about ripping out tiles and counters."

"You sound frustrated," Kevin whispers back.

Gee, Kevin, ya' think?! I scream in exasperation. But only in my head. From my mouth comes an exceedingly calm, "We've been looking at houses for six months. This is the best one we've found. The offer's been accepted. We did it. Yay."

Kevin sighs as he rubs his fingers over the stained counter. "At least with orange you have a color that presents itself: 'I'm orange. Deal with it. Like me or hate me, it's who I am.' Beige, on the other hand, says"—he switches to a whine—"'I can't make a decision. I'm just going to sit in the corner with the lights out and be the most boring color on the planet.'"

"It's just a counter."

"It's not just a counter. It's a compromise. And I don't want to compromise. It's bad enough I'm an accountant. Do I also have to be an accountant who comes home to a beige kitchen every day?"

Kevin's face is so contorted, he looks like he's in physical pain. I sigh and try to decide how to deal with his latest freak-out. (A quick lesson to you singletons out there: Just because a man's calm does not mean he's not freaking out.)

How'd I get myself into this hideously uncomfortable moment in my life?

The way so many uncomfortable moments start for a woman in her thirties: with someone else's wedding.

Six months ago, during a three-day weekend in Napa for a friend's wedding that wasn't the least bit fraught with, "Why isn't it us?" (right—you show me a woman who has been with a guy for over two years who is not secretly upset at another woman's wedding, and I'll show you a unicorn), Kevin got a bit giddy one night on too much champagne and suggested we start looking at houses.

That night, he gave me lots of great reasons for us to pool our resources and buy: Interest rates were still low, we could find a nice fixer-upper three-bedroom in an up-and-coming neighborhood. Since we're both accountants with stable jobs who are relatively frugal with money, why keep wasting thousands of dollars per month on two rents, when we could be investing in our futures with one mortgage payment? His hypothesis was completely logical—and not the least bit romantic.

What I heard was, "I'm ready to get married! Let's test the waters with a house. And let's make sure we have a second and third bedroom for our laughing babies."

The rest of the weekend became wildly romantic, and the following weekend, we began looking at houses.

Ew. Shopping for houses is the exact antithesis of romantic. It's one of those moments where your dream of where you want to be in your life crashes down like a tidal wave onto where you actually are. Kevin found problems with every single home. One house had no air-conditioning. One condominium had enclosed hallways ("I'm not spending the next twenty years of my life smelling Grandma Rosa's old spaghetti sauce from 2005"). One town house only had one parking spot. Some places were too expensive; others required too much fixing up. I was beginning to think I would be in rental and dating limbo forever. And I would never say it out loud, but I was starting to resent him for wasting every weekend of my life not moving us forward.

Then, just yesterday, we finally found the perfect home. It had been owned by the same couple for fifty-five years. After their mother died, the kids wanted to sell quickly. The house hadn't even gone on the market yet, but our Realtor knew their Realtor. The sellers were asking at least sixty thousand below market value, provided we make them an offer immediately. It had three bedrooms. Yes, one bedroom had two burn holes shaped like an iron that melted through the most hideous bronze carpet you've ever seen, another had a giant gold bathtub in the middle of the room (and cherubs peeing hot and cold running water), and the third smelled like a yeast infection. But the living room was huge, the walls had sconces, and it was up in the hills of Highland Park, with an amazing view of the city.

I was ecstatic. Kevin less so. But we made an offer on the spot for the asking price, and they accepted.

And now, less than twenty-four hours later, here was Kevin, standing in the middle of our soon to be beige kitchen, about to argue that we should keep looking.

"I just think we should keep looking," he says predictably. "We haven't put any money into escrow yet, and this is our last chance to back out."

I inhale a deep breath and try to stay calm. "I can have new counters put in the week we move in. Pick whatever color you want. Hell, at this point, you can pick orange."

"You mean the week *you* move in," Kevin corrects me. "I'm in Frankfurt for work starting next month. Do you really want to be going through the hassle of buying a house, plodding through all the subsequent paperwork, then moving, all by yourself?"

YES! I want to scream. *I'm desperate to move forward with my life. And if not now, when?* But instead all I can squeeze out is a defeated, "Okay."

I utter a lot of defeated "okays" lately.

Sometimes I say them aloud (like now), but mostly I say them to myself every day when responding to my inner monologue.

Innermost thought: *You can't take that pottery class. You don't really have time for it, and you'd suck anyway.*

"Okay."

You don't need to go to Italy this year. Venice will still be there next year, and by then you'll have more money to enjoy it.

"Okay."

Kevin's the best you're ever going to do. And if you don't agree with him, he'll leave you over this.

"Okay."

Half an hour later, Kevin is driving me back to my office. I stare out the passenger's window, in a daze, watching house after house on the hill whizz by.

"Are you mad at me?" Kevin asks gently.

Mad? That's the wrong word. He breaks my heart every day, but I'm not *mad* at him. I'm not anything anymore. I used to get mad when he wouldn't talk about marriage; now I'm just deadened to it.

Defeated.

It's like, every day that we don't buy a house and move in together, and every day that he doesn't propose, or talk about kids, he wins the fight. And I lose the fight.

It's not a yelling, crying, throwing things kind of fight, it's much quieter. But make no mistake—this is a fight. One of the biggest fights a couple can have.

And after almost an entire year of losing the battle and feeling emotionally beat up every single day, I'm no longer angry. I just have no fight left in me. I want to limp off the battlefield and head back to my castle to lick my wounds.

After several moments of silence, I finally lie to him with a succinct, "No."

Sensing he's not on solid ground here, Kevin asks, "Do you understand why I think we just need a little more time?"

To which I say, "Sure."

But really, of course not! And if he knew me even vaguely he would know that all that is racing through my head right now is, *Time. How much time? A week? A year? Another three years?*

Up until this point, I have never understood women who gave

their boyfriends ultimatums: As far as I was concerned, if a guy didn't want to be with me, I didn't want to be with him. And why would I want to have a wedding with a guy who had been strong-armed into it?

And yet . . . Three years is a long time. At what point will he realize that I won't wait around forever? And will he ever realize it on his own, with no prodding from me? Is an ultimatum really strong-arming someone? Or is it just a clarification of what everyone wants in life? "I want to be married. You either do or you don't. And if you don't, well . . . Peace. I'm moving on."

Kevin takes my hand and kisses it lightly. "Can I take you to dinner? Anywhere you want."

"Thanks, but I can't," I tell him apologetically. "I'm meeting Nat and Holly at Wine O'Clock tonight. The owner sold it, and tonight's the last night it will ever be open."

"Right. I forgot," Kevin says softly. "I love you," he reminds me.

"I love you too," I answer back, almost by rote, as I watch a little white house on the hill pass by my window.

I wonder who lives in that house. Is it some couple who decided six months into their relationship that they wanted to be together forever? Is it some fifty-year-old bachelor who was never able to make a commitment, and he still rents, because he'll never grow up? Is it a single woman who one day said to herself, "Fuck it! I don't need to be married to own a house"?

I turn to Kevin. He looks sad. Which I feel bad about, even though it's not my fault. "You can come with us tonight if you want," I tell him, hoping to God he doesn't take me up on my offer.

"No. It's your girls' night," he answers. "I get it. Besides, I have some work I should finish up tonight. Make up for my long lunch hour and all that."

"Okay."

More silence in the car.

"When I get back from Frankfurt—"

"I know," I say, cutting him off.

"It's only four months . . ."

"I know that too."

Kevin stops talking.

Just propose, I think to myself. *Let me know that I'm the one. That it's not me, it's the house. That I'm enough. That I deserve to get my wedding and my two kids and my trip to Italy for our honeymoon. And, yes, my home. Our home.*

I force a sad smile toward him. He forces an awkward smile back.

And don't do it because I prodded. Do it because you want to marry me. Do it because you're ready.

"There's an open house I'd love to go to Sunday, over in Silver-lake," Kevin says. "I figured we could go to brunch afterward."

The smiling is starting to hurt. "Sounds great," I say, trying to drum up some enthusiasm.

And the holding pattern continues. Today, once again, he wins.

Chapter Five

NAT

How the hell can a thirty-two-year-old woman explain still having sex in the back of a car?

Okay, if I were happily married with a couple of kids, I suppose that could be cool and retro. But I'm not, so it isn't. Although I am doing it with a married man.

And yes, I frequently hate myself. And yes, I'm an idiot.

Just like every other woman who ever has dated a married man. Because we're all idiots, and I'm the first to admit it (admitting it is the first step to recovery, right?).

Marc is charming, handsome, and athletic (but not annoyingly so), and has the sexiest accent on the planet. Actually, French is probably the sexiest, but British is a close second. Marc went to Cambridge, and listening to him is kind of like listening to Prince William speak.

Of course, also like Prince William, he's married.

Sigh.

So, how the hell did I get myself into this mess?

It started as a harmless crush. I am the head writer for *Million Dollar Genius!* (can't forget the !), a game show known for its difficult trivia questions and ridiculously high cash prizes. Last year, a woman won three million dollars in the time it took for us to tape four episodes. She was able to name the seventeenth president off the top of her head (Andrew Johnson), as well as the date of his inauguration (April 15, 1865), the numbers on the hatch from *Lost* (4, 8, 15, 16, 23, 42), and the first thing ever bought on eBay (a broken laser pointer). I can't remember where I put my keys on a good day, or where I stashed my birth control pills on a bad day.

Marc (with a *c*—I love that!) brought the show over from England two years ago and recruited me from another trivia show, where I swear I had men—good-looking, smart, *nice* men—surrounding me all day, and was never the least bit tempted. I promise I'm not usually a slutbag. This is so not like me.

I left my other job because Marc offered me a promotion with a better salary, better benefits, and a better contract. It had nothing to do with his clear emerald-colored eyes, his contagious smile, or his hug-inducing chest. Or his suits. He wears really fantastic suits. While most creative types in Hollywood seem to live in jeans, Marc wears tailored Savile Row suits on days when we tape the show. (Why is it that American men don't know that when a man looks good in a suit, the sight of him coaxes most women into thinking about how to get him out of said suit?)

Anyway, so yes, I did notice the eyes, the face, the body, the clothes, the accent, the wicked sense of humor, the charm, the intelligence, and his rather citrusy cologne that first year. But I also noticed the wedding ring, and that was enough to keep me from getting too close. We were friends for almost a year before anything got dangerous.

And we became good friends. He was smart. Funny. And thoughtful. He'd do things like bring me my favorite sandwich from Canter's Deli on a regular day (ham and Swiss on wheat, lettuce, and tomato only), and my favorite bottle of wine after a really stressful day. (And, okay, so maybe he routinely brought me a bottle of *his* favorite wine, not mine. But his favorite is Opus One, and if I could afford it, that could totally be my favorite wine.)

So, yes. We became good friends. But *just* friends.

Which wasn't a problem until I tried to fall asleep at night and couldn't help but dream about kissing him. Torturous as those thoughts were, they were also glorious: I could imagine exactly where we would be the first time he kissed me, and how it would feel. Those fantasies worked better than Ambien to send me off to a blissful night's slumber.

I would rationalize that they were just harmless daydreams (night-dreams? wet dreams?). I would tell myself that it's human nature to fantasize about someone at night, even someone you know. Really, what was the difference between thinking about Theo James, whom I don't know, or Marc, whom I do know? They're just thoughts, right? I've also thought about eating a pound of pasta followed by an entire cheesecake, that doesn't mean I will. Okay, bad example: I totally did that last week. But the point is there's nothing dangerous about what swims around in your head, as long as you don't act on it.

That was the lie I told myself at the time. Again, I know I'm an idiot.

So it started out with my thinking about kissing Marc. Just a fantasy about one little kiss. No sex, no making out, just a kiss. I just wanted to know how it would feel to kiss him.

And I'll admit, the obsession crept into my work life. I stopped eating in front of him, because butterflies flew into my stomach every time he walked into the room. During morning run-throughs, I laughed a little too hard at his jokes, and everyone else's jokes, because I was giddy with infatuation. And when he brought me wine, I invited him to join me in a glass at my desk.

He always did. Then usually a second. One night, we nursed the bottle until midnight, talking about everything and nothing for hours.

Then he walked me to my parking space, gave me a rather awkward hug good night, and watched me get into my car and drive away.

That was the first night I started wishing I could go back in time to when I was twenty-four, and he was still single. I made up entire scenarios in my head of how we would have met in a pub on my trip to London, or when he visited the States while studying abroad his junior year in college.

Talk about crazy thoughts.

Then, on the night of my thirty-first birthday, some thingama-bob switch on the set stopped working, and the crew and staff had to stay until eleven o'clock taping the show (we're normally out by six). Afterward, Marc asked if I "would allow" him "to buy [me] a drink on this most dreadful of birthdays."

I said, "Sure."

Frequently after we wrap our shows for the week, I go with several members of the staff to this sports bar down the street from the lot: It's loud, very well lit, very casual. I just assumed Marc would take me there.

Nope. The bar Marc took me to that night was dark, elegant, and romantic. Instead of a sound system blaring old AC/DC, a three-piece band quietly played jazz. And it was just the two of us who went.

We sat in a corner booth. I felt underdressed, but Marc told me several times how beautiful I looked. I flirted more than I should have. He told me stories that had me bursting out in fits of laughter, and he looked into my eyes when I told my stories, really listening.

I hadn't felt like that on a date in years. I didn't even know I could still feel like that—part of me was worried that after all of the years of bad dates, boring dates, and "S'up?" texts at two A.M., I couldn't feel much of anything anymore.

Around one, Marc leaned in and lightly kissed me on the lips.

It. Was. Amazing. Soft, sweet, perfect. My lips actually tingled.

Naturally, I reacted by saying, "I'm sorry. That shouldn't have happened." Then I grabbed my purse and bolted out the door.

As I ran away, I heard my phone ping in my pocket. I stopped running to my car to check it. Marc had texted:

Come back. I can't leave until I pay the check.

I immediately typed back:

Absolutely not. See you in the morning.

Then I continued on to my car. But I had stopped running. Naturally, my phone beeped another text:

I'm sorry. I promise not to kiss you again.

> **You didn't kiss me, I kissed you. And I'm the one who's sorry. It'll never happen again. I'll see you tomorrow.**

I kissed you. And I take full responsibility for it, even if it gets me fired for sexual harassment.

I stopped walking and stood in the cold, staring at that text for at least three minutes. It was exactly what I wanted to hear, and exactly what I didn't want to hear. I didn't know how to respond.

So he upped the ante.

I'm falling in love with you.

I leaned against a streetlamp, unsure of what to say to him, or what to do next. Barely remembering how to breathe. I had dreamt of kissing him so many times, but at no point did I ever dare to dream things could go this well.

Or this badly.

What was I doing?

After what seemed like a year, my phone beeped a fifth text:

You're not responding.

Fuck. Of course I wasn't. What was I supposed to say? Finally, I slowly typed back:

Don't say things like that. You're freaking me out.

Come back.

About a minute later, I was still staring at my phone when Marc magically appeared by my side. I looked up at him and said, "I don't date married—"

But he pulled me into his arms and kissed me, and I turned to jelly.

We spent the next three hours kissing like teenagers in my car and admitting that we thought about each other all the time. I warned him that this was just for tonight, that we would never go any farther, that I wasn't going to be one of those stereotypical mistresses who waited for a married man to leave his wife.

For the next two weeks, we stole kisses in each other's offices during the day and made out with our clothes on for hours in my car at night, with me breaking up with him the entire time.

Then we slept together.

And I've been hoping he'll leave his wife ever since.

"Are you all right?" Marc asks me gently, bringing me back to the present as he kisses my neck, a postcoital gesture I still find irresistible. "I seem to have lost you."

"I'm just thinking about Game 245," I lie. "We have a question about Sun Tzu that might be too esoteric even for our contestants. I think I need to switch it out," I say, killing time while I stare at the ceiling of his Mercedes. "Speaking of contestants, I have got to talk to the contestant coordinator about getting some prettier women. Seriously, he seems to think that women can either be pretty or smart, but not both."

Marc begins lightly stroking my hair. "Well, I think you've disproved that once and for all," he tells me flirtatiously.

I don't respond, instead continuing to stare up silently as he strokes my hair. "You're very sexy, you know," Marc continues. "There is something so wicked about having sex in a car."

Marc leans in to give me one of his elastic melting kisses. I kiss him back distractedly. Marc pulls back, squinting at me. "Are you sure you're all right?"

"Actually, I was thinking about your wife," I tell him apologetically.

Marc pulls away and sits up straight. "Hello."

"I know she's in London," I begin. "And I know you guys say you have an open marriage. But I'm starting to feel guilty again."

"Darling, we've been through this."

I put up the palm of my hand and give him an all-business, unemotional, "I know. I'm not telling you to leave her. I'm just having a moment. It'll pass."

Which sounds a little cold. But in my defense, I never ask him, "Where is this going?" or "When are you leaving her?" or plead, "Pick me! Pick me!" Because I'm a grown-ass woman, I already know where this is going: nowhere. I know when he's leaving her: never. And I know he will never pick me. So if there are moments when I seem cold, it's only because if I don't keep up those walls, my whole emotional world might crumble.

Marc looks pained. "Can I take you dinner tonight? We could head to that seafood restaurant you love with the view of the Pacific? Or that Italian place you like with the gnocchi?"

"I can't," I tell him as I sit up. "I'm seeing Holly and Jessie tonight."

Marc nudges me with his head like a cat. "Lobster risotto," he tells me in a tempting lilt.

"Sorry. Remember the place I told you about in Silverlake, Wine O'Clock?"

"The wine bar?"

"Yeah. Wine O'Clock's owner sold the place for, like, a bazillion dollars to some chain, and tonight is the last night the place will ever be open. Plus, Jessie and Kevin bought a house, and we're going to celebrate that. Kind of a whole end-of-an-era night."

"So is Kevin coming?" Marc asks hopefully, hoping to wing an invite. He's constantly trying to get invited to my events, and I'm constantly thwarting him. Bad enough I'm with a married guy—why flaunt it?

"No. Just us girls tonight," I tell him.

Marc looks hurt.

"Don't give me that look," I implore teasingly. "I've been with you every night this week."

"But Elizabeth comes to town tomorrow," he whines. "And I won't get to see you for nine whole days."

"Is that an argument in your favor? That your wife will be visiting?" I ask, trying to make the statement sound light and breezy.

Marc juts out his bottom lip. I can't help but smile. "Stop that. You'll still see me during the day at work. Come on. We should go back. We start taping again in half an hour."

And the two of us rearrange our clothes, drive his car back to work, and head back onto the set five minutes apart.

Sad emoticon.

Chapter Six

4:00 P.M.

Do you think people know when they're about to snap? Do you think it's like a snowball rolling down a hill that just gets bigger and bigger, until the ball is the size of a truck, and it's about to bitch-slap the next idiot who stumbles across its path?

Because my snowball idiot is sitting across from me at a table with his assistant, his commercial casting director, and some assorted randoms.

Ah, famous (infamous?) commercial director Joseph Chavez. How can I describe this guy? Talented? Very. Although you gotta wonder how much the people surrounding him pay for that kind of laser focus at work. Ridiculously handsome. Like, to the point where you're almost annoyed with him. His driver's license would merely describe him as a six-foot-two guy with dark brown hair and blue eyes. But that's like calling a Stradivarius a fiddle. I always wonder where in the world you find that glowing olive skin contrasting with electric blue eyes.

Personality? Ah. Here is where we hit the problem. A friend of mine who has auditioned for him on numerous occasions once described it as "does not suffer fools gladly." I think that's being generous. I would describe him as a raging narcissist, with a streak of OCD and a personality that can only be described as "chafing."

But I am a fan of his work, and I need this job.

So I close my eyes and let the world drift away . . .

Breathe, Holly. Take your time. Find your center. You are here to act. In this moment, you are an actress. Nothing else matters.

I open my eyes and burst into a dazzling smile. I lean into the casting assistant and tell her in a conspiratorial, yet excited, voice. "I'm wearing one right now."

"A diaper?" the casting assistant reads from her script in a deadened tone.

"Not a diaper, an adult undergarment!" I answer with a tone of voice normally reserved for finding unknown ice cream in the freezer. "Designed by NASA for discretion."

Before I launch into my lawyer-inspired monologue about how the product is not intended for use during periods (as you would when having lunch with a friend), I look over to see the director doesn't even know I'm in the room. He's too busy reading his phone screen and pensively thumb-typing back. The casting director nervously glances at him to glean a reaction of any kind.

Type, type, type.

I stare at the director, anger and hatred starting to simmer in my stomach. Yes, it's a crappy audition for a crappy product (no pun intended), but I drove forty-five minutes in bumper-to-bumper traffic to be here and get to act for forty-five seconds. His people called me, which means he called me, not the other way around. The least he could do is acknowledge me.

I watch the guy purse his lips as he reads the response on his screen, then thumb-type again onto his phone.

I slowly put down my script and lean in across the table, so my face is mere inches from his. "You've hit your breaking point, haven't you?" I ask him calmly. "That moment when you just can't take it any longer."

The director looks up from his phone, surprised to discover there is someone else in the room. "I'm sorry?"

"Yeah, you are," I agree. I interlock my fingers and let my chin rest on my hands as I look him right in the eye. "When you were a kid, you dreamed of becoming a director, didn't you?"

A bit startled, the guy looks around at his staff for a save. He gets dead-eyed boredom in response. I take that as a sign to continue. "It was all you ever wanted to do. I'll bet you spent hundreds of hours in your parents' living room, studying every detail of every Hitchcock, Scorsese, and Kubrick film you could find. The lighting, the sound, the camera angles each one chose."

The director slowly puts his phone down and stares at me. "Yeah," he admits suspiciously.

"And you kept studying," I continue. "And you started sacrificing. And when everyone else went to Europe after college, you took out student loans and went to film school. Then, when everyone else started moving in together and looking at rings, you stayed single, free from distractions, and spent every last dime you could get your hands on finishing your next short film. Maybe even maxing out a few credit cards along the way."

The douche bag widens his eyes at me like I have a crystal ball and just successfully guessed his weight, age, and third-grade crush. But then his tone of voice makes it clear that I am a piece of gum to be scraped from his shoe as he asks, "Where exactly are you going with this?"

"You had three roommates, a clunker that barely ran, and debt so high you didn't know why anyone would be stupid enough to loan you money in the first place. But you were a *director*. They weren't. You were sacrificing for your dream. And one day all of that hard work and sacrifice would pay off. You'd have your Academy Award, your hot wife, a couple of gorgeous kids who look just like her, and your house on the beach."

Now I have captured his attention. The guy considers my statement as though it were a question, "Well, I'm not sure if I thought—"

"And here you are, after all of those years of study, loneliness, and sacrifice, directing an adult-diaper commercial. Living the dream, huh?"

He's about to counter my statement, but I shut him up with the palm of my hand. "Tonight's going to suck for you, Joe. Because you're gonna go home and you're gonna be up half the night realizing what a waste of time your life has been lately. And that being an asshole doesn't make you an auteur, it just makes you unhappy, and it makes everyone around you miserable. It's time for a change, Joe. And as you stare at the bottom of your scotch glass tonight, you're gonna think about me, and you're gonna wonder, 'What do I need to change?' Well, the first thing is, when someone's talking to you, get off your fucking phone and listen. You might learn something."

I pick up my purse and leave.

Oddly enough, no one follows me.

Chapter Seven

HOLLY

"You just waltzed in and announced to one of the most successful commercial directors in town that he has wasted his life. What the hell is wrong with you?!" Karen, my agent, yells at me over the phone.

"Me? What the hell is wrong with *you*?!" I counter at the same decibel. "Who sends a thirty-two-year-old client out on an audition for adult diapers?"

"They were going for a younger demographic."

"You know what's a younger demographic? Babies. Seriously, I don't want to tell you how to do your job, but you need to be putting me up for younger things. There's got to be some happy medium between auditioning for parts as the college coed and going out for the teenager's mom. Or, in this case, grandmother!"

"Have you thought about starting a Botox regimen?" Karen asks me matter-of-factly.

"A regimen? I'm sorry, is Botox the new yoga?"

"Actually, yoga wouldn't be a bad idea either," Karen continues. "Let's face it: Your ass isn't as tight as it used to be."

"Wow. This coming from the woman who once hiked Runyon Canyon with me while sipping from a water bottle filled with vodka."

"I don't have to look fantastic every minute of the day—I'm not an actress," Karen points out. "No one's paying me to look great. I could wear battleship gray sweatpants from the '90s to work and have wrinkles as deep as trenches between my brows, and still have a job. You, on the other hand, are . . ."

Karen's voice trails off. I drive about ten feet on the clogged freeway before I prod her. "I, on the other hand, am what?"

I can hear a sigh on her end of the phone. "Holly, I love you. You're an amazing actress and one of my favorite clients. But you're not the dewy-faced ingénue I signed twelve years ago. It's not just time to think about going out for older roles, it's also time to think about what's next in your life. The time for you to be Hot Girl #3 is over. And that's not necessarily a bad thing."

The Prius in front of me moves up all of six inches. I put my foot on the accelerator and scoot right up to his bumper to keep any commuters from sneaking into my lane.

And I silently wonder how I got here.

Karen's voice softens. "I can keep putting you up for Mom auditions, and middle-management corporate roles, and you will book some of them. But only if you don't yell at the director."

I take a pinched breath. "Okay."

Karen continues patiently. "No, it's not okay. Hollywood is notorious for its age discrimination, and it sucks. I'm fifty—I get it. But at some point, you have to come to terms with who you really are."

"You don't mean who I really am," I correct her. "You mean how other people see me."

"How people see you is who you really are," Karen argues. "Look, I gotta go. I almost forgot, good news: You booked the part of the madam on that detective show."

Ugh. "I got a callback for the part of the escort," I remind her.

"Well, that's a step up, when you think about it. Who really wants to play a hooker? I'll call you Monday with the dates."

And she hangs up without so much as a good-bye.

I click off my Bluetooth and stare into the sea of cars blocking my way.

This is so *not* what I need today. But Karen's reaction was actually pretty tame for what I did.

And I admit my outburst was a little nuts. But my day has been hideous. Plus I've earned the right to be a little nuts for a while.

"Nuts" is probably the wrong word to be popping into my head. Or maybe it's a deliciously politically incorrect word for me to have in my psychological toolbox—I'm not sure.

A little backstory.

Six months ago, my father died from an overdose of an antidepressant that he had been happily taking for years. He was over sixty and should not have been taking more than twenty milligrams per day. His doctor had him on fifty milligrams. And slowly, the medicine built up in his system and killed him.

Up until six months ago, I didn't even know that you could die from a toxic buildup of antidepressants, and I certainly didn't know you could die from only fifty milligrams a day.

And while I may not have been taking fifty milligrams per day of my antidepressant, I had been taking thirty milligrams per day for years.

I started taking the pills just after college, and at the time they were a lifesaver. That first year of true adulthood was hideously awful for me. Auditions were hard on my ego, I was unceremoniously dumped by my college sweetheart, and I struggled to pay my bills. It was like all of the things that I just knew would fall into place after graduation instead exploded into five hundred different piles.

The antidepressant kept me grounded, and it was supposed to be temporary.

That was ten years ago.

And while I would never go Tom Cruise on anyone (and I think Brooke Shields's book was brilliant and took the shame out of post-partum depression), I have privately decided that, for me personally, if I have to pop a pill every day for the rest of my life to get through the day, it's time to change my life instead.

On the tenth anniversary of the day I started taking the medication, I chose not to refill my prescription. I weaned myself off by taking twenty milligrams a day for a week, ten a day during the next week, five the next, then stopping completely.

That was a few weeks ago. And, while I have not had any suicidal thoughts or any of the other common side effects associated with quitting, let's just say I've been a bit "passionate." Which is good and bad. Yes, in the past week I've yelled at a potential boss I should have been kissing up to. But I also broke up with a guy who I knew was a jerk right off the bat but whom I kept seeing because I was lonely. And I've started going for runs to calm myself down—despite the fact that up until three weeks ago, the only I time I ever ran was to the store for donuts.

I'm in this weird phase right now where I know what I don't want in my life, but I can't seem to figure out what I do want.

Although, as I slog through Los Angeles Friday afternoon traffic, I realize I do know one thing I want: a donut.

Maybe six.

Chapter Eight

NAT

Let me come over later.

No.

As I sit at the bar of Wine O'Clock waiting for my friends, I scrutinize my text. I worry it comes off as harsh, so I add:

I love you, but no.

What if I came to the bar at midnight
and drove you all home? I promise
to be very sober, yet very charming.

Your charm is how I got into this mess
in the first place. ;) But Jessie hates
you.

She doesn't hate me.

> Of course she does. She's just so polite,
> she might as well be British.

What does that mean?

> It means she hides her feelings really well. Holly,
> on the other hand, hates you but doesn't hide
> her feelings at all. Not sure which is worse.
> I gotta go.

Okay, how about this? You call me after
you get home, and I sneak into your
bedroom with a bottle of Bollinger and
your favorite chocolates. Then I'll sneak out
before Holly's awake.

I suddenly feel my gut clench. Marc isn't promising to leave before Holly wakes up because she hates him. He'll need to leave because he has to pick up his wife from the airport for her nine-day "fuck-my-boyfriend" vacation.

"You are so lucky to be single," Jessie announces, startling me as she tosses down her purse onto the bar and takes the seat to my left. "Please tell me that's not Marc with a *c*."

The scorn in her voice when she says "Marc with a *c*" causes me to immediately stuff my phone into my purse. "No. Just got a text from Holly. She's running late." (Seems like a safe lie—Holly's always running late.)

"What are you drinking?" Jessie asks me.

"Actually it's a lovely blend from Argentina. It's sixty percent Tempranillo and forty . . ." I stop speaking as I watch Jessie drain my glass. When she puts the empty glass down in front of me, I finish my thought. ". . . percent who the hell cares, you're just getting drunk."

Jessie makes a face. "I thought you said it was a blend. God, I hate Tempranillo. How can you drink that stuff?"

"Apparently I can't," I point out to her drily.

Jessie signals to Dave, our bartender. "Hey, Dave, can you get me a glass of Cabernet from Napa Valley when you get a chance? The one with the vintage from a few years ago that I liked?"

Dave nods. "The perfect choice, Jessie."

As Dave uncorks a fresh bottle, I shake my head at Jessie. "Honestly, could you be more predictable?"

"Dave said it was the perfect choice."

"You tip thirty percent. He'd tell you white Zinfandel was the perfect choice. Try something new. How about a Super Tuscan from Montepulciano . . ."

"We're not getting the house. Kevin got cold feet," Jessie blurts out.

"What?" I blurt right back. "Did he say why?"

"He hates beige," Jessie answers.

I'm confused. "He called you beige?"

"No, he didn't call *me* beige. He called the kitchen counters beige. Why would he call me beige?"

"Well, beige is boring. I thought he was saying you were boring."

Jessie's eyes widen into saucers. "You think I'm boring?"

I quickly backpedal. "I didn't say that. I was just asking if Kevin said that."

Jessie's jaw drops slightly. "Because, if he did, it would totally make sense?!"

"Okay, calm down. I'm on your side. Team Jessie. What happened?"

As Dave pours Jessie her glass of Cabernet, she quickly brings me up to speed on her shitty lunch hour and her shitty day. While she rants, Dave instinctively knows not to interrupt. He silently puts the drink in front of her, then points to my empty glass. I nod for a refill, which he leaves to get.

Minutes later, I sip my refill of Tempranillo-Garnacha blend as Jessie finishes her story with, "So now I have a ton of money saved up and nowhere to invest it. All because of an old counter we could have had removed and replaced while he was in Germany."

"Huh," I say.

Jessie narrows her eyes into slits. "What's 'huh'?"

Before I can answer, Holly magically appears, plopping down on the seat to my right.

I turn to her, welcoming the save. "Hey, there's our Happy Hooker."

"Yeah, bite me."

"You didn't book the job?" I ask, a little surprised. (She had three callbacks.)

"No. They went younger. I booked the part of the madam."

"Oh," I say, trying to sound upbeat. "Well, that's something."

"It's a one-day shoot rather than the guest-starring role. It sucks and apparently it's because I'm officially old." Holly turns to Dave, who is now leaning against the back counter, waiting to help the next customer. "Dave, what do you have that's yummy from somewhere weird?"

Dave thinks about her request for a moment. "Something along the lines of that Cava from Spain you liked?"

"No. I loved that, but let's go with something totally different. Tonight, I want to experiment. I'm done being beige."

Jessie throws up her hands silently.

Holly snaps her fingers. "Oh," she exclaims, pointing to Dave. "New Zealand. Bring me something from New Zealand."

"How is New Zealand somewhere weird?" I ask.

"Their Christmas is in summer," Holly answers, as though the answer is obvious.

Dave pours her a small taste of white in a large glass and explains, "This is a Sauvignon Blanc from the Marlborough region."

Holly slides two fingers over the bottom rim of her glass, then pushes the glass around counterclockwise, swirling the wine. She dips her nose into the bowl of the glass, sniffs, then sips. "Yummy. That's all there is to say about it."

As Dave smiles and fills her glass, I can't help but tell her, "You could say there are delightful notes of stone fruit and citrus."

"I could if I had any clue what a stone fruit even was," Holly jokes. She notices Jessie's sour puss. "What's wrong? Why the look?"

"Nat thinks I'm beige," Jessie accuses, jutting her chin in my direction.

Before I can remind Jessie that I never actually said that, Holly waves her off. "Oh, you're not beige, you're just predictable."

Not helping, Holly.

"What's the difference?" Jessie asks.

"Beige is for people who either can't or won't make a choice about things. You always make a choice. It's just always the same choice."

Jessie bugs her eyes out at Holly. "What? That's not true."

Holly points to Jessie's glass of wine. "Cabernet. Napa Valley. Probably a three-year-old vintage. Five to seven years old if you're splurging. Plus you have that bottle of Insignia Cabernet you've been saving forever. How old's that? Like, ten years?"

Jessie looks like she's going to cry. Holly seems surprised by Jessie's reaction and quickly clarifies, "That's not an insult. It's a good thing. You're like the solid person who knows exactly what she wants and loves, and has a step-by-step plan for how to get it. That's why you've got the stable career, and you're on a planned path to a house and marriage. I wish I was more like you. I wish I could be happy ordering the exact same wine every time, but I can't. Sometimes I need to go to New Zealand."

Jessie looks down sadly at her wine. Holly turns to me, confused. "What's wrong? What did I say?"

"Kevin backed out of the house," I tell her quietly.

Holly's shoulders drop. "Oh, honey." She hops off of her seat and walks around me to pull Jessie into a hug. "But I thought you guys already made an offer. What happened?"

"We went through the house one final time, and he freaked out over the beige counters in the kitchen."

Holly rubs her back sympathetically. "Did you tell him you'll just replace them with white granite countertops and blue and white backsplash tiles?"

Jessie does a bit of a double take at her apparent predictability but quickly recovers. "I tried. But he doesn't want to buy the house. The kitchen was just the excuse. He's not ready to make a commitment, but I am. That's it in a nutshell."

"I'm sorry," Holly tells her. "What can we do?"

"Nothing. But thank you."

Holly gives her another hug. Jessie pats Holly's arm, signaling she's fine, and Holly returns to her seat. Jessie takes a sip of wine, deep in thought. Then she turns to us, exasperated, "You know what's bothering me the most? It's not that we're not engaged yet—we'll get there. It's that he's robbing me of control of my economic future. I have money. I've been killing myself at a job that I hate for years, and sacrificing everything from great haircuts to exotic vacations, just because

I wanted to own something. I wanted something that was mine. And now, because of someone else, I don't get to have something that I've worked really hard for."

Jessie gestures around the bar. "I mean, look at this place. The owner bought it less than ten years ago, just as the neighborhood was really taking off, and now it's worth more than twice what he paid. I want what he has."

"You want a bar?" I ask her disapprovingly.

Jessie shrugs. "You know what? Maybe I do. It would certainly be more fun than accounting."

"That's not exactly a horse race . . ." I joke, trying to lighten the mood.

Jessie takes a sip of her Cabernet, then asks us angrily, "Do you have any idea how tired I am of getting up at five thirty in the morning every fucking weekday, forcing myself into an ugly suit, girdle-like panty hose, and barely there makeup that takes me half an hour to apply, just so I can trudge through fifteen-mile-an-hour traffic to get to my downtown office and marvel at my view of a back alley? Then I get to reward myself for the trip by downing three cups of black coffee, and brace myself to listen to a bunch of douche bag clients who either make ten or fifteen times what I do or, worse yet, have inherited or married money, yet still claim poverty?" She looks around the bar. "If I had any balls at all, I would take my six figures in the bank, sink it into a bar in Echo Park, and change my life."

"Sink is right," Holly tells her. "I've worked in bars off and on for over a decade. More than half of them fail by the end of the first year."

Jessie's face lights up. "That's right! You have bar experience. We should buy a place together. You could run it, I could handle the books. And we could both bartend."

"That's what you took from my statement?" Holly asks her incredulously.

"Really," I agree. "All you need now is Judy Garland and Mickey Rooney to fix up the barn and put on a show . . ."

"I have no idea what that means, but quit making fun of me," Jessie warns me. "Think about it: Echo Park is the next Silverlake. If we bought a bar and held on to it for ten years, like the owners did here, we'd be sitting on a gold mine."

"Is that your accounting background talking or the wine?" I ask.

"Both," she answers without hesitation or shame. "Real estate is a solid investment, whether it's a house or a business. And the only thing keeping me from moving ahead is fear." She looks around the bar, nodding slowly and smiling. "Do you have any idea how rewarding it would be to handle books for something I actually care about? To feel like I was moving forward in some area of my life, and not just treading water?"

She's serious. Clearly that Tempranillo blend has already gone to her head. I now feel bad for making jokes, so I try to make amends by indulging myself for a second and joining her in her pipe dream. "You should make it a wine bar. That way I can help you pick the wines," I say wistfully.

"You absolutely could," Jessie agrees. "You may have flunked out of sommelier school, but you'd be great at picking wines. You know your Sangiovese from your Syrah. Plus you know words like 'stone fruit.'"

"Stone fruit just means a peach, or a nectarine, or pretty much anything with a pit," I explain. "And I did *not* flunk out. I took a leave of absence."

"You can't smell," Holly reminds me.

"Which is *why* I took a leave of absence," I snipe at her.

Jessie looks around the bar again, but she soon deflates. "Never mind. I'm not really going to buy a bar and quit my job. I'm just having a bad day. So let's stop talking about it. I want to hear about yours, Holly. How did your tampon audition go?"

"It got moved to Monday. But you know what's funny: Remember how I told you just yesterday that I could not think of a more humiliating audition to go on than one for tampons?"

"Oh, God, condoms?" Jessie asks.

"Worse," Holly answers.

Jessie and I exchange a look. "Cat litter?" I guess.

"Lower . . ."

Jessie's turn. "A minivan?"

"Okay, as bad. I auditioned for a diaper commercial."

Jessie and I both take a second to absorb that. Really, that's not so horrible. Granted, in L.A. our generation is hitting the reproductive snooze button so often that the clock is bracing for the next hit, but most of the country is having kids by our age.

Jessie stays upbeat. "You know what? That's a good thing," she assures Holly. "You don't want to play college hotties forever. Nothing wrong with playing a cute mom. I'll bet—"

"Adult diapers," Holly clarifies.

Jessie's lips disappear. "Well," she begins, struggling to accentuate the positive, "at least you're not the younger wife in the Viagra commercials."

"That's Tuesday's audition," Holly tells her. "And before you ask, they're going after a younger demographic for that too."

"You know what works for younger guys' penises?" I ask Holly in a deadpan voice.

"Showing up with a six-pack and a pizza," Holly snaps.

"I was going to say showing up with your hair out of a ponytail. But, you know, pizza's a nice gesture."

Holly shakes her head. "Honestly, Jessie, I wish I had prepared for the future the way you have. If you really wanted to, you actually could go find a dive bar near here, redo the décor, hold it for ten years, and make a fortune. Me? My future's so bright, I gotta wear dentures and diapers."

"Man, I'd love to see the look on Kevin's face if I did that," Jessie says, almost angrily. "I have been researching neighborhoods for six months. I know exactly which block would work and why. I would actually do really well financially if I opened a bar."

"Well, if you need any help, let me know. I got an inheritance I don't know what to do with, and way too much time on my hands," Holly offers.

And that was all anyone said to anyone.

That night.

By morning, it was all we were talking about.

Chapter Nine

NAT

The rest of our evening was pretty fun. The owner was clearing out all of his old stock, so we managed to snag some tastes of bottles I could never afford on my own: everything from Ace of Spades champagne (not bad, but overrated), to a Shiraz from Australia that was so perfect I want to be buried with it.

Jessie seemed calmer by the end of the night, and even made up with Kevin, who picked her up around eleven. Holly and I stayed until about midnight, then took a Lyft home.

By two A.M., I am in a postcoital spoon with Marc.

I stare at his left hand, his fingers interlocking in mine. I rub his ring finger lightly. I know from experience that the plain platinum band is in his pants pocket, waiting to be put back on the minute he gets into his car. But for now, his finger is bare, and he's all mine. If it weren't for the ever so slight white tan line on his ring finger, I could almost pretend that it was just the two of us, a normal couple falling asleep in each other's arms after a long week.

"Have you ever been to Maui?" I ask Marc quietly.

"Yes," he answers uneasily, like I'm leading him into a trap.

I sit up and turn to him. "That was a strange tone of voice. What's wrong?"

For a second there, Marc looks nervous, a little jumpy. But then his face relaxes, and he's the same charming man I lov . . . well, like a lot. "Nothing," he says, lightly kissing my hand and then asking cheerfully, "What about Maui? What's on your mind?"

Instinct tells me to begin an interrogation about that nervous look. But I'm a woman in . . . fatuated. Let's just say a woman in-fatuated. So I give him a quick kiss on his hand and continue on with my mission. "After we finish shooting this season's episodes, we'll have two glorious months of hiatus to do nothing. Let's throw caution to the wind, get on a plane to Hawaii, and not come back until we have to be in preproduction for season three."

Marc smiles at me, a bit patronizingly. "Aren't you forgetting something?"

Obviously, I'm forgetting something. His wife. I try to forget her all the time. I am exhausted from all of the hours and energy I use up trying to forget her.

His wife, who will be here in less than eight hours. "On some level, she has to know," I answer.

Marc doesn't respond at first. He just stares at me like he can't believe I would say something so outrageous. But then he looks toward my bedroom door. "You know what? Maybe I should get going."

And that's just the match I need to start my powder keg. My voice simmers in frustration. "Why? Because I want something more than this?"

Marc opens his mouth to say something, then closes it. Starts to speak, then stops. Finally, he comes up with, "It's complicated."

"No. It's actually not. It's incredibly simple. You haven't seen her in three months. You don't have kids. You have nothing keeping you with her."

"Can we not do this at two in the morning when you've been drinking?"

"When should we do it, Marc? Should we do it tomorrow at the airport, when you're picking her up? How about at ten A.M. Monday, when we're taping and she's visiting the set?"

Marc quickly gets out of bed and grabs his underwear and pants from the floor. "I can't talk to you when you're being like this."

"Being like what? How am I being? Being like someone who doesn't want her boyfriend to go fuck another woman in a few hours?"

Marc gives me a look of patronizing disdain. Like I am a bug under his shoe that has to be scraped off and dealt with, "Don't use that word," he says, sounding like a bullying English professor. "It doesn't come naturally to you. It sounds awkward. As a writer, you should know that."

"Fuck you. Don't talk about my fucking writing. I'm a way better writer than you are a producer. If it weren't for my writing, you wouldn't even still have your show on the air here. No one in this country gives a fuck about Manchester's fucking soccer teams or Duchess Camilla."

As Marc slides on his pants, he admonishes, "Honestly, I absolutely loathe when you get like this. We can be wonderful together for weeks, and then I accidentally say something like I went to Maui on my honeymoon, and you freak out. I never know what to expect with you."

"What?" I begin. He thinks this is *my* fault? *Really?* "Are you . . . I can't . . ." I throw up my hands. "You're unbelievable. You are actually going to turn this around so that I'm the one being unreasonable?"

Marc grabs his shirt from the floor and quickly pushes his arms into the sleeves. "You *are* the one being unreasonable. It's so bloody obvious."

I will bite him. "The only thing I see that's *bloody obvious* is what a coward you are. I think you're right, I think you better get the fuck out before I lose it."

He stops dressing and looks me right in the eye. "Natasha, I'm not the bad guy here. You knew what you were getting into when we started. You're not a child. You got what every woman wants: you got romance, flowers, lovely meals, travel, mind-blowing sex. The only thing you didn't get was exclusivity, and I never promised you that."

Wow. I'm stunned. And heartbroken. And angry as hell. Does he genuinely think this is all my fault?

We stare at each other in silence. Marc, mostly dressed, standing in the middle of the room, probably ready to bolt. And me, naked in bed, making no move to stop him.

Is everything over? Did we suddenly break up and I had no idea it was coming?

Holly knocks and asks through my door, "Nat, is everything okay?"

I jump out of bed and grab a robe hanging on my office chair as I yell to her, "It's fine. Marc is here, but he was just leaving."

Marc also yells toward the door, "I'm not leaving, Holly. We're just having a bit of a lover's quarrel."

"Oh, he is *so* leaving!" I counter as I put on my robe. "And congratulate me! I just quit my job!"

For a half second, Marc looks startled. He stares at me. I stare back at him silently, but my face says it all: I'm out.

Marc moves toward me, saying softly, "Darling, you don't mean that."

He touches my arm, but I yank it away from him. "I do mean

that. I quit. You may not think I'm better than this, but that just shows how little you know me."

He sounds like a psychiatrist calmly handling a mental patient as he points out, "You have a contract."

"Yeah. I also have a lawyer who frowns on sexual harassment. And you have a wife who I have a feeling has no idea you have an open marriage. Should we call her now? Leave a voice mail for her to get the minute she lands in L.A.? No . . . I think I'll wait and call at the airport, just after you pick her up. I'm sure you guys can have your own lover's quarrel."

Another standoff. Me in my robe, Marc in his unbuttoned shirt and unzipped pants, both of us wondering what the other will do next.

I hear my bedroom door quietly open and then Holly say in a surprisingly menacing tone, "She asked you to leave."

Marc looks down at my hardwood floors. Purses his lips, debating. Finally, he says, "Holly, could you give us a moment?"

Holly crosses her arms and stares him down. "Nope. I may look like a cute little porcelain doll, but I have a black belt. And I have had the worst day. And I don't think you want to see me angry."

Marc turns to me to silently ask for protection. I shake my head *no* ever so slightly.

"Fine. I'll go," he says, as though it were his idea. He zips his pants, grabs his shoes and socks, then walks over and kisses me on the cheek. "We'll talk on Monday."

"No. We won't," I assure him.

Marc gives himself a moment to take that in, then turns to leave. "I'll call you," he says as he walks to my door. As he pushes past my roommate and out the bedroom doorway, he lies, "Holly. Lovely as always to see you."

And a few moments later, I hear our front door open and shut.

Holly takes a step back through the doorway to make sure he's gone. Once she's sure the coast is clear, she walks over to me. "You okay?"

"No," I answer honestly. "I just lost my job and my boyfriend."

She nods, then gives me a hug. "I'm proud of you."

"Don't be. I'm a slut and an idiot."

"You're human. You made a mistake. I don't judge people by the mistakes they make but by how they fix them."

"Thanks."

"You want me to leave you alone, or should we stay up half the night talking about how men are assholes?"

"Yyyyeeeeesssssss . . ." I answer, letting my head fall as we walk out of my bedroom. "You have a black belt? How did I never know that?"

"Sure. It's a Ferragamo. I got it at Bloomingdale's. Cute little buckle."

I smile, and almost laugh. "You are a great actress—I totally bought that."

Chapter Ten

HOLLY

Nat didn't fall asleep until after five. I stayed up with her, and we combined binging on a block of sitcom reruns on Netflix with binging on Tillamook rocky road ice cream and double-chocolate Milanos. Nat poured her guts out about how much it sucks to date a married man and how she couldn't face going to work Monday with him in the office right next door.

I didn't have any advice to give because, let's face it, every woman dating a married man knows what she should do: Dump the bastard. Delete all of his e-mails. Block his number. Block him from your Facebook, Instagram, and Snapchat accounts. Etc. But talking to a mistress about leaving her lover is like telling an overweight person how to diet: She knows what she is supposed to do, and she knows how she got herself into this mess. So don't insult her with advice. Just listen.

So I listened without judgment (and without a cell phone anywhere nearby—that's key) and sympathetically repeated various forms of "I'm sorry," "That sucks," and "He's an asshole" all night.

Eventually, I watched Nat drift off to sleep on our three-cushion couch. I put a blanket on her, then made myself comfortable on the smaller two-cushion love seat, staying in the living room so she wouldn't have to sleep alone.

Or maybe *I* just didn't want to sleep alone.

While I cannot imagine being so stupid as to date someone who right off the bat presents himself to be a liar and a cheat, I could totally relate to her "not-face-another-day-of-work" problem.

I know it's only Friday night (Saturday morning. Eek!), but I'm already dreading Sunday night.

When I have an acting job to go to the next day, my nights before are great. I get to read about another person and can immerse myself completely into a character, forgetting about my own life completely and just flying around fantasyland.

But when I know I have auditions on a Monday, the Sunday night dread borders on pathological. It's a dread that swims around so deep inside of me that I used to need pills to drown it out.

That dread doesn't exist the night before my "day job," which is delightfully mind numbing and a welcome break from my real job. I'm a waitress at a trendy restaurant in Hollywood. When I'm at that job, people are nice to me. I give them food and booze, so in general they're happy to see me. Rarely does someone take one look at me, say "Thank you for coming in," then wait for the next server to approach the table. (Notice that I'm saying "rarely" and not "never"? Hollywood people can be weird.)

So I usually don't mind that job. The one I really can't face is on Monday morning. My eight o'clock audition is for a two-scene role as a snooty receptionist. Absolutely nothing wrong with the gig— at least it's not diapers. But I didn't get into acting just so that I could practice saying, "And you are?" seventeen different ways, then rehearse various reactions for my character to have when the TV show's protagonist tells me that my boss is wanted for questioning. A reaction that I can get wrong, by the way. Some casting directors will want my receptionist visibly surprised, others cold and stone faced. Trouble is, I never know who wants what. My job is to guess, and I won't know what the wrong answer is until I drive to Century City Monday morning to find out.

I get myself so worked up some nights trying to guess what they'll want, and reading the sides so many times, that I end up looking over at the window to see the sun is coming up.

Speaking of sunrise . . . damn it. This is not the first time I have stayed up all night for no reason. Since getting off my meds, I seem to be making insomnia a habit (or a new addiction, but I can't think about that right now).

Well, as long as I'm up, might as well watch my favorite show.

A little after six, I hear my new favorite sound coming from outside: the front door gently closing next door. I pull back my curtain ever so slightly to peek through the window and check out my neighbor, who wears jogging shorts to reveal his perfectly toned legs.

He is ridiculously beautiful. He has to be an actor. Probably a former model who won the genetic lottery and spent his late teens and early twenties traveling the world, getting paid a fortune to get his picture taken so girls like me could dream that such men really do exist in nature.

Then, when he decided he was too old for the runways of Paris and getting thousands of dollars per day to have his image snapped on the beaches of Fiji (note that I said *he* decided—the world did not decide for him), he moved on to auditioning and quickly became a spokesman for a men's cologne, complementing that day job with roles in TV shows where the female lead gets to date him, even if she's not nearly as attractive, because his character loves her for her goofy personality and sparkling wit. And sometimes he plays the good cop or secret agent in action movies, since he's in such great physical shape.

The fact that I've never seen my neighbor on TV or in films is beside the point. In my mind, no one who looks like that goes on to be a health insurance administrator. He's 6'3" (I'm 5'8", so tall is important to me), with natural blonde hair, clear green eyes, and a body you want to bring to Vegas and hide in a suite with all weekend. What else could he possibly do besides model and . . .

Ohhhh . . . Looking at him stretch. Me want.

My mind revs up, and I begin lambasting myself for being too scared to introduce myself. The guy moved in almost three months ago, and I still have not so much as said hi to him. I don't even know his first name. I checked his last name on the mailbox: Erikson. Wonder if he's any relation to Erik Erikson, the famous psychologist who coined the term "identity crisis." He's the only really famous Erikson I found on Google.

Not that I would Google stalk my neighbor. That would be creepy. I prefer to think of it as Google research. I also discovered that he's not on IMDb, so maybe he still models full time.

I should go out there right now and say hi.

Or quickly change into my running clothes and be outside before he's done stretching.

We could jog together! There's an idea!

I quickly run to my room, throw on my cutest black yoga pants and matching top, lace up my sneakers, and head out.

But by the time I get out there, he's already gone.

Rats.

I drag myself back into the house, shoulders slumped, and fall onto the love seat. I should get some sleep anyway. My future conquest's first impression of me should not be half asleep, with un-washed hair and bags under my eyes.

Still . . . rats.

I pull on some covers, close my eyes, and let the daydream of hugging him wash over me and carry me to sleep.

Chapter Eleven

I awake to see Jessie hovering above me, holding up an eight and a half by eleven inch sheet of paper.

"I found our bar," she tells me excitedly. Then she holds up a pink cardboard box. "And I brought donuts."

I blink my eyes open. "How did you get in here?" I ask her sleepily.

"You still have a spare key hidden under your ficus plant," Jessie tells me rather maniacally as I struggle to sit up. "The place is on Sunset Boulevard, only a few blocks from three different trendy bars that all cater to the Eastside twentysomethings. We're gonna go thirtysomething, and we're gonna cater to women, although I also like the idea of middle-aged couples coming in on date night, but really, who are we kidding, married women pick the date night so married men can get laid, so we're still catering to the women. It also already comes with a Type 42 On-Sale Beer and Wine license."

She vomited that whole thought out in about twelve seconds. Auctioneers speak more languidly.

"A what?" Nat asks, keeping her eyes closed and still appearing dead on the couch.

"The license bars need to serve wine and beer," I answer Nat in my just-woke-up Elmer Fudd voice.

"Oh," Nat answers, clearly still in a fog. She pushes herself up, opens her eyes a bit, and tries to get her bearings. "We have a ficus plant?"

"It's the potted plant you think is an orange tree," I tell Nat.

"And it's dead. Get rid of it," Jessie commands in her rapid-fire patter. Then she practically thrusts the sheet of paper in my face. "Just look at this price! It's going for at least a hundred thousand below market value. Okay, so are we doing this?"

It's just too early. "Let's take a few minutes to let everyone wake up and have coffee," I suggest as I drag myself off of the love seat and head into the kitchen.

Jessie bounces like Tigger on his tail as she follows me into the kitchen. "From the pictures I could find online, it looks like the interior's all brick, which is the trend right now, so that's great. And I talked to a loan officer this morning who I use all the time. If we pool our money together and make an offer now, she promises me she can get us a thirty-day escrow! You have your inheritance, just sitting in the bank, begging for an opportunity like this and . . ." Jess yells toward the living room, "Nat, how much money do you have in the bank?"

"Enough to get me through until Wednesday," Nat answers groggily. "Wait. No, Tuesday. Holly, can I borrow some aspirin?"

"I have Advil in my purse," I yell to her as I pour some beans into our burr coffee grinder, and try to pry my eyes farther open without the use of toothpicks.

"I'm thinking Nat's right: a wine bar," Jessie bubbles, while opening the pink box and handing me a devil's food cake donut with chocolate icing and rainbow sprinkles. "Just wine. No food. No mixologists. Not even beer. Wine. All different kinds, from all over the world. And we cater unapologetically to women. According to this article I read last night, if you get the women in, the men will follow."

"Did you sleep at all last night?" I ask her.

"Sleep is overrated," she tells me in her sleep-deprived, manic state. "How do you feel about pink chandeliers?"

I blink at her a few times, then pick my words very carefully. "Jessie, I admire your enthusiasm. I do. I admire the hell out of it. But you haven't thought this through. Something like ninety percent of restaurants and bars fail in their first year."

Nat appears in the doorway, carrying my travel-size Advil bottle. "The ninety percent restaurant failure rate is a myth. The actual failure rate is closer to one in four." Nat walks to the donut box, gently pushing Jessie out of the way to get to her breakfast.

"How do you know crap like that?" I ask.

"Oh, I know a lot of useless crap," Nat mumbles as she scrutinizes the box to find her favorite. "Shame I quit my job. Where else can I get paid for knowing Sir Isaac Newton's dog's name?" She frowns. "Didn't you get jam-filled?"

"You quit your job?" Jessie repeats.

"I quit my job," Nat confirms. "And left my boyfriend. Maybe today I'll total my car and make it a screw-up-my-life trifecta." She takes a powdered sugar donut with red goo oozing out of the side. "Is this raspberry?"

"Powdered are strawberry, glazed are lemon. You seriously left Marc with a *c*?" Jessie asks her incredulously as Nat helps herself to a big bite.

"Please quit calling him that," Nat implores through a mouthful of donut.

"I'm sorry. Prick with a *c*," Jessie corrects. "So he's gone? Like gone-gone, or just gone like he'll be with his wife for the next week, then talk you into coming back?"

"I think this time he's gone-gone," I assure Jessie as I dump grounds into the coffee filter and pour water from the pot into the coffeemaker's reservoir. "Otherwise she would have kept her job."

"Perfect," Jessie exclaims. "This is a sign. Now you can cash in your IRAs and come work with us."

"Oh, wait. I stand corrected. *That's* what I'll do as my screw-up-my-life trifecta," Nat retorts sarcastically.

"More like blow up your life," Jessie promises with a joie de vivre in her voice that I haven't heard in years. "But in a good way. Do you still have stock in Apple?"

Nat's mouth drops open ever so slightly, and I'm surprised she doesn't answer with her driest, "Really?" Instead, she says, "Yeeessss. But that's a solid investment."

"So's this. How much did you spend on your sommelier classes?"

Judging from the look on Nat's face, a lot. "It doesn't matter," she answers. "I flunked out. Remember?"

"Ah, but the classes were an investment, because you were following your passion," Jessie points out fervently. "Wouldn't it be great to follow your passion again?"

While Nat takes a moment to consider that, Jessie moves in for the kill. "And think of all the other positives. You've been wanting to write a screenplay and get away from game shows. This way you'll have the mental energy to do it, because you won't be exhausting yourself ten hours a day coming up with a new way to ask about the Pythagorean theorem. And there will be zero chance you will run into Marc."

I can tell from the way Nat heaves a thoughtful sigh that she's thinking *Ouch.*

But then she slowly bobs her head up and down a few times, debating, and capitulates. "I suppose it couldn't hurt to look at the place."

"Yay!" Jessie exclaims, practically jumping into Nat's arms for a hug. "I love you! Thank you, thank you, thank you!"

Then she turns to me, a wicked smile crossing her face. "Holly . . ."

I cringe. "And she points the gun in my direction. . . ."

Jessie lowers her chin, gives me a look with fifty shades of serious. "What I am about to tell you is said with nothing but love and compassion."

"Careful," Nat warns me, "the last time she began a sentence like that, it was to tell me I'd gained ten pounds."

"It was more like fifteen," Jessie reminds Nat. "And you had started topping your Frosted Flakes with Pop-Tarts for God's sake." Then she turns back to me. (Gulp.) "You know we love you, and what we're about to say comes with no judgment or shaming . . ."

Nat's eyes widen at Jessie's statement. "We? Crap."

"Since you got off your pills, you've become a stark raving lunatic," Jessie begins.

For the next few moments, I watch my two best friends engage in the lamest silent communication ever.

Nat smacks Jessie in the arm. Translation: Shut! Up!

Jessie puts her palms up and raises her shoulders in a shrug. Translation: What?

Nat's eyes widen even more. Jessie's still not getting it.

Finally, Nat leans in to Jessie and says under her breath, "She doesn't know we know."

I don't know they know . . . what?

"Didn't you tell me that last week she went into the neighbors' yard, stole their rooster, and threatened to make coq au vin?" Jessie asks Nat.

Oh! The pills! Now I'm up to speed.

"Okay, I will admit, taken out of context, that is rather damning," I concede. "But in my defense, that fucking thing was crowing at six in the morning. What city dweller needs to raise chickens? Pretty sure our ancestors left the farm for the city specifically to get away from getting up at sunrise to the sound of livestock."

"Aren't you tired of having no control over your life?" Jessie asks me.

Whoa. Where the hell did that come from?

But she's right. I am tired.

I'm tired of giving it my all at auditions, then being forced to let someone else decide if I'm good enough. I'm tired of going to work for an idiot boss who knows nothing about running a restaurant and has the job only because she married a wealthy man who wanted to give his Beverly Hills trophy wife a hobby.

Speaking of men—I'm tired of dating. I'm tired of random men getting to decide if I'm good enough. I'm tired of never feeling good enough.

I'm tired of never getting to decide my fate. I'm tired of not having anything to look forward to. And yeah, Jessie's dead-on: I'm tired of not feeling in control of any aspect of my life.

I nod slowly. "You know what? It can't hurt to look."

Chapter Twelve

JESSIE

An hour or so later, three women walk into a bar.

"I came here with the lowest of expectations," Nat mutters, sounding almost shell-shocked. "And I'm still a bit disappointed."

"I don't think I've ever seen men drinking Pabst Blue Ribbon who didn't also wear skinny jeans a size too small, lots of plaid, ironic facial hair, and a fedora or newsie," Holly adds.

I, on the other hand, am oddly intrigued by this brave new world we have fallen into. This! This is different. How many women can say they've been at a bar at ten in the morning, hanging out with a clientele whose average age is about a million and two, with Methuselah tending bar?

"Ladies' room is out of order," Methuselah growls at us. "Everyone has to use the men's room."

"Oh. No, sir," I begin cheerfully. "You see, we are thinking about buying your lovely establishment and wanted to come by—"

BOOM!

Nat and I both jump a foot, then quickly turn our heads to the sound of the minor explosion. Holly appears in the doorway of the back room. "Okay, so apparently if you plug in the refrigerator back here, it blows a fuse."

"Circuits," the grizzled bartender says, shrugging.

I don't even know what that means.

I walk up to the jukebox, which I assume is busted, judging from the axe cleaved in the center of it. Just as well, as judging from the vinyl forty-five records I can see underneath the axe, all it would have played was honky-tonk from the 1970s. The floors are covered with a combination of ancient, ripped linoleum and something sticky. So sticky that Nat's Converse sneaker pulls up an entire eight-inch square.

As I run over to Nat to try to help her get the square off of her shoe, Holly politely asks Father Time, "Mind if I get behind the bar to inspect it?"

"Be my guest," he grunts. "Just make sure you don't make any sudden movements. Ralph hates that."

As Holly bellies up behind the bar, she smiles flirtatiously at an eightysomething dude wearing an old flannel shirt and jeans so ancient they may have been Levi Strauss's prototype. "Ralph, you're not afraid of me, are you?"

"That's Bob. Not Ralph," the old bartender tells her, making a show of checking out her butt as she bends down to see what we're dealing with.

As I unsuccessfully try to tug the linoleum piece from Nat's shoe, she asks Holly, "Well? How's it look back there?"

Holly pops back up, then leans on the bar. "The drainage back here is nonexistent . . ."

Methuselah shrugs. "So, be careful and don't spill anything . . ."

". . . the wells for the bottles all seem to be covered in maple syrup . . ."

Methuselah chuckles. "That ain't maple syrup . . ."

". . . and I'm pretty sure I saw a Chupacabra under the soda jet staring out at me suspiciously."

"That's Ralph."

As Holly reacts to Methuselah's piece of information, Nat lifts her nose in the air to sniff. "What is that smell?" she asks.

Holly takes a whiff. "I'm going with Eau de Retirement Home for the Neglected."

"Can we leave now?" Nat asks.

"Not until you say we're taking the place," I tell her firmly. (Good for me! I have no idea where this backbone came from, but I just need it for five more minutes.)

Nat opens her mouth, but I cut her off. "Fuses can be fixed, walls can be painted, smells can be bleached away, and Ralph can be . . ."

I turn to the bartender. "You can find a home for Ralph, right?" I ask him hopefully.

"This is Ralph's home," he says sternly.

"Ooohhhh . . . you do not want to let Holly near Ralph," I bullshit. "Did you hear about that pig in Silverlake that was reported missing?"

He turns to Holly, visibly surprised and horrified. "That was you?!"

It wasn't her, there was no pig, and I totally made it up. (Who am I? I don't know! But I'm so *loving* me right now!) But Holly smiles wickedly at him, shrugs, and confides, "I like bacon."

"I'll take Ralph," the bartender assures me quickly.

Point. Match. Game. "So what do you say, guys?" I ask, my heart jumping around in my rib cage like a pinball. "Should we do this?"

I watch Nat look over at Holly. Holly shakes her head, but she's smiling. "You know what? Why not?"

"Why not?" I repeat. "Really?"

"Really."

I then turn to Nat, put the palms of my hands together in a prayer sign, and silently beg.

Nat looks up and to the left. That means she's thinking about it. *C'mon, c'mon, c'mon . . .*

Finally, she nods. I grab her in a hug, nearly knocking us both over. "Yay! Okay, what do you think of the name 'Keep Calm and Carry a Big Drink'?"

"What a stupid name for a—"

"Okay, okay. That's okay, I have others," I tell her quickly. "You guys, take a moment to absorb everything around you. For this is our eciah."

"Our what?"

"Our eciah," I repeat. "You know, the point in your life when everything changes in a heartbeat."

The three of us share a moment of silence, in honor of the passing of our former lives and the beginning of our new ones.

Until one of the patrons interrupts our moment by telling Holly, "You know, you remind me of a hooker I used to date in Korea."

"Really?" Holly asks in irritation. "Was she half Japanese, this hooker?"

"No," he concedes sadly. "Actually, she wasn't even a she. I miss her."

Chapter Thirteen

Within the hour of touring the bar that Saturday, we had offered one hundred thousand dollars below the asking price (which was already way below market value), and by Monday we had raided every penny of our savings and retirement accounts, had formed a corporation called Girls' Night Out, Inc., and had officially gone into escrow.

Giving my two weeks' notice was great fun. Telling Kevin, on the other hand . . .

Well, I can't really say it's been fun. I can't really say it's been much of anything, seeing as I haven't exactly told him yet.

I've been trying. For the past several days, I keep opening my mouth to push out the words, "I quit my job and bought a bar." But all I can stammer out is inane gossip about the latest celebrity couple or talk about the weather.

It's now Thursday, and Kevin leaves for Frankfurt tomorrow morning. He'll be gone for three months, and it seems cowardly to tell him via Skype.

Why I am I being such a chicken? After all, it's my money, my career, my life. And people are supposed to support the people they love in their dreams, right?

Hah! Support their dreams—what a load of crap. How many women do you know willing to date a guy who does poetry readings at night and still lives in his parents' guest room? Well, it's just as bad with the guys these days. I recently read a statistic that said in forty percent of married households with kids, the woman is the main breadwinner. Which means that to almost half of the men in this country, a woman with no job and no savings is way less attractive than someone who hates her job but pulls in a six-figure paycheck. Whether they'll admit it or not, 2010s men have become the new 1950s housewives.

Armed with this information, I guess I felt like I was about to be much less attractive marriagewise, and I really wanted Kevin to propose at some point. So I just said nothing.

But I need to tell him. Now.

I decide to go with a celebratory approach.

As Kevin stands next to his bed, packing two large bags and a medium carry-on for his lengthy trip, I walk into his bedroom carrying two champagne flutes and a bottle of Prosecco from Valdobbiadene, a region in Italy that Nat has assured me makes the highest-quality Prosecco on the planet.

I put down the glasses and pop the cork. Kevin turns around from his suitcases, smiling. "I love that sound."

"Me too," I tell him as I tilt the flute slightly toward the bottle and pour him a glass. When I hand it to him, I try to sound really upbeat as I announce, "Plus, I figured we should celebrate. I got a new job."

Kevin's face lights up as he takes the glass. "Really? That's amazing. I didn't even know you were looking. Is it with that firm in Westwood?"

I turn away from him to pour my own glass (and avoid eye contact). "No. It's actually much closer to home," I eke out nervously. "It's in Echo Park." I plaster a smile back on my face, turn to Kevin, and hold up my flute. "Cheers."

Kevin clinks glasses with me. After we both take a sip, he says, "This is good. And I'm not usually a champagne guy. So tell me about the job. I don't know anything about the accounting firms in Echo Park. How big is it?"

"Little," I answer evasively. "Only three employees for now."

Oh, to hell with it—go for broke. "And it's actually not so much an accounting firm as it is a bar."

Kevin narrows his eyes and juts his chin forward in confusion. "I don't understand."

I can feel my heart pounding in my chest as I confess to him, "I bought a bar with Nat and Holly. We open in about eight weeks. Ten at the outside."

Kevin doesn't say anything. I watch him blink several times, then put down his glass. "I'mmmm . . ." He lengthens the *m*, then lets his sentence peter out. I worry about what's coming next as he opens his mouth to say something, then closes it without a word. Watching his reaction right now feels a little like clipping the red wire and wondering if the bomb is going to explode.

Kevin finally asks, in an exceedingly calm voice, "When did this happen?"

I take a healthy swig of bubbly for courage, then get it all out there. "We put the offer in Saturday. After you said you didn't want to buy the house."

Kevin's eyes widen. "I never said I didn't want to buy the house. I just said I needed a little more time."

"Well, either way, now you can take all the time you need," I counter in a tense, clipped voice.

Kevin fake laughs and shakes his head. "And passive-aggressive Jessica strikes again. So if I didn't buy a house that moment, we weren't going to buy a house at all? Thanks for letting me know what the stakes were. Thanks for lying to me and saying everything was fine."

I suddenly feel a rush of hatred for him flood over me. How is it that he can be the one to fuck up yet still make everything seem like my fault? "Everything *is* fine," I assure him coolly. "You chose not to make a decision, and that *was* your decision. So then I chose to make a decision—which was not to make any more decisions about my life based on how you felt about them. I love you. I want to marry you. But I am not spending my life waiting around for you to decide when the life I want gets to start."

Kevin inhales a deep breath. "You know, you may think you're being quiet and controlled here, but all I'm hearing is anger. Anger and an ultimatum."

I'm so angry that I begin laughing. "I assure you—there is no ultimatum."

I turn my back to him and quickly walk out of his bedroom, knowing that if I stay in there, I will say something I can't take back.

Unfortunately, Kevin follows me out to the living room. *His* living room. "Of course there is," he bellows. "And it's the worst kind of ultimatum, because I have to guess what you're going to do next. 'Yeah, Kevin, I'm gonna say, "Take your time," but then I'm going to blow our down payment and quit my job.'"

I whip around to correct him. "Not *our* down payment—mine. You're not married to me yet—nothing is ours yet. And I didn't blow anything. I chose to make an investment. A really solid investment."

"That's not an investment. It's a rash decision based on having a good time drinking with your girlfriends one night—"

I put up my index finger and point to him. "Okay, I'm going to stop you right there," I tell him warningly. "What about me . . . what in the last three years you've been with me makes you think you *ever* get to talk to me like that?"

To his credit, Kevin does stop talking.

I inhale a deep, cleansing breath, then finish the fight as calmly as I can. "There is no ultimatum, there's nothing to second-guess. I wanted you to buy a house with me because you wanted to, not because I guilted you into it. I want you to propose because you want to spend the rest of your life with me, and have kids with me, not because I'm pressuring you into it. But I've waited three years. If you need more time at this point, that's on you. And you're taking it at your own risk. Now, do you want me to stay and help you pack, or do you want me to go?"

Kevin sighs loudly, then shrugs. Simmering in anger, he says, "I don't know."

"Of course you don't," I agree. "Call me tomorrow."

I grab my keys and head out before he can convince me to stay.

It's not until I get to my car that I realize he isn't going to. Not tonight, at least. Was that his version of a counter ultimatum? I drive home miserable and second-guessing myself. After about ten minutes of silence in my car, I speed-dial Holly on my Bluetooth.

She answers on the first ring. "Didn't go well, I take it?"

"When did dating become like a chess match?" I ask her sadly.

"I don't know," she answers sympathetically. "But maybe that's why the word 'mate' is part of the winning phrase. Did you knock off his queen, at least?"

"Not sure. Think I may have gotten a bishop. I suppose I'll know more soon."

"Want to come over? We're making pizza."

"Be there in twenty minutes."

Six weeks later . . .

Chapter Fourteen

NAT

Remember a few years back, when the NSA was in trouble for "spying" on American civilians by listening in on their phone calls and reading their Facebook posts? I remember thinking at the time, *Well, maybe that means that at least one man is listening to me.* But based on my rounds of texts with Marc since I quit, I suspect it's mostly women listening. Women are just better at getting the subtle nuances of both oral and written conversation.

For example, they might know what I meant from my answers to an assortment of his texts during the past few weeks.

Work isn't the same without you. The caterer made your favorite chocolate chip red velvet cupcakes, and he was brokenhearted not to see you here to enjoy them.

Drop dead.

I'm truly sorry. I was terribly out of line.
Not to mention inexcusably belligerent and
defensive.
What can I do for us to be friends again?

Drop dead.

Did you get the flowers I sent?

Dude, I will cut you.

Now see, while I think a woman might pick up on my diplomatic hints and understated subtext, clearly what a man hears is, "Oh, my God, I love you soooooo much! Please don't call me or show up in person while your wife is visiting—just start to text me a million times a day the moment she leaves town."

He's been texting me, e-mailing me, and then calling my cell off and on for over a month, and I've surprised myself by managing to stay strong and (mostly) ignoring him. So I know what I should have answered when I saw this text yesterday:

Can I take you to dinner?
Just friends.

But after a "streamlined" escrow that cost us each an extra five thousand dollars in bank fees . . . (Seriously, how do banks get away with so many extra fees? We paid a fee to the bank just to give us a lower mortgage rate. Paid them money we were borrowing from them five minutes later. I was never great at economics, but by the third time Jessie explained to me how the process worked, I had a bottle of aspirin in one hand and a bottle of ibuprofen in the other.) . . . not to mention having to cash in my last IRA to pay for unplanned extra expenses for renovating the bar (Let's see: Spend my last few thousand dollars on a trip to Maui or on an ungraded sewer line? I'm such a clichéd romantic. What girl wouldn't choose the sewer line?), I felt like I was hemorrhaging money, and frankly a free gourmet meal in a posh restaurant with a remorseful hunk was not the worst way to spend an evening.

I vowed that I was not going to have sex with him. I was not even going to kiss him hello. I was just going to have dinner with an old friend and coworker.

A really expensive dinner. I'm thinking about ordering the veal.

Holly was out seeing a play, and Jessie was spending her night going over the bar's balance sheets, so sneaking out was not a problem.

But seeing Marc now, in his navy blue Prada suit, as he waits in front of my favorite high-end French restaurant? Huge problem.

"You look bewitching," Marc says seductively before kissing me lightly on my cheek.

At that moment I realize that I'm not just flirting with danger—I'm grabbing it, pushing it up against a wall, and jamming my tongue down its throat. This is a bad idea. What could I have possibly hoped to accomplish by coming? He isn't going to leave his wife just because I got decked out in his favorite bright red dress and sky-high sparkly red heels. And I cannot let myself slip back into pathetic mistress mode and sleep with him.

Soon we are seated and begin a two-hour, seven-course prix fixe tasting menu, with wine pairings.

During the first course, Golden Imperial caviar paired with Dom Pérignon, he is a perfect gentleman.

Which is making me uneasy. Why am I here? If he's not hitting on me, what are we doing?

"What's wrong?" Marc asks me as he scoops up and eats his last bite from the small porcelain plate. "Is caviar too traditional for a first course? Should we have gone somewhere else?"

"Are you kidding? No," I exclaim, scraping the small white plate with my mother-of-pearl spoon and downing the rest of my dish in one nervous bite. "It's fantastic."

"Do you think Dom Pérignon is too cliché for a wine pairing?" he asks, noting my flute has barely been touched.

"Dom Pérignon is perfect," I say, taking a healthy swig. "And clichés usually exist for a reason. Speaking of, how's your wife?"

Well, that came out wrong.

"You're being generous about the wine," Marc concludes, ignoring my jab completely. "What would you have paired this with?"

I shrug. "Honestly, I might have paired it with a sparkling from California, but that's probably just me overthinking it."

"So will your new venture be focused mostly on California wines?" Marc asks.

Ugh. Holly and Jess would kill me if they knew that I had told him all about our wine bar. But in the past few weeks, we might have talked a little more often than I cared to admit.

"No," I say, then finish the rest of the half glass of champagne. "I mean, I love California wines, particularly lesser-known ones from the Central Coast. But you can find a hidden gem from any country. You just need to know what you like."

Marc smiles. "You have always been a woman who knows exactly what she likes. I admire that about you: You never dither. You want something, you go after it. But perhaps even more important, once you're done with something, you're done. I've never seen you invest good time after bad. If you had a piece of writing that didn't work, rather than pore over it, racking your brain to try to make it palatable, you knew to throw it out and start fresh. It's a great quality in a person. Very rare."

Huh?

Soon, the waiter clears our first-course plates and glasses and brings each of us a large scallop doused in brown butter, paired with a Bourgogne Blanc. I take a bite of the scallop, which melts in my mouth. Then I sip the wine, which tastes decadently rich. While I would normally lean more toward a Sauvignon Blanc, this is lovely.

As is the company—I just won't let him know that.

Marc looks very pensive as he watches me eat. He doesn't touch his food. Just stares at me. "What?" I ask.

"I don't like scallops," he reminds me.

I reach over, pluck the scallop from his plate with my fork, and plop it into my mouth in one giant bite.

Marc chuckles at that. "Would you like to steal my wine as well?"

"Well, I did Uber. But, no. I think I may need to keep my wits about me this evening."

Okay, did I just tell him I Ubered to hint that I want a ride home, or did the last half of my sentence prove that nothing was going to happen? Wow, I can't even read myself, much less this evening.

Marc tilts his head and gives me that sexy look he knows makes me melt inside. "Really?" he asks flirtatiously. "Do I seem scary to you?"

"Scary? No. Dangerous maybe . . ."

"Oh, I'm not so bad once you get to know me," he says playfully.

"As opposed to me, who's *only* bad once you get to know me," I joke, wiggling my eyebrows up and down in an exaggerated Groucho Marx move.

"I very much liked getting to know you," Marc tells me, suddenly serious.

For a moment, we stare into each other's eyes, and I'm all jelly inside again. *Is he going to kiss me? He looks like he's going to lean in and kiss me. Do I really want him to kiss me? I spent six weeks getting over him. Do I want to start that process all over again?*

But Marc surprises me and, rather than make a move, breaks eye contact. "I almost forgot," he says, pulling an envelope from his jacket and handing it to me.

I look down at the envelope to see the familiar studio address in the top left corner. The clear plastic window with the recipient's name and address shows the familiar shade of light blue I associate with my paycheck. Confused, I open the envelope and pull out a check for eight weeks' worth of work. "What's this?" I ask.

"Your last paycheck," he answers. "You still had eight weeks left on your contract, so I decided to pay you in full for the season."

I hand him the check back. "I can't accept this . . ."

Marc puts out the palms of his hands in a show of *no contest.* "Legal says you can, after a rather lengthy conversation with the Writers Guild."

"But I quit," I say, confused.

"They didn't see it that way," he tells me, quickly adding, "You had a contract for a specific project that was supposed to take thirty-nine weeks. You finished it in thirty-one. Lots of writers finish jobs early."

Despite myself, I examine the check and debate accepting it. As I said, since the day I committed to this bar, I have been hemorrhaging money, and I'm sure it will only get worse. Between bank fees, building permits, liquor permits, contractors, and trips to Home Depot and furniture stores, I wonder how anyone who opens a bar makes money. So far, it has just been a very expensive hobby.

"I can't accept—"

"You can. You must. You shall. If you don't take it, the studio keeps the money. Haven't you made enough for them?"

He's right. I did have a contract. My boss has decided to pay it off, with the studio fully supporting him. Why am I fighting this?

I slip the check in my purse. "I'm not sleeping with you," I tell him sternly.

"I didn't offer," he reminds me.

And yet, clearly we're both thinking about it.

The next few courses are spectacular. With a seared wagyu beef filet, we sample a Barolo from Italy that makes me want to grab my passport and fly to Piedmont.

During that course, Marc tells a gregarious story that makes me burst out laughing, and the tension between us instantly dissolves.

The mushroom course features chanterelles, an earthy Burgundy, and a compliment on my dress, followed by a sexy, lingering gaze from Marc.

As we finish the lamb course, which includes a cru Beaujolais that is so tasty, it is making me rethink that I hate Beaujolais, he leans over and kisses me on the cheek. It's very sweet and innocent. There is nothing sexual about the gesture. But, oh, my God, I missed that kiss. It made me feel loved and accepted. Not necessarily hot and bothered, but cared for.

Women aren't supposed to want to feel cared for. We're supposed to be independent: capable of changing our own tires, buying our own houses, zipping up our own dresses, and rubbing our own feet. But I think everyone—male, female, gay, straight, young, old— wants the luxury of just resting for a moment and letting someone else put in the effort.

I get hot and bothered during the cheese course, when we both flirt over the last bite of Camembert. Marc smiles, spreads the gooey ambrosia on a cracker, and feeds me.

By the time we finish with the chocolate mousse paired with Sauternes, we are all over each other.

I miss him so much, I ache. Logically, I know this is a bad idea. But I can't remember the last time I felt this way when I was around a guy: that heightened feeling of not knowing if something will happen or not, and desperately wanting it to. Followed by the flood of relief from being truly wanted and cherished.

A few minutes later, with Marc wrapping his arms around my waist and nibbling my neck from behind, I text Holly to say I'll be out all night, but I don't tell her why.

I'm sure she knows why, and I'm sure I'll be paying for it tomorrow. But right now, I don't care. Right now, I'm with the guy I dream about at night. How many women can truly say that?

Chapter Fifteen

NAT

I lie in the king-size bed in Marc's bedroom, post coitus, listening to him take a shower, and stare through his floor-to-ceiling windows at the city glowing pink with the sunrise.

How did I let myself fall back into this second ring of hell?

It's a weird mind trick we women play on ourselves: How we are secretly convinced that a man must love us if he wants to sleep with us. We whip up dubiously plausible scenarios in our heads where the guy is just as tormented over the thought of being separated from us as we are from him. He must love me—how could he want to have sex with me so hungrily if he weren't totally in love with me?

Now, of course, deep down we all know the answer: *Uh, dork, because he's a dude and dudes want to have sex. And since said dude is married, he has to work harder for sex than the single dudes. That doesn't mean he loves you. If he loved you, he would have said it by now.*

In Marc's case, instead of those three words, he plied me with compliments, good food, and lots of booze, just like men have done for thousands of years. Plus he gave me a check. Which technically makes me a . . .

I really should not be left alone with my thoughts. All I need is five minutes to myself, and the familiar gut-wrenching guilt rages back full force.

I hear Marc turn off the shower, and I debate what to do next. Should I call Lyft, or get him to drive me home? Should I put on last night's dress and feel like Mata Hari as I make my way home, or steal a pair of his jeans, a belt, and a crisp white button-up shirt to go with my heels? (Okay, I'm not borrowing jeans. Fuck it, the Walk of Shame is an antiquated, not to mention ridiculous, notion: Yes, world, I had sex last night. For all we know, the president can say the same thing. For all we know, your mother can say the same thing. Bazinga!)

Should I stay in bed until tonight, bat my eyelashes, and talk Marc into a bed day one more time before I break up with him finally, once and for all?

Marc walks out of his bathroom wearing a fluffy white Pratesi robe that I gave him for his last birthday. As usual, he's adorable, which is just making me a little sad. "What would you like to do today?" he asks me cheerfully.

"Do you love me?" I blurt out as I sit up in bed.

Marc looks surprised only for a moment, "Um . . . sure," he says awkwardly to me as he sits on the bed.

Huh. He sure coughed up that word like it was a hairball.

Oh, shit. He's lying. I don't know how I know, but I can tell. He doesn't love me—he's fond of me. There's a difference.

Marc leans in to give me a light kiss. "Do you love me?" he asks, and somehow when the words come out of his mouth, they sound dirty.

"Yeah. I do," I tell him.

I don't know if he hears the sadness in my words. Because I love him so much, I ache. This isn't lust anymore, and it's not fun anymore. It's love, and it's toxic, and it hurts all the time. I tilt my head a bit and make sure to make eye contact when I tell him calmly, "You know what? I gotta go."

As I bolt off the bed, Marc turns to me, confused. "You're leaving? Why? I just told you I love you. What more do you want from me?"

I turn to him, naked, emotionally and physically, and tell him the truth. "I want you to be someone you're not. I want to have a baby with you. I want to wear the white dress and go to Hawaii with you. I want to meet your mum."

The words don't come out angrily: Unlike so many times before, I am neither picking a fight nor avoiding one. I'm just not hiding the real me anymore.

Marc sits there on the bed, looking just as pained to hear the words as I am to say them.

I retrieve my clothes from the floor. Marc is silent as I dress.

Once my second heel is strapped on I say, "I guess I should call Uber or something."

Marc forces himself to move. "Don't be silly. I'll drive you home."

"No, I think . . ." My sentence peters out. We stare at each other again in silence. "I think I should be by myself," I finally say.

Slowly, I walk out of his bedroom and head to the front door. Alone.

Finally, clearly after some debate on his part, Marc emerges from his bedroom. "I have to go to London," he says in a rushed tone. "Come with me."

Of course he didn't tell me that last night when we were making out like teenagers. "For how long?" I ask.

He doesn't answer. Just smiles apologetically at me.

Shit.

I nod slowly. "Wow. That long."

"I took a new job," he tells me. "Producing a British version of a new game show, which we hope to bring to America in a season or two. Part of the reason I took you out last night was to offer you the job as the show's head writer."

I can feel my eyes widen. "You took me out on an insanely romantic date because of work?"

"No. I took you out because I miss you and want to be with you. The job was just a good excuse to see you."

"Except you never offered me the job."

"I got sidetracked."

"'Sidetracked'? Is that supposed to be cute, Marc? Am I supposed to be flattered that you see me as fuckable before you see me as employable?"

"Of course not," Marc says, coming up to me and gently taking my hands. "I'm not offering you the job because of us. You're really good at what you do. And this is an incredible opportunity."

I shake my head in disbelief. "So . . . when I was telling you all about my new business, and my new life, you thought . . . what?"

"Come on, Nat. You're a writer, not a bartender."

I pull away from him, stunned. Too much is happening. I feel like my brain is about to explode. "Now I really need to be alone."

"I'm offering you weekends in Paris," he rushes to tell me. "Theater in the West End. A pub crawl in Dublin. Hiking on a cliff in Ireland. A romantic gondola ride in Venice."

"Are you offering me a baby?" I blurt out before my brain has a chance to stop me.

That gives him pause. Marc has to think about his answer. "I don't know. Maybe?"

I walk over to my purse and pull out the envelope he gave me last night. The one with eight weeks' pay.

"Sweetheart, don't . . ."

"When your 'maybe' changes into a real answer, give me a call," I tell him as I scribble something down on the envelope and leave it on the side table by his door. Then I turn to him. "You have no idea how lucky you were."

Then I silently open his front door and walk out of his life.

I only wrote three words on the envelope: *Don't follow me.*

He didn't.

Chapter Sixteen

HOLLY

I miss my dad. I've managed to go seven months without talking to him, but I still feel like an addict missing her hit of heroin or cocaine. I'm a Dad addict. I just need one hit of Dad. Just five minutes with him, and then I can go another seven months without talking to him. I just want to really quickly catch him up on everything going on in my life. Let him know that I dumped that guy he couldn't stand, that I'm taking a break from auditions, and that I'm opening a bar with Jessie and Nat. That I got off the antidepressants. I want him to make a joke about the week I tried yoga because, let's face it, nothing about my personality says, "Breathe."

I want him to know that I have a huge crush on a guy whose last name is Erikson, and that I'm the worst stalker ever, because I can't even figure out how to Google him. And that I'm so shy I've never even spoken to him. I want to bore Dad with details about how I went jogging one morning just because I saw Mr. Erikson stretching outside, and that after he smiled at me and said "Hi" as I passed him, I was so nervous, I gave a quick wave, then broke out into a run down the block that caused me to pull a hamstring, and surreptitiously limp back home once I knew he had left.

When I tell my story while getting my five-minute fix, Dad would laugh and shake his head. He would listen to me drone on about the guy, then hear me vent about how hard it is to date nowadays, because between texting and carrying our phones with us at all times, and Instagram and Facebook and that new site that a twenty-year-old at work told me about, now we girls have to wait by the phone 24/7. Dad would tell me that I sound ridiculous—that I might as well be one of those old biddies who said the world of dating had gone to hell now that men couldn't stop by their homes with calling cards. He then would remind me that I am worth at least four goats, two chickens, and a mule, and to not stress out so much, because any guy worth his salt is going to do everything he can to be with me.

My father was my biggest fan in the world. He was always convinced that if the men didn't know what they had, they didn't deserve to have it.

This time, during these five minutes, I wouldn't roll my eyes when he told me that I was as pretty as my mom. (I remember as a teen thinking that was the worst compliment ever. Yeah, Dad, genetics. Duh.) Instead, I'd say, "Thank you. I look like you too."

And then, I would ask for Dad's advice about the guy. And he would tell me to just talk to him. He'd say, "Just get on with it! Go smile and say hello to the guy. We really don't like being the aggressors. We may say we do—we lie. Really, we want the beautiful woman to think we're amazing, right off the bat. Most of us just want to know where our chair is. We want to ask you out. But in order to do that, it would be nice to get a little encouragement."

Yup, that's what Dad would say.

But, truth be told, if I had those five minutes, I wouldn't talk about dating or finding a new man. I'd still ask for his advice, but it would be about a different man. It would be about him. And I would ask, "How do you ever get over losing your first love?"

And he would say, "You're being a martyr. Knock it off. Life is for the living. Go open that bar. I'll be there that first night, beaming with pride."

There's not a doubt in my mind, that's exactly what he'd say.

I look over at his urn, a dark wood cube with a picture of a sailboat carved on the side. I kiss my index and middle fingers, and put them on the urn, then I sadly rest my head on the urn.

Yeah, Dad, I know: I am being a martyr. And an addict. Because I would still give anything for just five more minutes.

Chapter Seventeen

A few days later, it is early evening, and I am at our dining room table with Jessie and Nat, pouring a flight of wines for us to taste. Nat has a pad of paper in front of her (how retro!) and has just crossed off another suggestion from her list. "Okay, Holly's idea, 'Once Upon a Wine,' is out, as is 'The Vintage Point.'" Nat looks over at Jessie as she continues, "You also killed my idea, 'Que Syrah, Syrah.'"

"Because we're not serving only one type of wine," Jessie pipes up defensively.

"Which is the same reason you didn't like 'Don't Get Me a Cab,'" Nat says as she crosses out another line on her page.

"No, I just found that one to be a passive-aggressive snipe about my taste in wine."

"I don't think it was passive . . ." I think aloud.

Nat continues reading from the elimination round. "Holly made a face at 'Wined-up Dolls.' And 'It's Ireland Somewhere' doesn't even make sense—they don't make wine in Ireland. Next."

My face lights up, "How about 'Corkscrewed'?"

"We are not putting the word 'screwed' in the name of our bar," Jessie tells me firmly.

"Why not? People will want to go there either because they already feel that way . . ."

"Too dark . . ." Nat says, shaking her head.

"Or they want to get—"

Jessie shuts me down with, "I'll give you a thousand dollars not to finish that thought."

I shrug, finish pouring a Meritage from the Central Coast of California, then watch quietly as Nat and Jessie take a minute to stare into space with writer's block. We've been working on the name of the bar since the day we bought the place. So far, we could have started each morning with a pitcher of margaritas and a TV remote ready to hit "Play Next Episode" twelve times in a row, and been at the same place we are now with the name.

Some days the Muse not only refuses to visit, she texts you to say she went to Cabo for the week.

Dead silence in the apartment. I separate my index and middle fingers into a V, press down on the bottom of the wineglass of a relatively young Pinot Noir from Oregon, swirl the glass a few times, and stick my nose in the bowl, giving myself something to do while I rack my brain for more ideas.

"'Pinot envy'?" I ask, raising my voice an octave at the end.

Nat winces. She absentmindedly runs her fingers through her shiny, dark brunette pixie cut as she stares off into space, thinking.

I realize I am absentmindedly twirling my own long straight hair.

I take a sip of the Pinot. "This one needs a few minutes to breathe."

Nat sniffs it. "That one needs a bottle of orange juice and some brandy, fruit, and ice cubes."

Jessie eventually snaps her fingers. "Oh. How about 'A Clean, Well-Lighted Place'?"

"You want to name the bar after a short story about the inevitability of death?" Nat asks, mildly horrified. "Why don't we just call it 'We're All Gonna Die. Everybody Drink'?"

Jessie's eyes widen. "Wait. That's what that story's about?"

"Yeah. Remember, the old man sits in a corner by himself getting drunk, and the young waiter with the hot wife waiting for him at home just wants to call it a night, and the middle-aged guy is all pensive because he knows he'll be the old man one day."

Jessie looks crestfallen. "Crap. How depressing. See, this is why we shouldn't read the classics at sixteen. No one should take AP English until they're thirty. How about 'Grapes of Wrath'?"

Nat narrows her eyes at her. "Honestly, would you ever go into a bar with the word 'wrath' in its name?"

"I would before I'd go to one with 'screwed' in its name," Jessie counters. "'Grape Expectations'?"

"Do you want to know what that book's about?" Nat asks in an almost threatening tone.

"I'm gonna say no," Jessie answers tentatively. "'Waiting for Merlot'?"

"I am seriously going to make you take an English class," Nat threatens.

Jessie shrugs her shoulders sheepishly, then takes a sip of one of the reds. "This one's good. We should definitely have it on the menu on opening night."

Nat barely suppresses an eye roll. "A Bordeaux. How original."

"Don't give me that look. At least I've moved on from Cabernet Sauvignon," Jessie announces proudly.

Nat sighs. "That particular Bordeaux is made from almost fifty percent Cabernet Sauvignon grapes." She points to a different glass of red. "Try that one. It's a Carménère from Chile."

Jessie sniffs it and makes a face. "It smells like cigarettes."

"Tobacco," Nat tells her. "Nicely done. What you're smelling are notes of leather and tobacco. Now take a sip."

Jessie moves her glass up to sip, then promptly does a spit take back into her glass. "Ewww!" she exclaims, then grabs a napkin, sticks out her tongue, and scrubs. "Why on earth would someone want to drink tobacco?!"

"For the same reason you might want to taste cow dung. Because it shows you have a sophisticated palate."

Jessie stops her tongue scrubbing just long enough to snap, "So there are people out there drinking wines tasting like poop to be sophisticated? I call that bullshit."

"Cow dung," Nat corrects.

"It's still on my taste buds," Jessie howls, grabbing a flute with a small amount of sparkling wine in it, gargling with it to kill the taste, then spitting it in the cardboard spit cup in the center of our table. Jess looks over to me. "Holly, help me out here. Can we agree not to put any wines with cow dung notes on our menu?"

I shake my head. "Are you kidding? A lot of Burgundy lovers like the complexity that it adds, and at over a hundred dollars a bottle, I like the extra tip it adds."

"Wait. You guys are not seriously telling me we're going to serve a wine that tastes like cow dung, are you?"

"It's your third wineglass from the right," Nat tells her. "Whole-sales for thirty-six dollars a bottle, we're charging twenty-eight a glass."

"Ka-ching!" I say happily as Jessie takes her third-from-the-right wine stem, gingerly dips her nose into the center of the bowl, and cautiously takes a whiff. She eyes Nat. "I'll admit I don't smell poop." She dips her nose farther into the glass. "But I'm not smelling anything fun in here either."

"It's not your thing—that's totally fine," Nat says. "There's no right or wrong wine to love. Everyone's taste is different, and that's a good thing. It's like men: If we all wanted the Jared Letos, the Ryan Reynoldses, and the Idris Elbas would wither on the vine, and that would be a shame." She pushes a glass of white in front of Jessie. "How about his one?"

Jessie leans in and sniffs. Her face lights up. "Oh, now, see, this one smells like bubble bath."

"That's a Triennes Viognier from France, and what you're getting there is a combination of honeysuckle, orange blossoms, and flowers."

"Huh," Jessie murmurs. "Turns out I like white wine too. Okay, more ideas for names. Go!"

"'Something Fabulous'?" I throw out.

Nat juts her chin back and forth quickly, debating. "It's like, it's good, but not great. I'll date that name, but I won't marry it."

"Oh! 'Nice Stems'?" Jessie suggests.

Nat begins doodling a flower on her pad. "We're a wine bar, not a florist. 'Hollywood and Wine'?"

"We're in Echo Park, not Hollywood," I point out.

And we're back to thinking. I take my small pour of Viognier and head over to our living room window. It's almost 7:05. Time for my nightly peek at perfection. I pull the curtains back slightly to make sure he's not home yet.

I sniff the white Jessie likes. It's okay—smells a bit too flowery for me. But, like Nat says, we can't all like the Jared Letos. My tastes these days run more toward the Chris Hemsworths of the world.

"'Love the Wine You're With,'" Jessie suggests quickly.

Nat eyes her dubiously. "Like the Crosby, Stills, and Nash song? What are we? Seventy?"

"No. Like when you come here, we will find you the wine you will love. The wine that you've been searching for, dreaming about. Your wine soul mate. You might not like the wine everyone's drinking this month, the Jared Leto wine, if you will, and that's okay. When you come to our bar, we will introduce you to the wine you love, your Justin Trudeau wine, or even your Chris Hardwick wine, and you'll love the wine you're with."

Nat makes a face, "Justin . . . the Canadian prime minister?"

"What? He's hot."

"I suppose. Anyway, what you're saying is the opposite of loving the wine you're with: It's being introduced to the perfect wine. The winning wine—like the winning guy. Oh! How about 'FTW: For the Wine'?!"

Jessie mulls it over in her mind. "I don't hate it," she says cautiously, then turns to me. "Holly, what do you think?"

I look out the window. Still nothing. Maybe he got a last-minute modeling gig that ran late.

I turn to Jessie and pout. "I think that you are so fucking lucky to have a great guy like Kevin, who is a decent human being and loves you more than anything in the world and takes you to the opera, even though he can't stand it, and who knows to buy you cookie dough ice cream, and makes you breakfast in bed on Sundays."

Nat points to Jessie and deadpans, "Or we could go with Holly's suggestion. Maybe shorten it to 'Cookie Dough Ice Cream.'"

"I'm sorry," I exclaim in exasperation, "but Kevin's amazing, yet you're barely talking to him right now just because he was scared of commitment, which most men are. You don't even get how lucky you are and the world is so unfair and when is it my turn to be loved?!"

Jessie seems at a loss for words. She stammers a bit, "I told you . . . after he left town, he called me and we made up."

I eye her suspiciously. "Actually, your exact words were, 'We pretty much made up,' which really means, 'Yeah, I say he's my boyfriend, but I'm still pissed, and now, subconsciously, I'm looking.

Whether I'll admit it to myself or not.' It's like the opposite of when Nat tells us she'll never see Marc again: We know subconsciously she's not looking, which means she'll see him over and over until someone new shows up unannounced."

Nat rubs the bridge of her nose, silently wincing at my indiscretion as Jessie's jaw drops. "You didn't break up?"

"Yes, we did," Nat tells her conclusively.

Jessie frowns and asks in an accusatory tone, "Last month?"

Nat shrugs and grabs a glass of wine to hide her face behind. "I may have had a minor slip-up. Hardly worth mentioning."

Not deterred from my rant, I tell Jessie bitterly, "To paraphrase Paul Newman, it's like you have filet mignon at home, and even Nat has a fast-food hamburger out. I don't even have a juice cleanse to look forward to in my life."

Nat turns to me. "You're not by the window waiting for that guy to come home from work and get his mail, are you? Because if so, that's creepy."

"Not nearly as creepy as what I'm going to dream about him doing to me tonight," I confess. "Oh, wait! Here he comes!" I immediately throw myself down on the couch in splayed position so that he can't see me through the window.

"That does it," Nat decrees, pushing her chair away from the table and standing up. "This ends today."

"Sounds like the tagline from a bad action movie," Jessie says as Nat marches to our front door in determination.

I panic as Nat opens the door. "Wait! What are you going to do?"

But Nat's out the door before she answers.

I quickly run out the door. "Nat!"

"Holly, I just need to check my mail before we head out on that double date," she says to me a little too loudly, then she flashes her mail key for me and Hot Neighbor Guy to see.

Oh, my God. He's right there. He's standing there, less than five feet from us. Nat, please don't say anything. Please, please, please . . .

She does. "Hey. You must be the new neighbor. I'm Nat. This is my roommate Holly."

Adonis puts out his hand to shake Nat's hand as I scoot in behind her. "Nice to meet you. I'm Sven."

Like he couldn't be more perfect—he has an accent too! It's . . . actually I have no idea what it is. I just know it's hot.

"Sven?" I repeat, mentally filing that information away for Google later. "You seemed more like a . . . Lars?"

Nat turns her head to me slowly and widens her eyes at me so wide she looks a girl from a Margaret Keane painting.

Sven smiles, clearly not sure what to make of me. "No, it's Sven. I'm from Sweden."

"Sweden. See, I would have guessed Norway," I say.

Nat shakes her head ever so slightly at me to signal: *For the love of God, stop talking.* Then she turns back to Sven. "Did you grow up in Sweden?"

"Just until I was ten. I was born in Gothenburg," Sven tells her, pronouncing Gothenburg the way we would pronounce it here.

Nat beams happily as she exclaims, *"Yeutebory."*

Sven is visibly surprised. *"Du talar Svenska?"*

"Nej," Nat answers, then switches to English. "But I can pronounce pretty much every major city in Europe. I need to for my job."

"Oh, What do you do?" Sven asks, clearly interested.

"I'm a . . . was a . . . game show writer for *Million Dollar Genius!*"

"Really? I love that show. I used to watch the British version when I lived in London. Is it true that they tell the contestants what types of questions to expect ahead of time?"

"No, no. That was made illegal in the 1960s. Sadly, the guy who knows the name of the dog from *GTA* really doesn't have a life."

"Chop!" I answer proudly.

Sven seems intrigued. "I'm sorry. What?"

"The dog from *Grand Theft Auto*," I answer. Then I add, "I don't really have a life."

Good, Holly. Tell the man you're in lust with that you don't have a life. Really sell it.

Nat takes pity on me and turns to Sven. "She's kidding. Holly leads an incredible life. Did you ever watch *CSI: Seattle*?"

"Yeah . . . a couple times."

"Holly played Veronica on that show."

Sven's face lights up in recognition. "Were you the tattooed computer prodigy?"

"Yes," I say, my mind bursting with the thought: *He knows me. Wheeeeeee!!!!!* "But I would never have a tattoo in real life. That would be ugly. Like putting a bumper sticker on a . . . Unless you have one, in which case I'm sure it looks sexy as fu—"

"Holly . . ." Nat interrupts me loudly.

I catch myself. "Sorry. Are you a model?"

Sven smiles. And maybe blushes a little? "Um, no. I'm a computer programmer. Well, that's an oversimplification. I write code for computers that are used both for American as well as European companies. It's very dull, compared to what you do. So what else would I have seen you in?"

"A bar," I answer truthfully.

At this, Nat laughs. "She's kidding," she tells him as she walks behind me and grabs both of my shoulders. "We own a wine bar that's opening in Echo Park in a few weeks. Would you like to come to the grand opening? It's on the twenty-seventh."

"That sounds fun. I'd love to," Sven answers sweetly as Nat pulls me away from him and leads me back toward our apartment.

"Perfect," Nat says, continuing to haul me away. "I'll slip an invitation under your door. You're in Apartment 6, right? Erikson?"

"Yes. Sven Erikkson. Two *k*'s—the mailbox is misspelled."

That's why I couldn't Google him! I think to myself as Nat continues to lead me away from my future conquest.

"Great," Nat tells Sven as she pushes our front door farther open to make our escape. "Should we put you on the list as 'Erikkson and guest'? Do you have a girlfriend? Or boyfriend?"

Brilliant. I could not love her more right now.

"No. It's just me. Like I said, I just moved here," Sven answers. "Do you want me to bring a coworker or something?"

"No, no. Just bring yourself," I can hear Nat say behind me as she shoves me inside. I escape to the sanctuary of our living room.

"So nice to finally meet you. Have a great evening," Nat tells Sven cheerfully, then practically slams the door shut, turns around, and falls into the door in exhaustion.

"How'd it go?" Jessie asks.

Nat appears pained as she asks Jessie, "You know how you have certain friends who are absolutely in-fucking-credible, and you have no idea why they're still single?"

Jessie turns her chin to the left while keeping her eyes on Nat. "Yeeeeah."

Nat shakes her head pityingly. "Holly's not one of them." She turns to me. "Wow."

"I know . . ." I whine apologetically, letting my body drop onto the couch.

"I would have guessed Norway?" Nat continues.

"I short-circuited," I admit in frustration. "What is wrong with me? Why can I not be myself around hot guys? I can be cool . . ."

"Apparently, you can't," Nat counters. "Like, on so many levels."

I raise my index finger and point to Nat as I tell Jessie, "On the plus side, thanks to my awesome roommate, I now have a sort of date to the grand opening, not to mention a full name to research online: Sven Erikkson, two *k*'s, from Sweden. And for that, I am eternally grateful."

Jessie looks up hopefully. " 'Eternally Grapeful'?"

Nat ignores the suggestion to ask me, "How on earth did women date before Google?"

" 'Who's Drinking Gilbert Grape'?" Jessie presses on.

"I don't know," I answer, also ignoring Jessie. "You think they had to, like, listen to what the guy shared with them over dinner or something?"

Jessie, mentally exhausted, begins desperately suggesting names in rapid-fire. " 'Dinner Is Poured,' 'Wine Girls,' 'Wine Notes,' Quit Your Whining,' 'Winenot?' Snickers!"

"Snickers?" Nat repeats. "You want to name our place after a candy bar?"

"No, I'm getting snickers from both of you. If I were to name the bar after a candy, obviously it would be 3 Musketeers."

Nat opens her mouth, but Jessie shuts her down before she can speak. "And don't tell me what that's really about, because no, I've never read it, and the only thing I know is the 'All for Wine and Wine for All!' " And if you tell me they all die at the end, I'm just going to get upset and have to eat some Snickers."

Nat shakes her head. "Seriously? Next time you get the urge to watch Bravo, promise me you'll crack a book instead. The line is—"

"Wait," I tell Nat. "I think Jessie just came up with our name."

"I did?!" Jessie blurts out happily, her face glowing. "Oh, yay! Good for me! Which one was it? It wasn't the Gilbert Grape one, was it? Because actually I hate that one."

"'All for Wine and Wine for All!' No matter who you are, and what you like, we will find a wine for everyone."

And, with that, we finally had our name.

Now all we needed to do was get the sign made, get it out on social media, finish redoing the ladies' room, move in the rest of the furniture, teach those two how to use a cash register, and pick some wines for opening night.

And I had to Google Sven Erikkson. With two *k*'s.

Chapter Eighteen

Two weeks later, I am sitting in the back office of the bar, wondering what it was like to date Prince William.

I mean to date the actual guy: the six-foot-three-inch dude who back in college had morning breath, occasionally got the flu, and may very well have left his socks on the floor.

Most women grew up knowing who the future king was. And probably, at least on one occasion, they fantasized about going out on a date with him, either because they were dreaming of getting photographed by the paparazzi, or dreamt of being a princess, or maybe simply because the guy wasn't always going bald—at one point he was a cute blond. Point is, millions of women around the world had an idea of what going out with William would be like. And most of them were probably dead wrong.

Because you can't know what a relationship is really like unless you're one of the two people in it.

And I would like to think that there is at least one woman out there who, while dating the guy that every girl wanted, finally tired of him leaving his dirty socks on the floor, or not proposing, or wasting every Sunday watching football or rugby or whatever, and thought, "Fuck it. I can do better."

Maybe not. But I'd like to think so. I would like to think that no matter how perfect the guy is to the outside world, there is at least one moment in every relationship when his girlfriend thinks, "Screw this. I'm out."

At least that's what I'm feeling like right now, sitting by myself in the back office of the empty bar, Skyping on my computer with Kevin and wondering how Cinderella would deal with her Prince Charming if they dated in this day and age. Would she swipe left?

"You hate it," Kevin tries to get me to admit.

"I don't hate it," I counter.

"Why can't you just admit that you hate it?"

"Kevin, whatever ring you want to get me is fine. You could put a Band-Aid on my finger and I'd still say yes."

"No. No, no. Don't do that. I know you, and if the ring isn't perfect, you're going to spend the rest of your life staring at your hand, obsessing over the symbolism of my not getting you exactly what you wanted."

I sigh. Loudly. Then I scratch my head. "Fine. The truth is, I would prefer platinum to white gold."

"So why didn't you just say that in the first place?" Kevin asks in exasperation.

Why didn't I say that in the first place? My God, men can't really be that dense. What I want to tell him is that I didn't say it because I just want to get married. I want to tell him that I hate the fact that just getting engaged is this much work. And that I hate feeling like I haven't even heard the starting pistol for this marathon, and I'm already exhausted.

Instead, I lie and say, "I just don't want you to spend so much money."

"Compared to the cost of a house, this is nothing," Kevin jokes.

I must have flinched, because he immediately backtracks. "That came out wrong. I just meant, in terms of our long-term goals, this one isn't very expensive."

We then have one of those awkward pauses in conversation that can be bad in person but deadly half a world away. Eventually, Kevin changes the subject. "So, did you find a pink chandelier you like?"

I'm still inwardly flinching, but I try to get the conversation back on track by saying enthusiastically, "Actually, Nat found this really cool chandelier at the Brewery Art Walk near downtown. It's made out of hanging glass wine bottles. The artist hung wine bottles around an iron chandelier she welded, then put a low-energy light bulb inside each bottle. They're from a bunch of different wineries, so you have clear ones, green ones, even a few purple ones." I catch Kevin glancing at his phone but decide to ignore the intrusion. "It's neat. Really works with the brick and exposed pipe." Kevin can't help but focus on his text, and I've lost him completely. Nonetheless, I plod on. "It's like . . . even though I had a great fantasy in my head of what everything would look like when I started, the reality looks even better."

I wait for a response—nothing. He's immersed in the text now. "Is that work again?" I ask, trying not to sound irritated.

"I'm sorry," Kevin says, popping his eyes back up to me. "This is the problem with working for an American company in Germany. I get calls from nine to five my time, and nine to five their time." He sighs loudly. "I've got to send them a quick e-mail in response. I'm really sorry. Can I call you back in five?"

"You know what? It's okay," I say. "Get your e-mail done and try to get some sleep. I have a million things to do here before we open Thursday anyway."

"Are you sure?" Kevin asks.

"Yeah. I love you."

"I love you too. And I miss you. And I'm sorry I can't be there opening night. Send me a picture of that chandelier?"

"Will do," I promise, smiling.

"Okay." He flashes me his patented adorable smile. "Phone sex tomorrow?"

I laugh. "Not on your life."

"Eh, it was worth a shot. Same time tomorrow?"

"Unless I call you first," I say lightly.

Kevin smiles again. "I miss you, you know."

"I miss you too."

"No, I mean . . . I really miss you. I can't wait for you to walk along the Danube with me. It's like I keep seeing all these things here and thinking, 'Jessie would love this. Jessie would think this was cool. Jessie would think this was fun.' It's weird to think I'm not going to hang out with you for almost two more months."

The way he says that last sentence does sort of melt my heart. "I miss you like that too," I assure him. "I wish you could see everything we've done here. I think you'd be pretty proud of me."

"I'm always proud of you," Kevin tells me.

But before I can bask in the glow of his praise, he's back to his phone. "Crap, this is getting worse. I gotta go. Love you."

"Love you too."

And he's gone.

I look around my new office and sigh.

Why are relationships such hard work? Why can't anything be easy?

I mean, I love Kevin, I really do. But there's a part of me that wishes it could all be effortless. That I wasn't the first one to lean in for the first kiss. And lean in for the first date. And lean in for the ring.

There's a part of me that wishes guys would be more assertive these days. More sure of who they are and what they want. Less likely to keep checking their phones for the latest call, text, or ESPN alert, desperate for the distraction of what else is out there.

I get up to refill my coffee cup, sit back down to focus on my computer, and try to concentrate on ordering glassware.

While Nat picked and ordered five different shapes of glasses for wine (out of more than one hundred styles sold by the bar supply distributor—yikes!), she completely forgot about water glasses. Turns out there are over fifty types of water glasses. Who knew there were so many ways to serve water?

Fifty. And I have to look at a picture of each one. Talk about a distraction from what's important in life.

I'm not only tired of stressing over each decision we have to make, I wonder how many of them our customers will even notice. It reminds me of a wedding my coworker planned for almost two years. For months on end, I'd hear her in her office next to mine fretting: "Should the party favors include candy? Do we want lilies on the tables, or roses? Salmon or filet mignon?" Two years of her life, and for what? I'll bet the main thing her guests remember is whether or not they got laid that night.

Shit. Now I'm thinking about weddings. Which is making me think about Kevin's and my possible wedding.

I'm saying "possible" because I don't want to jinx it. But I'll admit, this last month has been nothing short of amazing. The guy went from refusing to buy a house with me to obsessing over my perfect ring. Maybe there really will be a wedding. Maybe all those relationship gurus are right—if you focus on yourself and what you want, the perfect man will follow.

Speaking of perfect . . . is a curvy water glass perfect if it looks sexy, or is a sturdy solid water glass with a heavy base more to a girl's liking? Probably depends on the girl. Our All for Wine and

Wine for All! philosophy of finding the perfect wine for each woman could probably also apply to water glasses. Everyone likes something different—half the battle is figuring out what you really want.

I set my sights on choice number twenty-eight. It looks perfect. But, then again, what is perfect? And how do I know when to quit looking, click the "buy" button, and get on with my life?

"Good afternoon," I hear a deep voice say from my office doorway. "Can you tell me where I can find Natasha?"

I look up to see the Roman god Bacchus, in all his perfect-bodied glory, standing in my doorway.

Ho-lee crap.

Tan skin that's so flawless, it's like someone Photoshopped him. Glittery brown eyes with long black eyelashes. Wavy dark hair that's a little too long, a little unkempt, but just enough to make a girl think about keeping this guy in bed for two weeks straight.

Bacchus is wearing dark blue jeans, a white button-up shirt, dark jacket, and black Italian loafers. He holds a pile of glossy brochures in one hand and wheels a small suitcase with the other. If he were a character in a foreign film, it would inspire me to read subtitles. (Who am I kidding? It would inspire me to pay eighteen bucks for the movie to just stare at him and not read a damn thing.)

I think the elastic in my underwear just melted a bit. "Natasha's not in yet," I tell him, trying to keep my voice from catching. "Can I help you with something?"

"I'm Giovanni Caro. I represent six Italian wineries that export to the States. I called a few days ago to arrange a tasting of several of my favorites, and to give everyone at your establishment some information about our wines. I thought she said to come at three o'clock Monday. I have an Orvieto that I believe your customers will be very pleased with."

The way he says "Orvieto" makes me wonder what swooning actually feels like. And am I doing it now? (That would be embarrassing.)

"I can help you with that," I say, quickly hitting Sleep on my computer and standing up to walk over to Giovanni. "I'm one of the owners, and have the authority to make purchases."

Giovanni puts out his hand. "Perfect. And you are?"

"Jessie. I mean Jessica. I mean . . ." I start to put out my hand, then quickly pull it back to wipe the sweat off on my jeans. "Sorry," I say, then put out my now dry hand for him to shake. "It's Jessie. I'm a little scatterbrained today. I wasn't expecting you, and you threw me for a loop."

That's putting it mildly.

Giovanni shakes my hand. "Delighted to meet you. Now, what can I interest you in?"

Oh, I don't know. A house with a view of the water, two bilingual kids with beautiful eyelashes, and whatever dog is popular in Italy?

"Um . . . that Orvieto sounds good. Is that anything like Cabernet?" I ask him.

"Actually it's a white, but I think I can find you something you'll like in red."

Perhaps you, nestled between some red silk sheets.

Oh, my God . . . What is wrong with me? I'm acting like a fifteen-year-old with a crush on the Varsity quarterback, I tell myself as I accidentally sniff him. He smells woodsy. Like, woodsy enough to make a girl consider camping for the night.

"Are you an adventurous person?" he practically purrs.

Not even vaguely. "Sure."

Giovanni smiles brightly. "If you like reds, I have everything from a Montepulciano d'Abruzzo to a Super Tuscan to a Barolo from

Piedmont. What would you say is the characteristic of Cabernet that most appeals to you?"

I would say that it gets me drunk. But that's probably not the answer I should give a wine rep. "You know what? I'd really like to try that Orvieto. Do you want to come out to the bar area, and then you'll be all set up once Nat gets here?"

"Wonderful," he says cheerfully. He wheels his suitcase out of my office, toward our open-concept bar.

I follow him out, unable to ignore the fact that he looks just as good from behind as he does in the front.

Okay, obviously I can't date him, because I have Kevin. But Nat *must* date him! He's gorgeous. He's charming. And, unlike Prick with a *c,* he's not married.

Wait, I don't know if he's married. I realize I need to look for a ring as he walks to one of the large wooden butcher block tables in the middle of the room, and stands at attention by a pink cushioned barstool. I scrutinize his left hand as he pulls out the chair for me to sit. No ring. (And also—how cute. When was the last time a guy actually pulled out a chair for a lady? I'm guessing 1958.)

"Thank you," I say, feeling my face heat up as he pushes in my chair, then makes his way around the table. "So do you need to put the bottles in the refrigerator for a bit to get them to the proper temperatures?"

"That's not necessary. I installed a wine refrigerator into the trunk of my car so that my wines are always ready to serve and the perfect temperature."

I watch Giovanni open his suitcase, which holds six bottles of wine.

"Really?" I say, impressed. "Did you install it yourself?"

"Actually, yes. I like to tinker with cars."

"Wow. The guys I know can't even install a dimmer switch, much less a refrigerator. So . . . what do you drive? Like . . . a minivan or something?"

Please say no, please say no, please say no.

Giovanni begins fanning out the brochures on the table, "No. I don't have kids yet, so I haven't quite hit my minivan stage. Don't judge—I drive a Porsche."

"A Porsche? Yowza!" I exclaim.

"Yowza?"

"A man who looks like you *and* drives a cool car *and* can fix one? Yowza. Times ten."

Giovanni laughs. "I wish my ex-girlfriend saw things your way. I picked up a 1994 model last year, cheap but very beat-up, deciding I was going to restore it. It has since become known as *foro di denaro.*"

I let my jaw drop and my shoulders sink in exaggeration as I sigh, "Ooohhhh, that sounds so romantic."

"It's Italian for 'money hole.'"

"Oh."

Giovanni pulls out a green bottle with a green-and-cream-colored label and gold lettering. "Orvieto is a city in southwestern Umbria, and the Orvieto zone is known for its limestone and volcanic soil. Orvieto wine is probably the best-known wine in Umbria. Have you been to Italy?"

"No," I am disappointed and embarrassed to admit. "I've always wanted to go, but life just keeps getting in the way. You?"

"Oh, many times. My father also works in the wine industry, and my mother will use any excuse to travel, so we went back and forth a lot as a family. Plus I did a semester abroad at the University of Padua."

"Wow," I say as I watch him pierce the green foil top with his corkscrew, then peel it off. "I almost did a semester abroad, but I didn't think my French was good enough. Where did you go to college?"

He smiles mischievously as he screws in the corkscrew with a smooth and practiced flourish. "The University of Hawaii at Manoa."

"Seriously?" I blurt out enviously. "You got to live in Hawaii? Did you surf?"

"I did," he tells me proudly. "I surfed the North Shore on Oahu and windsurfed in Maui. I also flew to the Big Island to ski on Mauna Kea, and I even went to Lanai to lounge at the pool at the Four Seasons for a long weekend and pretend I was a millionaire."

"That's amazing," I say, genuinely impressed. "So does your family live in Hawaii?"

Giovanni pulls out the cork and hands it to me to sniff. "No, they're up in Sonoma. Truth be told, I applied to Yale. But when I didn't get in, instead of wallowing in self-pity, I decided, 'Okay, life didn't work out how I planned. Now what can I do to be happy anyway?'" Regarding the cork, he asks, "So what do you think?"

To be honest, I never could get into the sniffing-the-cork thing. I never know what I'm supposed to be smelling (I'm guessing wine?), but I make a show of putting it up to my nose and taking a big whiff. Honestly? It smells like . . . crushed grapes. "Smells great," I declare, as though I have the slightest idea what I'm talking about.

"Excellent. Now, what glass would you use to serve your guests this type of wine?"

Ummm . . . not a clue. I turn the question back on him. "What glass would you recommend?"

"There are several that can do the job well." He points to the area behind the long pink bar. "I'd love to see what our choices are. Do you mind?"

I motion for him to go ahead. "Please."

Giovanni heads behind the bar. As he peruses his choices, I take his silence as an opportunity to continue my interrogation. "So you said 'ex-girlfriend.' Is there a current girlfriend?"

"No."

"Boyfriend?"

He chuckles a little. "I'm going to assume you think I'm gay because I'm so well dressed and charming."

"You didn't answer the question."

"No."

"No, you're not gay, or no, you didn't answer the question?"

"No, I'm not gay," he tells me, then bends down and disappears behind the bar. "Why? Are you?"

"I wish!" I blurt out. "So can you find anything back there?"

Giovanni pops back up. "Absolutely. You have great taste in glassware." He holds up one of our narrower stemmed glasses. "And this one is made for Orvieto." Giovanni walks back to my table, places the glass in front of me, and pours a small amount of the wine into the glass.

Then he waits.

Oh. That's my cue.

Okay, I've been a customer at enough wine bars to be able to pull this off, I tell myself. I place my index and middle fingers under the bowl of the glass and swirl the wine a bit. Then I raise the glass and stick my nose into it.

I inhale deeply, and fall in love immediately. The wine smells like a combination of apricots and peaches. I could put whipped cream on this thing and call it dessert. (I could also put whipped cream on . . . never mind. Nat. He's for Nat.)

I take a sip, expecting it to be too sweet for my taste. But, contrary to what I thought it would taste like, it's not cloying, but instead tastes clean and crisp.

"That's . . . really fantastic," I say, not bothering to hide my surprise. I put out my glass. "Can I have more?"

"Of course," he says, filling my glass halfway. "Now, the trick with this wine is never overpour. You need to give it lots of room in the glass to bring out its fragrance."

What I want to say is, "Hey, what are you leaving room for? Cream and sugar?" because it's so good, I want more. But instead I ask, "Aren't you having any?"

"No. I have to drive. Plus I have two more calls today. I only enjoy wine in the evenings."

"Would you like to enjoy some wine this Thursday?" I ask abruptly (not to mention rather clumsily). Before Giovanni can answer, I quickly add, "That's our opening night. Lots of beautiful single women will be here, and you could enjoy an Orvieto with one of them."

My mind wants to take half a second to try and read his reaction to my invitation, but my mouth refuses to stop talking. "Or we could serve your favorite wine, and you could have that on Thursday. What's your favorite wine?"

Giovanni thinks for a moment. "I've recently grown fond of our Montepulciano d'Abruzzo."

"Great. We'll take six cases of that."

He seems almost startled. "Don't you want to sample it first?"

"Great idea!" I agree, hitting the table twice. "Set me up!"

What am I saying? Who is this girl?

"Okay, then," Giovanni says, clearly pleased as he pulls a red from his wine suitcase. He fetches a wider wineglass from the bar. "Now you'll want to let this one breathe for a bit . . ."

I hear our back door open and Nat yell out, "I managed to track down a stud finder at the hardware store! Wouldn't it be great if they sold those in real life? Go to the grocery store and tell it, 'I'd like a young Stephen Colbert type . . . and the stud finder could *beep beep beep* until, 'Oh there he is. In the frozen foods section.'"

I jump up from the table and tell Giovanni, "That's Nat. You have *got* to meet her. You are going to love her. And if you stay for the next hour and pour us tasters, we'll take six cases of everything."

As I quickly trot over to the storage room in the back, I hear Giovanni say, "That's fantastic. What should I pour after the Montepulciano?"

"Whatever else you plan to drink this Thursday," I yell over my shoulder to him as I enter the storage room and quickly slam the door.

"I'm your stud finder!" I exclaim proudly (yet very quietly) to Nat once the door is closed. "And you don't even have to pay me. I'm thinking you'd make an amazing October bride and . . . Oh, Jesus. What are you wearing?"

Nat is wearing old stretched-out, elephant-gray yoga pants, a ripped battleship gray T-shirt, and—the pièce de résistance—a scrunchy. She turns to me. "Well, since I was heading out to the hardware store, naturally I spent quite a while debating between the Prada and the Gucci. You should see my room—clothes all over my bed."

I race up to her, so we can whisper. "Do you want to change and come back?" I suggest. "Maybe put on that purple dress that shows off your boobs."

"You're all flushed," Nat tells me as she puts her hand on my cheek. "I hope you're not coming down with anything."

"Just a case of matchmakeritis. I have the perfect guy for you. He's single, well traveled, drives a Porsche, and knows a ton about wine. Go home and change. Maybe pair your red mini with a kicky top."

"'Kicky'?" Nat repeats, furrowing her brow. "How much wine

have you had? Anyway, I'm not changing for some guy I've never met. Particularly not some douchebag who drives a Porsche."

"Oh, I'm sorry. I forgot Prick with a *c* rides his bike to work," I pipe back sarcastically. "I'm telling you, this is the most amazing man I've met in years. And he's so cute, there should be a Disney prince modeled after him."

She gives me a dubious look. "You and I really don't pick the same . . ."

"He's so good-looking, he could be a pharmaceutical rep," I continue.

"I'm sure he's very nice looking. But I'm just getting over Marc and . . ."

"He's so cute, he served me an Orvieto. And I drank it."

"Plus I . . ." Nat stops, turns her head slightly to the right, then narrows her eyes into a squint. "Wait. *You* drank white wine?" she asks. "You?"

My eyes light up, and I grin as I nod vigorously.

"And a wine that doesn't come from California?" she asks dubiously.

"Yes. And I liked it so much, I bought six cases. Apparently, it comes from Italy."

"I know where Orvieto comes from," Nat assures me testily. "Okay, I gotta see this guy." She creeps over to the door, opens it ever so slightly, and peeks through. I can't help myself—I tiptoe next to her to take another look. So, so pretty . . .

Nat closes the door gently. "He certainly is very good-looking," she concedes. "But, wait, if he's so great, why don't you go out with him?"

"I have Kevin," I point out, taking offense.

Nat shrugs a bit like she's not convinced.

"Oh, for God's sake! We're practically engaged," I say as I yank the scrunchy out of her hair and fluff up her roots with my finger-tips. "Now go! Let me live vicariously!"

I yank open the door, put my hand on the small of Nat's back, and shove her out to meet the father of her future children. "Giovanni, this is Natasha. And she would love to try your Orvieto!"

Chapter Nineteen

NAT

Jessie shoves me forward into the room so fiercely that I stumble and have to regain my balance. I then hear her slam the door shut to give us our privacy.

Subtle.

I know this dude Giovanni saw her do that. But clearly he's trying to make a big sale, so he'll pretend he didn't. "Hi," I say awkwardly, forcing a smile. "I'm Nat. And I'll be the one thrust upon you this afternoon."

"Giovanni," he reciprocates, smiling. "So is there a wine I can interest you in?"

"I believe Jessie would like me to try your Orvieto," I say, trying to couch my embarrassment as I walk up to him.

"Yes. I find her enthusiasm quite refreshing," he says, pulling out a chair for me at the center table, which is now filled with six wines, each in appropriately shaped glassware.

As I take the seat and allow him to push my chair in, I realize this is sooooo not going to work. I'll admit: The guy is very, very cute. Like so much so, you expect a film crew to pop out of nowhere and say, "Surprise! You're on that NBC show where we secretly record single women to see how they'll react when we put a former prom king right in front of them."

The prom king looks make me uneasy, and not in the fun way. Too handsome. Notices-the-mirror-before-I-do handsome. Does-yoga handsome. Tries-too-hard handsome.

So I decide to get that exquisite elephant out of the room. "You know, if you had longer hair, you could be on the cover of a romance novel."

"What makes you think I haven't been?" he asks, deadpan, as he makes his way to his side of the table.

"Really?" I ask, a bit intrigued.

Giovanni smiles. "No. I just didn't know what to say to that. It's like you're passively-aggressively complimenting me."

"Oh, it's not *like* that. I *was* totally passive-aggressively complimenting you. I'll try to control myself."

"Most women have to around me," he says, opening his mouth and rolling his eyes to show me he's just joking. "So, Natasha, which wine can I tell you about first? The Orvieto is the first glass on your left . . ."

"I'm actually more in a red mood, if that's okay. What are in glasses four, five, and six?"

"Those are a flight of Brunello di Montalcino. I have a couple of good years here. Perfect with a rare steak and a gratin dauphinois."

"You'd mix a French potato dish with an Italian wine?" I ask him haughtily.

Back off, Nat. The guy's just doing his job. No need to pick a fight.

Giovanni puckers his lips as though debating his answer. Finally, he gives me an almost wicked smile. "See, I believe it's important to mix things up when you can. Indulge in a little bit of everything. And, like the contrast of a French cheese with an American potato, American beef, and an Italian wine can be just as intriguing as an exquisitely beautiful woman clothed"—he eyes me lasciviously, despite the sweats—"in a deceptively casual ensemble."

I narrow my eyes at him. "I'm sorry, do you *write* romance novels in your spare time? Who talks like that?"

"Oooo . . . she doesn't like the compliment," he pretends to say to himself. "I made her uncomfortable." Then to me, "Try glass number four. It's been aged five years."

I take a sip. Much like him, it is smooth, gorgeous, and I could roll my tongue around it for a while. "That would actually be very tasty with a medium-rare filet," I concede.

"See, I'd have pegged you for a rare girl," he jokes.

"Oh, I'm a rare girl indeed," I counter effortlessly.

"And your tastes lean more toward filet mignon than rib eye?"

"Actually, I'm more of a Chateaubriand for two, for one, kinda gal," I say, playing along. "But a perfectly cooked rib eye can make me happy."

"I notice you didn't say 'well done.'"

"Not before the date, no," I say, sniffing the second Brunello di Montalcino.

Giovanni laughs. "So there's going to be a date? Will I be cooking for you on this date? Or will you be cooking for me?"

I smile slightly. "I think you should cook for me. I hate cooking."

"Really? Why?"

I shrug and smile bashfully. "There are just so many more enjoyable activities one can do in a kitchen."

It's amazing how easy it is to flirt with someone when you don't really give a shit.

"Oh, for God's sake!" I hear Jessie mutter from the back. I jump up from my seat and race toward the storage room as I hear her complain, "I practically gave him to you gift wrapped and you—"

And I quickly open and slam the door. "Ow," Jessie yelps from the other side.

Giovanni's eyes widen in surprise. "Is she all right?"

"She'll be fine. She's a drama queen. Look, I'm sorry. This was fun, but I can't keep this confident Bond Girl thing going any longer. You're awesome. But you don't have to keep flirting with me just to make a few wine sales. Jessie means well. She's pretty much engaged and wants everyone else to be in a relationship too. I'm sorry. I'll be good now."

He looks up at the ceiling in thought, then looks at me. "So, is this the moment where I continue the banter and say, 'I'd prefer you bad' or are you really telling me to back off?"

I want to shake my head a bunch of times really fast and say "Wha—?" Instead, I say, "You can continue flirting. I just didn't want to put you in an awkward position." Then I sip my wine.

"Once again, you've given me the perfect setup."

I try to suppress my laugh, and wine goes up my nose. Giovanni chuckles. "Sorry."

"Of course you are. How dare you be funny while I'm drinking?" I tell him mock sternly.

Giovanni laughs a little more. "So . . . I wouldn't be able to cook for you, but would you like to go out tomorrow night? I have an extra ticket to the opera if you're interested. Do you like *La Traviata*?"

I have no idea. I've heard of it but never seen it live. I know it was written by Giuseppe Verdi in the mid-1800s. I also know I hate opera.

But the Universe (or Jessie) has presented me with a good-looking, funny guy who's easy to talk to. And no, he's not Marc (whom I kind of miss), but he's probably better than Marc. "You know what? I'd really like that," I tell him.

"Great. Are you a night owl? Maybe we can do a drink beforehand and dinner afterward so we're not rushing through dinner to get to the opening curtain?"

"Sounds perfect," I say to him.

And it really kind of does.

Then my early thirtysomething woman brain kicks in (damn her), and I start thinking of all the reasons I shouldn't go out on the date.

"I know this sounds like crazy-girl behavior," I begin awkwardly. "And I'm sorry about that. But I just got out of a rather complicated relationship, so I have to ask up front: You don't have a girlfriend, do you?"

He smiles. "That's not crazy. And as of now, no. But I met this really beautiful woman today. So I'll have let you know after to-morrow."

I look away from him and smile nervously. Though I can't see him, I'm positive he's still looking at me.

Then crazy brain takes over again. I snap my head back at him. "Wait. You mean me, right?"

I seem to amuse him. "Yes. I mean you."

I grin. "That's a coincidence. Because I met this really handsome guy today. Like, insanely handsome. Beauty-that-should-not-be-found-in-nature handsome."

Giovanni nods, turns the corners of his lips down to signal, *Not bad.* Then he jokes, "Except his hair is too short."

"Oh, so you saw him too," I joke.

And we smile at each other.

Okay, he seems nice. And I wouldn't kick him out of bed and all that. This might be just what I need.

I raise my voice to acknowledge Jessie, whom I see peeking out of the storage room. "We set up a date. You can come back now."

Jessie charges out to us. "Yay!" she says while quickly taking a seat next to me. "And you're going to love *La Traviata*. It's all in Italian, but the opera company runs subtitles on a lighted board above the stage."

"I do love Italian things," I admit to Giovanni as flirtatiously as I can.

Though actually my mind is racing. *Subtitles? Crap. I hate subtitles. Why can't he take me to a Lakers game like a normal guy?*

Chapter Twenty

Giovanni was perfect for Nat! He likes opera, Jonathan Franzen, Thai food, and *Casablanca*. (Okay, he admitted he hadn't seen *Casablanca*. But how cool would it be for Nat to see that movie with a newbie?) This was definitely going to work out. Good-bye Prick with a *c*!

Nat had to leave for a dentist's appointment but gave Giovanni her number and said she was looking forward to their date tomorrow.

That left him all for me. Just as a friend. Obviously, not as a date or anything, since I'm with Kevin. But how cool to find a new friend who likes opera and Thai food.

I was really feeling a connection with him. He laughed at all of my jokes and really listened to me when I talked about all of the problems we were encountering three days before the bar was set to open. He even offered to look at our floor-to-ceiling wine fridge, which we bought used, and which didn't seem to want to work.

"We have a repairman coming," I tell Giovanni as he examines the back of the unit. "But he can't come until tomorrow—and we're desperately hoping he can fix it and we can get our bottles in there before our soft opening on Thursday."

As I watch him tug at some silver wiry thingie, he assures me,

"This is an older unit, but it's still in pretty good shape. You just need a new coil back here. If you want to go to Home Depot with me, I can fix this in about an hour."

He's asking me out! I think happily.

Where did that come from?

I quickly lambaste myself, *No, he's asking you to join him at a hardware store. So he can impress your best friend. Dork.*

But I'm still excited. New friend and all that.

"Let me grab my purse," I tell Giovanni, then practically bounce out of the room into my office.

As I pull my purse from the bottom drawer of my desk, my Skype beeps that Kevin is calling. I quickly answer. "Hey, I can't talk right now. We found someone to fix the refrigerator, but I have to go to the hardware store with him."

"What do you think of this?" Kevin says, holding up a picture of a ring with a large blue sapphire in the center surrounded by diamonds.

Wow. I mean, seriously, yowza.

I put down my purse and stare at the screen. "It's really pretty. It looks a lot like Duchess Kate's ring," I tell Kevin.

"That's because it is. I looked it up online because I remembered you said you liked it a while back. Kate's ring is white gold, but we could get you something in platinum. So what do you think? Is a big colored stone maybe something we should be looking at? Then we could afford to go bigger than a diamond, plus it's not what every cookie cutter bride is wearing."

"It is really pretty," I say, intrigued. "But the blue one is so associated with Princess Diana. What do you think about an amethyst instead? Like a super-dark one?"

Giovanni walks up to the doorway silently as Kevin answers me, "That could be cool. I'll do some research on amethysts."

I look over at Giovanni and suddenly feel guilty. Which is weird, because I'm not doing anything wrong.

"Sounds awesome," I manage to sputter out to Kevin while nervously watching Giovanni. "I really have to go, though. Can I call you tomorrow?"

"Wait—I have one more to show you. It's a pink diamond in the shape of a heart."

I look at the picture and want to scream, "Oh, God no!" But I also don't want Giovanni to see what a bitch I can be. *Jesus, Jessie, snap out of it. How about you don't want the guy who wants to buy you a diamond to see what a bitch you can be?*

I glance over to the doorway to see Giovanni has disappeared. "Um . . . that's really not my style," I tell Kevin awkwardly. "But . . . can we talk about this later? I really need to get to Home Depot."

Kevin's unfazed by my brushoff. "Sure. Call me tonight when you have a minute. Or I'll call you when I wake up. Maybe I can catch you before bed. I love you."

"I love you too. Bye," I tell him, and I wonder if he's bothered by the rush in my voice.

Huh. I've told Kevin I love him a million times. Why did I suddenly not want to say it? Why did it just sound like words coming out of my mouth due to a social contract: like "How are you?" and "Have a nice day"? And did he notice?

I decide I'm overthinking, quickly click off Skype, grab my purse, and head out of the office. Giovanni is waiting for me by the front door, holding it open for me. Oh, my God, he's so cute AND he's a gentleman. Where was this guy when I was surfing match.com and wondering if I'd ever find anyone? Nat is so fucking lucky. "Thank you so much for doing this," I tell him. "I don't know how I can repay you."

"Not a problem. Maybe it will win me points with your friend Nat. So, was that your boyfriend?"

I don't know why, but I suddenly feel a twinge of nausea. "Yes. He's in Frankfurt right now for work."

"Ahhhh, nice this time of year," Giovanni says, not showing any trace of disappointment that I have a boyfriend. "For how long?"

"Four months. Although now they're saying maybe five."

"Have you visited him yet?"

"No," I answer uneasily, feeling a wave of guilt come over me again. "I should have by now. I just got so busy getting ready to open the bar. Plus, it's expensive."

Giovanni doesn't answer. Instead he silently follows me out of the bar and onto the street. "I will, though," I continue. "He said if I came we could also spend a few days in France. I'd really like to see the Louvre. Plus, of course, the Paris Opera House." I close the front door and lock it. "Speaking of opera, how did you get to be such a fan?"

Giovanni smiles, leans in to me, and whispers, "Can I let you in on a little secret?"

He smells delicious. It that woodsy or more citrusy? I turn to him, and for a brief moment I think about kissing his neck. "Sure."

"I originally bought tickets to impress women. Particularly on third dates. But then, the older I got, the more I started to enjoy it."

"What are you wearing?" I ask him out of the blue.

"Excuse me?"

I shake my head, embarrassed. "I'm sorry. I meant your cologne. What is that?"

"Oh. Chanel for Men."

"Really? Which scent?"

"Bleu de Chanel," he rattles off in perfect French. "An old

girlfriend got it for me back in college, and I just kind of stayed with it. What do you think?"

"You smell fantastic. I should definitely get some for Kevin."

Good save, Jessie.

"Glad you like it," Giovanni tells me easily. He beeps his car unlocked, then opens the passenger door for me. "I'll be sure to wear it tomorrow night."

Tomorrow night?

Oh, yeah. Right. His date with Nat.

Chapter Twenty-one

HOLLY

That Tuesday, two days before our big opening night, I return from yet another introductory yoga class to see a letter taped to our front door. I untape the letter from the door and examine it. There's no address or postage, just a handwritten "Nat and Holly" chicken-scratched in black ink on the front of the envelope. I open the letter and read.

> Hi, guys,
>
> I'm so sorry. I got your invitation, but I have to miss your opening night. I have been called to San Francisco on business. I was very much looking forward to seeing you both again and supporting you in your oenophilic endeavors.
>
> I have the address and plan to come by as soon as I get home. Please accept my apologies. And good luck Thursday!
>
> Best,
> Sven

Damn it! I've been waiting for almost two weeks to see him again, specifically keeping my distance so that I could make a great impression this Thursday. Since the disastrous first encounter at the mailbox, I've been rehearsing what I would say to him and coming up with lots of questions to ask him about Sweden, and computer code, and Cambridge (which is where he went to school, even though I'm not supposed to know that, because Google stalking is a little creepy). I bought a new dress. Got new perfume. Went to the Mac counter to try to find the perfect lipstick.

All that effort, just to get rejected.

Damn it. There's that familiar anvil feeling in my gut again. Why can't just one thing in my life go the way I planned?

I shouldn't have asked, because my brain immediately starts blasting me with all of the usual insults: *He doesn't like you, you know that. If he did, he would have called. Suddenly had to go to San Francisco for business? What does he think? You're an idiot? You've watched Marc and Nat long enough to know that Sven obviously has a girlfriend there. Men like that don't go for girls like you. You're an actress. You're never going to be smart enough for him, and let's face it, you're not twenty-two anymore: You can't con a guy into liking you just because he thinks you're hot. That was twentysomething Holly, the idiot who didn't know all the good men would be picked off by the time she was twenty-five.*

You should have gotten married when you had the chance. You're going to die alone.

Isn't it amazing what our brains are constantly telling us? If I had a roommate who started in on me like that before I'd even had a chance to get my coffee in the morning, I'd have her stuff out on the curb by noon. If a boyfriend said such horrible things, I'd be out the door and have his Facebook blocked within the hour.

But my inner voice? She knows exactly what to tell me to make me want to get back on those pills. And my inner voice has been way louder since I got off the meds.

Right now I desperately want to run to the drugstore and pick up a refill. I need to feel better.

So I do what addicts have done for years.

I head to a meeting.

"Hi. I'm Holly," I begin cautiously. I take a deep breath and (finally) admit to the group, "And I'm a drug addict."

Because that's what my antidepressants were for me. They were drugs. Like most drugs, they could do good or harm. Penicillin: good. Heroin: harm. Vicodin: somewhere in between. Usually necessary, but can be abused. My pills? Probably (for me at least) closer to Vicodin than the other two.

"Hi, Holly," the rest of the group responds in soothing voices.

I look around the room at the twelve or so people here at the Narcotics Anonymous meeting. "I'm sure some of you recognize me. I've been to a few of these meetings and I . . . um . . . I never talk because I don't know what to say."

I make eye contact with a sixtysomething woman. She is this week's group leader (people take turns) and has dyed jet-black hair and kind brown eyes. I decide to talk to her.

"I'm addicted to painkillers," I begin, having decided before I started coming to these meetings that that's what antidepressants should ideally be: painkillers. "It's nothing you get high from—trust me. But they are addictive, and in the long run, they were hurting me, and I knew they had to go. I've been off of them for a couple of months. And even though I know they might kill me, I don't think I'm going to be able to stay off of them."

I turn my attention to a twentysomething redhead, wearing jeans and a bright white T-shirt. He too, has kind eyes. "The thing is, since my dad died, I've tried really hard to do the things that will be good for me, and to avoid things that I know will hurt me. I've stopped auditioning for TV roles, because it's just not making me happy anymore. I'm trying to take up yoga. Although, frankly, I don't get the appeal: It leaves me way too much time alone with my thoughts. I'm opening a business with my two best friends in the world, both of whom are amazingly loving and supportive and always wish the best for me." I stare down at my fingernails and nervously pick at a cuticle. "I'm actually surrounding myself with love and support all the time. Not just from them, but from old acting buddies, college friends, from anyone who I know is good to me and wishes me well."

I take another breath and continue. "But even with all of this love in my life, I'm still hurting. And I don't know how to fix it. And there was this guy . . . half the time it's a guy, right? . . . I don't know him well, but I wanted him to like me, and when he didn't, all my brain could tell me over and over again was, 'That's because he saw the real you. And ick. Who would want that?'" I flit my eyes over to a middle-aged man wearing a suit. "I'm so tired of my inner voice. She's mean, and she never cuts me any slack. And the only thing that ever shut her up were the painkillers. So how do I keep her quiet without them? How do I make her like me?"

I look around the room, hoping for an answer. The problem with these meetings is that no one's supposed to answer you—they're just supposed to let you talk. I nod knowingly. "So I guess that's why I'm here. I need to learn how to quiet down the mean girl of my inner voice without going back to the painkillers. Thanks for letting me share."

Well, that didn't help at all. But I suppose it bought me three extra minutes without popping a pill.

I spend the next half hour listening to stories from people whose drug addictions sound so much harder to fight than mine and wondering why I dared to come at all. Seriously, how dare I? Who do I think I am to consider myself in the same group as a person battling a heroin or cocaine addiction? I don't belong here. No one ever divorced me over my crutch. I never lost my job or my kids. I have this minor problem that I am clearly blowing way out of proportion . . .

And suddenly I realize: There she is, my inner voice, telling me yet again that I'm not worthy. Nobody here thinks I don't belong— that is all coming from me and my thoughts.

So I tell my brain to Shut. The Fuck. Up.

Just for now. Just long enough to really focus on the other people's stories, the way they did for me.

And my revelation? She did simmer down. For the first time in a long time, my inner voice shut up.

Huh. How about that? Maybe these meetings are working.

Chapter Twenty-two

NAT

I ask this without judgment. Why the hell do people go to the opera?

La Traviata is Italian for "the Fallen Woman." And that makes sense, since *this* woman almost fell asleep at least four times before intermission. Everything sounded like a Bugs Bunny cartoon set up. Duh-daaaahhhh, duh, dah, dah, duh-dah-dah-dah-dah-dah-dah what the fuck are they singing? Oh—right—read the subtitles.

Despite the fact that it's in Italian, it's about this Frenchwoman named Violetta, who is a courtesan, which technically means she's an entourage member from the French court, but really I think it means she's a hooker. Albeit an elegant one, swimming in velvet.

As far as I can tell, Violetta is getting over tuberculosis in Act 1. Usually a deadly and frightfully contagious disease tends to dissuade gentlemen from pursuing a relationship, but not so in Violetta's case. She must have looked like Beyoncé back in her day, because everyone is in love with her, despite the whole TB bugaboo. One of the doe-eyed suitors, Alfredo, declares his love for her by trying to put her to sleep with his grandiose singing. It certainly put me to sleep.

I suppose she inexplicably likes his singing, because she does go to the countryside to live with him in Act 2. Chaos ensues: He can't marry her, so they break up. But then he comes back when she's on her deathbed (again—did TB mean nothing back then?). If I am to understand the subtitles correctly, first the two sing together, then she sings about being revived, then she promptly drops dead in his arms. (Because—hello? I really hate to beat a dead horse here, but the girl has tuberculosis. In the 1800s. No one survives TB in the 1800s. Or do they? I should look that up. Marc would know . . . Stop thinking about Marc.)

I find myself staring longingly at the prop wineglasses during all of the party scenes. If only I had a drink, maybe this would go faster.

And the opera finally ends. Thank fucking God.

As the lights come up, I have already decided that this date is going nowhere. Yes, Giovanni is a great guy, very sweet, and hotter than a New York sidewalk in August. But clearly we have nothing in common. I don't like Porsches, opera, or the Boston Red Sox. Plus, on the way over he said he liked "anything by William Faulkner," so clearly he's a moron.

The question is, which is more polite? To tell him the date is over now and save him the cost of dinner? Or to go through with the dinner so he won't feel rejected?

I am debating this when Giovanni gently takes my hand, and we walk up the lush red carpet aisle together. "What did you think?" he asks me.

I'll admit that his hand feels nice. Soft, warm, kind of comforting. It's been a long time since I had a man around who would willingly take my hand in public.

"Well," I begin cautiously, "I found Alfredo to be . . . a little pitchy?"

Giovanni laughs lightly. "Wow. You're really on first-date behavior.

The guy sounded like he'd had whiskey and cigarettes for breakfast, then broken glass for lunch."

I exhale a giant breath of relief. "I'm so happy you said that. So that's not what the men are supposed to sound like?"

"Not at all. Fortunately, Violetta was good."

If you say so, dude.

"I have tickets to *The Barber of Seville* in a few weeks. If you're free, the man playing Figaro has some serious pipes on him."

Did he just ask me out for a few weeks from now? Like . . . already? He hasn't even kissed me yet. How would he know if he wants to see me again at all, much less in a few weeks?

"I'm not sure if I can," I hedge. "The bar opens this week. I have no idea how busy we'll be, or what my schedule will be once we get going."

Giovanni pauses for a second, as though he's trying to figure out if my hedging is code for something. "Fair enough," he finally tells me as we walk hand in hand into the grand lobby. "So I've made a reservation for us at this amazing steakhouse nearby. There's a piano bar that goes until one. And I'm told they do a fabulous Chateaubriand for two for one."

I laugh. "I was kidding about that. Well, kind of." I stop walking and turn to him. "Have I apologized enough yet for acting like a freak when we met?"

"No, you haven't," he tells me in all seriousness. Then he leans in and kisses me gently on the lips. "But maybe you can over dinner."

His lips are soft and warm, and I can't help but close my eyes and revel in the moment.

He pulls away from me, and I smile and look away shyly. The kiss was very innocent, very respectable here in the land of the well-dressed octogenarians. But it is leaving me wondering what it would be like to have more.

Giovanni smiles back, then the two of us stroll hand in hand outside. Once we get outside, he asks, "So, did I pass the kissing test?"

"The kissing test?" I ask, hoping to God he's not referring to what I'm absolutely sure he's referring to, and trying to cover the panic and embarrassment on my face. "What are you talking about?"

"Jessie told me you have three tests for men: the kissing test, the phone test, and the brunch test."

I'm going to fucking kill her. I close my eyes super tight, hoping this will all go away. "Oh, my God. I'm mortified."

Giovanni laughs. "Don't be. I'm looking forward to the brunch test."

To that, I open my eyes and challenge, "Really? So you think you'll pass the phone test well enough to get to the brunch test?"

"I have three sisters and a mother. Bring it."

"Oh, I'll bring it," I promise, leaning my head lightly to the left to hint that I would like him to kiss me again. "So do you want to take me home so I can call you?"

"Your home? No," Giovanni says as he puts his hands around my waist and pulls me in for a kiss so passionate and perfect, my whole body feels like it might melt into goo. I wrap my hands around the back of his neck and wonder what I did to deserve having a man this wonderful come into my life.

And then Marc pops into my head.

Damn it!

Chapter Twenty-three

JESSIE

"So then what happened?" I ask Nat excitedly as we unpack wines into the new (to us) floor-to-ceiling refrigerator.

"Then we went to this really great steak place, which I wouldn't have thought I would have liked because it's all dark wood and red leather booths and old guys hanging out. But it was fun, and Giovanni was cool and easy to talk to and . . ." She shrugs. "I don't know. It was fun."

"So did you sleep with him?" Holly asks Nat as she polishes glasses behind the bar. "Get under someone to get over someone and all that?"

I crane my head forward a little, jealously waiting for Nat's answer.

"No," Nat snaps, slightly offended. "He kissed me a couple of times before dinner, and we made out for a couple of hours afterward. He was really sweet. Oh, that reminds me . . ." Nat proceeds to smack me on the arm. Hard. "By the way, thanks a lot for telling him about the kissing test."

"I was helping you," I assure her. "It's weird that you get rid of a guy if he doesn't kiss you by the middle of the first date."

"It's not weird. It's survival of the fittest. If a guy doesn't make a move, that means he's not an alpha male. And I need an alpha male."

"Yeah, because that's been working out so well for you," I point out sarcastically.

"You hush."

I decide to back off.

Holly takes a moment to put down her polishing cloth and stare into space. "A couple of really sweet kisses, then dinner," she says, then shakes her head and goes back to work. "Man, what I wouldn't give for a night like that. I don't even remember the last time a guy took me on a real date. I mean, what straight man do you know who's willing to go to the opera?"

"Your time is coming," Nat promises. "Sven will be back soon, and this will work. You just need to calm down a little when you're around him." Then she quips, "And if he really likes you, he won't subject you to the opera."

"How can you say that?" I whine to Nat. "*La Traviata* is one of the most emotionally stirring, beautiful pieces of all time."

"A story about a hooker with TB who still has an easier time finding a guy than me," Holly deadpans. "I'll admit, that certainly stirs up some emotions."

"Your time will come," Nat repeats. "We're gonna make that happen if I have to use a pound of bacon and a trip wire."

"So what were the kisses like?" I press, not wanting to hear details at all and yet desperate for them.

Nat shrugs, embarrassed. "They were nice. He's nice."

"Why are you being so coy?" I ask in frustration. "You didn't sleep with him already, did you?"

"I said no!" she exclaims, appalled. "It was our first date."

"Didn't you sleep with Marc on your first date?" Holly asks her.

"I most certainly did not," Nat insists.

Holly narrows her eyes at her. Nat rolls her eyes in response. "Okay, maybe *technically*. But we had known each other for months and months. So it was practically, like, a twenty-sixth date or something."

"So, has he asked you out again yet?" I press.

"Yeeeaaahhh, that was almost a little too alpha. He asked me to see *The Barber of Seville* with him in a couple of weeks before our date was even half over," Nat tells me. "Plus I'm going to his place for dinner tonight. And he's coming to the opening Thursday. I think he was going to ask me out for Saturday night, but obviously I'll be here, so that won't work."

I squelch my urge to exclaim, "I LOVE *The Barber of Seville*," but only because I can see that won't help Giovanni's case any. Damn, Nat gets to see a glorious opera with an even more glorious man, and she doesn't even know how lucky she is. I kind of resent her for that.

"*The Barber of Seville* won't be so bad," Holly tells Nat.

"Will there be subtitles?" Nat asks with a tone of dread.

Holly counters with, "Yes. And there will also be a good-looking guy buying you dinner, so who cares? Some women have to go to sporting events that last an entire Sunday afternoon just to get that kind of attention."

"Fair enough," Nat concedes. She reads one of the wine bottles. "When did I buy us Sauvignon Blanc from Fresno?" she mutters to herself.

As Holly and Nat start conversing about wine, I can't help but stare at Nat and fight off a tinge of jealousy. How can she be so nonchalant? She landed the perfect man, and she's acting like it's nothing.

And then I start to get a little angry. I have practically gift-wrapped this exquisite present for her, and she seems reluctant to even pull off his first ribbon.

But as Nat said just a few days ago, sometimes you know exactly why your girlfriends are still single. "So, is tonight the night?" I ask her.

Nat seems almost startled. "TMI. But no. With a little luck, I'll be straddled on top of him on his couch all night, getting all hot and bothered while fully clothed."

Holly looks up to the ceiling as her shoulders fall, then says wistfully, "Oh, the climbing all over each other like you're teenagers. The first few dates are always so fun. Like when you make out in the car."

"That reminds me a little too much of Marc. Since we sometimes snuck out at lunch—"

"No Marc!" Holly and I exclaim to Nat in unison.

"Jinx," Holly says to me. "You owe me a Coke."

And suddenly, like a crashing wave, the idea that Nat gets to make out with Giovanni is making me very jealous, and I don't want to hear any more details. I decide to change the subject by asking her, "So, are you going to wear your red dress on opening night?"

Nat shakes her head. "Nah. That only goes well with a superspiky pump, and we'll be running around serving all night. I figure jeans, my purple Converse sneakers, and a black T-shirt that says I DRINK WINE BECAUSE I DON'T LIKE TO KEEP THINGS BOTTLED UP."

I can feel the wrinkles forming between my brows. "That's what you're wearing on opening night? Jeans and sneakers?"

"That's what I'm wearing every night," she tells me. "I bought tees with an assortment of phrases: FORGIVE ME FATHER, FOR I HAVE ZINNED. That shirt's red. HOW MERLOT CAN YOU GO? Obviously, that's in a Merlot shade of purple . . ."

"What is wrong with you?" I snap at Nat. "It's opening night. And there are going to be a ton of men here, including Giovanni."

She shrugs. "Technically, it's the third date tomorrow. How much effort do I really have to put in here?"

I want to bite her.

Holly turns to me and says, "My T-shirt is pink and says I LOOK FABULOUS FOR MY VINTAGE in glitter."

Nat points to Holly. "You know, I think you are the one woman I know who could pull that off."

"The pink or the glitter?" Holly asks.

"Well, yes," Nat answers.

"Well, no!" I exclaim. "So am I the only one here who is dressing up? Holly, didn't you buy a new dress?"

She shrugs. "I did. But without Sven here, it just suddenly seemed kind of pointless."

"Pointless? By that argument, the only time you'd ever wear nonperiod underwear and a matching bra is when you knew a guy might be spending the night."

Judging from Holly's wide-eyed expression in response (imagine her saying, "Duh," with her eyes), I can't help but groan. "Gross."

Nat unloads the last two bottles and puts them in my row, where there is still room. "Jess, if you want to dress up, no one's stopping you," she tells me. "It's not a big deal either way."

"But it *is* a big deal!" I argue/whine. "In about twenty-four hours, all of our lives are going to change. When was the last time that happened? College graduation? When you moved away from home to go to college? Holly: when you had your first opening night? Or Nat: the first time you saw your 'Written by Natasha Osorio' credit on TV? We don't get a lot of moments anymore when we get an eciah, and see our futures suddenly get brighter. Particularly not at our age. I want to celebrate that."

I give both of my friends my best cocker spaniel don't-you-want-to-share-that-cupcake? pleading eyes. Holly breaks first. "Fine. If it's that important to you, I'll dress up."

"Thank you!" I say, clapping my hands several times and running over to hug her. Then I set my sights on Nat. She makes a show of sighing, "All right. I'll wear the red dress. But just on opening night. Then I'm right back to my Chucks and my puns."

"Yay!" I say, trotting back to pull her into a hug. "I love you! Thank you!"

Without thinking, and still hugging, I give her advice. "And you should not sleep with Giovanni on the third date. It makes you look easy."

"Yeah, guys hate that," Nat deadpans.

Chapter Twenty-four

HOLLY

The three of us spent the next few hours setting up for tomorrow night's "soft opening," which is sort of like a dress rehearsal for restaurants. We extended our invitations to friends who we've supported over the years by going to every insufferable ninety-nine-seat theater play, pseudo-intellectual art gallery opening, book party, and bad movie premiere they had ever done.

Now it's payback time.

We're expecting over a hundred people during the course of the night. Plus, the bar will also be open to the public, so I am hopeful we'll have extra business.

By the time we close up Wednesday, All for Wine and Wine for All! looks like a real bar. The interior's a lot of exposed brick (and some fake exposed brick, Los Angeles being earthquake territory and all), with wood beams and exposed pipes. One wall is the floor-to-ceiling wine refrigerator that Nat's new boyfriend managed to fix. The wine chandelier Nat found looks like a piece of modern art, bathing the middle of the room with a romantic glow. And scattered throughout the place we have wooden signs in various colors that say things like IT'S WINE O'CLOCK, WINE: THE WAY CLASSY PEOPLE GET TRASHED, and COME. SIP. STAY.

We did it. We actually pulled it off.

I feel like such a grown-up.

And if Jessie's right, in less than twenty-four hours, the next phase of my life begins.

That's exciting. Or scary as hell. Either way, the not knowing what's happening next is rather thrilling. This is the most alive I've felt in years.

I hate Pollyannas who say things like that, my brain points out.

Now normally, I would cow down to that inner voice. But just for today, I'm going to listen to Jessie instead.

And that night, armed with my newfound courage to quell my inner voice, I do something I consider very brave: I Facebook Sven Erikkson, with two *k*'s, and friend request him.

I then reward myself with two cupcakes and a can of pink frosting I find in the back of the pantry. I'm following the unspoken rule every woman knows: A girl can be brave for only so long, and then she needs a treat. Because in this day and age, bravery isn't about storming out onto the battlefield; most days it's just about putting yourself out there. And that frequently requires frosting.

I hear my computer ding, and can't help but run back to it, my arms full of the modern girl's dating provisions.

Oh, my God! He accepted my friend request! Gorgeous neighbor accepted my friend request.

Within ten minutes!

Paydirt!

I suppress the urge to hide under my desk. Shit just got real.

No. I have my cupcakes and my frosting—I can do this. Time for some recon, Sweden Boy!

I immediately click on his page to discover that his relationship status is single (hallelujah!) and that he really is in San Francisco on business. One of his male friends checked in at a local bar and tagged him. Five guys and a girl—and the girl has her arms around a different guy. I move my head toward the screen to get a closer look at the girl. It looks like she's wearing . . . Yes! An engagement ring! Which means she can't be with him, or he'd have changed his status.

Then I begin reading his previous posts. He was recently in New York for a wedding, he recently became an uncle for the third time (very cute baby pic), and he is inexplicably a San Francisco 49ers fan. (Not that I don't like the team, but how did a guy from Sweden become a fan of a football team that doesn't use a soccer ball?)

As I am going through his old pictures, I see a message pop up in my in-box.

From Sve . . . Get the fuck out of here—no way!

I click on the message box to read:

Hey! Was trying to figure out how to e-mail you yesterday. I saw you on TV.

He saw me on TV? Crap. Doing what? Please not the show where I kill my boyfriend and they only discover it because of my nail polish. That might send a bad message about how I feel about men who work late. And not the one where my little Half Asian self inexplicably has an Irish accent. A baaaaddd Irish accent.

I bite the bullet and ask,

One of the CSI ones?

No. You're a firefighter, and you're the girlfriend of
that guy who's now the sexiest man alive.

St. Louis Fire. Wow, I haven't thought about that job in years.
Okay, that's not a bad one. I was off dairy for five minutes and kind
of looked okay back then.

Pointed to you on the television at a pub I was at
with my friends earlier tonight. I said, "That's my
neighbor!" I haven't been on Facebook in
several days. Glad you caught me.

Pointed me out at the pub? To whom? Maybe to the girl with the
engagement ring? Okay, that's a good sign, right? I mean, pointing
out a girl to an engaged person must mean something.

So what did your friends think of me

Michael, who just moved here from London,
said if the women in Southern California look like
that, he needs to make sure his transfer to
America is permanent.

I grin at the screen. Ahhh . . . England. An entire nation of men
who look and talk like James Bond.

That's very sweet. I'm sure he'll do great here, if for
no other reason than his accent is an aphrodisiac.

Well, that's why I moved to Los Angeles. There,
my accent is an aphrodisiac. (Even if no one

> seems to know what it is. One woman asked me
> if I was from Brooklyn!) Maybe I should go to
> where you're from. Do you think my accent could
> be an aphrodisiac?

It took until after I hit Send to realize how ballsy I was sounding.
He immediately writes,

> **Indeed. The men wouldn't know what hit
> them. You would kill it, in London, Sweden,
> San Francisco . . .**

> **I don't have an accent in San Francisco**

I type back, a little confused.

> **You don't need to. You are the aphrodisiac.**

Okay, that was fantastic. I will be dining out on that in my head
for at least a week.

And then the flirting continued—for five hours.

Nat has this thing she calls "the phone test." Basically it just
means that if a man really likes you, he'll want to talk to you on the
phone all night. She has this theory about how you should never
have sex with anyone unless you're both so into the other person
that you talk until the sun comes up.

And because I stopped listening to my inner voice long enough
to take a risk, Sven and I talk (well, type) until the sun comes up.
For hours and hours. we talked about everything and nothing. I
learned that he hates vanilla ice cream, and he learned that the first
time I tried to golf I accidentally hit myself in the head.

The evening flew by, and it felt both exciting yet effortless. It was so easy to talk to him. Somehow, just typing (instead of actually talking) allowed me to write whatever I felt like sharing. I didn't second-guess myself at every turn, because I wasn't staring at a great-looking guy, stressed out about the outcome. And I listened, really listened, to what he had to say.

I passed Nat's phone test.

You know, I hear a lot these days about how society is wrecked because people aren't going on real dates anymore, how they aren't seeing each other face-to-face, and they're all on their phones at dinner. And that might very well be true.

But, for tonight at least, it sure was a relief to hide a bit. Because it gave me the courage to be myself. To admit, "Here's me! I'm weird."

Which allowed me to find someone I didn't want to hide from.

Chapter Twenty-five

NAT

I'm thinking about how sexy you look in that
red dress.

> Well, maybe if you weren't in London,
> you could see me in it at the opening.

And now I'm thinking about unzipping you in
that red dress.

> Don't say things like that right before I
> go on a date.

What kind of gentleman doesn't pick you up
for a date? I'm telling you, it's not proper.

> The kind who can invite me to his apartment and
> not have to worry about his wife answering the
> door. Gotta go.

And I click off my phone.

Well, that was stupid. After my really nice date last night, filled with laughter, good food, and a lot of kissing, Giovanni dropped me off at my house, and in a moment of weakness, I texted Marc.

I don't know why I did it.

Yes, I do. I wanted him to know that I was over him. I wanted him to know that only a few weeks after I became available, someone had snatched me up and taken me out of the rotation. I wanted him to know what a big mistake he had made and that there was no turning back.

Stupid. I know. But at least the conversation didn't end in phone sex.

But Marc and I did text back and forth for an hour. And we've been texting off and on until now, right before I leave for my date with Giovanni.

Which was a huge mistake, and I won't do it again. Marc has to be treated like an addiction: fun at the time, but absolutely destructive for my life in the long run. And I need to get rid of my addiction. If you're addicted to heroin, you don't just text it at two in the morning for a little fix, do you? You stop taking it altogether. Or you go under a doctor's supervision and get yourself some methadone.

Giovanni is my methadone, I think to myself as I drive through the winding streets of his hilly neighborhood.

No, that's not right. Giovanni's sexy as fuck . . . He's more like crack than heroin. Bad analogy. Crack is bad for you too. No, Giovanni's more like reading a great book: deliciously distracting and possibly life changing. Yes, much better.

About twenty minutes later (thank God for Waze, or I never would have found this place), I park my car and take a moment to scrutinize Giovanni's house. It looks cozy, like a little sanctuary, nestled in the hills high above the Sunset Strip. I like how quiet it is up here—all I can hear are trees rustling with that late summer/fall tease that happens with our Santa Ana winds. I grab the dark purple tulips I bought at Trader Joe's from the passenger seat, get out of the car, and beep my alarm. It almost echoes in the quiet. I can hear the clicking of my high heels as I walk up to Giovanni's front door and ring the bell, which sounds melodic and peaceful.

Everything about this home looks peaceful.

Giovanni opens the door wearing dark jeans, a long-sleeved shirt with his sleeves rolled up, and a bright red apron with white letters reading MANGIA BENE. He's all smiles as he greets me, "Welcome!" He kisses me very quickly on the mouth, then backs up, saying quickly, "I'm afraid I've had a kitchen mishap. I don't want to get melted butter on you. Come in."

I follow him through his front doorway, which steps down into his living room, clearly done in early to mid-twenty-first-century no-woman-has-helped-decorate bachelor pad. A gray sectional sofa on a white shag rug, thrown over dark hardwood floors. A gas fireplace blazing over glass pebbles glistening with the light of the flames. Against the wall is a vintage record player, which fills the house with a beautiful soulful jazz ballad.

"Is that Lena Horne?" I ask, utterly charmed by the song, the atmosphere, and the man.

"Etta James. Are those for me?" Giovanni asks, referring to the purple tulips.

"Yes," I say a little nervously as I hold them out for him. "I figured bringing wine to a wine rep is a little like bringing cookies to a baker, so I thought I'd come up with a different gift."

"Great. Let me see if I can find a vase to put them in." Giovanni walks into his kitchen, which looks out onto his living room. He points to a barstool on the living room side of the counter separating the two rooms and says, "Have a seat. I've already poured you a glass of the Neprica you ordered at dinner last night."

He remembered what I ordered last night? Well, of course he did, he's a wine rep. Nonetheless, I am pleasantly surprised to see a glass of red on the counter waiting for me, along with two cheeses on a cheese board, accompanied by fruit, nuts, and crackers. A happy "Oh" escapes my mouth. "This looks amazing."

"Crémeux des Citeaux, which is a triple-cream cow's milk from France and a Saint Agur, which is a blue, also made from cow's milk. I noticed at the restaurant last night that when we ate the cheese plate, you steered clear of the goat's milk cheese. Some people shy away from sheep's milk, so I figured stick with the cow."

I spread a bit of the Saint Agur onto a cracker and take a bite. "Mm. This is gorgeous. Thank you."

I watch Giovanni's shirt hike up as he reaches for a vase on a top shelf. From what I can see, he has a very nice back. Makes me want to lift his shirt up more. You know, just to make sure I'm right.

"I hope you're hungry," he tells me as he fills the vase with water. "Per your request: I'm doing a filet mignon au poivre, medium rare, potatoes au gratin, and an arugula salad."

"Wow. Are you sure you don't have a wife and kids tucked away somewhere? Or a husband and kids?"

He smiles, toasts my glass with his, and says, "I'm sure."

We spend the next fifteen minutes talking as I happily sip my wine at the counter and watch him putter around the kitchen. Daaammmmnnnnn. It is just occurring to me for the first time: Why do men waste all of that money taking us out to nice restaurants when they could be cooking for us? It would save them money and would be so much closer to the bedroom. I mean, to think of all the times Marc took me to Nobu when he could have . . .

Stop it! Don't think about Marc!

"So where do you see yourself in ten years?" I ask Giovanni as I try to push Marc out of my subconscious.

"Ugh. Please tell me you're not one of those kind of women," Giovanni says as he throws the filets into a sizzling cast iron pan.

"One of what kind?" I ask, already knowing the answer. "You mean the reads-the-self-help-books-on-dating kind?"

"I do," he says, smiling to himself. "Honestly, why can't women just live in the moment?" He turns from the steaks and asks me, "Or is that the wrong answer?"

It is, but I decide it's too early to hold that against him. "No, I tend to agree with you. How's this: On what date can a woman sleep with a man and not be considered a slut?"

"The first."

"Not true," I counter.

"Absolutely true," he assures me cheerfully.

"Can I finish off the Crémeux des Citeux?"

Giovanni walks over to me and leans in for a kiss. "I love the way you say that."

We kiss. "Oh, you do, huh?" I stretch out the words. "Crémeux . . . des . . . Citeux."

And we kiss again. People on the first few dates are silly.

We continue to make out for a few minutes. Giovanni pulls away to flip the steaks, giving me one final quick kiss and smile.

I return to my original mission. "Okay, so, Jessie says I'm terrible about not asking enough questions on the first few dates . . ."

"She thinks you're too busy kissing?" Giovanni teases.

"Yeah . . . let's just say she said 'kissing.' Anyway, I'm trying to . . . sort of . . . date differently than I usually do. So . . ." I try to figure out where I'm going with this. "The ten-year plan was Jessie's question. What do you think is a good second-date question?"

Giovanni takes a moment to think about that. "What would you do if you knew you couldn't fail?"

I open my mouth.

"And don't say 'Play the lottery,'" Giovanni tells me quickly.

I close my mouth. Damn, that was a good answer.

"Hmmm . . ." I consider, taking a sip of wine. "I just blew my savings and my job to open a wine bar. Does that count?"

"It can," Giovanni turns to me. "Was there a particular reason you quit?"

"My boss didn't appreciate me," I say, truthfully.

"Good reason. So, anything else you'd do?"

Hmm. I think some more. "Sadly, other than the wine bar thing, I can't think of anything. What about you?"

"Come on," Giovanni prods, "you can't think of anything?"

"Okay. Well, I've quit writing for now. But I have this screenplay I wanted to write about Elizabeth Cady Stanton. She was the first woman to demand a woman's right to vote, yet no one's ever done a movie about her."

Giovanni breaks into a huge smile. "That's awesome. So why haven't you written it?"

"Because there's no point. No one watches historical films. Plus, who has the time? I get paid to write game shows. If I'm going to go back to writing, I should be paid for it."

"Are you passionate about game shows?"

"God, no," I blurt out. "I mean, don't get me wrong. The people I work with are amazing, and the money is great. It's not a bad life. At. All. I was very lucky to get that job."

Giovanni watches me as I try to think of some other way to justify what I've been doing for the last seven years of my life. But instead, I just nervously sip my wine.

"Write the script," he tells me.

"And what if I waste six months on it, and no one ever sees it?" I counter.

Giovanni raises his shoulders slightly and puts up the palms of his hands. "Then you'll be the exact same age as you would have been, if you hadn't done it. But you'll have created something you care about."

Huh. He's right—he's totally right. Why don't I write something just because? Why does there have to be a paycheck at the end of it? I have a new job that won't drain me intellectually, I don't have kids or a boyfriend right now to distract me. The roadblocks aren't there. Why not go for it?

"You know what? I think I might," I say. I put my arms around him and kiss him on the cheek. "This time next week, I'll try to have the first five pages."

"You mean you *will* have five pages," Giovanni encourages. "And I can't wait to read them."

And we make out again. This guy is seriously cool. I think I could get used to him.

Giovanni breaks away from me to take the steaks off the pan. As he puts them on a platter to rest and throws some aluminum foil on top, I ask, "So, what about you? What would you do if you knew you couldn't fail?"

He smiles mischievously. "I'd kiss a beautiful woman I've had my eye on."

Well, obviously that leads to a mini make-out session.

When we pull away, I press on. "At the risk of calling myself a beautiful woman, you've already done that. So what else do you want to do?"

Giovanni takes a moment before confessing, "Actually, I would go to dinner."

I'm confused. "Wait. What? Aren't we having dinner?"

"No. It's a particular dinner. A twelve-course tasting menu served on the beach. You know what? It's not important."

Whoa, I hit a nerve with dinner? "It sounds important. So why don't you go?"

He shrugs. "First of all, it's really expensive. Like, insanely. Mostly . . ." He sort of stumbles over the rest of his sentence. "It's nothing. It's just . . . I want to go with the right person. And it's something I've fantasized about for years, and what if my date didn't appreciate it or the food wasn't all it's cracked up to be? Plus I'd have to drive all the way to Santa Barbara and get a hotel . . ."

"Are you passionate about . . ."

Giovanni wraps his arms around my waist, smiles, and rubs the small of my back. *"Silenzio, mio bella."* Then he kisses me to accomplish his goal.

But when we finally stop kissing, I narrow my eyes and joke, "Just so you know, that'll work six . . . seven years tops."

Giovanni chuckles, then turns to make the sauce. He pours some brandy into the pan, then tilts the pan down to the gas flame, igniting the brandy into the most amazing flambé. The flames die down, and Giovanni adds cream.

Seriously—is there anything sexier than a man who knows how to cook?

"Wow."

Giovanni whisks the cream sauce until it bubbles. "So, do they serve steak during this twelve-course meal?"

"Yes. A Kobe beef short rib," he tells me as puts the steaks back in the pan and coats them with the decadent sauce.

He answered me easily and without hedging, but I still can't read him. I decide to change the subject. "Well, maybe if the bar does well, I can go and take you as my arm candy."

"Maybe," he says. "Ready to eat?"

"Always," I deadpan. "And this looks amazing."

He carries the platter of meat in one hand and his wine in the other. I grab the potatoes au gratin and my wine and say, "Just to warn you, I'm not nearly as good of a cook."

"Yes, I believe you were quite candid about excelling in other rooms." He sets down the platter in the middle of the table and holds out my chair. "So what are you reading these days?"

For the rest of the night, the conversation flowed as easily as the wine. We talked about books, movies, synthetic CDOs (all right, I'll admit he mostly talked about those), women's shoes, and politics.

And yes, there was kissing, but we talked a lot. The guy is interesting. He's smart. Well read. Well traveled. And I wouldn't have known any of that if I had just blown him off at the bar because I didn't immediately feel the hots for him the way I did with Marc.

I'm starting to think that Jessie is right: Maybe with dating you should lead with your head and not your heart. Actually, it's not usually our heart that normally makes these decisions either, is it?

I did spend the night, but slept in a borrowed T-shirt and boxer shorts. I tucked into his arms and fell asleep around one, content.

The evening would have been perfect if I hadn't woken up at five to a *ping!* on my phone, which was in my purse in the other room.

I should have known when I tiptoed out to check it that it would be from Marc.

I waited all day for you to text me back. Did you get home okay?

I quickly delete Marc's message and go back to bed.

Chapter Twenty-six

JESSIE

"Slut!" Holly jokes to Nat, putting her palm up for a high five as Nat walks into the bar on the morning of our grand opening.

"All you know is that I never made it home last night," Nat tells Holly rather sheepishly, though she does give her a weak high five. "You don't know what happened."

Although obviously we do know what happened, I think to myself as I work on our financials from my laptop, which I've placed in the middle table near the bar so I can bitch to Holly about how much more this is costing us than we planned.

She got to sleep with him. She is the luckiest fucking woman in the whole world right now, and I mean that literally.

Damn it. I love Kevin, and I'm going to marry him. What is wrong with me?

I once read in a bridal magazine that it is completely normal to have a crush on someone right after you get engaged. That it is a healthy . . . normal (repeat: normal!) . . . reaction to being spoken for. And realizing that you are never going to have a first kiss again, ever, for the rest of your life, and now I'm fantasizing about my first kiss with Giovanni and . . . Damn it! I have got to get hold of myself.

"Well, I have faith in you," Holly tells Nat. "Nice shirt, by the way."

Holly is referring to a souvenir T-shirt Nat is wearing from the Napa Valley winery that I've been dying to go to. Seriously? She has his shirt? It's been less than a week, and they're already at the point in their relationship where she gets to wear his clothing?

"Isn't it cool?" Nat agrees. "I stole it from Giovanni's dresser this morning, and he said I looked so cute in it, I could keep it."

I stare intently at my computer screen, trying not to writhe in jealousy. Damn it, I'm positively writhing. *Nat gets to wear his T-shirt like it's a normal, run-of-the-mill thing. Like things like that just happen. Like in the real world, a guy that ridiculously perfect just gives you his T-shirt, which also probably smells like him a little, or at least smells like the Costco detergent he must use because, yes, I recognized the scent on him when we were at Home Depot, and now even doing my laundry reminds me of him, and no, I'm not obsessed.*

"So, did you talk to Sven last night?" Nat asks Holly as she lugs a box of Syrah over to the bar.

Plus he told her she looked cute in it. Seriously, what makes her so great that he picked her over me? What's wrong with me? Why didn't he want to give me his shirt? And, while we're on the subject, why did he agree to go out with her when I saw him first?

"No, but we have been sending e-mails. I don't want to look too crazed," Holly answers.

She got to see him naked! He must look perfect naked. Like a statue or something—just beautiful. He likes her. I don't have a shot. I missed my opportunity.

"I agree," Nat affirms. "You know, I'm starting to realize that if you don't obsess about a guy, you have a much better shot at happiness . . ."

Thanks a lot for the great advice, Nat. I'll try not to obsess.

"And it's all thanks to Jessie," Nat tells Holly.

"Why? What did I do?" I blurt out, trying not to sound defensive or jealous.

"You introduced me to a really cool guy," Nat tells me gratefully. "Someone I would never have thought was my type. You practically forced me into his arms, and for that I'm indebted to you."

"Well, I know a thing or two about dating," I say a bit snootily. "So, did you ask him about his ten-year plan?"

Nat winces at my question. "You know, I tried. But he thought it sounded a bit too interviewy."

Does that mean he doesn't see her in his long-term plans? Hmmmm . . .

"The ten-year-plan question is so stupid," Holly declares, shaking her head. "I blame the self-help books."

"That's pretty much what Giovanni said," Nat tells her.

"Hm. Maybe I should date him," Holly jokes.

You do, and I'll break you like a twig.

"He cooks, he cleans, he has a nice house in the hills. You could do worse," Nat jokes right back.

Seriously?! How can they joke about that?

Nat turns to me. "Instead, Giovanni suggested we should ask our dates: 'What would you do if you knew you couldn't fail?'"

"See, that's a much better question," Holly says. "That focuses on what a person wants to do right now, not on what someone thinks they might want to do, maybe, in ten years."

That's a dumb-ass question. So I give the obvious answer, "I'd play the lottery."

Nat points to me. "Me too! But he told me I wasn't allowed to answer that."

Holly looks up and scrunches her lips, thinking. "I think I'd swim with sharks."

Nat frowns. "Damn. That's a better answer than what I said."

"What did you say?" Holly asks.

"Elizabeth Cady Stanton," Nat answers.

Holly nods, knowing the whole backstory of Nat's stalled script idea.

"Wait. Giovanni thinks we should judge our dates by what they haven't done? That's ridiculous," I insist. "That question tells a person who you're not, instead of who you are."

Nat furrows her brow and scrutinizes me. "Wooowwww . . . you clearly have something you want to do, but you're afraid to. What is it?"

"Don't be silly. I just quit my job and started a business. I'm not afraid of anything."

"Whoa. Minnie Mouse voice," Nat says, as though I've given her some sort of tell.

Holly smiles as she shakes her head and says to Nat, "I was just thinking the same thing. Damn, I'd like to get her in a poker game."

"What are you talking about?" I ask them, careful to keep my tone dismissive.

"Whenever you don't want to talk about something, your voice goes up two octaves and you start talking like Minnie Mouse," Holly enlightens me. "Spill! What is it?"

Kiss Giovanni—obviously. Hm . . . If I knew I wouldn't fail, would I actually kiss him?

Well, this sucks. I'm supposed to say go paragliding, or learn to play piano, or even open a wine bar. I'm not supposed to wonder if my best friend's new boyfriend would kiss me back. That makes me a truly awful person.

"I want to open a wine bar," I answer emphatically, making sure to deepen my voice as I shut my laptop and head toward the back office. "And if I don't get this work done, I'll be no help tonight for the soft opening."

"Oh, come on," Nat implores. "Why are you being like that? I told you about my screenplay, and Holly about her sharks. Just tell us one thing you'd do if you knew you couldn't fail."

"I'd get out of this conversation," I say, making my way into the office. "You guys keep doing setup. I need an hour of quiet, and then you're free to ask me whatever second-date question you want."

Thankfully, the girls let me go.

I use my quiet time to set up my laptop, reopen QuickBooks, and do my job.

And quickly check Giovanni's Facebook. And his Instagram. And Twitter.

No new posts, and no change in relationship status.

Sigh. What is wrong with me?

Chapter Twenty-seven

HOLLY

At 4:28 P.M., we officially open the doors of All for Wine and Wine for All! and begin our new lives.

Well, okay, we don't officially open our doors. But that's when Karen, my agent, perpetually on the phone, begins pounding on the door incessantly, so I guess we're opening early.

"It's just Karen! I got it!" I yell to the girls, who are getting ready in the back.

I quickly run up to the door and unlock it to stop Karen's banging. "You're early," I tell her.

Karen whisks in, looking like her usual fabulous Neiman Marcus self: Tory Burch jeans with a six-hundred-dollar "kicky" top and Louboutins so high I wonder if she had to take a class in stilt walking before she put them on. "Darling, it's not going any farther," she says into the phone.

It's not going any farther is agentspeak for, *You had an audition and two callbacks and they still didn't hire you. Go get a brownie.*

"I know, it sucks. Now promise me you won't indulge in *Kummerspeck*. Just go for a nice run to get all of your feelings out. Call you tomorrow." She hangs up her phone and throws it in her bag as she air-kisses me on the cheek. "I'm sorry, darling. What did you say?"

"I said you're early," I repeat. "And what's *Kummerspeck*?"

"It means 'grief bacon.' And if I'm not ten minutes early, I'm late," Karen says, walking to the center of the bar and doing a slow spin to check out the place. "Just put me to work. Do you need some candles lit?"

Before I can answer, she exclaims, "Well, isn't this charming? I love it. Let me make some phone calls—let's get some more people in here."

"Okay . . . sounds good," I say.

Karen pulls out her phone and looks at her screen. "Fantastic. Who do you want? Famous people or paying customers?"

"Yes. Can I get you a drink?"

"Dirty martini, two olives."

"Pinot Gris it is," I tell her, heading behind the bar as she texts. "So how's work going?"

"It's not as much fun without my favorite client," she tells me as I pull out a bottle of Pinot Gris from the Marlborough region of New Zealand. "But of course I wouldn't dream of pressuring you to come back."

As I pour her a glass, I ask bluntly, "Is that your passive-aggressive way of telling me you're firing me, or your passive-aggressive way of asking me when I'm going back to work?"

Karen is laser focused on her phone as she absentmindedly sits down on a stool across the bar from me. "It means I'm proud of you but I miss you. No hidden agenda." She hits Send, then tosses her phone on the bar and smiles at me. "By the way, I happened to invite a few casting agents tonight. Maybe a director or two . . ."

I wince. "Damn it! Karen, I'm nervous enough about tonight . . ."

"Which is why I'm here. To soothe you yet encourage you. And if part of what I encourage you to do is cheerfully ply a few job cre-ators with booze and then pour them into an Uber . . ."

"Crap. Who did you invite?"

"Fans. People who love you. Forget I said anything," Karen says, taking a big sip of her white wine. "This is lovely, dear. Thank you."

I take a deep, cleansing breath, then exhale my nerves out. "Ex-cellent. Now if you'll excuse me . . ."

"That's what you're wearing?" she asks, referring to the tasteful sleeveless black dress I bought when I thought Sven would be here.

"Yes, Karen, this is what I'm wearing," I tell her patiently.

"Black? What do you think that says to people?"

"I don't know. That I'm opening a bar?"

"And where's the cleavage?"

"I'm opening a bar, not a brothel."

"But I have people coming to see you."

"Yes, and I'm not auditioning anymore, remember?"

She crosses her arm and pouts. "Fine."

"Thank you," I say, turning on the cash register to make sure everything works.

Karen waits all of ten seconds before saying, "You could at least color in your eyebrows a little more . . ."

"Karen!"

"And that's all I'm going to say about anything. Forget I'm here."

Yeah, that'll happen.

Chapter Twenty-eight

JESSIE

4:35 P.M.

I am standing in our new pink marble ladies' room, trying to decide if (1) pink marble is quirky or tacky and (2) my makeup is cute or tacky. Can I pull off red lipstick? The Nats of the world can pull off red lipstick. She has that shiny, dark brown hair and glowing slightly tanned skin, and (most important) a personality that says, "Fuck, yeah, I wear red lipstick."

I'm more "barely there" beige, possibly an "oh so subtle" pink. I lean in to my reflection to debate.

Nope, can't pull it off. I grab a Kleenex and wipe off the red as Nat pops into the doorway, looking super cute in her bright red dress and matching lipstick. "Your computer has been beeping off the hook. I think it's your Skype, so I assume it's Kevin."

"Okay, thanks," I tell her.

She walks over to me. "How come you're not wearing the lipstick?"

I shrug sheepishly. "Not my style."

"Don't be silly. I wear it all the time."

"Yeah, *you* do. And it looks great on you. But women like me . . ." My sentence trails off as I look in the mirror again. "I don't know. I'm already a little out of my comfort zone tonight. Let's not push it."

Nat furrows her brow. "You okay?"

No, I'm not okay. I wish I could wear red lipstick. I wish I was that woman. But I'm not—I'm a big phony. I'm an accountant who is pretending she can own and run a business, and I'm acting (meaning pretending!) like this is a great idea. I'm a woman who wears knee-length dark blue dresses, not short red ones. Keeps the same shoulder-length, dirty blonde hair that she's had since college, because I would never have the nerve to get Nat's "I'm fierce" pixie cut. I'm a woman who never gets the Giovannis of the world. So we make ourselves happy with the Kevins.

"Yeah," I lie. "I'm just a little nervous."

"You just sank your life savings into this place. If you weren't a little nervous, I'd be worried about you."

I pull out my glossy beige lipstick. "Thanks."

"Stop," Nat says cheerfully. "I have a thought." She runs out of the bathroom, then reappears less than a minute later with her makeup bag. "I just got one of those free-with-purchase lipsticks that would look great on you." She pulls out a black plastic tube, opens it, and twists it up to reveal a dark purple lipstick.

"Purple?" I react. "No, no, no. I don't wear purple."

"Let's just try it," Nat says, getting right up to my face so she can swipe the lipstick onto my lips. She pulls back and looks me over. "Nice. One more thing to make it pop, though." Nat pulls out another, thinner black tube, and opens it to reveal a liner pencil in the same shade of purple. She begins drawing studiously. "Let's just open those lips up, give you a little pouty Brigitte Bardot thing."

After another thirty seconds, Nat pulls back to examine her work. "Perfect. Take a look."

I turn to the mirror to see my reflection. "Huh. Who knew I could wear purple? It's cool. It's, like, it's not exactly me, but it's kind of a cooler version of me."

Nat squints at me a bit. "So that's good, right?"

"It's awesome," I assure her. "I need to buy those. What's the color called?"

"Curious Cabernet," Nat says, handing me the lipstick and matching liner pencil. "It's fate, I tell you."

I wave my hands. "I couldn't. That brand's expensive."

"Don't be silly. Like I said, it was a freebie," Nat reminds me, pushing the lipstick and liner into my hands. "Now go call back your boyfriend, show him what he's missing tonight, and meet me at the bar."

A minute later, I am in the back office, waiting on my computer for Kevin to pick up. He clicks on after the third ring.

It's the middle of the night in Germany, but I can see when he answers that his lights are on. "Hey, just returning all of your calls. Did I wake you?" I whisper.

"No," he says, slurring a little. "I actually just got home from celebrating. I've been promoted to management accountant."

Management accountant? I didn't even know he wanted to be a management accountant. "Wait, so you're coming home early?" I ask him, confused.

"Not exactly. The job's in Copenhagen. I'm flying up to see the offices tomorrow morning. You should hop on a plane and come meet me. Copenhagen this time of year is supposed to be magical."

I'm stunned. For a bunch of reasons. "Obviously, I can't come now. We open the bar tonight," I stammer out.

Kevin smiles warmly. "Oh, that's right. How's it going? I'm sorry to miss it."

"It hasn't actually opened yet, we don't open until five," I tell him quickly. "So I don't understand. How long will you be in Copenhagen?"

Kevin pauses. (Damn it. Here it comes.) "I've been offered a contract for three years."

"What do you MEAN three years?"

"Minimum," Kevin says.

"Minimum?!" I shake my head. "And you're telling me this now? Less than an hour before opening night . . ."

"Shitty timing on my part," Kevin says quickly, and it occurs to me that maybe he didn't intentionally just ambush me. "I'm sorry. I was just excited, and I didn't think it through. Let's talk about it tomorrow. You go do you tonight. I'm proud of you. Have a great time."

I'm blinking, and slightly shaking my head. I want to get up and start pacing. But then I'd move out of my computer's camera range, so I stay seated. Finally I ask, in a seething voice that surprises me, "What about us?"

"It's an amazing offer," Kevin tells me. "Tons of money. We could get married here and start having babies right away. And you could stay home with them, just like you've always wanted. Can you imagine what an amazing opportunity it would be for a child to grow up in different places around the world?"

Copenhagen. I'm not even completely sure where Copenhagen is. I mean, I know it's in Denmark, I'm not an idiot, but if I had to point to it on the map I could just as easily hit Sweden.

"So what do you say?" Kevin says, smiling warmly. "You wanna get married?"

Wow. I pause. Look down at my desk, thinking. Realize my tongue is thrusting itself against the back of my top teeth. Do I want to get married?

Three months ago, when we were looking at every house imaginable, and I was worried Kevin was getting cold feet and about to leave me, I would have died for this moment. But now . . .

Now I feel nauseated. "You knew this was a permanent move before you left, didn't you?" I suddenly realize.

"No," Kevin insists.

I narrow my eyes at him. "I think you did."

Kevin looks down, and I see him take a deep breath. "I will admit, I thought there was a chance. That's why I was so nervous about buying a house."

"And yet you didn't tell me," I say, and another puzzle piece falls into place. "Because you were thinking about leaving me."

Kevin's eyes dart to his left, and I know that's exactly what happened.

I shake my head. "You bastard."

"Don't get like this. I had a few moments when I wasn't sure, but that's normal. I'm sure now. I want to marry you."

"You know what? I'm gonna go," I say, "because now I'm the one who's not sure. And you're not going to call or Skype me for the rest of the night."

"Jess—"

"No," I interrupt, slightly raising my voice. "Tonight is *my* night, and you're not stealing it from me. I worked my ass off for it, and I deserve it. I will call you when I'm ready."

"Jessie . . ."

I roll my mouse to click Off and immediately shut my laptop.

Then, in a moment of self-care I didn't know I had in me, I click on my cell phone and block all of Kevin's numbers.

I open my top drawer, pull out a mirrored compact, then check my lipstick.

Purple. Nat's right. It is perfect.

And I'm sure as fuck done with being beige.

Chapter Twenty-nine

NAT

Standing behind the bar, I proudly survey the room. The party is going great! The hors d'oeuvres are a hit (Jessie is right—you really never can go wrong with prosciutto). We are selling tons of wine, and everyone seems to be having a great time.

Naturally, this is the moment when I'm set to get unmistakable proof that there is no benevolent God. Because if there was a benevolent God, the really good-looking guy would not be walking into my bar right now.

Wait! Crap! No fucking way! Shit. Shit. Shit. Why, God, why?

Of all the wine joints in all the towns in all the world, he walks into mine.

I quickly walk over to Holly's half of the bar and whisper, "Can you take care of that guy? I need to get some more pretzels from the back."

Holly eyes me with concern. "Suuurrreeee. Everything okay?"

"Everything's fine. I just need to—"

"Natasha?" I hear Chris (the really good-looking guy) ask behind me.

Damn it. I turn around and smile weakly. "That's me."

"Natasha Osorio?" he clarifies.

For a split second, I debate saying no, but then I decide to confront this problem head on. "Yup. Hey, Chris."

He smiles, then asks, "Wow. You filled out a little. Going through another breakup?"

Less than three seconds. That's a new record, even for us.

"On the contrary. I'm in a glorious relationship and this is happy fat," I tell him, trying not to clench my jaw. "Of course, I can always lose the weight, whereas your hair won't be coming back anytime soon."

Holly looks to me, then Chris, then back to me. "Okay, so I'm guessing you two know each other. Natasha, would you like to help the ladies at table six?"

I cross my arms and stare down Chris. "Oh, no. I got this."

Holly smiles at Chris and, as she passes me leans in to whisper, "Paying customer. Be nice." Then she heads to table six, where a group of cheerful women are debating their next series of flights.

Chris takes a seat at the bar. "What kind of beer do you have on tap?"

"None. Did you read the sign out front? We're a wine bar. We have water on tap. And soda."

Chris squints at me for a quick second, then flashes me an easy smile. "Okay, what wine would you recommend?"

"That depends. Do you prefer red, white, or rosé?"

"I prefer beer."

"Then go home and call Pink Dot."

He smirks with confidence. "You do know we're gonna sleep together, right?"

Typical Chris question, designed to shock and intrigue. I hit his volley back without missing a beat. "You do you know you're gonna propose to me, right?"

I can't tell if he's amused by or hates my comeback. Never could read his face. He takes a moment, then says, "Red."

"What types of reds do you like? And don't say red ale."

"Hah," Chris says, pointing at me. "You remember I like red ale."

"You just tried to order a beer, you moron. What are you doing here, anyway? This is a wine bar for women."

He looks around. "First off, there are men here too. Second, I'm meeting a woman."

"Lucky her," I say, making a show of an eye roll.

There is absolutely no reason why I should have a tinge of jealousy about that. But a small part of me—a part of me I hate—can't wait to see what she looks like.

Okay, I suppose it's time for a little backstory. Chris and I met my junior year of college, at a friend's party.

He was my friend's new roommate, and we hated each other almost immediately. He was smug. Thought he could have any woman in the room. In all fairness, he could get a lot of them, which just made him all the more annoying. I suppose one could say Chris was kind of handsome. You know, if chiseled features, an effortless smile, and clear hazel eyes are your thing. And as long as he didn't open his mouth and show you his personality. In college, he did a couple of national commercials, and the girls at school acted like he was the best-looking man they had ever seen. They'd flirt, they'd giggle at every stupid thing he said, they'd toss their hair around.

I was not impressed. And he wasn't particularly impressed with me either. So we sparred. He'd try to get my goat and show he wasn't interested. I made it clear I wasn't interested. Unfortunately, his roommate was dating my roommate, and we saw each other all the time.

And, over time, ever so rarely, I let my guard down around him. I talked about a bad date I had, and Chris told me the guy was an idiot. I opened up about not wanting to go to my dad's wedding to his fourth wife (a woman all of three years older than me). Chris offered to go with me. At one point, he admitted he was failing a literature class, and I tutored him.

And then one night, right before winter break, we all celebrated the end of finals week with shots of something stupid, and I got hammered. Ham. Mered.

I remember the tree, and Chris and me walking out onto his balcony to look at Christmas lights across the street, and then the song "Baby, It's Cold Outside" came on, and I sang one of the woman's lines and he started singing the man's lines, and we quietly sang the banter to each other for a verse or so. Then he took me in his arms for this spontaneous slow dance. And for a brief few seconds, I forgot I hated him and just closed my eyes and enjoyed the warmth of his body and the smell of his cologne.

When the song was over, Chris pulled back to say, "You're a pretty good . . ." and I kissed him. Yeah, I know it's all my fault.

We made out for a while, and I remember thinking I could be in his arms forever, and that I could not ask for a more perfect evening. (Let the record show I was twenty. Only twenty-year-olds are so naïve.)

Anyway, late that evening/early that morning, I woke up in his bed, not remembering much after that perfect kiss.

First, I looked down at myself and was relieved to see I was fully clothed.

But then I looked over at him, shirtless. He was covered by a sheet, and although I was tempted to look, I resisted. Instead, I did something I am not particularly proud of: I snuck out. Totally pulled the coyote-ugly asshole-guy move. Just grabbed my shoes and purse and tiptoed away.

In my defense, it's not like he ever called me afterward. But he should have known that I didn't really leave because I didn't like him, that I was just embarrassed by how the night went. He should have known that he could have easily picked up the phone to ask me out, that I would have been relieved that he didn't think I was "that kind of girl" and that I would have been thrilled to go on an actual date with him.

Instead, my roommate broke up with his roommate over Christmas break, and Chris and I never saw each other again.

No, that's not true. We did see each other once, at a party toward the end of the year. He smirked that smirk guys get once they've nailed you and teased, "Good morning, sleepyhead." I pretended to trip and spilled a drink in his lap, and that was all that anyone ever said to anyone about anything.

Until now.

"Give me something Spanish," he says, then asks, "So how's the writing career going?"

"Aces," I nearly spit out as I angrily pour him a red. "This is a Bobal from central Spain. Some wine aficionados are calling it Spain's hidden gem. If you don't like it, I'll be happy to punch you in the throat."

"In that case, it looks . . . What was that word you used? Aces. Thank you." He smiles as he raises his glass to me.

Tool.

I put down the bottle, and the moment Holly returns behind the bar, I tell her, "I need to check on the corner tables."

I bring the bottle of Bobal with me, planning to ask some people in the corner if they would like a refill. *Seriously, what is he doing here? And why didn't he leave the minute he saw I was here?*

I don't mean to, but I accidentally glance over in Chris's direction, and suddenly I'm an insecure coed again. What is it about our first loves that we never completely get over them? And make no mistake—I was totally infatuated with this man. The first time I saw him, I couldn't breathe. It must have taken five trips back and forth across my friend's living room and three red Solo cups of beer before I finally had the nerve to talk to him.

At which time he was a jerk. I walked up to him only to hear him say to another girl, "It's perfectly fine to ask a guy out. It's awesome even. You just need to make sure he's a good guy. No one needs an asshole in her life."

Okay, that sounds like a nice-guy thing to say—but you had to be there! The tone was manipulative and calculating. And his calculation paid off: Twenty minutes later, the girl had him pushed up against the wall, having her way with him and causing several guys to yell, "Get a room!"

They did.

I walk up to Giovanni, who is giving a table of women an in-depth lesson on the Orvieto he distributes to us. "Can I borrow you for a second?" I ask.

"Of course," Giovanni says happily, then turns to the women and slightly bows. "Ladies."

They wave to him as he leaves, clearly checking out his backside as I take him by the hand and lovingly bring him over to Chris. "Giovanni, this is Chris. He's an old college friend of mine. Chris, my boyfriend, Giovanni."

Chris puts out his hand, "Chris Washington. Nice to meet you, man."

"Pleasure," Giovanni says. "What are you drinking?"

Chris looks down at his glass. "I don't know. Something Spanish."

Giovanni turns to me. "You didn't offer him one of mine?"

Before I can answer, Chris says, "That was my fault. I just got back from Barcelona for work, and I wanted a little reminder."

"Barcel—" Giovanni's face lights up. "Hey, I know you," he says, suddenly realizing. "You're a sports reporter, aren't you?"

Chris actually seems surprised. "I am. How did you know that?"

"I recognize the name," Giovanni tells him, then he points to Chris while talking to me. "This guy was wrote an amazing article for *Esquire* a few years back about the increasing influence of soccer here in the States. Got to interview Messi and everything."

I have no idea what he just said to me.

"So, are you still with *Esquire*?" Giovanni asks Chris.

"No, I only freelanced for them. Actually, I took a job at Fox Sports last year. Decided I wanted to sleep in the same city for more than two weeks at a time, maybe have more than four dollars to my name."

"So you must get to see some really great stuff live."

"A lot of it I just watch on the feed. But I can get tickets to anything local. If you ever want to hit up a Galaxy game, let me know."

Before Giovanni can answer, I stop him cold by saying, "Honey, we're almost out of Super Tuscans. Could you go to the storage area and stock a few back into our wall-of-wine fridge?"

Giovanni smiles at me. "Sure." He shakes Chris's hand. "Nice meeting you. I'm sure we'll see you again soon. And let me know about those Galaxy tickets. I'd love to tag along to a game with you."

Giovanni heads toward the back room, then makes a detour over to Jessie, who is opening a bottle for table eight. Once he's out of hearing range, Chris says, "Cool guy. Think he knows anyone for me?"

I don't try to hide my disapproval. "I thought you had a date."

"Yes. A date. Not a fiancée."

"You're a pig."

Holly leans over the bar to me and whispers, "Rather than insult the customers, feel like heading over to the center table and waiting on a few of them?"

"No problem," I say, and head over to a long community table bisecting the large room.

He's still just as smug and gross and phony as ever. I dodged a bullet leaving that one.

Despite myself: I spend the next hour scoping out Chris, vaguely keeping tabs on him yet wishing he'd leave.

Particularly after I watched him take a small corner table toward the back with a stunning blonde.

I make Jessie wait on them and feel a little betrayed when I see her burst out laughing at a joke he makes.

I really do hate him. Men like that act like they're nice guys, and that's the most dangerous kind of guy to date, because his eventual betrayal is the most insidious. It's one thing to know you're dating Lucifer right off the bat. But guys like Chris sneak into your heart by acting like they're into what you're saying, and being all nice and funny. And then just when you let your guard down, they screw you over.

Believe me: I will never let my guard down again. Screw me once . . .

Chapter Thirty

JESSIE

Okay, Jessie, you gotta keep it together. Nobody knows, and you don't want anyone to know. You can do this. It's just for a couple more hours . . .

I was doing so well for the first few hours. After Kevin and my conversation, I felt powerful. In control. Angry as hell, but in a good way. I didn't even bother to tell my friends what was going on. I just marched out of my office and began the night. I greeted old friends, helped customers, talked about wine. I took cheerful pictures with the girls, posted the hell out of them on social media (#allforwineandwineforall), and in general pushed Kevin out of my mind.

But then I overheard a woman at the table I waited on complaining to her friends about a destination wedding she had just been invited to, and how pissed she was that the bride and groom required everyone to spend thousands of dollars and several vacation days to head out to some island halfway around the world. And I immediately wanted to tell Kevin, "See, this is why we shouldn't have a destination wedding: Instead of your closest friends, you get your richest friends."

And then it hit me like a punch in the gut: I won't be debating destination weddings with Kevin anymore. Or any kinds of weddings. I won't be talking to him about my engagement ring ever again. We won't playfully argue about whether our formal china should be patterned or plain. Or whether our kids will go to public or private school.

Because there won't be an engagement. Or a wedding. Or kids. There will just be me, by myself, on the other side of the planet.

And suddenly I felt completely alone.

The table asked for another bottle, and I was grateful for the escape. I am now at the wine fridge, staring at the sea of bottles and feeling the tears start to well up.

I angrily wipe a tear from my right eye, grab the bottle of wine with the gold-and-black label, plaster a smile to my face, and walk back to the group. "Are we ready to keep this party going?" I ask them, and I'm greeted with cheers. I present the bottle to the ladies before I open it, making sure to hold it in such a way as to show off the label. The alpha of the group seems convivial and tells me to pour. I am about to pierce the foil when Giovanni appears out of nowhere to put his hand over mine and subtly pull the corkscrew away from the bottle. "Now, ladies, you promised me for your second bottle you'd try one of my Sangioveses. I have a 2012 that I'm so sure you'll love, that if you hate it, I'll take it back free of charge."

Okay, that was kind of an asshole move. Maybe Giovanni isn't the perfect guy after all.

A few of the women giggle (of course they do), and they agree to try his Sangiovese. "Excellent. Jessica will be happy to get that for you. Jessica, a word?"

He then takes the bottle out of my hand, places his hand on the small of my back, and begins gently pushing me toward the storage area in back. Feeling his hand on me is making me even more sad, and I'm not sure how much longer I can keep it together.

The moment we are in the storage area, Giovanni turns me to face him. He knits his brows in worry. "Everything okay?"

"What? Yeah, why?" I stammer.

He holds up the bottle. "I think you grabbed the wrong bottle. This is a three-hundred-dollar bottle, wholesale, that you guys are selling for twelve hundred. I can't imagine anyone would order it as their second bottle of the night."

I grab the bottle from him and stare at the label. "Shit!" I say, and I can feel the tears mudding up my mascara. "God, I'm a space cadet. I'm sorry. I'm so sorry."

"You don't need to apologize. No harm done. It . . ."

Without thinking, I walk right into his arms for a hug. "I broke up with Kevin."

"What? When?"

"A few hours ago." I look up at him and beg, "Please don't tell Nat. Don't tell anyone. I'm not ready to deal with it yet."

"Oh, sweetheart," Giovanni whispers to me empathetically as he hugs me and rubs my back. "I'm so sorry."

"Thank you," I say, putting my hands around his neck and hugging him harder than I probably should. I can feel his warmth and his heartbeat. It's nice.

Eventually, I can feel him wanting to pull away, but hesitating, so I pull away first. "I may be overreacting," I say, dabbing at my eyes to make sure they're not wet. "I'm not even sure if this is really it. I just . . . I don't know . . . it feels like it is, though."

Giovanni's eyes crinkle in sympathy. "What can I do?"

"I don't know. Set me up with your brother," I half joke. He tilts his head, confused. "I know, you only have sisters. Maybe you can set me up with one of them for a while. God, that was a bad joke. Never mind. I'm just trying to lighten the mood, and I'm doing it superbly badly."

Giovanni pulls me into a soft hug again. Bleu de Chanel mixed with deodorant and the smell of . . . what? . . . him, I guess.

I hear the door open behind us and turn to see Nat carrying a tray of giant glasses, each one half filled with red wine. "Honey, can you also get . . ."

I pull away from Giovanni faster than a babysitter's boyfriend when the car pulls up.

"Everything okay?" Nat asks. (Suspiciously? Or is that my imagination?)

"Fine," I say quickly. "I was just telling Giovanni here that . . ." How do I explain being in his arms? And, more important, never wanting to leave. For my save, I blurt out instinctively, "Kevin and I broke up."

Nat's jaw drops. "What? Hold on, let me get rid of these." And she disappears behind the door.

Giovanni and I share an awkward silence as we wait for her to come back. Neither of us moves. We just stand there, a few feet apart, looking like two awkward middle schoolers at their first dance. Finally I break the silence with an embarrassed, "I'm sorry to emotionally vomit all over you like that."

"Don't be silly. If you can't talk to your friends, what are we here for?"

Friends. Right. To add insult to injury, I just told the guy I like that I am now available, and he hasn't even thought about asking me out. I mean, of course it hasn't; he's dating my friend. But damn it! I wish it would cross his mind. Like, if only we lived in another universe . . . a universe where ice cream was considered health food and the fact that I saw him first meant something.

The door swings open again and Nat reappears. "Okay, what happened? When did it happen? Do you need to go home?"

"It happened right before the bar opened tonight, which I don't think was a coincidence," I tell her. "Kevin was offered a three-year job in Europe, and he's taking it. And I think he's known about it for a long time. It just took until I actually had my own life before he had the motivation to tell me."

Nat and Giovanni exchange a quick look. "I'm fine!" I insist. "Really. Actually, I'm better than fine. I'm angry and determined to move on as soon as I can. I just made a mistake and had a weak moment, but Giovanni gave me a hug, and I'm better now."

Neither of them looks convinced.

"Seriously, lock up your sons. I'm back on the market."

Nat tilts her head and looks at me quizzically. I shrug my shoulders and mildly shake my head to signal I know the joke was lame.

"Actually, I have a great guy for you when you're ready," Giovanni tells me.

"Really?" I say, intrigued.

"She's not ready. They've been broken up for two minutes," Nat chastises him.

"No, no, of course not yet," Giovanni tells her quickly. Then he turns to me. "But when you are: He's an investment adviser, but not like one of those asshole hedge fund guys in New York or anything. Stable, but dabbles in the arts. Very well read, likes to travel. Great sense of humor. I think you guys would really hit it off."

I want to ask, "Is he as cute as you?" but am quickly upstaged by Natasha. "A good sense of humor? No woman wants to go out with a guy with a good sense of humor."

"I thought every woman wanted to go out with a guy with a good sense of humor," Giovanni says.

"Maybe not as my rebound guy," I admit while Natasha simultaneously declares, "No, he's gotta be hot. The rest is icing."

"Hold on," Giovanni says, taking out his phone. "He's an occasional buyer of mine at the private tastings I do. Let me find a picture." Giovanni swipes his screen a few times, then shows me. "Here."

I grab the phone and stare at the screen, "Whoa. Cute. He looks kind of like Justin Trudeau."

"The Canadian prime minister?" Giovanni asks, confused.

"It's her thing. Let it go," Nat advises.

"Guys!" I hear Holly yell, as the door swings open again. "As intriguing as this threeway is, I need help out here. Get back to work."

"Jess broke up with Kevin," Nat tells her.

Holly grimaces, then tries to read my face. Finally asks me, "Devastated or pissed?"

"Oh, pissed," I assure her.

She points to me. "Great. Use it. Tomorrow morning, we'll eat cookies and make sure every whipped cream can in the house has beige lipstick around the nozzle. But for now—"

"Purple," I interrupt.

"What?"

"Purple. I'm wearing purple lipstick."

Holly moves in for a closer look of my lips, them beams at me proudly. "That's my girl."

And she turns and heads back to work outside.

That was Holly/Jessie shorthand for a lengthy conversation that could be summed up in three words: You got this.

Nat and I exchange a look and a nod: Our shorthand is even quicker. But she doesn't believe me. "If you want to take some time—" she begins.

"I've given him enough of my time," I interrupt. Then I head for the door. "And now, if you'll excuse me, I have a Sangiovese to pour."

I'm a terrible person. I should say I felt better because my girls made me feel supported and loved, and that I was happy everyone checked up on me. But that wasn't it.

The truth was, the second Giovanni hugged me changed everything.

In that one second, I knew Kevin didn't matter anymore. He was a placeholder: a frequently nice, kind of funny, solid guy who I had a lot in common with. But in the three years I dated him, I never once felt the way I had just felt in Giovanni's arms.

But now what?

Chapter Thirty-one

HOLLY

I first see Joe around nine thirty that night. He is dressed in the L.A. single guy standard uniform: button-up shirt, nice jacket, expensive jeans. He doesn't seem to be there with anyone, but I don't give that much thought: It's a women's wine bar. Single guys love to find easy ways to be near women.

"What can I get you?" I ask, after he waits politely for a few moments while I finish a large order.

"Holly, right?" he asks me, and I notice his cute smile. "I'm Joe. I'm a friend of Karen's."

I return the smile. "Hey, Joe. Thanks for coming. What can I get you?"

"How about if you tell me? I like my wine the way I like my women—dark, a little bitter, and totally out of my league."

I laugh. "Sounds like you could use an aged Cabernet," I tell him, describing our eighty-dollar-a-glass Cabernet which Jessie was appalled to learn has notes of cow dung. "But that might be a little steep pricewise." I hand Joe our one-page "wine by the glass" list. "Tell me what you normally drink and I can find . . ."

"No, no. That Cabernet sounds perfect. I'll take that."

"Great. Do you want to start a tab?"

"I do," he says, handing me a black AmEx. "And can you get me a glass of whatever Karen is drinking, and then a glass of whatever you're having at the end of the night? My treat."

Hmm, I think. *He must be European. I've seen Europeans buy their bartenders a drink.* Still, a little strange. "That's very sweet, but I can't drink while I'm working. But thank you. Really."

I pour him his Cabernet and Karen's Pinot Gris, start his tab, then focus on my other customers.

About half an hour later, Joe returns. "Karen says to buy a bottle of Dom Pérignon, and to tell you that before you say that it's a boring choice, she wants to remind you that she just made you a four-hundred-dollar sale."

This is the first time I've noticed how good-looking he is. One might say "handsome." Not my type of handsome: His dark brown hair has a little too much product in it for my taste, and there's something a little too put together about him. But there's a light in his clear blue eyes, a passion. And I like his smile. It's genuine, unforced. "Do you really want a bottle of Dom Pérignon?" I ask.

"No," he admits. "But Karen says having a bottle at my table is a good way to meet women."

I laugh and nod. "Fair enough. So are you here tonight to meet women?"

For a split second, I think he gives me a weird look. But then he's normal. "I'm here to meet a woman, I suppose. What about you? Do you hope to meet a man?" He quickly backpedals. "Or a woman?"

I pull out the bottle of Dom Pérignon from the white wine fridge (set to forty-five degrees exactly) and give him another smile. "You're sure you want this?"

He nods and smiles. "I'm sure." As I begin the process of

unscrewing the cage surrounding the cork, he asks, "So . . . man? Woman? One of each?"

I chuckle as I say, "Neither. Truth be told, there was a guy, but I don't think it's going to work out. Which is par for my life—no dating has ever worked out. Probably for the best—I'm here to start my new life. I've had some stuff go on in the past year that has made me realize that I need to make some changes. The bar is step one." I reconsider my statement. "Or maybe step seven or eight, I don't know, I've lost count. Point is, I'm making changes. Not dating I guess is either step two or nine."

I toss the cage in the trash, put a towel over the cork, turn the bottle, and make everything go *pop*.

"What's gone on in the past year?" Joe asks me.

"Ah, great question. But I'm swamped. Another time?"

"I'll be here until closing," he says, smiling to me warmly as he takes the bottle and two champagne flutes from me.

"Thanks. And good luck."

He cocks his head. "With what?"

"Meeting that woman."

"Ooohhh," he says quickly. "Right." He lifts the bottle slightly and says, "Well, thanks."

I wave happily and . . . I don't know. Something.

Something swirls around in my brain. But then I hear, "Can I get a refill?" and I get back to work.

About half an hour after that, Karen trots up to me. "Well, what do you think?"

"I think ordering Dom Pérignon is cliché," I tell her, as I pour several small glasses of white from southern Italy.

"Not as cliché as the sommelier criticizing my choices," she counters. "I meant about Joe."

"Your friend? Uh . . . he's nice."

"Not my friend. Business associate. And what do you mean, 'nice'?" She flicks her head back toward his direction. "He's thirty-five, single, successful, and intrigued as hell by you. But he's not nice."

"Three tours of Italy flights, and one rosé flight, table three," Nat calls out.

"On it!" I call back as I pull out more small glasses to finish the Italian flights. (One thing I'm good at is predicting who will be needing what in the next few minutes. And the gaggle of thirtysomething women at table five will be tasting flights until their Lyfts get here.) "Karen, I'm flattered. But if you wanted to set me up, maybe a night when I'm not completely overwhelmed with guests . . ."

"He's also the director you told off a few months ago."

"What?!" I exclaim, grabbing her arm and pulling her toward me. "Joe is Joseph Chavez?" I whisper. "Are you out of your fucking mind?!"

Karen's face lights up. "There's that passion I saw when you walked into my office at twenty-two."

"Why?" I stammer out. "For all that is good and holy . . . why?"

"For the same reason I invited three casting directors and a few network executives: You suddenly weren't available for auditions. People are intrigued. I'm just trying to build up heat."

"I don't want you to build up heat. I'm taking a break from acting."

"And I'm taking a break from Dysport. But we both know neither of us can stay away long."

"How are you coming with those flights?" Nat asks as she pours a large Australian Shiraz into a goblet and puts it on her tray.

"Give me a second," I say, pulling a Rosato from the Veneto region out of the wine fridge below me and quickly pouring it into three glasses. "Seriously, Karen, I cannot handle this stress tonight. Please make him go home."

She rolls her eyes, then assures me, "I'll see what I can do."

Meaning she'll do nothing. Argh . . . .

I so do not need this tonight.

I place Nat's flights on a tray, trying not to look over at Karen and Joe in the corner. (Meaning, of course, I'm looking over at Joe in the corner.)

Okay, yes, he's good-looking. Kind of has a baby face, which would be annoying at twenty but works on a guy in his midthirties. And he's smiling as Karen tells a story with her customary wild gesturing and theatrics. Nice shoulders. I have a thing about shoulders.

"Can I get another glass of this Pinot when you have a chance?" a woman sitting at the bar asks me pleasantly.

"Absolutely," I tell her, and get back to work.

A minute or two later, Joe returns to the bar. "I have been told that I must close my tab."

I place my palms together in a prayer and apologize, "I am so sorry for telling you off at my audition. You did not deserve my unloading on you like that. I was going through a lot, my dad had recently—"

"Stop. I was the asshole," Joe interrupts. "I was on the phone dealing with . . . you know what, it doesn't matter. Just please accept my apology. I had my casting director call your agent to bring you back the following week, and she said you were on a break. We've been asking about your availability for months. I'm a fan of your work. What can I do to get you to come in and read for me?"

One of the hottest commercial directors in town wants me to come in and read. I should be thrilled. But instead I hedge. "It's just not the right time," I tell him. "I can't work on any other characters right now. I'm taking time to work on myself. But thank you."

One of the double-edged swords in acting training is if you are really paying attention, you can tell exactly what the other person is feeling. And despite him nodding pleasantly and saying, "Cool. Cool. I get it," I can tell that my very minute rejection broke a tiny part of his heart. "Can I close out?"

I have to force a smile as I say, "Sure." Then I run his card, bring it back, and wait for him to sign.

"I see you guys close at one," Joe says. "Want to grab some breakfast with me afterward?" Before I can answer, he quickly says, "I know you're not dating. I'm not asking you out. I just . . . I don't know. I just want to get to know you better."

"It's opening night I kind of have to hang with my girls after we close."

"I get it. Of course," Joe says immediately. "How about tomorrow night?"

"I don't get off until two or two fifteen in the morning," I tell him apologetically.

"And I can name five places that are open that late. What will you be more in the mood for? Deli? Coffee shop? Diner? Thai food?"

So this is why this guy is such a successful director—he's tenacious.

Yet I think I'm blushing. Why am I blushing? I surprise myself by answering, "You know that coffee shop in Silverlake? I'll meet you there at two thirty."

"It's a nondate," he confirms, then pulls out his phone. "What's your number?"

"323 . . ." then I give him my cell number.

He types it in. "Perfect. Texting you now . . ."

My phone beeps. I check and read the text . . .

Idiot #7 to hit on you opening night.

I chuckle. "Were you hitting on me?"

"I might have been. But not anymore. Nondate."

I hold up my phone. "But should I put Idiot #7 as your contact information?"

"I would."

I smile, kind of tickled, and type in "Idiot #7."

Tickled. That's actually how I'm feeling right now. Maybe this guy's not so bad.

We say good-bye, and he heads back to Karen's table.

As I head to the register, I open the check to see he left an outrageous tip. Out. Ra. Geous. So much so that the credit card company probably won't allow it.

Hm. Maybe I should have let him stay later.

Chapter Thirty-two

NAT

The second I saw the delivery man come through our front door with the explosion of white and purple roses, my heart dropped into my stomach.

Well played, Marc. The bouquet must have set him back at least five hundred dollars. There are at least a hundred white, lavender, and dark purple roses nestled among other smaller flowers in a Waterford crystal vase.

I think I'm going to be sick as I watch the delivery man walk up to Holly at the bar. I quickly excuse myself from table three and race over to greet him as I hear him ask Holly, "Natasha Osorio?"

"That's me," I tell him, grabbing the vase from him as I say to Holly, "Can you sign for these and give him a tip? I'll pay you back." Then I scurry into Jessie's office in the back to hide the flowers (and, more important, the card).

I walk into her office, practically slam the door, put the flowers on her desk, grab the envelope, and rip it open. Inside the card merely reads, "Congratulations on your newest endeavor! Wishing you all the success in the world. (And if you ever decide to go back to writing, remember London is calling!) Much Love, Marc."

Crap. That was actually very sweet. Now I miss him again. Damn it.

I look at the bouquet and feel a tinge of yearning for my old life. Purple is absolutely my favorite color, and the floral design is exquisite. I feel positively spoiled as I lean in to sniff the buds. The aroma is decadent.

Marc does love me in his own way, maybe even as much as he is capable of. And in many ways, he tries to give me everything. And maybe if I just waited a little longer, he might actually leave. I mean, clearly he still misses me.

I pull my phone from my apron pocket and am about to click on to text him a thank-you when I am interrupted by a knock on the door.

"Come in!" I say, shoving my phone back into my apron.

Giovanni pops his head in. "Everything okay?"

"Yeah. Perfect. Why?"

Giovanni walks in. "Most women don't react to flowers by racing away and hiding."

"Huh? Oh, no. It's just . . . roses are so fragrant, you don't really want them near wine. Messes up the bouquet, no pun intended." I nervously hold up the card. "Just reading the card. They're from my old boss at *Genius!*"

I show Giovanni the card. After he reads it, his face seems to relax. "Well, that was nice of him. What's in London?"

"A new game show's he producing there," I say quickly, the lie of omission just gliding off my tongue. "He actually offered me the head writing job on it before we opened the bar. Obviously, I turned it down, but I guess it's still available if I want it."

"Are you rethinking your decision?" Giovanni asks me.

"Not at all!" I assure him. "I mean, yes, the offer's very tempting.

And I'm sure lots of women would kill for that opportunity. But it's not a healthy . . ."

At that moment, I almost slip and tell Giovanni the truth. What's it going to hurt? We've just started dating, and I'm going to have to tell him about Marc at some point.

I look at the flowers again. It's painful to me how beautiful they are. And how much I miss Marc.

I chicken out. "It just wouldn't be a good fit for me anymore. People change, people grow. What was great a year ago isn't where I am supposed to be now. You know what I mean?"

I try to read his reaction. He nods. "Sure. But I also know that it can be hard to say good-bye to your past. It's normal to wonder, 'What if?'"

"Really?" I ask, grateful for his understanding. "So you don't think it's weird that the flowers are bittersweet for me?"

"Not at all," he says, pulling me into a hug. "It's actually good to want to revisit your past every once in a while. It means, for the most part, you've led a happy life."

And that is exactly what I need to hear. That is beyond a glass-half-full way of looking at it. Who is this guy? And how did I get so lucky? I hug him back, hard. "Thank you."

"No problem. I just wish I had thought to buy you flowers. Now I feel like a jerk."

I shake my head. "You are *so* not a jerk. You are, by far, the least jerky guy I've ever dated."

He kisses me, and we begin making out. He is such a good kisser. I wonder if we have enough time for . . .

"Are you kidding me?" I hear Holly exclaim from the doorway.

"Sorry," I apologize, pulling away from Giovanni, grabbing his hand, and heading out. "Back to work. I know."

As we pass Holly, she mutters/jokes, "I was more referring to the fact that you got flowers and get to make out with a great-looking guy. Honestly, God may sometimes give with both hands, but never to me."

Chapter Thirty-three

HOLLY

Around eleven thirty, Sven walks in. He's dressed casually in jeans, a light blue button-up shirt, and a puka shell necklace. Huh. Who wears . . . ? Must be a Swedish thing.

"Oh, my God! You're here!" I exclaim, shocked. I immediately walk out from behind the bar to give him a big hug. When he hugs me back, he smells of . . . what is that? Pot? Patchouli? What does patchouli smell like? You know, besides awful.

What am I saying? He looks gorgeous, with freshly washed hair, still wet, and glowing skin. Half the women in the bar have already snuck a glance, and the other half are staring at him with their eyes almost popping like Roger Rabbit when he sees his wife, Jessica.

"I finished the work I needed to do early and literally took the last plane out for the night. I couldn't miss your opening," he tells me as we hug. Then he pulls away and looks around. "This is amazing."

"Thank you," I say bashfully. "What can I get you to drink?"

"What are you having?" he asks. (Not such an odd question: In Europe the bartender frequently has a drink with their customers.)

"Nothing yet," I say as I return behind the bar and he grabs a free barstool. "We might have a glass of champagne to celebrate the end of the night, but that's not until one."

"Well, hopefully you'll allow me to stay until one, then," he says, smiling brightly at me.

I return the smile, and my insides get a little gooey. "Of course you can."

"You made it!" Nat says cheerfully to Sven, giving him a quick hug and a kiss on the cheek. "You rock." As she heads behind the bar, she asks. "What are you drinking?"

"I don't know yet," he tells her, while staring at me with those clear blue eyes. "Holly is going to help me decide. And she's invited me to join you in a celebratory drink after closing."

"Perfect," Nat says, quickly filling two glasses with something red. She points to him. "Closing time. You. Me. It's happening."

And she gives him an easy wink, then walks away to serve other guests.

Why is it so easy to talk to men when you don't care?

"So," I ask with a catch in my voice, "what type of wine do you like? Red? White? Do you have a favorite country?"

He shrugs. "I'm pretty easy-going. What would you choose for me?"

Before I can answer, an obnoxious twentysomething stumbles over to Sven. "Oh, my God! Did anyone ever tell you that you look EXACTLY like Chris Hemsworth?"

She's too cute. *Go away, go away, go away* . . .

Sven smiles pleasantly. "That is very sweet, thank you."

Her eyes widen. "Oh, my God!" she yells like a sorority girl as she places her hand on his forearm and begins rubbing. "I loooov-vveee your accent. Where are you from?"

"Pittsburgh," he answers without missing a beat.

I suppress a laugh as the girl's friend appears behind her, places a hand on each of her arms, and twirls her back to their table. "Sorry about my friend. I dared her to come talk to you," she tells Sven, then says to her friend in a tone of voice we reserve for preschoolers and drunks, "Okay, say good-bye to the good-looking Thor."

Drunk cute girl makes a show of waving, "Bye, good-looking Thor."

"Bye," Sven says, still smiling. When they're out of hearing range, he asks me, "Why do American women keep comparing me to Thor? I don't look anything like Thor."

"So you're upset that you're being compared to a god?" I ask him, only half joking.

"No. But it's a little like if someone said you looked like . . . Who do people say you look like?"

I rattle off the usual suspects. "Jamie Chung, Lucy Liu, Chrissy Teigen, Beyoncé . . ."

"Beyoncé?"

"Just the one time. But it made my day."

He laughs as the smarter, less drunk girl comes back. "Hi, I just wanted to apologize for my friend. I'm Tracy."

She puts out her hand, which Sven graciously accepts. "Hi, Tracy. I'm Sven."

"Sven," she repeats, looking charmed. "Sven, our table is getting so estrogen heavy, I'm afraid we're about to become a pack of birth control pills. Would you like to join us for a drink?"

She's got to be a scientist, that was a strange joke. And by that I mean, *Go away go away, go away . . .*

"I don't know, maybe," Sven says, grimacing his face in debate. He turns to me, "Honey, how late did you say the babysitter could stay?"

Score!

I smile and bat my left hand like a cat swatting a string of yarn.

"She said to stay out as late as we want. After all, it is our opening night."

Tracy's face falls, and she turns to me in apology, "Oh, my God. I am so sorry. I had no idea Sven was your husband. So, so sorry. I swear I looked for a ring."

"Don't be silly," I say, waving it off. "He gets that all the time. And he won't wear a ring. Hates the feeling on his hand."

She ran away so fast, I felt bad.

Well, I felt bad enough to send over a free refill of the Sauvignon Blanc she was nursing.

But, really, I felt awesome.

Chapter Thirty-four

NAT

The evening could not have gone more perfectly. It was crowded, but not so much that people couldn't find seats. We sold a ton of wine, broke only one glass, and the refrigerator Giovanni fixed held up nicely.

We had hugged friends good-bye, thanked all of our new customers, sent any of the people who needed rides home in an assortment of Ubers, Lyfts, and cabs (oh my), and had just sat down at a table by the brick wall to open a bottle of bubbly and celebrate.

I pop open the champagne and Holly grabs four glasses while Jessie waves good-bye to our final two customers of the night as they step into a black Prius. Jess yells out a happy, "Good night. Get home safely!" then locks the front door, flips around a wooden sign Holly had made from a picture of a cork popping from a champagne bottle (open) to a picture of an open of red wine being vacuum sealed (closed).

Jessie immediately turns around to Holly, me, and Sven, and runs excitedly over to the table, "Postparty car analysis. Go!"

"What is a postparty car analysis?" Sven asks Holly as I pour them each a flute.

"You know how when you're a couple, right after you leave the party and get into your car, you start gossiping about everyone who was there?" she answers.

He seems genuinely confused. "Why would I do that? That sounds mean."

I hand him his glass, then make a joke of waving him off. "Okay, Sven's too nice to play. But speaking of cars, that reminds me: Sven, I'm going to go to Giovanni's tonight. Would you mind giving Holly a ride home?"

"So that we can gossip in the car?" he asks jokingly.

I shrug. "Or whatever else you want to do in the car," I suggest, giving him a fun wink as I hand Holly her glass of champagne.

I watch Sven gently take Holly's hand and give her a shy smile. "It would be my pleasure."

Jessie knows what's up. "Holly, we can handle cleanup if you guys want to leave after our toast."

"Oh, I couldn't do that to you," Holly insists. "There's way too much to do."

"Nonsense," Jessie counters as I hand her a filled flute. "The cleaning crew will be here in an hour for the heavy lifting. We just need to get the glasses into the dishwasher and things like that. You should go."

Holly sneaks a quick look at Sven. "I don't know . . ." she says awkwardly. "Jessie, you just broke up tonight. We need to rally around you."

"It's a breakup, not an election," Jessie points out. "And I'm fine. You should go."

Sven kisses Holly's hand lightly. "I'm happy to take you."

"Well . . ." Holly hesitates.

"Oh, for God's sake," I mutter. I raise my glass and quickly toast, "Here's to us! Good people are scarce." I down a fast gulp like I'm doing a Jell-O shot, then turn to the two of them. "Now get the fuck out."

Both Holly and Sven laugh before drinking their champagne. "Let me grab my purse," Holly says, practically giddy.

In less than two minutes, Holly is out the door with the man of her wet dreams, and Jessie has relocked the front door and is heading back to me. "I feel like I just finished finals week in college."

"Me too," I say. "I am exhausted and wide awake all at once." I take a sip of champagne. "So where did you leave things with Kevin?"

Jessie looks down at her drink. Looks back up at me. "Would you be mad if I didn't drink this?"

"Of course not. If you don't feel like celebrating, I totally understand."

"I do . . . I just . . . I want my head to be clear right now."

Jessie doesn't say anything else, and I know her well enough to know that she is not a typical girl: If she doesn't feel like talking, pushing her along won't help.

"I totally understand," I tell her, giving her a smile as I pick up Holly's, Sven's, and my glasses, and walk them toward the dishwasher. "Let's just clean up and get out of here."

Jessie picks up her glass and the bottle, and follows me. "Man, that agent of Holly's is a piece of work. I felt like I was serving Auntie Mame."

"Make no mistake, you were," I tell Jessie as I dump the champagne into the sink. "I could tell you stories. Did Holly tell you about the guy her agent was with?"

"I don't think she was with him," Jessie says. "He's too young for her. Really cute, though. I kept trying to figure out a way to introduce myself to him."

"That's the commercial director Holly told off," I tell Jessie as I rinse the glasses and put them in the dishwasher.

"No!" Jessie exclaims.

"Yes," I confirm. "And he asked her to meet him for dinner tomorrow after work."

"You do the glasses. I'll wipe down tables," Jessie says as she wets a rag and begins scrubbing down the bar. "Well, she's with Sven now, so: friends or date?"

"Not sure. I don't think Holly knows either. But he . . ."

My phone pings, which startles me a little. I pull my phone from my apron pocket and check the screen.

Did you like the flowers?

Shit. I have to admit, even after all this time, that man still manages to surprise me. From the time the flowers showed up, I was bracing for Marc's text. I didn't want Giovanni to hear my cell pinging like crazy, or see a flood of texts on my phone.

But Marc never called, texted, or gave any indication that he had even a passing interest in me.

Jessie walks around the room, picking up stray glasses. "Giovanni's waiting for you. You should go."

"No, no," I say, neither lying nor telling the truth as I quickly text back.

They were lovely. I'm with my boyfriend. Gotta go.

Then I put my phone on vibrate.

Half an hour later, Jessie and I have finished cleaning up, and I am headed to Giovanni's.

Well, I should say as far as Jessie knows, I am headed to Giovanni's. In reality, we drive off at the same time, then I follow her car

until she makes a right turn while I go straight, en route to Hollywood Hills.

I pull over a block later, turn my phone ringer on, and check my
screen. Three text messages and two voice mails.

> I'm in town next week for business. When
> can I take you to dinner?

> Hello? I just left you a message.

> You're not answering, so I checked your bar's
> Web site. You appear to be closed on Mondays.
> Can I take you out then?

And immediately, I'm nauseous. I sit in my car for several minutes, shoulders slumped, absentmindedly watching cars whiz past
me, the drivers anxious to be home and in their beds.

Finally, after mentally preparing myself, I listen to his voice
mails.

The first one is just as I expect. His voice is smooth, he's charming . . . He's a snake. "Darling, it's me. I hope the florist got you exactly what I asked for: I told them a woman like you deserves
millions of roses, but to also add a surprise or two. I also said nothing but purple and white."

He pauses, but the message keeps playing. Finally he says, "I miss
you. I didn't realize how much until recently. Please call me back."

The messages ends. I take a deep breath and play the next one.

"I'm getting a divorce," Marc begins. "I'm telling her everything.
I didn't want to tell you over voice mail, but I was afraid otherwise
you wouldn't call me back."

I don't even wait for the rest of his message before I call him back.

He answers on the first ring. "I'm so glad you called. It's over."

"What happened?"

"I miss you is what happened. This marriage feels like a hollow shell. I feel like we're pretending to be a happy couple, and it's all an act. I want out."

For a few moments, I'm speechless. "When are you going to tell her?"

"Before I leave for Los Angeles. I want it all out in the open."

"Wow," is all I can manage.

"So, the question is . . . Will you still have me?" Marc asks.

"I . . . I'm sorry. I'm just stunned," I stammer. "Of course, I love you. I'm thrilled about this news. Not thrilled. What a terrible word. I just mean . . ."

And the words sort of disappear. Marc finally asks, "Would you like to have dinner with me on Monday?"

"I would LOVE that," I answer immediately.

"Good. I kept my apartment, so maybe we could stay in . . . Wait. Hold on," Marc says.

I wait for a few moments.

"Elizabeth just walked in," Marc says, lowering his voice. "Can I call you back?"

"I'm actually . . . going to bed," I half lie.

Marc gets quiet. "The boyfriend."

"He's not my boyfriend," I quickly insist.

"Are you sleeping with him tonight?"

"You know what, Marc, until you actually break up, you're not allowed to guilt-trip me," I snap, surprising myself with my sudden backbone.

"No, darling, I'll be right there," I hear Marc say, presumably to her. Then he whispers to me, "I have to go. Wish me luck."

And he clicks off the phone.

I have no idea what to think. I have no idea what the right answer is. Do I even want Marc anymore? I mean, sure, I love him and there's a chemistry . . .

Actually, do I even love him? Or am I just in love with the romance? I've been wanting him to be free for years, and now that he's about to be, I feel . . . clenched.

Why aren't I happier about this?

But I am happy. I'm just in shock. Supposedly, some women who get proposed to need a few days to let everything sink in. It's probably that. My phone beeps a text. I immediately check it.

> **I'm passing out on the couch, trying to stay
> awake. If I don't answer the door, knock harder.**

Giovanni. Right.

Beautiful, super-nice Giovanni. Really one of the good ones. Jessie did an amazing job picking for me. I text him back:

> **Perfect.**

> **Oh, and I made you the Italian hot chocolate
> we talked about. It'll be waiting for you when
> you get here, Nice and warm.**

> **Just like you.**

> **I wasn't going to say that, but yes. Now
> stop texting and get over here.**

> **Be there in 20.**

The kind of guy who gets up in the middle of the night to make me hot chocolate. The kind of guy you build a life with.

I'll cancel my dinner with Marc.

Why couldn't things have just worked out with Chris back in college? Then I wouldn't be dealing with any of this drama.

Where did that come from? Probably because I miss college. I miss having the certainty I had at twenty that my knight in shining armor would make my heart flutter, without being a dick. Without breaking my heart.

I sure wish I could get that certainty back at thirty-two.

Chapter Thirty-five

HOLLY

After saying good-bye to Jessie and Nat (and mouthing an exaggerated *Thank you* to them when Sven wasn't looking), I follow him to his car, parked about a half block away. Ick. A white BMW. I don't know why, but I find BMWs annoying. They don't cut me off in traffic quite as often as Audis, but pretty close. Somehow, he didn't seem like the type to buy a . . .

What is wrong with me? I am on a date with the guy I have had a crush on for months, and the little voice in my head is already trying to find fault with him.

Wait, is this a date? Is he just driving me home because Nat asked him to? I mean, he did come to the bar and hang out with me, but lots of my friends showed up tonight. That doesn't necessarily mean anything. How can I figure out if this is an actual date?

"So . . ." I begin awkwardly as he clicks his car alarm and opens the passenger door for me. "Are you hungry? If you're still awake, we could go get something to—"

Sven leans in and kisses me hungrily. So I guess he was hungry—just not for food.

I'm so not mad at that. Yay! I'm on a date!

We immediately begin pawing each other out there on the street. Disgusting, lustful open-mouth kissing that makes any accidental spectators look away uncomfortably, and makes your friends disdainfully advise, "Get a room."

"Do you want to go somewhere a little more private?" Sven asks me between hyperventilated breaths.

"Mm-hmm," I mumble as I come up for air between kisses. We pull away from each other just long enough for me to get into the car and for him to close my door and walk around to the driver's side . . .

Where I am already leaning over from the passenger's seat, waiting for my next kiss. Sven gets in and pulls me onto his lap. The make-out session gets even hotter. I unbutton his shirt as he unzips the back of my dress and unhooks my bra.

Yikes. Slut alert.

I pull away from the tongue trading, smile, give him a closed-mouth kiss, and return to my seat. "I would love to see your apartment."

Sven grins and turns on his car. "We'll be there in five minutes."

We make out at every red light. At one point, the car behind us honks angrily. Green light.

We make out after he parks, we make out as we walk the pathway to his apartment. We stop kissing at his doorstep only long enough for him to find his keys.

As he fishes around in his pockets, I notice I smell like . . . what the hell is that? Patchouli?

Never mind. He finds his key, opens the door, and pushes me up against his doorway.

I wrap my legs around him, and he carries me through the dark living room to his bedroom.

Wait—right to the bedroom? We're not even going to make out on the couch for a little while? Aren't we going to do a little bit of the dance of seduction?

"Do you want to slow down a little?" I ask as he moves his hands up my dress.

"I don't need to. Do you?" he asks as he pulls my dress over my head in one quick maneuver.

Fortunately, I'm wearing pretty underwear. I mean, no, it's not the red lace I just bought, because I didn't know he was coming to opening night, but it's still . . . Oh, hello, he's really good at that.

Let's just say the next thirty minutes are very nice.

Which I wish I could say about the thirty minutes after that.

I am lying in Sven's bed in pitch dark, waiting for him to return from the bathroom. He jumped up the moment we were done, said, "Can you excuse me for a moment?" then left me in the dark to run a shower.

First off, that's weird. But also, he didn't ask me to join him. And now I smell like whatever the hell cologne he was wearing. I lift my arm to sniff. Yuck.

But wait, I think I'm also smelling rotten food. What is that? Pizza? Very old pizza? Very young blue cheese? Dirty socks?

I sit up and look around. My eyes have adjusted to the dark enough to see his floor is completely covered in clothes. God knows what's under those clothes. I hear the shower go off and lie back down as Sven takes his time coming out of the bathroom.

The moment his door opens, I am slammed with the stench of that cologne. Seriously, how have I not noticed that before? It makes Axe body spray seem subtle.

Sven lies down next to me and puts out his arms, silently inviting me to rest my head on his chest and fall asleep.

I kiss him once, then take my spot. I must say, I sure like this spot.

Except his heart is beating fast enough to rocket out of his chest and onto the ceiling. I move my ear over to listen. "Your heart's thumping like a jackrabbit."

Sven doesn't respond. Both of us just lie there awkwardly in silence.

"Would you mind going to your own bed?" Sven asks me out of the blue.

I pop my head up, more shocked than I guess I should be. "You want me to leave?"

Sven quickly sits up, clearly relieved to have me off of him. "It's nothing personal. I just have a problem falling asleep with someone in my bed. It's not you, it's me."

Well, of course it's him. WTF? Who doesn't want to have a naked woman in his bed? Hell, in a few hours I'll be ready for Round Two. Does this mean nothing????

"I normally I wouldn't ask," Sven says apologetically. "But it's not like I'm really kicking you out. You're just next door. You can just go home, shower, we'll both get some sleep, and then in the morning you can come back and we'll have some more fun, and then I can make you breakfast."

Wait, I'm the one who needs the shower?

Twenty-two-year-old me would have gotten emotional. Would have wondered what she did wrong.

But I'm too old for this.

I immediately get up and grab my clothes. "You smell like a wet grave," I announce as I throw my dress over my head, not bothering to take the time to put my bra back on. "And your room smells like a combination of cat litter and feet."

"Okay, never mind. You're mad. You can stay."

"Can I?" I ask sarcastically as I shimmy into my underwear. "You know . . . I have to ask, no judgment," I begin, with judgment seeping through my pores, "as good-looking as you are, what on earth makes you think it's okay to have sex with a woman for the first time, then immediately jump out of bed, shower, then ask her to leave?"

He tells me something in Swedish.

"Oh, my fucking God!" I exclaim as I yank my bra off the floor and storm out of his bedroom.

"Wait," he yells from the bedroom, "I'm trying to think of how to translate my explanation into English."

I grab my purse and let myself out. "Instead, why don't you tell me how to say 'Go fuck yourself' in Swedish."

Pretty sure he answered me as I slammed his front door.

Chapter Thirty-six

It's amazing how much can change in only a few hours. I'm not talking about the major things: life and death, birth, seeing *Love Actually* for the first time. I'm talking about how bipolar we are during the hours immediately following a breakup.

At two this morning, when Nat and I were cleaning up, I felt giddy. Empowered. Hear me roar!

But now it's five in the morning, and I'm lying alone in my California king-size bed I picked out with Kevin, taking up only the right side, and wondering, *What the hell am I going to do?*

I'm too old to start over. I can't go through the anguish of a first date ever again. I don't want to fall in love with someone new. A whole new set of failures and 'coulda beens' and 'almost but not quites.'

Kevin had been sending me texts and e-mails for several hours after I hung up on him. At the time, I didn't want the distraction. I didn't want to think about anything other than all of the great things that were happening to me at that moment. So on the advice of a (male) customer, I texted:

> I'm swamped with work. Can't talk. Get some
> sleep.

And the text worked. Kevin stopped bugging me.

But now, in the silence of dawn, I desperately want to talk to him. I'm terrified of losing him. Or maybe I'm just terrified of being single again.

Maybe this is for the best.

No, I should be terrified. I want kids. And if I start over again with someone else, that could mean having kids three years later than I want. Or maybe only being able to have one kid, because I'll be so old when I start trying. Or maybe never getting to have a kid at all, or a husband, ever, and being single for the rest of my life.

Then Giovanni pops into my mind. What a depressing reminder of what I'll never have. When he left tonight, he kissed me goodbye on the cheek, and my knees gave out a little.

Knees turning to jelly. I hate that feeling, I crave that feeling.

I miss that feeling.

Now that I think about it, it's been years since my body went limp from a guy. I don't remember ever having that candle-in-the-sun feeling with Kevin. But I must have. I wouldn't have stayed with him for three years, I wouldn't want to marry him, if he didn't make my heart and my loins ache with desire, at least at the beginning.

Loins ache with desire? I have got to quit reading romance novels. You know who would make a really good novel cover boy . . .

Stop thinking about Giovanni. He belongs to her. He picked her. And she's my friend.

Which makes me a really terrible person, because I am obsessing over the riddle of how to kiss him without getting into trouble.

I wonder what they're doing right now. Probably having sex. I mean, seriously—how could they not be having sex every minute of the day? He's the most beautiful man in the world. How can she not just bide her time all day waiting to get him back into bed? Or onto a couch, or in the backseat of a car. The backseat. I only thought of it because Nat did that with Marc with a *c*. I wonder if I could get her back together with . . . Jessie, stop that! It's bad enough you want her boyfriend—do you have to wish Marc back on her besides?

I should text Kevin. It's daytime there, and he'd be happy to hear from me. He's sorry. He wants to marry me. Yes, he had a few moments of doubt, but didn't I as well? I bought a bar, for God's sake. First stone and all that.

I should text Kevin. Shorthand the apology. Figure out our next step and get to the wedding planning.

I pull my phone off the charger on my nightstand and look at it. For a while.

What do I really want? If I could do anything in the world and not fail, what would I do?

Finally, I type:

You up?

I wait.

Nothing. Then . . .

Indeed. How are you holding up?

**I can't decide what to do about Kevin.
Any advice?**

Holly would say what's your heart telling you?

I can't tell Nat that my heart is telling me to go after her man. But I can tell a half-truth.

What my heart is telling me is that I don't want to move to Copenhagen.

That actually is the truth. I have no desire. I don't know what I do want, but I'm absolutely positive about what I don't.

Well, there you go.

Thanks. Am I keeping you from Giovanni?

Nah. He's asleep. I kept him up too late, which I feel little guilty about. (Yeah—not at all.) Have I thanked you for finding him for me?

She kept him up too late. Right.

And it's all my fault.

The heart doesn't really get to decide much in life. If it did, we would all live in Paris, painting for a living during the day and sleeping with the father of our children, Ryan Reynolds, at night.

Maybe there's some way to convince Kevin to come home.

Chapter Thirty-seven

NAT

My Friday started out so promising. I got to wake up to a beautiful man, who's still happy to only make out with me for hours on end. I have a man leaving his wife for me (which I assume he did last night, based on his texts. All he told me was that things at home had blown up and he'd see me Monday), and I was at a job that I liked, working with people who I love.

And then at five oh five, just as our first happy hour is officially under way, Chris strolls in.

My shoulders sink. "Oh, good Christ, what are you doing here?"

"I have decided to become the Norm to your Diane," he chirps happily as he plops down on a center barstool. "Did you get beer yet?"

"Get out," I mutter menacingly.

"We still don't have anything on draft," Holly answers. "However, we do have bottles of the local craft brewer's IPA and stout."

"Whose side are you on?" I ask her.

"The side of the customers," she answers. "Always. Particularly the ones willing to pay ten dollars for a bottle of IPA."

"And I am willing to do that," Chris tells her, smirking at me.

I swear, that's not an exaggeration. He's smirking.

Holly points to him and flirts, "I like the way you think. So I'm assuming you like your beer the way you like your women."

"How did you manage to buy dumb beer?" I ask her.

"I was thinking bitter," Holly tells me as she pops open the cap of a bottle of IPA and pours it into a pint glass.

"I like the way you think," Chris tells her playfully.

"Where did you find pint glasses?" I ask Holly accusingly.

"BevMo!" she answers. When I glare at her, she doubles down. "And the best was on sale for ten ninety-nine a six-pack."

"So you are really making a killing off of us beer drinkers," Chris says.

He holds up a credit card, which Holly cheerfully plucks out of his hand. "Thank you, baby. Start a tab?"

"Yes. I plan to be here late."

As Holly walks to the end of the bar to start Chris's tab, I follow her and whisper, "Why are you acting all friendly with him?"

"Um . . . I'm a bartender. It's what I do."

"But . . ." I turn to look at Chris, who surveys the room, checking out the women here for happy hour. "He's an asshole. We don't need a guy like that hitting on our customers all night."

"Actually, we do. Do you know why women go to bars?"

"Yes. To hang out with their friends and decompress."

"Sometimes. But frequently it's to dress up and flirt and feel pretty amid hot guys. And I hate to break it to you, but your friend over there is a hot guy."

I make a face. "Ick."

Holly shakes her head at me. "He's so not an Ick. What's your problem? Did you sleep with him?"

"What?! No! Ick."

"So he didn't fuck you over in any way?" Holly clarifies.

I look up at the ceiling, trying to find a way to tell her what happened in college without actually telling her what happened. Holly continues, "Trust me, I know Ick. Sven's an Ick. And if he ever shows up here again, I apologize in advance for all of the glassware that gets broken and the tables that splinter apart when I tackle him and haul him out by his ear. But your guy? He's fine."

Holly grabs a huge bag of peanuts from beneath the counter, pours some into a pink wooden bowl, and walks them over to Chris, who asks me, "So which station are you working tonight? I want to be at your table."

"She's working the bar," Holly tells him as she puts down the peanuts, then walks away to serve other happy hour guests.

Chris's face lights up. He turns to me. "Excellent."

"Chris! Yay!" I hear Jessie exclaim from her table near the window.

She quickly walks up to us and hands Chris her phone. "What do you think this means?" she asks.

He studies the text for a moment, then winces. "Oh. Stage one of the negotiation. He's trying to be nice but still make it seem like it's all your fault. I would steer clear for at least another three days. Give him time for it to sink in that he really fucked up."

She looks at her phone. "Okay, but I can't keep not talking to him. And I don't even know for sure what I want yet. So what should I . . ."

Chris types into her phone, then hands it back to her to scrutinize. "What do you think of that?"

Jessie's eyes widen. "Oh, my God—you're brilliant." She hits Send, then heads behind the bar to pour two flights of Central Coast reds.

I follow Jessie over to the reds, lean in, and try to whisper, "Okay, what the hell was that about? Since when are you and Chris friends?"

"Since last night, when I told him about what happened with Kevin when I was waiting on him and his date. And he was so helpful. I mean, as nice as you and Holly and Giovanni were, Chris just immediately turned it into a chess match, which was much more productive. He has such fascinating theories on dating."

"Jessie, the guy's a tool. We need to get him out of here so he doesn't hit on our clients."

Jessie fans out her eight glasses perfectly and begins pouring the first red. "Why is he a tool? What did he do?"

I loudly sigh. "Nothing outright, he just . . ."

"Did you sleep with him?"

"Why does everyone keep asking that?"

"Who's everyone?"

"Holly."

Jessie shrugs. Switches to bottle two and pours. "So you didn't sleep with him. Do you plan to sleep with him?"

"No. Ick. Besides, I have Giovanni."

"Then what's the problem?"

"Am I allowed to bring a pizza in here?" Chris raises his voice to ask from his side of the bar.

"Actually, that's not a bad idea," Jessie tells him. "The place next door delivers; we should get some sort of promotion going with them."

And she switches to bottle three.

I give up.

I make a point of ignoring him when a group of women walk in and sit a few seats away from him. We do the usual polite banter: How long have you guys been open? The place is beautiful. What would you recommend? Etc.

I hook each of them up with different glasses we have on special, start tabs, then try to keep myself busy and away from him.

"Can I get some water over here?" Chris asks, pulling out his iPad and the latest issue of *Sports Illustrated*.

Sigh. Trying not to grimace (well, not trying too hard), I scoop some ice, shoot some water into a glass from the soda gun, stick in a red straw, and bring it to him. "You brought a sports magazine into a women's bar?"

"Some women like sports."

I suppress a laugh. "Schyeah, that's why sports bars are crawling with women on a random Tuesday."

Chris turns off his iPad. "Do you want to know the difference between a man dating two women and a woman dating two men?"

"Oh, good, dating thoughts from a man who's still single . . ."

"If a man is dating two women at once, it is either because (a) he is an asshole, (b) he's trying to be an asshole, though he'll soon realize he sucks at it: think swipe left, or (c) he is trying to break up with the old girlfriend, but he wants a place to land after everything explodes, so he sets up the new girlfriend before he's completely done with the old girlfriend."

"So, in other words, (a) because he's an asshole," I drone.

"Great, we're on the same page," Chris tells me with mock cheer. "Do you know why a woman dates two men?"

"Because one of them is you?" I ask drily.

"Awww . . . I love that you acknowledge women want to date me."

"I didn't say that . . ."

"The reason why a woman dates two men at the same time is that neither of them is 'the guy.'"

Shit. How does he know about Marc? But I cover, "That's ridiculous. Women are just as capable of setting up a landing pad."

"Yeah, they are," he acknowledges, "but they usually don't. See, most women don't see dating as a game. If they find the guy—that's it. Chase is over! Let's start obsessing over dresses and cakes. So the only reason why a woman is dating two men at once is because one of the guys is a jerk who she knows she should break up with, but who for God knows what reason still holds some sway over her. And the other guy, the nice one, is just the chump she's using to try and get over the first guy."

I clench my jaw.

A happy Jessie walks up to Chris. "You're brilliant. Look what he wrote back." She hands him the screen, then looks at me. "Oh, my God, this guy is amazing. He knows everything about dating!"

"Rook to e5," Chris says, scrutinizing her screen. "So has he sent you flowers yet?"

"No," Jessie says, intrigued. "Am I getting flowers? I love flowers."

"In this case, you might not," Chris tells her. "When men give flowers at the beginning of the relationship, it's to be suave and romantic." Then he looks directly at me as he says, "But if he's already sleeping with you, it can be manipulative. Be very clear on what you want, both with yourself and him. No one's on solid ground right now."

Wow. He thinks Marc is sending me flowers to establish territory? Fuck you, Chris.

Jessie looks at me. "He's brilliant. He knows everything about men. How have you been keeping him from us this long?"

God, it's going to be a long night.

I quickly pull out my phone and send a text of my own. To Marc.

Can't wait to see you Monday. What can I bring?

Chapter Thirty-eight

JESSIE

Around nine o'clock, I am on my first break of the evening and am sitting at my desk, staring at my computer, and absentmindedly stuffing my face with my third Twinkie. I receive an e-mail from Kevin that I'm intrigued by.

It is titled "No beige in sight." And when I click to open the e-mail, up pops a picture of a bright blue three-story building, smushed between a bright yellow building on one side and a bright red building on the other, with a canal and small boats out front.

Below the picture Kevin wrote:

This is Copenhagen. Specifically, a very picturesque neighborhood called Christianshavn. This is a three-bedroom home for sale there, complete with boat slip.

Below that is a series of pictures of bright white rooms with light wooden floors. Everything is pristine and spotless, but also very cozy. I could vaguely picture myself walking around barefoot in that house, a fireplace roaring in the background. Which is a lot more than I could have said about Copenhagen an hour ago.

As I rip open the plastic wrap of another Twinkie, I end up going down a rabbit hole, researching Copenhagen.

The city is actually made up of a bunch of islands, so I could get the benefits of both worlds in terms of living near water and living in the city. Most Danes actually speak English, so it is possible to get around the city without feeling like Scarlett Johansson in *Lost in Translation*. The signs all seem to be in Danish, but it's easy to get a smartphone translator to help with that. And, yeah, the weather sucks in February (it's cold!), but the weather sucks in lots of places in February. I can't believe how blonde everyone is there.

Nat pops her head in. "Jess, can I ask you a favor?"

I gulp the bite of my Twinkie, nearly causing myself to choke. "Shoot."

"Wait, is that your dinner?" she asks with a hint of disapproval.

"Last week I saw you wolf down two slices of cold sausage pizza with a plastic cup of chocolate pudding and a horchata," I remind her.

"Fair enough." She trots in and leans on my desk. "So how would you like to see *The Barber of Seville* on Monday night with a hot Italian?"

My heart stops, and my breath catches. God, more than anything. "What? Why?"

"There's this panel I really want to go to at the Writers Guild about writing for subscription TV, but it's on Monday night. Unfortunately, Giovanni asked me to go to some black tie opera benefit, which I totally forgot about. "Pllleeeaaasseeee. I will so owe you."

I'm sort of at a loss here. "Won't Giovanni get upset?"

"Why would he get upset? He loves you. And you actually know about opera. Plus you won't preorder your cocktail three hours beforehand just to get through Act Two." She puts her palms together in prayer. "Please, please, please?"

I shrug, trying to look nonchalant. Like I'm doing her a favor. "Sure. Sounds fun."

"Really? Oh, my God! Thank you!" Nat hugs me so hard that I nearly fall over. "I'll call him right now to tell him," she says, pulling out her cell and racing back out of the office. "I owe you!"

As the door closes behind her, I can hear Nat saying, "I just talked to Jess. She'd love to go."

I have a date. I can't breathe. I know it's not a real date, but . . . what am I going to wear? What am I going to say to him? How am I not going to kiss him all night?

A new e-mail pops up from Kevin, with the title "Or maybe Norrebro. Or Frederiksberg."

Nat pops her back in. "Holly says break's over. And Giovanni says that sounds great. Is it okay if I give Giovanni your phone number so you guys can coordinate Monday?"

"Did he ask for my number?" I ask, trying not to sound giddy as I turn off my laptop and stand up.

"Yeah. Is that a problem?"

"Of course not," I say, trying to sound breezy. "I like talking to him."

You know, kind of like how I like taking my next breath.

Giovanni's texts start almost immediately and continue throughout the night. The first one dinged when I was taking an order for a party of eight. I was so swamped, it didn't occur to me to check it for at least five minutes. But then I saw it was him, and I was hooked.

> So I know you say you like the opera, but you
> don't have to go if you don't want to.

Are you kidding? I'm thrilled! I haven't seen the
Barber of Seville in years.

Did Nat explain what this is? It's a variety of arias
performed for a charity benefit, including Figaro's
aria. But also Violetta's aria from La traviata, Un
bel di vedremo from Madame Butterfly, and I'm
not sure what else.

Sounds exquisite.

I begin typing. Then I decide to test the waters, adding . . .

Can I take you to dinner afterward to thank you?

You don't have to. There will be tapas and
cocktails at the benefit.

He sensed it. He knew that I was asking him out, and he shot
me down. Which is totally fair. I deserved that. So I lie . . .

Perfect.

Even though it's not perfect. It's not even vaguely perfect. I feel
utterly humiliated.
But then an hour later he writes again.

I looked up the menu, because I'm a geek,
and it does seem a bit sparse. Maybe we
should nibble on a little something beforehand.
Where do you live?

I'm near Santa Monica. Is the benefit downtown?

Yes, so I'm going to have to pick you up early.

You don't have to go all the way out there. Traffic
will be a mess. Plus I'm used to driving to the
Eastside. I'll come meet you.

No. I'll come get you. Is 5:00 too early?

"Jess, tell Kevin we say hello, then get the hell off your phone,"
Holly chastises me.

5:00's great. Gotta go. Swamped here.

Tell Nat I say hi.

And that should have been it. I was already dancing with fire.

Leave it to Nat to douse the woodpile with gasoline and a bright
new torch after closing. "Shit," she says as the three of us pile into
our cars an hour after closing. "My phone is dead, and I forgot my
charger." She looks over at me. "Can you call Giovanni and tell him
I'm on my way?"

"Sure," I promise. And we all head out in opposite directions.

It takes me at least five minutes of driving to get up the nerve to
dial him into my Bluetooth and press the little green phone button.

Giovanni answers on the first ring. "Hey. Is everything okay?"

"It's fine," I assure him nervously. "Nat just wanted you to know
that her phone is dead, but she is on her way over."

"Cool. So how was your night?"

"Good," I answer. "Yours?"

"Good. I have a wine and food festival I'm presenting at tomorrow in Santa Barbara, so I'm just packing for the weekend."

"Fun!" I say, with a crack in my voice that makes me sound like a thirteen-year-old-boy going through the change.

Fun? Who says "fun" like that? Try to sound intelligent. "So, are you going to go do that twelve-course meal you told Nat about when you're there?"

There's silence on the other end. Crap. What did I say?

Finally, he answers, "No. There won't be time."

We share an awkward pause I quickly try to fill. "Oh. Well, it sounds amazing. I always wanted to do that dinner with Kevin, but he never wanted to. The scallop course alone would have me happily slogging up the PCH on a Friday afternoon for three hours."

"Wait, you know about this meal?"

"Oh, I've fantasized about it for years. I think I'd most want to do it in the fall, when the chef pairs the scallops with a fresh pumpkin risotto."

"Whoa. You really do know this meal," Giovanni says, clearly impressed and warming up to me. "Fall would be great. Although in the spring, she pairs the lamb chops with what's supposed to be an out-of-this-world roasted asparagus."

"Well, now see, we'll just have to go in the spring *and* the fall," I say, without thinking.

And he gets quiet again. God fucking damn it. Why can't I just let a nice moment happen?

Giovanni changes the subject. "So, have you heard from Kevin?"

And the moment is gone. Damn it. "Yeah," I answer. "Well, just via text and e-mail. I'm not ready to talk to him. He sent me pictures of a house in Copenhagen."

Why did I tell him that? What do I possibly hope to gain by letting him know Kevin is still very much in the picture.

"Why didn't Kevin want to go?" he asks.

For a moment, I don't understand the question. Then, "Oh, you mean to the restaurant in Santa Barbara? Kevin and I never went to places like that. It was way too expensive. And we were always saving up to pay off student loans and buy a house."

"So four-hundred-dollar meals weren't really in the budget."

"God, no. If it wasn't happy hour or we didn't have a Groupon, we stayed home."

"It's always a balance, isn't it?" Giovanni states. "I'm guilty sometimes of only living in the moment. But then the credit card bill will come due at the end of the month, and you have to think about that too."

"So is that why you haven't gone? You worry at the end of the month it wouldn't have been worth it?"

"I do worry about that. But not because of the money. It's . . ." He seems to struggle with how to put his next thoughts into words. "Have you ever traveled with a friend?"

"Sure."

"Okay, me too. To me, the coolest part about traveling with someone is that, for years afterward, you have this person you get to share that memory with. And they'll remember details about the trip that you totally forgot about. And when you talk about this memory years later with your friend, it all comes rushing back and you get to relive those happy feelings again, like it's the first time."

"Hm. I never thought about it that way. But yeah, you're right."

"So back when I was in college, and for a little while in my early twenties, I had all of these experiences in Hawaii and Europe with friends who can bring me right back to that time, and that's awesome. Unfortunately, I also had some experiences with now ex-girlfriends, one in particular who cheated on me, and those memories . . . Well, they're just not as good."

"Got it," I say, intentionally not asking about the ex-girlfriend memories so I don't ruin another moment. "You want to make sure you go with the right person."

"Exactly."

And then I say, truly, just as a friend, "Well, if you ever decide you want to go up there with a friend who can rave about the roasted asparagus with you in ten years, let me know. Because I'd love to be that person."

Can I hear smiling on the phone? I think I hear smiling. "That sounds pretty cool. I'll think about it." And then another ninety-degree turn: "You know what wine they pair with the pasta course? Orvieto."

"You're kidding?" I say brightly. "Well, see, now I have to go."

And the conversation easily flowed from there. We mostly talked about food. I admitted to hating duck breast, and he pulled the usual guy thing of, "Maybe you've just never had the right duck breast." But I let him. And he recommended a gourmet food truck he insisted served the best duck tacos on the planet. He said there was even a Groupon for it sometimes, which made me smile.

And okay, so maybe I wasn't going to get a boyfriend out of this. Maybe I would just get a really cool new friend who enjoys a lot of the same things I do. That's still pretty good, right?

At least that's what I told myself twenty minutes later, when he hung up to go have sex with my friend.

Chapter Thirty-nine

HOLLY

Okay, let me just break down the punishment I received today for being a totally clueless slut last night.

At nine A.M., Sven texts me. (Note: I do not say he comes over to speak to the woman he had sex with less than six hours before. He doesn't even call. He texts.)

Hey. Ended up oversleeping and had to quickly get my run in before work. (Talk about a mad dash—LOL.) What time are you done tonight? We can hook up, and tomorrow I promise breakfast.

Of course, the proper response would be, "Are you fucking kidding me?" Or, better yet, "Fuck off." But, being a doormat, I spend the next thirty minutes lying in my bed, trying to figure out a nicer way to play this. I finally write:

I actually have a date tonight after work.

Granted, I did not actually have a date tonight; I was just seeing Joe. But here was my theory: Men prefer women who are wanted by other men. They need to pursue a little bit. I did not give Sven the chance to chase me enough. Therefore, I have to reset the clock.

Thoughts like that are one of a myriad of reasons for why I'm still single. Sven's response?

Cool. Want to come see me afterward?

Say what now? I tell myself, *You know what? Don't even answer his text. He doesn't deserve it.*

Unfortunately, four minutes later, my compulsion to always have the last word kicks in.

No, I don't think so. I think last night may have been a mistake.

And Send! Good for me!

Don't be silly. I don't care if you're seeing other people. And if this guy you're seeing does, just don't tell him about us.

Is he fucking kidding me? I quickly text back:

This has nothing to do with him. You slept with me and then totally blew me off. Gentlemen don't do that.

I'm sorry. I thought we were just going to
be fuck buddies. I didn't realize you wanted
anything more.

Why on earth would you think that?!

Because the character you played on CSI
had five boyfriends.

I have no words. Wait, yes I do.

That was a character, you moron! I was acting. I
have also played a hooker on a show. Does that mean

I quickly backspace "hooker" . . . out of the text.

mother of two preschoolers on a show. Does
that mean you saw a tricycle outside of my
house?

Clearly I've offended you. Let's talk later,
after you've calmed down.

We will never talk again. I promise you.

Granted, I spend the day seething and vowing never to date
again. But I don't text or call him back. I go to work, listen to other
people's problems and dating dilemmas, and try to immerse myself
in my new, wonderful life.

Then at two thirty in the morning, just as I'm getting into my
car to drive over to Astro coffee shop to see Joe, I get a *ping*.

If you change your mind, just knock. I
bought eggs for the morning.

Livid, I drive into the parking lot of Astro coffee shop, where I see Joe standing in front of the restaurant, waiting for me. He immediately walks to my car.

He opens my door as I am turning off my car. "Right on time," he says cheerfully.

I get out and slam my door. "Can I just vent to you for a minute?" I ask him with a kind of nervous energy I constantly try to suppress. "Why is dating so fucking hard? Why do men . . . perfectly nice men, I'm sure, to their friends and their women friends and their mothers and their friends' daughters . . . why do they either become complete assholes or completely clueless when they finally accomplish their goal of sleeping with a woman?"

"Do you ever lower the heat to a simmer?" Joe asks.

"I'm serious! Think about it. You're being really nice to me right now. You looked me up, you tried to call me in for an audition, you came to my opening night. Hell, you're up at almost three in the morning for pancakes just to see me. But that's because we're not dating. I can guarantee you, if we slept together, you'd either be a jerk in some way—like you're dating three women at once or you make us go dutch for dinner—or there'd be some weird thing about you that would just come out of left field. Something I could never figure out in a million years: like you have five cats, or you talk to your mother four times a day, or you're a complete slob, or you can't fall asleep with a woman in your bed!"

I wait for his reaction to my statement. He stands there, in the middle of the parking lot, staring at me. Finally he says, a little sarcastically, "Oh, I get to talk now?"

The way he asked was actually find of funny. I smile. "Yes. Thoughts?"

"I think it would be exhausting to date three women: I try to only disappoint one woman at a time. I talk to my mother about once a week, usually on Sundays. I occasionally talk to her a second time during the week if my sister calls to say, 'Call Mom,' or if my mother calls me with a computer question. I don't believe in people going dutch for dinner for the most part, male or female, because I've been lucky in my career and have some money, so I like to treat my friends. But if they have a problem with that, we take turns buying coffee, or food, or whatever. I am a slob, particularly when I'm on a project, but I have a cleaning lady. I have a dog, who seemed very confused that I went out this late, and I will be ordering the steak and eggs because I don't like pancakes."

"Can you fall asleep with a woman in your bed?"

"It's pretty much been my life's goal since I was fourteen."

I smile again. "I'm sorry. You seem to keep seeing me at exactly the moment when I'm exploding. I'm really sorry."

He shrugs. "No worries. Sometimes when you're around a bomb, you get hit with shrapnel. Doesn't mean the bomb was meant for you."

I think I must look startled. Joe's chin juts forward as he asks, "Now what?"

"No . . . I . . . it's just . . ." And in that moment, I suddenly realize Joe is going to be in my life for a while. "My dad used to say that. It was his way of saying not to take things personally. I've just never heard anyone else say that before."

We begin walking toward the restaurant. "Huh. My dad used to say that all the time too," Joe tells me as he opens the diner door for me. "You said 'used to.' Did your dad pass away?"

"Yeah. Close to a year ago," I tell him as I walk through the entrance. "I thought it was going to get better, but it still sucks."

"For me it's been almost five, and I still have a hard time on his birthday," Joe tells me. He looks at the hostess/waitress and puts up two fingers. "Two please."

She tells us to take a seat wherever we want, and we take a booth by the window. She brings us menus and we both order coffee.

"Do you have a place where you can visit him?" I ask after the waitress leaves. "Not to be a Debbie Downer, but honestly, I don't know many people who have lost a parent yet. It's nice to be able to talk to a fellow member of one of the suckiest clubs in town."

"Dad wanted his ashes scattered in the water of a beach in San Francisco where he proposed to my mom. Actually, it took Mom a really long time to finally part with them. We didn't all head up there until the second anniversary of his death. It was really hard for Mom, she cried a lot."

"My dad wanted his ashes spread on the water too. On a buoy just outside Newport Harbor, in Orange County. I know I'm a terrible daughter, but I just can't do it. It's him. How can I let him go?"

"Well, this might not help, but my dad would have said it's not him, it's an old apartment he used to live in. He moved out awhile ago."

I laugh a little. "Sounds like my dad and your dad would have liked each other." Then I decide to change the vibe. "Okay, enough about death. Back to why dating sucks."

"Ooohhhh, I'm all in," Joe tells me with a spring in his voice. "You want to know why I was on the phone the day you auditioned for me?"

"I'm all ears," I tell him cheerfully. "And have I apologized enough for my outburst yet?"

"You have. Have I apologized enough yet?"

"You have. Go!"

"The girl I was seeing broke up with me via text," Joe begins.

"That sucks."

"Not done yet. From Las Vegas . . ."

"Uh-oh."

". . . where she had just eloped . . ."

"Good Lord."

". . . with my producer."

"Shit."

"Yeah," he agrees. "I had only dated her for a few months. But I had worked with him for over five years. It's like a bad version of a Rodney Dangerfield joke, 'I really miss my producer.'"

I have no words. Finally I just shake my head slowly and say, "That might be the worst breakup story I've ever heard. And you're a dude."

"Thank you. Although it didn't make me hit the scotch that night like you predicted . . ."

"Well, that's good . . ."

"I went with a dirty martini the size of a measuring cup. But on that night I realized: My dating life has been fucked up for years. I have tried dating every kind of woman: smart but boring, funny but neurotic, beautiful but dumb—as was the case of the latest ex—way too young, slightly too old, and occasionally, very occasionally, someone awesome who was totally out of my league. And every time, it's failed. And every time it gets worse, because I'm older. I'm in my midthirties, and by this age, and I know you're going to tell me I'm an asshole for saying this, but most of the good women are taken. It's not like when you're in college and have the pick of the litter. And I don't want to be that clichéd guy who hits forty and starts dating a twenty-two-year-old yoga instructor. But it sure seems like I've been setting myself up for that eventuality."

I suppress the urge to tell him he's an asshole for saying that all of the good women are taken. Instead, I say, "You're right. That sucks."

"So what about you?" he asks. "Why aren't you happily married with two beautiful kids yet?"

"I actually used to be one of those lucky women who always had men around. I loved college: If there was a straight man you liked, you just batted your eyes and presto! Easy make-out session. My problem was that I could never keep the guys I wanted around, and the ones I could keep around I didn't want. I inevitably dated actors, musicians, and comedians. Do you know who are the worst?"

"No," he says.

"Neither do I."

The waitress interrupts our conversation to take our orders. Joe orders the steak and eggs, and I tell her to make it two. After the waitress leaves with our menus, Joe looks at me, surprised, "Steak and eggs at three in the morning? I'm impressed."

"Well, it's not a date, and I don't have an audition tomorrow. So praise be to God, I may never order a salad again."

I give him a proud smile. I think my favorite part of taking a break from acting is taking a break from all the guilt trips about what I eat. The camera really does put on ten pounds, which means I didn't struggle just to maintain a healthy weight, or even a runner's weight. I have spent my entire adult life trying to stay ten pounds too skinny, and it's been so freeing to give up that daily struggle.

"So, you're serious about the 'no-dating' thing?" he asks.

I consider his question. Am I really? Or is this a knee-jerk reaction because I'm pissed? "I think for now," I tell him. "While I miss acting, not auditioning has given me a break from worrying about what total strangers think of my life choices, and it's been quite liberating. It very quickly led to five-dollar rainbows like ordering steak and eggs if I want, or going out of the house without makeup. I normally walk around Echo Park Lake every day, and it's something I enjoy. But I always used to push myself to do one more lap around the lake than I wanted to. This week, I went around three times instead of four, then picked up a latte at the boathouse, grabbed a table outside, and people-watched. So while I sometimes miss the rush of acting, overall, giving it up for now has made me a lot happier. And if I give up dating, yes, I'll miss the rush of the third date—like the rush of the acting. But if I don't have to go through the mild trauma of the first date for a while, maybe overall I'll be happier."

Joe nods. "That make sense, actually. Be nice to avoid that first date for a while."

"Yeah, I suppose those can be stressful for guys too."

"Are you kidding? Way worse for men than women. First off, you have to ask her out . . ."

"You don't just swipe right?" I joke.

"I tried that. Very briefly. One date in particular got really weird. Anyway, let's say you've asked the girl out, and you're going on a first date. Now everything is on you: We start with the choice of restaurant—can't be too nice, or she thinks you're trying too hard—"

"Not true," I interrupt. "We never think that. That's an urban myth, along with the woman who slept with the guy on the first night and still married him, and the emotionally available thirty-something man."

"Really? So all of those guys who were around but you didn't want? Did any of them try too hard?"

I am forced to concede, "Actually, one of them showed up in a limo."

"Oh, geez, I actually feel sorry for the guy. Anyway: restaurant. Can't be too nice, but can't be too cheap either. And you also want to make sure it's nothing she'll find vaguely offensive, like pizza, burgers . . ."

"A diner . . ." I joke.

"Ahhhh, but as you have pointed out, this is not a date. Next: clothing. What's too much? What's too casual? Invariably right before I go on a first date, I try on half of my clothes. And I'm a dude. Then there's the first kiss . . ."

I raise my hand. "May I give my opinion on that?"

"You may not. Because no matter what your opinion is, some other woman vehemently disagrees with you. Next, do you offer to take her back to your place . . ."

"On a first date? Never!"

"Again, you'd be surprised. I live in a nice house by myself. Some women have roommates. One even had her ex-boyfriend as a roommate. So apparently, I am supposed to figure out whether or not I should invite her to my place, or take her to her place and make it clear that I want to be invited in, or drop her off on her doorstep, kiss her good night virtuously, then head home. This is all based on what she says over dinner and the movie, if there is a movie, which to some women is good and to some bad, and how the hell do people ever get together and get married in the first place? By the way, what's a five-dollar rainbow?"

"Oh. A five-dollar rainbow is something that doesn't cost a lot or take much time but that makes you happy. It can be anything from a silly sparkly headband you bought at Disneyland for five dollars, a box of Girl Scout cookies, a black pen that just glides when you use it, or a hike on the beach. It's just something that makes you happy."

Our meals soon come, and we talk about everything from the upcoming elections (big no-no on a first date), to our mutual disdain for German food, to our mutual obsession with the TV show *Bojack Horseman.*

And the easy conversation really drove home my point in my head: I do need to take a break from dating. This is the best time I've had with a new guy in I don't know how long.

"So, because this is a nondate, we should order the pudding cake for dessert, right?" Joe suggests.

"It's like you read my mind," I say.

Dinner lasted two and a half hours. Dessert talk included family members, religion, even exes. It was fantastic.

When the check came, I try to grab it before he can. He beats me to it by less than two seconds. "What are you doing?" he asks in mock irritation.

"You said you take turns with your friends buying dinner," I tell him. "I had a really great time tonight. I want buy you dinner."

"Not happening," he says while handing his credit card to our waitress. "But you've just reminded me of the last bad part of a first date: trying to figure out when to ask the girl out for a second date. Since it's not a date, I'll just ask: Would you like to buy me dinner sometime?"

I smile. "You know what? I would like that a lot."

"Perfect. You guys are closed on Mondays, right?" Joe asks.

"We are."

"Want to have dinner Monday? Like, at a normal time?"

"Yup. And I'm taking responsibility for picking the place."

"Just no German food."

"It's a nondate."

The waitress comes back with his credit card and slip, which he quickly signs. As I stand up, I notice he tipped forty percent.

Huh.

"Do you always tip so much?" I ask him as he opens the door for me and we walk out into the parking lot.

"Why? Is that a bad thing?" Joe asks. "Do you think I'm masking some secret insecurity or something?"

"No," I say quickly. "I've been a waitress off and on for years and love customers like you. I guess I just assumed when you left that big tip for me . . ." I pause, sort of losing my way in the sentence. "That was stupid. Never mind."

As he walks me to my car, he says, "Okay. Well, first of all, maybe I did leave you a big tip because I was using it as an apology. Which, now that I say it out loud, is an asshole move. But mostly, I spend some days, all day, rejecting people for reasons that have nothing to do with them: The actor read well but is the wrong height. I can't use the first AD I want because the commercial house has a must-hire. Or the amazing writer I know wasn't approved by the ad agency. Tipping is one of the few times in my day when I have total control over letting people know how much I appreciate what they're doing. And, let's face it, if you are working at five in the morning at a coffee shop and you're still cheerful, you've earned your tip."

We get to my car, and I beep the alarm. Joe opens my door for me, flashing me that smoldering look he's famous for around town. I wait a moment to get in. Not sure why, I'm not waiting for a kiss or anything. I guess I just feel like scurrying in and leaving quickly would be rude.

But also, I can see from the expression on his face that something is on his mind. "Debating whether to invite me back to your place?" I joke.

"No. It's not that. There's something I need to tell you, and it's probably going to be one of those out-of-left-field things, but I think I better just get it out there."

Crap.

"You actually do like German food."

Joe smiles. "No. We've met before. As a matter of fact, we've worked together before."

"Oh," I say, not quite sure how to react. "When?"

"You did a music video . . . it was probably five or six years ago . . . and you were supposed to be dead for part of it, and the makeup artist had to put this egg solution over your eyeballs for a close-up to prove you were dead."

I remember the video—it won some MTV awards that year. But I don't remember . . . "Wait. You were the PA on that," I suddenly remember.

"Yeah, the thirty-year-old production assistant. But I needed the money and my roommate was production managing, so I took the job."

I shrug. Why the confession? "Okay. Hope I was nice."

"You were really nice. I cut my hand on something, and you were on a break. But you found a first aid kit, cleaned up the wound, and even put on the Band-Aid."

I wait for him to continue. Joe stops making eye contact. He looks off to the traffic light, then down to the ground, then back to me. "Well, anyway, I just wanted you to know that."

"Okay. Thanks for telling me," I say. "Good to know I'm not always a raving bitch."

"No. You're not," Joe says.

And for a second there, I think he might lean in to kiss me. Instead, he reiterates, "So Monday. It's a nondate!"

"Indeed Monday. Don't dress up."

"Wouldn't dream of it. Good night." Joe kisses me on the cheek, gives me a hug, then not only watches me get into my car but waits as I turn it on, back out of my spot, then drive out of the lot.

Is it bad that there might have been the teeniest, tiniest part of me that wanted to kiss him good-bye?

Chapter Forty

JESSIE

It's a perfectly beautiful Saturday afternoon, but I still can't motivate myself to crawl out of bed to make coffee. It's already one o'clock. I guess I haven't quite gotten used to my new life as a night owl, because I feel like I've wasted the day. But honestly, if your day doesn't end until four A.M., this is the new normal, right? How do artists, doctors, and insomniacs do it?

My phone rings that someone is trying to FaceTime me. I grab it, hoping against hope it's Giovanni, wanting to continue our conversation from last night when we were interrupted by Nat. I know I'm being ridiculous, but I still grab the phone, wishing.

Kevin.

Nat's friend Chris said to wait three days to talk to him if I want him back, so I let the call go.

I drag myself out of bed, slip on my favorite Tweety bird character slippers, and putter over to my kitchen for coffee. As I fill the water reservoir, my phone beeps a text from (310) and then a number I don't recognize.

Your floral arrangement has been delivered.

What? I didn't hear a delivery man. I open my front door, and there on my doorstep is a beautiful bouquet of a dozen pastel pink roses. I pick up the arrangement and read the card as I walk back inside.

> *These look like some of the roses you'll find in the springtime in Paris's Jardin des Tuileries.*

Love,
Kevin

Just like Chris predicted, Kevin sent me flowers.

Hm. Chris said to wait three days, but I rush to my computer and hit Skype.

Kevin's face pops up. I forgot how cute he was. "Did you get them?"

"Yes. And they're beautiful," I say, feeling all gooey inside. Then I remember. "But I still just can't wrap my head around Copenhagen."

"I know," Kevin says. "Which is why I've asked them to transfer me to Paris instead."

My jaw drops. "What? That's amazing. How did you manage that?"

"Believe me, it took a bit of convincing. But I pointed out that while I am fluent in both German and French, I know zero Danish. When that didn't work, I said I'd take a pay cut—"

"Kevin, you—"

"And when that didn't work, I told them my wife wouldn't move to Copenhagen, but she'd move to Paris."

Paris. I've always wanted to visit Paris. I thought about going my junior year, but didn't. Then thought about it after graduation, then when I was twenty-five, then thirty. But it was never the right time, or I never had the money. And now . . .

"You'd move to Paris for me?" I ask, my voice quivering a little.

"I'd do anything for you," Kevin answers. "I love you. I want to spend the rest of my life with you. I'm sorry I took so long to figure that out, but I will spend the rest of our lives making that up to you."

I take a moment to absorb his answer. "Wow." And then, "I love you too."

Kevin smiles. "Good. So when can you come look at houses?"

"We can afford a house there?" I ask him, surprised.

"Well, no. Not if we want to live in the city. But we can afford a Paris apartment. Somewhere near the museums, where you can have a coffee in the middle of the city and people-watch. Then have wine at night at a café and people-watch."

Wine. Sipping wine in one of those little Parisian bars with the highly polished black-and-white floors and . . .

The bar. For a second there, I totally forgot about our bar.

"Kevin, what about my bar?"

"We'll figure it out," he assures me. "We can give your friends a great price on your share, or you can just be a silent partner. Whatever you guys decide."

I do not see that going over well. I can already hear the fight in my head: Holly prodding me to continue to pursue my dream. Nat trashing Kevin, bringing up all of his sins over the past three years that she only knows about because I told her.

"It's going to be complicated," I warn Kevin.

"Life's complicated," he points out. "But they love you. And I guarantee you that when they come out here as your bridesmaids and see your new place, and see how happy you are with your new life, they'll be fine."

I'm not so sure about that.

Kevin continues his pitch, "And the minute she finds out you're pregnant, Holly will inundate us with clothes from Baby Gap."

I smile again. Babies. Parisian babies. Wearing Baby Gap. I can take them to museums every week, start them early on art. And the Paris Opera House. (Is that the same thing as the Opéra Bastille? I guess I'll know once I live there.) And the food. Ohhh . . . The food. I'll bet even the baby food is better in Paris.

"I wonder how quickly we could plan a wedding," I say wistfully.

"As quickly as we want. Pick a place, tell people when to come. We can do whatever we want. Where would you like to get married? Paris? London? Venice?"

That's right, I could get married wherever I wanted. I mean, granted, it would technically be a destination wedding (which Nat hates; she once referred to a destination wedding as "rich people fuckery"). But I'd be living there, so it would be okay.

"I think London," I tell Kevin happily. "And I want to stay at the Goring Hotel. That's where Duchess Kate stayed the night before she married Prince William."

"I'll make a reservation for the two of us when you come out. We can scope out wedding locations."

"Oh, my God, that would be amazing."

My phone pings a text.

"Is that from you?" I ask.

"Is what from me?" Kevin asks.

I look at my phone screen and see the text is from Giovanni.

They just changed the eleventh and twelfth courses. Thought of you. Maybe we should go now.

Below his text is a picture of a pastel pink background with words on it. I tap the pic and expand it with the flick of my thumb and forefinger. It's the menu from Gauguin, the restaurant we've been talking about. The eleventh course is now a mini cheese plate, with small bites of a Blu del Moncenisio (going to assume that's a blue cheese), something called Brebirousse D'argental, and a Gouda made in San Francisco. For the twelfth course, a chocolate-avocado mousse.

I quickly text back.

> Okay, the cheese plate sounds amazing. But why would anyone want to add avocado to a perfectly good chocolate mousse?

Fine. I'll eat your mousse, and we can pick up a donut for you on the way home.

> Fair enough. Or you can just trade me your duck breast.

Get away from my breast, woman!

"Are you looking up the Goring?" Kevin asks.

"No," I tell him. "Sorry. Just texting a friend. I . . ."

"Whoaaaa!" Kevin balks.

"What?" I react. "What's wrong?"

"Did you see how much the Goring Hotel is?" Kevin exclaims, reading his phone. "And that's just for one night. Maybe we should rent an Airbnb while we're in London."

"Oh," I say, disappointed.

But then again, what was I thinking? I'm not Kate. I'm not marrying a prince. I'm marrying a very nice man who wants to live with me in Paris. Not a bad life. Time to get my head on straight.

My text pings from Giovanni again. I click on it and see a picture of an ocean view. Underneath the text . . .

And the perfect room to stumble back to.
Don't worry—two beds.

> **Well, if we do that, we have to do Sunday brunch.**

> **My very thought!**

Giovanni then texts me a picture of a luscious Sunday brunch that includes lobster tails and champagne.

> **So what you're saying is we'll need that hotel**
> **room for two nights then.**

> **Ha! Did you see they pair the duck with**
> **the Syrah you guys carry?**

"Looking up hotels now," Kevin says. "There's an Airbnb flat that has a small kitchen, so you can make your coffee in the morning before we head out. I'm e-mailing you the link."

"Can I take a minute to make coffee? I'm starting to get a mild headache."

"Sure," Kevin says, his voice now all business. "In the meantime, I'll send you some more links of other flats in London."

My phone rings *La Bohème. "Je vous parle . . ."* I quickly hit the off button on my phone, then click it to vibrate.

"What was that?" Kevin asks.

"Nothing. My phone. Not a big deal."

Kevin doesn't seem fazed. "Oh. Okay."

Yikes. Good thing I didn't download Beyoncé's *50 Shades of Grey* version of "Crazy in Love" for Giovanni like I wanted to.

"Get your coffee," he tells me cheerfully. "I'm gonna pour myself a scotch. Call me after you check out the links. I'll also send you a realty Web site for Paris apartments."

I can feel my phone start vibrating.

"Great. Let me call you back in ten," I tell Kevin.

"I love you," Kevin says, sounding all soft and gushy.

"Me too," I rush to say. "Let me call you back."

I click off Skype, and the moment I know I'm off, I look down at my phone. Giovanni's call has already gone to voice mail. Instead of checking to hear what he says, I immediately call him back.

Giovanni answers right away, sounding cheerful. "The chef at Gauguin is about to begin his lecture. They're doing a live feed if you want to watch; we can text back and forth about his take on blood oranges."

"Oh, I can't," I say, disappointed. "I have some errands to catch up on before work. E-mails and stuff."

"Come on, play hooky," Giovanni teases. "Don't you want to know what about the soil makes local asparagus better than shipped asparagus?"

"Tempting. But I should go."

"Okay," Giovanni says, sounding not only disappointed but also perplexed. "Well, I'm looking forward to Monday. We can talk asparagi then."

"Is the plural 'asparagi'?" I ask him. "Is it Latin?"

"Honestly I don't know," he tells me, still sounding upbeat, but less so. "Just sounded smarter to say 'asparagi.'"

I smile into the phone, as though he can see me. We both wait through an odd pause. I give him an upbeat, "Okay, well, looking forward to Monday. I'm gonna go make some coffee and get my stuff done."

"You do that," he says.

And then neither of us hangs up. "Okay, so I'll see you Monday," I repeat.

"Okay," Giovanni says.

"And thanks for the pictures."

"No problem."

He's still not hanging up. Then again, neither am I. "Okay, bye," I say.

"Bye," he says.

And this time he's off. I look at my cell and sigh. Why did he have to call now? At a moment when everything was perfect?

I putter over to my kitchen and pop a pod of dark roast into the coffee machine and press Brew. My phone vibrates again. It's Giovanni again. (Yay!)

I pick up. "Hey."

"I'm sorry," Giovanni says. "I walked out of the lecture, and I'm in the hall. I know this is none of my business, but did Kevin call you again?"

I seem to have forgotten how to breathe. "I talked to him today. Yes."

"Oh," Giovanni responds. "So, how did it go?"

"I told him I couldn't see myself in Copenhagen," I announce truthfully.

A surprised, "Oh . . . Well, good."

I'm going to hate myself for my next sentence, "And then he asked me to move to Paris instead."

Another, "Oh."

"He requested a transfer. Just for me," I tell Giovanni.

"Huh," Giovanni says. "And what about the bar?"

The bar. Shit. "Please don't tell Nat!" I beg. "I haven't told her yet."

"No, I mean what about the bar? You're not going to let it fold less than a week in are you?"

I feel like he ripped out my lungs with that question. I mean, I can actually feel my chest constricting. "No, of course not. I would never do that. I'll just be a silent partner or something."

"Huh," Giovanni says. "Well, it sounds like you've got it all figured out."

"I never said that," I joke in a self-deprecating tone.

"What will you do in Paris?" Giovanni asks me.

It's a rather out-of-the blue question, and I don't know how to answer it. "Spend my days wandering the Louvre and the Musée d'Orsay. Stare for hours at the Monets and the Manets. Go to dinner in the Latin Quarter. Take walks along the Seine. Visit Versailles."

"And what would you do the third week?" he asks me, his voice picking up a distinct note of hostility.

Plan a wedding, I think to myself. But I can't quite get up the courage to tell him that. "I don't know. What did you do your third week there?"

"I went down to Provence and studied wine. Met a lot of the winemakers."

"Well, maybe I'll do that too," I say defensively.

"So you're just going to traipse around Provence? And then what?" he asks.

Which makes me snap. "Oh, I see. So it's okay for you to traipse around the world and it's okay for all of my friends to travel everywhere and have adventures. But I'm just boring, reliable old Jessie. Am I just supposed to stay in the same place forever? Am I also supposed to stay in the same part of my life forever?"

"That wasn't what I meant," Giovanni says quickly.

I immediately feel bad for barking at him. "I know," I say much more calmly. "I'm sorry. I wish . . ." I take a second, trying to figure out how to put it into words.

I wish I had met you three years ago. I wish you weren't dating my best friend. I wish life would occasionally not be so much work. That something would just fall into my lap.

"I wish I knew you better," I finally say. "Then I might feel more comfortable talking to you about this. But you barely know me, and I don't want to burden you."

"You can burden me," he promises. "I walked out of the lecture. Seriously, maybe I could help."

"You can't," I assure him sadly. "And I've got a lot to think about, and a lot of stuff to do today. Can I just talk to you later?"

There's a pause. Finally, he says, "Of course. Let me know if there's anything I can do."

"Thanks," I say. "Promise me you won't tell Nat about our conversation?"

"What conversation?" he asks.

"I mean I hate for us to have a secret but . . ."

"I'm good with secrets," he assures me.

"Thanks."

I don't want to get off with Giovanni but . . . "I really have to go."

"Go. I'm around if you need me."

"Thanks. Bye."

"Bye."

When my cup of coffee is ready, I grab it and run back to my computer. I check my e-mail to see that Kevin has sent me several links already. I open the first one, an Airbnb in London that looks . . .

Small. And nowhere near the part of the city I want to be in. Sigh.

Kevin's Skype rings, and I click on, then look at his next link: an apartment in Paris.

"Okay, do you see the link for the two-bedroom in the eighth arrondissement?"

"Looking at it now," I tell him. The moment the first picture pops up, I sigh in contentment. "Oh, my God, it's stunning."

"Yup. And the kitchen is a nice size for Paris too. Look at the fourth picture."

"Oh," I blurt out, not able to contain my disappointment. "It's all beige. Even the counters."

"Yes. But according to the real estate agent the company recommended, everyone who buys in Paris needs to include money in their budget for renovations. I figure you can redo the kitchen in whatever colors you want."

I spend the next five minutes scrolling through Paris apartments and fantasizing about my new life. And I happily decide: *Okay, Universe, maybe I was wrong. Maybe my life is easy occasionally. Maybe some days I effortlessly get everything I asked for.*

And the Universe burst out laughing. Because then I get this text:

I went to all of those places when I was young because I was lost and trying to find my niche in the world. To figure out what I was supposed to do, and where I belonged. I was twenty. I was a baby. I just wanted to find home. I think you are home. You've found your calling. Your passion was one of the first things I noticed about you. Paris is stunning, and you should go. Travel is amazing. But there is still no better feeling than at the end of an exciting adventure, when you fall into your own bed.

And we're back to our regularly scheduled life. What the hell am I going to do? I type back:

> Thank you. I'll keep that in mind. And hey, we still need to go to that amazing dinner at Gauguin.

"Are you happy now?" Kevin asks.

I give him a big smile and lie, "Absolutely."

Chapter Forty-one

NAT

Saturday night. A bachelorette party (a good sign that our reputation is already preceding us), a few dates, and a good mix of men and women flirting and having fun. Unapologetic girl music playing on the soundspeakers. (Jessie has this theory that might be panning out: no male singers. Our iPod playlist has Lady Gaga followed by Paula Abdul, then Britney jumps in. Fall back to vintage Rihanna, come back to the present with a little Beyoncé, then on to Christina, Pink, and the list goes on.) By the time "I Will Survive" starts, half of the women in the bar are singing to their friends or dates, and/or boogying in their seats. I'm bopping my hips behind the bar, snapping, getting my shoulders into it as I pour a flight of Pinot Noirs. Life is good.

Another bonus? Chris didn't come in tonight.

Actually, maybe that's not a bonus. I'll admit, I do sort of keep looking over at the front door to see if he might show up.

"So let me get this straight," Jessie says to Holly as she opens a new bottle of Sauvignon Blanc to finish filling a glass. "You ate steak in front of the guy and talked for almost three hours, but it wasn't a date?"

"Right," Holly concurs as she pours a glass of Merlot. "Can I have that Sauvignon when you're done?"

I continue Jessie's thought, "And you let him buy you dinner?"

"That doesn't mean anything. I actually tried to grab the check, but he wouldn't allow it," Holly clarifies.

Jess hands the Sauvignon to Holly. "So was it a real grabbing of the check? Or was it like when you start to reach for your wallet to get a credit card but secretly you're hoping he'll tell you he's got this, so you'll both know you're on a date?"

"I really tried to grab the check. And we really weren't out on a date."

Jessie shakes her head. "So cute. What a waste."

"Having a good person in your life is a waste?" Holly asks.

"Oh, when he looks like that? Totally," I assure her.

Holly corks the bottle of Sauvignon, then places her stemware on her tray. "I just can't face dating anymore. I'm too tired, and I don't have the strength to take the disappointment one more time. The patchouli alone could kill me. So back off."

"You know, the not dating could be a good sign," Jess says, putting a filled glass of Cabernet on her tray. "You know what they say—love happens when you're not looking." Jess heads out from behind the bar and over to her table.

"That's not love. That's getting hit by a bus," Holly tells Jess, following her.

Chris walks through the door, hyperfocused on a text. He takes his usual seat at the corner of my bar. "Can I get an IPA, please?" he says, rather distractedly.

I walk over to the small refrigerator where we keep the beer and pull out a bottle. As I walk it over, I enlighten Chris. "If she's telling you how crazy her life is right now, it means she's not coming. And you're in the friend zone."

He looks up, confused. "What?"

"You're not the only one who has theories on dating," I tell him, then open his beer and pour it into a pint glass. "And while you may know what men really mean, I know what women really mean. That look on your face? It's confusion. Mixed with a touch of anger. It's you wanting to get your two cents in, but you can't. Because she does not give a fuck what you really think. You are never getting laid by that woman."

I toss down a coaster, put down his pint glass, and smirk at him. One point for me.

Unfortunately, he comes back with, "It's my sister. But thanks for the heads-up."

Oh. I slink away to help another customer. About a minute later, Chris asks me, "Can you watch my beer and make sure no one takes my spot?" Then he goes outside to take a call.

I'll admit, I'm kind of intrigued. I watch him pace in front of our large picture window. At one point, he takes his phone and repeatedly hits it against his forehead. He then disappears from view.

I go back to my other customers for about five minutes. When Chris finally returns, he is holding a laptop. He sits down, flips open the computer, and pouts while he reads.

I'm not taking the bait. I refuse to engage. He can talk to me when he's ready.

Jessie, on the other hand, walks right up to him, giving him a bright, "Hey, you made it."

"Hey," he returns. "I could use your help. What's your Wi-Fi password?"

She types it in for him. He looks flummoxed. "That is seriously your password?"

"Holly picked it. She's secretly into otters. And One Direction."

Chris's eyes widen as if to say, *I'm gonna let that one go.* "Jess, you're a girl, so obviously you've thought about this: If you had to get married in Los Angeles, where would you go?"

"In Los Angeles?" Jessie asks, giving him a strange look.

"Yeah, like you'd ever elope in Vegas," I snark.

"Fair enough," Jessie concedes. "Well, it depends. If I was only having twenty guests, I'd get married in the gazebo of the Hotel Bel-Air, in front of the swans." Her answer motivates Chris to begin typing vigorously on his keyboard. She continues, "Or maybe at the Montage, and have a nice luncheon afterward. Something with salmon or striped bass. If I was having fifty guests, there's this lovely venue in Santa Monica I am in love with: I'd get married on the beach, then rent out the venue and bring in a caterer. If I was having a hundred people, I might go with Duke's in Malibu, but I'd definitely go with the buffet there, not the seated dinner, and if I were having over two hundred—"

"Hold up," I stop her as Chris continues to type like a madman. "Why would you ever have over two hundred guests at your wedding? You don't even know two hundred people."

"We're talking about my dream wedding. I'm not really thinking about who the guests are . . ."

"Schyeah," Chris mutters to himself.

She makes a joke of saying, "Fine. Then I'm not telling you where I'd get married if I had over five hundred guests either." She rubs his arm to let him know she's not really offended, then heads back to her work.

Chris projects his voice toward her. "Thank you. That's very helpful." Then he says, "Holly, where do you want to get married?"

"I like the idea of downtown. You know, the Biltmore if we went traditional, maybe the Ritz-Carlton if we wanted to be more modern. Of course, there are so many cool hotels constantly opening up down there, I'm sure I'll have lots of good choices."

He types away. "Biltmore, actually now called the Millennium Biltmore, and the Ritz-Carlton. Thank you."

And she goes back to work.

I watch Chris focus on his screen and begin using his index finger to move around the mouse box on his keyboard.

He doesn't even acknowledge me. Finally, I ask, "Aren't you going to ask me where *I* want to get married?"

He looks up. Throws me a sarcastic, "You? With your fear of intimacy? Right."

"I don't have a fear of . . ." I throw up my hands. "You know what, Chris? I think you should go. I'm done. I don't know what this is, but I'm done."

Chris takes a deep breath, then closes his computer. "You're right. I apologize. I actually meant it as a compliment."

"You think telling me I have a fear of intimacy is a compliment?"

"No. I think you are a level-headed woman who could just as easily go to City Hall on a Tuesday morning to start her marriage, than turn everything into a spectacle at the expense of the sanity of everyone who loves her. Again, I apologize."

I debate throwing him out anyway. But instead I decide, "I accept your apology." Then I decide to be nice. "It sounds like you've had a bad day. Do you want to talk about it?"

"I spent the day, starting at eight in the morning, driving my mother and two sisters around the city looking at wedding venues."

"Okay," I say. His sentence was loaded with exasperation, but instead of jumping in with more questions, I give him the space to go on.

"My sister lives in San Francisco with her fiancé. He's from Boston, she's from L.A. So, instead of doing a big wedding, they announced last month that they were going to elope in Bora Bora. Get married on a beach at sunset. Have their honeymoon in an overwater bungalow. Swim with dolphins during the day, drink too much champagne at night. Sounds perfect, doesn't it?"

"Bora Bora sounds lovely, yes."

"That's what I thought. And nobody had to go. No tuxedos to rent, no dates to try and find, no planes, no hotels, no rubbery chicken for dinner. They go. When they get back, they send out a wedding announcement. I send a gift. One click of a button on the Bloomingdale's registry, and I'm golden."

Jessie suddenly reappears. "Wait, you wouldn't go to your sister's wedding just because she was traveling out of town?"

"Please," Chris says as he returns to typing. "Anyone contemplating a destination wedding must be comfortable with the idea that not one single guest will be pleased to hear that."

"Huh," Jessie says. "Okay, thanks." And she walks away again.

I decide to ignore Jessie's weirdness and focus on Chris. "I take it your mother did not approve of your sister's choice."

He seems surprised by my observation. "How did you know that?"

"Well, I have a mother," I tell him.

"Mom basically threatened to show up to Bora Bora with a flashlight and a machete looking for them. She then reminded all three of us of how long she was in labor with each one of us. Apparently, she sailed through the day with me at only eighteen hours. My sister was forty-two. That was on Day One of the fight. By Day Two, we got a very graphic, not to mention rude, description of how bad potty training went all three times. Day Seven was a trip down memory lane on the horrors of driver's education. By Day Fifteen, my sister capitulated and agreed to get married here. Only she doesn't live here anymore, so she decided to come down for one weekend to pick a venue. And somehow, her soon to be husband got to stay in San Francisco and get out of helping her. So now the lovely job of picking a venue, choosing a menu, and negotiating with my mother has fallen onto both her maid of honor and, much more important, her man of honor."

"That would be you?" I surmise.

"Yes. Because she didn't want to, and I quote, 'hurt my feelings' by not asking me to be in the wedding. Can you honestly tell me women get offended if they're not asked to be in a wedding? Which part would be offensive? The not having to listen to your friend lambaste you because you don't know the difference between squab and pigeon, or the paying six hundred dollars for a taffeta dress that makes you look like a prom date from 1988?"

I am ready to answer, *Hell, yes! Of course our feelings would be hurt, you unfeeling cad.* But I can't get a word in edgewise.

"And don't even get me started on the bachelorette party. I'm not going. If I technically have to host it, fine, here's my credit card. Go nuts. But I'm not going."

I nod my head. "Well, I can certainly see why you're feeling agitated . . ."

"The second I learned what Bachelorette Party Bingo was, I started planning my appendectomy to fall on that weekend. Then there's the male strip show. Where women actually pay money . . . I can't even . . . Do you know what it takes to get the average man to take off his clothes?"

"A six-pack of microbrew?" I answer.

"I was going to say, 'Asking,' but I like your answer better. Oh! And then, for God knows what reason, in the middle of the after-noon they suddenly decide we need to go dress shopping. Like, right this minute!"

I try to help his sister by explaining to him calmly, "They deci-ded to go because the groom wasn't there. It's bad luck for him to see the bride in her gown ahead of time."

Chris narrows his jaw. "Oh, my God, that's what they said. What is wrong with you people?"

"So I take it you didn't like dress shopping . . ."

"I don't even like shopping for my own clothes. Why on earth would I want to go shopping for hers? And do you know there is something called a 'mermaid dress'? Why would anyone want to show up on her wedding day dressed as a fish?"

"A mermaid style is actually form-fitting until you get to the—"

"I am sad to say I now know exactly what a mermaid dress is. And it made her ass look huge, although not as big as the dress, which can only be described as the dress that made her look like Glinda the Good Witch."

"You didn't actually tell her that her ass—"

"I'm not done talking."

Fair enough. I shut my mouth and let Chris continue his tirade. "You know, many years ago, I thought I wanted to spend my life surrounded by women. God has a sense of humor, because after one day of this, I'm toast. Seriously, why do women like weddings?"

"For the same reason men like victory parades," I tell him. "Because the war is over. And in our case, we get rewarded with cake and pretty jewelry."

Chris takes a deep breath. "I'm sorry. I will be calm now. Thank you for listening. How was your day?"

I'm about to answer when his cell phone rings the first line from "Lady Marmalade": "Hey sister, go sister, soul sister, go sister." He picks up and consciously tries to keep his voice level, calm, and supportive. "Okay, what do you think about Malibu? There's a place called Duke's . . ."

I walk away to give him his privacy. And for a brief moment I decide that he's actually kind of cute. I mean, I always knew he was good-looking in that prom-king, -girls-will-do-whatever-I-want kind of way. But listening to him talk to his sister is actually rather sweet.

Chris spends the next several hours dealing with the female members of his family, and I must say, it was quite entertaining to hear him losing the war of the sexes. My favorite lines of the night being, "If your groom wants me to wear a magenta cummerbund and tie, that's fine . . . I'm not taking his side. And there shouldn't be sides, if . . . Seriously, magenta's purple? It sounds like it should be yellow. Or discovering new worlds for King Charles I of Spain . . . I am paying attention . . . Fine. Black. Nothing says 'We wish your marriage well' like black."

Also, "The way you're using that in a sentence, it sounds like a chicken."

And finally, a defeated, "Brunch. Yes, by all means, let's day drink . . . I wasn't being sarcastic. When can I meet you?"

At twelve forty-five, Holly loudly announces, "Last call." I walk over to Chris and ask, "One more?"

"Yes," he says very pleasantly as he closes his laptop. "And I so need to call Lyft. Is my car safe out there?"

"Yeah. Meters don't work on Sundays," I tell him.

As I go to the refrigerator to get him his IPA, he asks, "Actually, can I get a glass of champagne?"

I smile. "The man is full of surprises. Do you want actual champagne, or a sparkler from California?"

"Whatever you choose. You're the boss." As I rifle through our selections and go with a dry bubbly from Northern California, he asks, "Care to join me?"

"Can't really drink while I'm working," I tell him, and I take down a flute hanging from a metal rack in the ceiling. I bring the flute and the bottle over to him for inspection, then pour a small taste.

He smiles and nods. As I pour the drink, he asks, "So where do you want to get married?"

A teeny part of me braces. I smirk and give him a sarcastic, "I have a fear of intimacy, remember?"

"I'm sorry about that. Really. I'm curious. Where do you want to get married?"

Yeah, I'm not telling him that. "You know, I've got other customers I have to close out. Maybe we'll talk another time."

"Okay."

Chris nurses his drink, waiting until every other customer has left the bar. At some point, Jessie walks over to him, and he asks her, "Am I allowed to be here past closing?"

She shrugs. "Sure. Just finish drinking that so it doesn't look like we're still open."

I overhear them but pretend not to.

A little after one, I put his credit card and receipt into a clear glass and place it on the bar. I nod at his champagne flute. "You done with that?"

Chris downs the rest, then hands me the glass, smiling. "Absolutely. So, everyone's closed out. Nobody here but us chickens. Where do you want to get married?"

I deflect him by flipping his question around. "Where do *you* want to get married?"

"Wherever I'm told."

"Oh, come on. You don't have any opinion about where you are going to spend one of the best days of your life."

"I'm assuming if I'm with the woman I want to spend the rest of my life with, it's going to be one of the best days of my life anyway. I could be at a One Direction concert, and it would still be great."

"What's wrong with One Direction?" Holly snaps kiddingly from the other side of the room.

"All respect. Although it wouldn't kill you to pick up a Beatles CD," Chris tells her teasingly. Then to me, he asks softly, "Seriously, I want to know. Where do you want to get married?"

Don't tell him. He's just going to file away the information and use it against you later. "The Hotel del Coronado," I can't help but answer.

His face is expressionless. "In Coronado?"

"No. In Wichita. Never mind."

"No, I'm just surprised. Coronado's beautiful. I just assumed . . . I don't know what I assumed. I guess that you'd get married here."

"My family's in San Diego," I tell him. "I grew up there. I'm getting married there. And the Del is absolutely gorgeous."

"Her colors are going to be red and white," Jessie tells him in passing as she gathers a bunch of glasses to bring to the dishwasher in the back.

Chris nods approvingly. "Hm. I like red. Everyone knows that color. You say your colors are red and white, we're all on the same page. It's not like vermilion or . . . Zaffre. Do you plan to do it on Valentine's Day?"

"No. I hate Valentine's Day. I just like red."

He puckers up his lips a little as he says, "Hm. Explains the lipstick."

I don't know what that means, so I decide to let it go.

Chris pulls out his phone and types, at the same time asking me, "So have you told Giovanni about your plans?"

Was that a dig or a genuine question? "It's a little early for that. Most men spend the beginning of the relationship trying to get laid, not trying to pick a groom's cake."

"You know us well," Chris admits, then puts away his phone. "I just called Lyft. Michael, my Lyft driver, will be here in four minutes." He gets up from his seat, and he does seem to be swaying a little. "Good night, ladies."

Jessie and Holly both say good night. Chris looks at me and smiles. "Lovely as always to see you, Miss Osorio."

"Hold on. I'll walk you out," I tell him.

We make our way outside and stand in front, silently waiting for his ride. Finally, I tell him something that's been bothering me all night. "I don't have a fear of intimacy."

He turns to me as though he's going to argue but then says, "Okay."

"I don't. I don't know why you would say something like that. I'm actually really nice."

He thinks about my statement, nods a little to himself, but then he tells me, "Women who date married guys usually have a fear of intimacy."

I brace for a fight, ready to lay into him. How dare he say I'd date a married . . . Oh, wait.

"It's complicated," I explain.

"It always is," he says sympathetically.

I want to hide. How did he figure that out? I shrug and quickly lie, "Anyway, I have Giovanni now, so it's ancient history."

Chris nods, agreeing with me. "He seems like a really good guy. Decent guy."

"He is," I quickly agree.

A black Prius slowly pulls up to us.

"There's my ride," Chris says. "See you tomorrow?"

"Yeah, okay."

And then he just stands there, staring at me. "What?" I ask.

"When you hear the word 'sex,' who do you think of?"

I smirk and shake my head slowly. "None of your fucking business."

He smiles and puts his hand on the passenger's side car door handle. "Fair enough, Miss Osorio. Fair enough. I'll see you to-morrow."

"Fair enough, Mr. Washington."

He gets in the car, and I watch it slowly pull away. When I come back in, Holly mocks, "Chris and Natasha sitting in a tree . . ."

"Stop it," I mutter, heading back behind the bar to clean up.

"Seriously, what was going on there?" Jessie asks.

And the way she asks makes me feel guilty as hell. Which is ridiculous, because I didn't do anything wrong. "Nothing. I was just walking a drunk customer out and making sure he got home safely. Geez."

The conversation soon turns to gossip about the night's custom-ers, more ribbing of Holly about her new guy (whom she clearly likes), and a very odd rendition of "Heard It Through the Grape-vine," which we all decide has to go onto our all-girl playlist, even if Gladys Knight is backed up by the Pips.

Overall, a very good night.

Then, around three o'clock, I get a text.

I'm here. I miss you. Are you available now?

It's from Marc.

I turn off my phone.

Chapter Forty-two

JESSIE

I don't think there is a more lonely time to be awake than four A.M. I'm lying in bed in pitch darkness Saturday night, staring at the ceiling, wide awake, and wondering how long it will take to adjust to my new nightlife.

It's not the early hour, though. It's the guy I'm thinking about.

After my last text to Giovanni, Kevin and I spent a few hours online looking at Paris flats. Kevin gave in to every demand I had: I wanted to make the kitchen my own, I needed at least two bedrooms, I needed to be in the city. It's almost like I was trying to find fault with the places, and I couldn't.

It didn't help that Giovanni texted me about an hour into my apartment search.

Are we still going to the fund-raiser Monday night?

I wrote back truthfully.

Of course. I can't wait.

> I can't either. I have to go present my wines now
> to a hundred people. Will be out of commission
> for a while. But call later if you want to talk.

I did want to call. I ached to call.

But then I felt guilty for how I felt. Kevin didn't deserve that. Here he was, giving me Paris, marriage, a life. Magic.

But would it be magic? And isn't everyone's definition of "magic" different? Isn't that what we talked about with loving the wine you're with—that it's not going to be the same wine for everyone. It's the same with men. It's the same with magic. You have to find your wine. Your magic.

What's my magic? If I dreamt of doing something I knew I would never fail at, what would it be?

If I was the heroine in a romantic comedy, who would I want running after me in the rain?

It's noon in Paris. I should be talking to my future partner about how torn I am. I sit up in bed, turn on my light, and text.

> You up?

I wait at least ten minutes for an answer. Nothing.

Finally, I call Kevin.

"Hey there!" he says, and I can hear the smile in his voice.

"Hey," I say back. "Do you have a few minutes?"

"I have all the minutes in the world. What's up?"

Just rip off the Band-Aid. Take a breath and then spill. "I can't move to Paris."

That's it. That's all I say. I want to inundate Kevin with a million reasons why. But when it comes down to it, there's no point. I can't move to Paris. What more is there to say?

Kevin doesn't say anything for at least a minute. I know because I watch my phone's timer click 0:31, 0:32, 0:33 . . .

He finally asks me a question, and it throws me. "Is there someone else?"

"No," I tell him honestly. "There's the idea of someone else. That there's someone out there who I can be effortless with, if only for the first few months. Where, yeah, maybe five years and two kids in we're exhausted, or overdrawn at the bank, or finally getting a vacation, and it's at a hotel with waterslides. But where everything with us isn't always such a struggle. It's not supposed to be this hard, Kevin. We're not even married yet, and these last three years have already been so hard. I just need something easy. And living in Paris, while it's a really great dream, it's not my dream. And it wouldn't be easy. And it wouldn't be home. And I'm home. This is where I'm supposed to be."

"You would never be overdrawn at the bank," Kevin says, deflecting my heartfelt statement.

"You're not getting it," I say, a little angry. "So let me make it even clearer. I want someone who wants to be with me. From Day One. Who doesn't go halfway around the world without telling me the real reason why. Who doesn't need to be talked into spending the rest of his life with me. Maybe I don't deserve that guy. And maybe the guy isn't even out there. But it's what I want. And I'm going after what I want. And hopefully I won't fail."

Kevin doesn't say anything for a bit. Then he says, "Okay. I'll stop bothering you."

Another zinger, designed to bait me into saying, "You're not bothering me Kevin." Instead I say, "Thanks." And then, for lack of anything better, I add, "You have a good life."

More silence. Then Kevin makes a final mistake, which just shows me I made the right choice. He says, "Take care of yourself."

Most people have a favorite line from a movie. Mine is from the 1970s sitcom *The Mary Tyler Moore Show*. In the pilot, Mary breaks up with her boyfriend after she realizes he's never going to propose. After the breakup, as he is leaving, he says, "Take care of yourself."

And she responds with my favorite line ever (which I now say to Kevin): "I think I just did."

We're off the phone within a minute. I'll admit as I stare at my cell, I feel a wave of sadness start to flood over me.

And then I hear the *ping.*

I am. I just got off the phone with Nat.
Can you talk this late?

And the wave of sadness immediately dissolves.

Giovanni and I spend the next several hours talking, and before I know it, the sun is out.

Which, okay, sounds a little suspicious, but we were just talking.

I am never going to do anything physical with him. He is Nat's, and I know that.

Around seven, we fall asleep by putting our phones on the pillows next to us.

I am out in five minutes.

When I wake up a few hours later, I ask him, "Are you still there?"

"Hm?" he grunts sleepily over the phone. "Yeah, I'm up. How did you sleep?"

"Better than I have in weeks."

We talk throughout the morning, taking only bathroom breaks. We finally get off the phone as I park my car at the bar just before two for our early open on Sunday. I know I am texting him more than I should throughout the afternoon.

But I can't help myself. Life is short. How do I not be with this amazing man, at least in spirit?

You can be with someone emotionally, and not physically, right?

Right.

Right?

Chapter Forty-three

HOLLY

Joe and I spent much of Saturday texting, which was fun. We also decided to Facebook and Google stalk each other, which was even more fun.

You got to meet the prime minister of Canada?

I did. It was a fluke—I was guest starring on a show the week he came to Vancouver. You've been to the Gobi Desert? Impressive.

Not really. I was shooting a car commercial. And it was so cold, my snot froze.

Charming.

Hey, if you were a date, I would be much more genteel.

I had a blast learning all about him and seeing all of his pictures. I found some intriguing ones of his last commercial.

> You worked with sharks? What was that like? Did
> you get to swim with them?

Yes. And I'm kind of chuckling right now. The
difference between men and women: My male
friends were impressed that I worked with
Margot Robbie. You're impressed with Jaws.

> Very. And I'm so jealous. I was recently asked
> what I would do if I knew I couldn't fail, and I said
> swim with sharks.

You're a strange and wonderful woman.

As much fun as I was having, I specifically didn't talk to him on the phone that day. This was intentional. There was a small part of me that had thought about kissing him Friday night, and I needed to silence that part of me. But texting seemed okay. Until Saturday night, while I was at work, and he wrote this:

Hey, you don't have to be at work until 4 on
Sunday, right?

> Actually, we open at 3 on Sundays, so I need to
> be in at 2. Why?

Any chance your friends could cover for
you for the first few hours?

I glanced at the text while I was behind the bar listening to Chris and Nat spar.

"So you're telling me you would spend five hundred dollars on a blender," Chris asked in dismay.

"If I was the maid of honor and my sister registered for it, yes," Nat insisted.

"It's a blender. Forget it, I'm giving her cash."

"Of course you are. Because nothing says, 'I don't know a thing about you,' quite like cash."

At the time, I decided to suppress the urge to blurt out, "You guys are so going to hate fuck." Instead I asked Nat, "Is there any chance you guys might be able to cover for me for a few hours Sunday?"

Jessie was suddenly beside me excitedly asking, "Why? Do you have a date?"

"How did you . . . No."

"Then why are you looking at your phone?"

"Look, can you cover for me or not?" I snapped.

Fortunately, Nat saved me without requiring further explanation by saying, "Jess, leave her alone. And yes we can. Have fun, whatever you're doing."

I happily typed . . .

I'm good to go.

Awesome. We're going somewhere casual.
Wear a swimsuit under your clothes. Oh,
and bring rock shoes.

> **Wow. It's a nondate, and the man is still trying to**
> **get me out of my clothes. Why on earth do I**
> **need rock shoes?**

(1) I said "Under your clothes." I'll pick you up
at 10. (2) Not telling.

I spent the rest of the night trying to figure out where he was taking me.

Sunday morning, I spend about half an hour getting ready and debating which swimsuit to wear. I have a hot pink bikini that I really love. But when I try it on and look in the mirror, all I can see is my stomach protruding out like I'm two months along. I quickly change into a dark blue one-piece, which pushes everything in but makes my hips look huge. Next, I change into a pastel blue bikini top with matching swim skirt, which looks ridiculous. Why did I ever buy this? What idiot designer said, "You know what women really need when they're swimming? A skirt to float up around them and make them feel like the hippo ballerina in *Fantasia*?"

I change back into the hot pink bikini, but add a cute light pink cover-up. I throw my rock shoes into my bag, but wear sparkly sandals that show off my pretty pedicure. Then I spend at least fifteen minutes on makeup, and I'm good to go when Joe rings my bell at exactly ten A.M.

The second I open the door, I wish I had spent a little more time on my makeup. I hate myself for thinking this, but damn! He looks cute. Nothing noteworthy about the outfit, just a dark blue T-shirt with khaki swim trunks and black rock shoes. But it shows off his semi athletic build: you know, in shape but not Schwarzeneggery about it or anything.

"Hi," I say, giving him a quick peck on the cheek. "Am I dressed appropriately?"

"You are, and you look amazing."

"Thank you. You too." I hold up my straw beach bag, "Rock shoes are in the bag."

As we head out and I lock the door behind me, I once again ask, "So, will you tell me now?"

"Nope. I said it was a surprise."

"But I hate surprises," I tell him as we walk out to his car.

"Why?"

"Because I'm neurotic and need total control over everything in my world at all times."

"So naturally, you became an actress," he jokes.

"That's the neurotic part. Speaking of neurotic . . ." As we walk past Sven's apartment, I grab Joe's hand, pick up my pace, and command, "Let's go! Let's go! Let's go!"

Over the weekend, I told Joe every (nongraphic) detail about my disastrous night with Sven and even described how I've been avoiding him with the maturity of a fifteen-year-old.

Joe and I hightail it to the curb and stop in front of a bright blue Mercedes-Benz. "Wait, this is your car?"

He sighs. "You hate Mercedes."

"No, I hate white BMWs," I tell him. "A blue Mercedes is okay. I mean, ridiculously overpriced—"

"I'm sorry—am I sleeping with you?" Joe interrupts.

"What?" I ask, a little thrown.

He smiles and repeats his question, slower this time. "Am. I. Sleeping with you?"

"No," I answer, a little offended.

"Then you don't get to make fun of me for my car," he says jokingly, as he opens my door for me.

"Touché," I concede.

He walks around his car, gets in and turns on the ignition with the press of a button.

"It's a hybrid," I say, a little surprised.

"It is. And in your favorite color."

As Joe pulls his car into the street, I ask, "How did you know blue was my favorite color? That can't be on Google."

"You told me after I told you my favorite color was plaid," he tells me, referring to one of our many text conversations. "And speaking of things you told me . . . Behold!" Joe turns on his radio, and a screen pops up on his dashboard showing his Bluetooth has connected to his iPhone. Joe presses the square that reads "Playlist for Holly."

And on comes Panic! at the Disco's "I Write Sins Not Tragedies."

"Whoa!" I squeal like a teenage girl. "You made me a mix tape!"

"I did. Not one song I would normally listen to on my own. Everything from Taylor Swift to *NSYNC . . . Pretty much if an artist could be asked to perform during the Super Bowl halftime show, it's on there."

I press the button on his screen to read the list. "Oh, Madonna! Where on earth did you find 'Causing a Commotion'?"

"iTunes. I also found that song you mentioned from Morris Day and the Time. I kind of liked that one—sounded like Bruno Mars."

"You like Bruno Mars?" I ask.

"He's all right. Not as much as the Arctic Monkeys, but good."

"Did I request the Arctic Monkeys?" I ask.

"Well, when one of their songs came on at the diner, you said you liked them, so . . . let's say you did."

An hour of midlevel Los Angeles traffic later we are on the 710 heading toward Long Beach. Joe pulls into the left lane, heading toward downtown.

I am intrigued. "Are we going to the pier?"

"Sort of," he says, and pulls into a multi-tiered parking structure for the Aquarium of the Pacific.

"Hey, I've always wanted to come here," I say, my face lighting up. "Do you know they have otters here?"

"Really? They also have sharks," Joe tells me, giving me a smile.

I narrow my eyes at him. "Wait. This wouldn't have anything to do with my wanting to swim with sharks, would it?"

He shrugs playfully. "Maybe."

It totally did. On Sundays, the aquarium does what they call "Animal Encounters." For a fee, you can go behind the scenes of the exhibits and interact with sea lions, penguins, sea otters, or (drumroll, please . . .) sharks.

As Joe and I sign liability waivers, I share my fear of sharks with our guide for the tour. She quickly calms me down by pointing out that there are over four hundred different species of sharks, but only ten to twelve of them are actually dangerous to humans. I tell her that makes me feel better, but in my head I'm hearing John Williams's score from *Jaws*.

Well, if you can't conquer the fear, feel the fear.

Our guide soon takes us on a behind-the-scenes tour, where we learn what it takes to care for and feed the many different types of sharks who call this home. We also get the opportunity to feed cownose rays and target feed trained bonnethead sharks.

Next, we are on to the main event: the big shark tank.

Okay, so we don't scuba-dive into the huge tank filled with blacktip and whitetip reef sharks, and sand tiger sharks. What are we—mental?

Instead, we go to the shallow holding area (also knows as the husbandry area), off to the side of the large tank, which is about waist deep in water.

First, our guide puts out fish to try and coax a particular zebra shark into visiting us, and we watch a blacktip shark swim through, grab the food, and swim out. Eventually, a spotted shark slowly ambles in.

As the shark slowly swims around her, our guide closes the gate between the big tank and the holding area, then invites us to come in.

The zebra shark is actually spotted, not striped. If I had to guess, I would have called her a leopard shark, and I would be right. Scientists originally gave zebra sharks their name because when they are babies, they have stripes. Eventually, as they mature, their stripes disappear and spots begin to appear. Hence the confusion.

For the most part, zebra sharks are not dangerous to humans. There has only ever been one case of an unprovoked attack. These are odds I am willing to chance as Joe and I step in.

"Take a quick swim now," Joe jokes, as the water is only waist deep. I kneel and mock-swim over to my guide.

And now, despite my fear, I have officially swum with sharks.

We are soon allowed to feed the shark (a female) with the help of light blue tongs holding larger pieces of fish that she seems to slurp in like a vacuum.

I ask Joe if he wants to take a turn feeding the shark, but he is too busy with his GoPro. "Come on," I prod. "Are you going to live your life or film your life?"

"Fine," he says, handing me the camera so I can film him feeding her. Our guide then turns the shark over and Joe rubs her belly (the shark's, not the guide's).

The tour is soon over (boo . . .). We thank our guide and head to our respective locker rooms for showers.

Half an hour later, I am practically dancing as we pass an aquarium of otters. "I can't believe we did that!" I tell Joe. "I can't believe you knew how to do that!"

"What can I say? I'm a man of many surprises."

"I just realized," I say as I watch an otter flip out of the water and onto a pile of ice cubes, "I never asked you: If you knew you couldn't fail, what's the one thing you would do?"

Joe watches a mother holding a baby at her side and being pulled by an excited toddler in a bright red dress. "Not sure. I think I've tried all of the things that are really important to me. Workwise, anyway."

"What about in your personal life? Somewhere you're dying to travel to?"

He gives me a weird look. "Actually, I want that," he says, pointing to the mother.

"Pretty sure she's taken," I joke.

He raises his eyebrows as if to say, *Oh, well. You win some, you lose some.* But we both know what he meant.

"So kids," I say. "Good for you. Have a number in mind?"

"I used to want all boys. Now I think I'd like to have a boy and then a girl. But I'm the oldest, with a younger sister, so that probably just shows a complete lack of imagination on my part. You?"

"I've always wanted three. I grew up an only child, and I always wished I had a sister."

He nods. "Two girls and a boy, or all three girls?"

"My dad used to say, 'I never cared. I just didn't want a seven-pound foot.'"

"You had a very wise dad."

"I guess I did," I say proudly, but with a teeny bit of sadness washing over me. Which is a shame, because I'm having such a good day. "He'd have liked you," I tell Joe. "You remind me a little of him."

"Really?"

"Yeah," I say. Then quickly add, "But not the bald part. I like that you have hair."

"I like that I have hair too," he says, then stands up and puts out his hand to help me up. "You know what we should have for lunch? Ice cream."

"They have ice cream here?"

"They do. Let's grab some and keep walking."

So we have ice cream for lunch and then see a room full of jellyfish, tanks and tanks of tropical fish, and a tunnel that goes through the seal tank. There is nothing more soothing than watching a seal glide past you on an easygoing Sunday.

Soon we have to leave. Sad emoticon.

On the trip back, I stare contentedly into space, listening to my music and being very happy to find such a cool new friend.

And then a song comes on that I recognize but can't quite place. The song from the diner by . . . ? What did Joe call them? The Arctic Monkeys?

As the song continues, I realize he is ever so quietly singing along. "I'm sorry to interrupt, it's just I'm constantly on the cusp of try-ing to kiss you. But I don't know if you feel the same as I do."

He looks over to see me watching him, and smiles.

Then he stops singing.

"You can keep singing, you know," I tell him.

"Nah. It just sort of slipped out. I don't really sing."

"Okay," I say pleasantly, smiling and looking at L.A.'s downtown skyline ahead.

Twenty minutes later, Joe is dropping me off at the bar. "I had an amazing time today," I tell him as I grab my bag filled with the change of clothes I need for work. "Do you have time to come in for a drink?"

"I actually have an eight-hour workday ahead of me," he says (apologetically?) "I'm in preproduction and probably should not have taken today off. But they only do the tour on Sundays, and I couldn't wait to bring you."

Rats.

"Okay, well . . ." *Hmmm . . . Should I kiss him good-bye?* "Are we still on for dinner tomorrow night?"

He nods. "Absolutely. I'll pick you up at seven."

"And I'm buying, right?"

He smiles. "We'll talk about it after dinner."

"I'm buying!" I repeat.

"I'll think about it."

"Don't make me call my new friends the sharks to convince you."

He laughs. "Okay, fine. You can buy me dinner."

I stare at him, hoping he'll be able to read my thoughts and kiss me.

He just stares back.

Finally, I give up. "Okay, bye," I say, giving him a quick peck on the cheek, then quickly getting out of his car. He watches me use my key to go in the back way. I turn and wave to him, and watch him pull away.

Less than five minutes later, I use Jessie's computer to download the song "Do I Wanna Know?" by the Arctic Monkeys.

It's on our (now almost) all-girl playlist five minutes after that.

Sunday night, I play it over and over again until I fall asleep.

Chapter Forty-four

NAT

Sundays are our early days, and we decide to open at three instead of five, and close at eleven instead of one. Holly wasn't scheduled to come in until four (her new "we-are-so-not-dating" beau asked if she could come in late). So it's just Jessie and me.

Chris never shows up. Which is fine. The end of last night probably put him on alert as much as it did me. I mean, we didn't do anything. I have nothing to feel guilty about. But maybe there was something there? If he had leaned in to kiss me, what would I have . . .

Nothing. I would have done nothing.

When Holly comes in at four, we have all of six customers in the place. I don't know if it's because it's a Sunday afternoon or because we're new, but it's kind of nice not to have to zoom around all day.

"You know, we might be able to get away with only two bartenders on Sundays," I suggest to Jessie, who's hyperfocused on her phone.

I seem to startle her, and she throws the phone into the air a bit, then catches it. "What?" she stammers. "Oh, well, uh, it'll probably pick up later in the evening." She looks around. "If it's okay with you though, since Holly's here now, I'd love to get some accounting work done in the back until it gets busy."

"Sure. Go for it."

An hour later, Chris comes in, carrying his laptop.

I suddenly remember that today was another wedding day with his sister! He wasn't ignoring me. He was with his family. I walk up to him and ask, "The usual?"

"Not yet. Do you have coffee?"

"We do. And I won't even ask you how you like your coffee."

I pour him a cup of black coffee, drop in two sugar cubes, stir, and bring the cup and spoon to him. He looks at the cup. "Do you have any—"

"I already put two cubes in and stirred," I interrupt.

"Oh. Thanks," he says, looking confused for a brief second, then returning to his work.

Yeah, moron! I remember how you take your coffee from twelve years ago! Don't I get points?

I wait.

Nope—no points.

By around six, we have a few more customers, and things are picking up. Holly and Jess both have full tables, we got a little Adele playing in the background. Things are good.

Except for the guy at the corner of the bar, who is antagonizing me by, well, ignoring me.

I mean, I don't care if Chris is ignoring me: It's certainly better than him engaging me in a heated debate over fake boobs, or enlightening me on his theories about the battle of the sexes. But he seems to be working, and I don't understand why he's come to a relatively loud bar on a Sunday night just to work.

I want to ask him, but I also don't want to engage. So every few minutes I glance over at him, nursing his coffee and working very studiously on his laptop. When his cup is empty, I mosey up to him.

"Refill?" I ask.

He looks up. "Hm? Oh, yeah. Thanks." Then he focuses on his work again.

I grab two sugar cubes, toss them into the cup, pour coffee over them, stir, and place the cup next to his computer.

The sight of me doesn't register.

"Okay, fine. You win. I'm intrigued. What are you doing here?"

Chris looks up from his computer, not seeming to understand the question. "Working."

"I see that. Why here?"

"I like it here." He takes a sip of his coffee. "Plus I said I'd see you today, so . . ." He wiggles his fingers in a wave. "Hi."

Then he goes back to typing.

Seriously, I can't get a read on this guy at all. Every night he has been here, he has baited me with conjectures on flowers, weddings, and my fear of intimacy. The first night, after not seeing me in over ten years, he greeted me with an insult. And now, here he is, doing . . . what exactly?

"So does Giovanni feel like going to a Lakers game with me tomorrow?" Chris asks without looking up from his screen.

"No. He's going to the opera that night."

Chris looks up at me, surprised. "Since when do you like the opera?"

"What is that supposed to mean? You don't think I'm cultured enough to like the opera?"

"Sorry. So who's your favorite soprano?"

"That would be Tony," I answer, only half kidding. "Actually, Giovanni's going with Jessie."

"Oh. Well, then, would you like to go to the Lakers game with me?"

"I have a"—oops, I almost said "date"—"previous engagement."

He narrows his eyes at me. "I see. That previous engagement wouldn't have anything to do with a certain floral aficionado, would it?"

"What a bizarre question. No."

He shrugs. "Okay. Well, if that engagement falls through, or you change your mind for some reason, they're really good seats."

Jessie walks behind the bar, texting Kevin. I make my way over to her. "Hey, do you think . . ."

Once again, she nervously pops her phone out of her hands. I try to catch it, but when I do, I accidentally hit a glass, which shatters all over my hand.

Before I can even figure out what happened, Jessie is screaming, and there's blood everywhere.

Shit. My blood.

Oh, crap. My hand is split open like a canned ham. From my wrist to my thumb.

"What happened?" Holly asks, running up to us.

"Nat's bleeding. Call nine-one-one!" Jessie screams.

"Do not call nine-one-one," I say firmly as I quickly wrap a white towel over my hand. "It's just a little blood. I'll be fine."

Chris has already closed his laptop and started walking behind the bar. "Let me see."

The white towel immediately begins to blossom red. I raise my hand because I read once that that slows down bleeding. "I'm fine."

As Jessie runs to the back room, Chris takes my hand and slowly unwraps the towel. "Let me take a look."

The towel only partially comes off before I spurt blood. "Shit!" Holly says. "You need stitches."

"I'm fine," I repeat as Jessie dashes out of the back office with my purse. "Chris, you have to take her to the emergency room."

"We're on our way," he says, holding up my left arm with his left hand, and wrapping his right hand around my waist to guide me out of the bar.

"Maybe we should just wait a few minutes and see if the bleeding stops," I suggest.

"You can wait a few minutes while we drive to the hospital," Chris counters. "If the bleeding stops by the time we get to the ER, I'll be happy to admit you were right and I was wrong. Bye, guys! We'll keep you posted."

Appearing to be outvoted, I grudgingly go with Chris to his car.

Within fifteen minutes, the bleeding has not stopped, and we are at the local emergency room, with Chris filling out forms for me.

"Name," he begins. "Natasha Lila Osorio. Address?"

"I'm right-handed. I can do it."

"Your adrenaline is pumping like crazy, and your hands are shaking. Let me do it. Address?"

I look down at my hands. Which are shaking like San Francisco in 1906. Damn it. I give him my address and various other information. For my emergency contact, I list Holly.

He looks up. "Holly?"

"Yes. She's my roommate. Why?"

He shakes his head slowly. "Just a little surprised is all. I need your insurance card."

"It's in my wallet," I tell him.

He waits for me. "What?" I ask with a note of irritation.

"Don't you want to get it out?" Chris asks.

"Oh, I'm sorry," I snap. "I'm doing my best impression of Captain Hook right now. Maybe a little help?"

"I just didn't want to invade your privacy," he says, taking my purse and opening it. "Most women don't want you rifling through their purse."

"There's nothing in there that would embarrass me," I tell him as he pulls out my wallet, which unfortunately has two condoms stuck to it. He looks over at me.

"What?" I repeat in the same irked tone.

Chris puts up the palms of his hands as if to plead *No contest.* He takes my insurance card and my driver's license from my wallet, then brings them and the clipboard over to the receptionist.

I look down at my red-clothed hand. That is going to leave a mark.

My phone texts. Crap. I grab the phone with my good hand and read:

Jessie told me you're in the hospital. Should
I come back early?

I start typing back with one hand.

No, I'm fine. She's overreacting. I'm only here
because she and Holly made me go.

Chris walks back to me and takes a seat, telling me, "She said they'll see you soon."

"Sir," the receptionist says, "you forgot your wife's insurance card."

"Thanks," he says to her as he walks back to retrieve my card.

My phone beeps again.

She said you're bleeding like a stuck pig.

Chris comes back. "Can you do me a favor and type a text for me?" I ask him.

"Sure," he says, taking my phone.

"Type, 'Jessie doesn't even know what a stuck pig is.'"

Chris looks up. "I'm sorry?"

"Read what she told Giovanni. I am *not* bleeding like a stuck pig."

Chris reads the text. "How about if I tell him everything's going to be fine, you're at the ER with me. No need to panic, we will keep him posted."

"And I'm not a pig," I add.

He looks up, sighs, then returns to typing, "How about all of what I just said, and you're not a pig." After typing, he asks, "Do you want me to tell him you love him?"

"Give me the phone," I say, putting out my good hand.

"*Now* what did I say wrong?"

"Just give me the phone."

He does. I hit Send—without the "I love you." "Thank you for your help."

The doctor calls us in. Long story short, I needed six stitches, and it could have been a lot worse. Why do doctors always say that?

As we're making our way out of the hospital and through the parking lot, I click my speed dial and get Holly. "Okay, everything's good. Just needed a few stitches. I'll be back in about fifteen minutes."

I hear her say, "Wrong. Go home. What did they give you for pain meds?" at the same time Chris says, "No. You need to get your antibiotics and your Vicodin and go to bed."

I put up my stump to shush him as I say to Holly, "Wait, what did you say?"

"I said go home. What did Chris say?"

"That I'm totally fine," I say, but the phone disappears from my ear.

Chris took it away from me to tell Holly, "She's not fine. She's had stitches and she's hyped up on adrenaline. Any minute now, she's going to have an adrenaline crash and be in hideous pain."

"You guys are being ridiculous. I . . ." This time he shushes me, answering Holly. "Yes. Vicodin . . . I have both prescriptions, she also needs an antibiotic. We're going to the pharmacy now."

"Seriously, you don't have to . . ."

"Great. And I will. Thanks," he says, then hangs up and gives me the phone. "Do you want to call Giovanni?"

I take the phone. "What did she say and what will you do?"

"She said the two of them will handle the bar, because it's not that busy. And to make sure you take your Vicodin, because apparently you hate the feeling of being spacy and sometimes won't take your medicine."

"That's pretty judgmental coming from . . . Never mind. I need to call Giovanni."

I dial him, and he answers on the first ring. "How are you? Jessie says she accidentally cut open your hand."

"Yeah. She fumbled with her phone, and I tried to catch it and hit a glass. I'm fine. How are you doing?"

"Well, I didn't cut open my hand. Are you sure you don't want me to come home early?"

Chris presses the alarm for his Prius and opens my door first. "No," I tell Giovanni. "You have wine to sell, and I'm just going to take my medicine and go to bed early. Stay in Santa Barbara. I'll see you Tuesday."

"Well, do you want me to cancel the fund-raiser? I don't have to go," Giovanni tells me. "I can come straight to you tomorrow afternoon."

Shit. With everything going on, I totally forgot about my dinner with Marc. "No, Jessie's really looking forward to it, and I'm going to be drugged out and resting anyway. I'll just see you Tuesday."

"Okkaaayyyy . . ." he says reluctantly. "Are you sure? I feel bad."

"Don't feel bad. You're being the perfect boyfriend. Go. Sell wine. See opera. Have fun."

We talk for another minute, and I think I have him convinced that I'm not dying.

He seems to be the only one I've convinced. After I hang up, Chris tells me in an urgent tone, "We'll stop by the pharmacy, then pick you up some food. What are you hungry for?"

"In-N-Out."

He turns to me, surprised.

"What?" I ask.

"I just thought you were going to fight me about the meds. In-N-Out it is."

Chris runs into my local Walgreens to drop off my prescriptions, then we head to the nearest drive-thru of In-N-Out. I order a double-double with everything on it (including the grilled onions), french fries, and a chocolate shake. Chris gets almost the same, but no grilled onions.

We grab our bags, and he starts to drive away from the restaurant. "What are you doing? Park," I command.

"We should get back . . ."

"No, no, no," I insist. "This is In-N-Out. You don't save In-N-Out. You thank the gods for this blessed ambrosia, and you wolf it down like you still have the metabolism of a fourteen-year-old."

Chris capitulates and parks in the lot. I hand him his double-double, then tear into my burger. For my first bite, I close my eyes and have a culinary orgasm. "Oh, my God, that's good," I murmur. "They should not tell us it's six hundred and seventy calories. Nobody wants to know that."

"Leave some food to have with your meds."

"Yeah. That's not happening," I say through a mouthful of delicious burger.

Chris takes his first bite. "These really are the best. Some East Coast people say Five Guys—"

"Oh, they're so wrong," I tell him, then take another bite and savor. I lean back in my seat and let happiness wash over me. "Man, I don't even know the last time I got this with the grilled onions. I'm always worried about my breath."

"Never know when there might be a man around to kiss," Chris jokes.

He watches me as I continue to scarf down my burger with just my right hand. "What?" I ask, not able to read his facial expression. "Am I making a mess?"

"Well, yeah. But it's In-N-Out. That's expected. No, I was looking at . . ." He smiles, take his napkin, leans into me, and gently wipes sauce from my lip and chin.

Okay, that was sexy as hell. Where did that come from?

I smile and take a few (nonmessy) french fries. We stare at each other until . . .

I look away from his stare. "So, you never told me how the rest of your wedding weekend went. Did your sister find a venue?"

"She did. In downtown. It's happening Valentine's Day weekend. Now I just have to dry-clean my tux and find a date."

"And the bachelorette party?"

"As of now, I'm still hosting. Maybe I can find a date for that too."

I let his statement lie there, because there's a tiny part of me that thinks, maybe, he was referring to me?

My phone buzzes a text. I put down the burger, wipe my hands, and check it to see . . .

We have 7:30 reservations at

I quickly turn off my phone and stuff it into my purse. Chris pretends not to notice my panic.

But he knows. I know he knows.

I nervously offer him the white box of french fries. He takes a few.

The car is deafeningly silent. Finally, he asks, "So how long have you and Giovanni been dating?"

"Not long," I say. I am hoping those two words form a whole sentence.

Chris waits for more.

"Less than a week," I admit reluctantly.

"Oh. So he's not really your boyfriend."

"Really? What constitutes a boyfriend?"

"Having sex."

"Sex does not constitute a boyfriend."

"Yes, it does."

"No. I've had plenty of boyfriends I didn't have sex with."

"Not after the age of twenty-five you didn't."

"How do you know?"

"Oh, come on."

More silence. Finally I have to ask, "How did you know we haven't had sex yet?'

Chris smiles, clearly very proud of himself. "I didn't until just now."

Damn it! He keeps entrapping me. "I will have sex with him soon, though. And, unlike you, he passed the kissing test."

"Do you want to explain . . ."

I cross my arms. "It's none of your business."

Chris debates prodding me, then surprises me by saying, "Fair enough." But you could cut the tension in the car with a knife.

We finish our food and head back to the pharmacy in silence.

As Chris pulls the car into a spot in the Walgreens parking lot, I say, "I'll get everything. You wait here."

As I open the passenger door, he asks, "So you can text your married boyfriend?"

Ouch. I turn to him and clearly enunciate every word. "No. So I can talk to the pharmacist in confidence and take my pill." I haughtily grab what's left of my chocolate shake and head out.

Surprisingly, Chris lets me go in by myself. I get in line for prescription pickup, turn my phone back on, and use my good hand to text.

> I can't wait. Pick me up at 7:00. I'll be wearing the dress you like.

> Will you be wearing the bra and panties I sent you?

The pharmacist calls out, "Next," and I give him my name and wait for my meds. It kind of hurts to type, because I have to rest the phone on my bad hand, so I type back . . .

> If I can get them on. I actually had to go to the hospital because I hurt my hand. I'm fine but have people around me. See you tomorrow?

I hit Send and then wonder why I wrote that. Because I want him to come over and take care of me? But I don't want him to meet Chris? Or know about Chris? Or maybe I want Chris to take care of me?

I wonder what the definition of neurotic is. Thirty-two-year-old single woman?

The pharmacist hands me my pills, explains the proper dosage and side effects, and sends me on my way. On my way out, I rip open the antibiotic bag and take my first dose with the chocolate shake. I leave the Vicodin alone for now. I get loopy on that stuff.

Then I head back to Chris.

We drive to my place in silence. Out of the blue, Chris asks me, "So did your married guy pass the kissing test?"

My initial inclination is to give a resounding, "Oh, yeah." But instead I shrug.

More silence. Five blocks later, "So, did I pass the kissing test?"

Whoa. He remembers. He remembers that night, the night I left. But he's still here taking care of me. Why?

"Actually, no," I answer, thinking back to his balcony, and our dance, and that magical first kiss. The one that I initiated.

"Wow. How bad was I twelve years ago?" he asks.

"No. It has nothing to do with the kissing itself. I just have a rule that a man has to kiss me by the middle of the first date. If he doesn't, it means he's not really interested, so we both need to move along."

He smirks and shakes his head. "That is the dumbest rule I've ever heard of."

"Of course you would think that, because you always force the woman to put herself out there. Look, I'm sure there are perfectly good men whose wives or girlfriends asked them out or made the first move or whatever. But I need a man who will put himself out there. I want a man—"

"You want a man who you don't care enough about to have an actual relationship with, so you definitely don't want the guy who you like so much, you're stressing out the entire date trying to figure out if he's going to kiss you or not. And by the way—I did not flunk that kissing test. I kissed you."

"Wha . . . You most certainly did not."

"Like hell I didn't. I pulled you into a slow dance and totally worked up to it."

"You did no such thing! I pulled *you* into the slow dance. Me! I did that!"

I wait a moment before stating one more time, "And *I* kissed *you*."

Chris shakes his head slightly, seemingly having an entire conversation in his head. "Fine. Maybe I'm remembering it wrong."

I narrow my eyes at him as I watch him drive. I can't tell if he's placating me. I look down, feeling bad. "Well, if this were a date, just for future reference, the next red light might be a good time to kiss the girl." I turn away. "Not that I mean me, of course. I'm just giving you pointers."

"I think pointer number one would be, 'Don't start your date in the emergency room,'" Chris says, trying to lighten the mood. "And I can't kiss you now anyway. You're hopped up on Vicodin."

"I haven't even opened the bag yet. I just took the antibiotic."

"Why haven't you taken your Vicodin?" he exclaims with a little more exasperation than I think is warranted.

"I don't like the feeling when I'm on the stuff. I get woozy."

"You're *supposed* to get woozy. Your hand is currently resembling a fifth-grade girl's needlepoint project. Take your damn pill."

"Fine," I say, ripping open the bright white bag and pulling out the bottle. But my left hand is a bit bandaged up. "I can't get it open."

Chris stops at the next red light and puts out his hand. "Here. Let me."

He opens it, hands me the big white horse-size pill, then hands me my shake. I can feel it slog down my throat. Yuck.

A minute later, Chris slowly pulls his car up to my house, and stops.

"You want me to help you inside?" he asks.

"No. I'm fine." I put my hand on the car door handle and start to open it. "Thank you for taking me to the ER. You're not so bad. I'll see you soon."

I let my statement hang there, making no motion to actually open the door. I turn to him, a little sad. "You know, I feel like if we were in a parallel universe, we'd . . . I don't know."

Then, as I open the door, he becomes his usual antagonistic self. "If I kissed you right now, you'd secretly be afraid that I wouldn't come back Tuesday, and you can't stand that. That's why we haven't kissed yet."

I slam the car door back shut. "What?"

"It plays into your whole fear-of-intimacy thing. Which is cool, I get it. It's also why you have three men around and you don't know what to do with any of them."

I sigh loudly. "You know, if I'm so awful, why do you keep show-ing up to see me every night?"

He shrugs. "Honestly? I don't know."

I open my door again, but not completely. I want to say a million things to him. I want to tell him to go away. I want to say I'll see him Tuesday. I want to ask him in.

I slowly close the door again. We stare at each other. I lean in and kiss him. Tentatively. Hesitantly.

What the fuck am I doing?

His lips are so soft, and he opens his mouth slightly. He doesn't stick out his tongue, and neither do I.

So what does that mean? Is he being polite? Is he being nice to me because I'm in pain? Does he feel sorry for me?

I quickly pull away. "I'm sorry. I don't know what I'm doing."

He gives me a sexy smile. "I think you know exactly what you're doing."

I shake my head slowly, sadly. "You give me more credit than I deserve." Then . . "You need to not come into the bar anymore."

Chris seems to give my request some consideration. Then he answers, "I'll see you Tuesday."

"No. Seriously. I don't know why I just did that, because I don't want you. I want Marc."

Chris doesn't seem offended. He asks me in a neutral tone, "He's the married guy?"

"For the record, how did you know he was married?"

"A single guy shows up with flowers. A guy with a girlfriend sends flowers. Only a married guy sends a bouquet the size of a kid's jungle gym."

I can't help myself—I focus on his lips. And before I know what I'm doing, I fiercely lean in and kiss Chris again. Race cars have less velocity.

This time he kisses me back and, make no mistake, he's not just being polite.

I rip myself away just as fiercely. "My God. Giovanni. I have to break up with Giovanni."

Chris calmly leans in, puts his arms around my waist, and kisses me again.

I melt. I absolutely melt. There might as well just be a puddle of Nat on his passenger seat.

Eventually, I come up for air. "I have to go," I tell him, and this time I manage to open the door fully. And yes, okay, so maybe my knees are weak and I can barely get out of the car. But I'm out of the car.

He starts to get out of the car too.

"No, no, no, no," I stammer and point. "Stay in the car."

"I just want to make sure you get in okay."

"No you don't. You want to make sure . . ." I look at my white bag, then point to him again. "And I'm now on drugs. You said so. So that's . . ." I whirl my index finger around, not quite sure what to say next. "That's what that is."

And I turn on my heel and racewalk to my door.

I have not heard his car turn on yet. "Go!" I command without looking behind me.

"I'll go when you're safely inside."

"I'm safe. Go," I yell behind me and fish through my purse for my keys.

Fuck. Noooo . . . Not when he's looking. Where are my damn keys?

"I'm not fishing for my keys as an invitation!" I yell toward him.

"Okay," he yells back.

There they are. I pull them out.

Then stare at my fist full of keys.

Silent night out here. Just a cricket and some faraway freeway traffic noise. I still don't hear his car. He still hasn't moved.

I could invite him in. Crawl into his arms. Softly kiss him until the Vicodin kicks in and I fall asleep.

Jesus, Nat: Marc, Giovanni, now Chris? What's the matter with you?

Determined not to further screw up my life, I slip my key into the lock, and turn it. I quietly let myself in and close the door. I fall against the door, desperately wanting to invite him in, yet knowing what a horrible idea that would be.

Still quiet outside. I remain with my back to the door and wait for what could be two minutes or twenty. Finally, I hear a car start and slowly drive away.

Holly's still at work, so I decide to lie down on the couch and breathe.

Seriously, what's wrong with me? Who kisses two guys within thirty-six hours of each other, knowing she's about to finally get the third guy she has pined over for years?

I hear my phone ping a text.

Chris.
Of course.

See you Tuesday.

I start to write back.

No, you won't.

I delete that. Type . . .

I'm sorry. That won't happen again.

Delete.
Finally . . .

Okay.

And Send.

Chapter Forty-five

HOLLY

You know how, after your first real heartbreak, when the guy you were totally in love with leaves you, you see him everywhere? It is so much worse when the guy who leaves you dies. Just like after a bad breakup, it's not the big things that send you down an emotional spiral: a birthday, an anniversary, or some other date that you can emotionally prepare for ahead of time. It's the little things that remind you of the person that ambush you: You find yourself bursting into tears because "Teach Your Children" plays on the sound system at Target, or you pass your beloved's favorite museum or football stadium, or someone is wearing the same aftershave he wore. (Dad wore Old Spice. I used to joke that every time I smelled that on a man, I had the uncontrollable urge to miss curfew. Now I have the uncontrollable urge to vomit.)

In this case, the trigger is a catalog that came in the mail this morning from his favorite candy company. Every year at Christmas, I bought him a pound of milk chocolate and a candy called bear claws (his favorite) from this little chocolate shop in Dad's hometown. So every year, they sent me a catalog, usually around Christmas, occasionally before Thanksgiving, and then once or twice a year other than that.

The catalog came in the mail today, and I've been crying off and on for the last three hours.

It's my own damn fault. I really wanted to leaf through the catalog the way I used to as a kid. My favorite pieces were always the chocolate-covered Oreos. In the fall, they hand-decorate each cookie with a sugar pumpkin or turkey or cornucopia. In the spring, Easter bunnies and chicks.

Without thinking, I opened the catalog to peruse next season's decorations.

And now I'm sitting in the corner of my bedroom, cheeks wet from tears, feeling like I've just been punched in the gut.

Because the candy made me miss him, which made me want to hug him, which made me take down his urn from my bookshelf, because (stupidly) I thought hugging the urn might feel the same. Which, of course, it didn't.

And also now I feel guilty, because I'm not even supposed to have the urn.

I didn't steal it from his grave or anything. I mean, I totally would have done that—I was nuts right after he died—but my parents have been divorced forever and I'm an only child, so I got the urn.

I also had very specific instructions in his will that I have chosen to ignore. Hey, it's not the first time he ever gave me an order I skirted around.

My dad had wanted his ashes scattered over the Pacific Ocean. He wanted me to take his old kayak, which he had made from a kit, out into his favorite harbor, then past the rocks making up the jetty, and over to a particular buoy where we met a seal one day that tried to jump into our boat. I should have scattered the ashes months ago. But I just can't part with them yet.

In my head, I can hear my dad say, "Don't be a martyr. That's not me in there." Dad put himself through college by working at a mortuary, and he always thought people spent way too much time, money, and emotional energy on the remains of a body. He used to tell me that the body was the vessel that housed our soul, and to give any significance to a body would be like going to someone's old house once they had moved out: They were already long gone. And the house was just a house.

I look down at the wooden urn and decide to open the top. Maybe if I just kept, like, a baggie's worth and scattered the rest of his ashes, Dad would be okay with that.

The top won't budge. I get my fingernails under the lip and really yank. Nothing. Okay, just make your hands into a claw and really pull upward . . .

I flip the entire urn up several feet into the air, then cover my hands over my head instinctively to shield myself when what goes up inevitably comes crashing back down, in this case onto my hard-wood floor.

Well, it's not the most elegant way to open the damn thing, but at least it's done. I grab the top and . . . it's still completely sealed. What did they use on this thing? Krazy Glue?

I walk to our kitchen, pull a flat-head screwdriver from our tool-box, and try to pry the top open. Nothing. I grab the hammer from the box and bang it into the screwdriver, trying to chisel underneath the lid. Still nothing. The ashes might as well be encased in Fort Knox.

Okay, clearly I need to look at the problem from another angle.

Dad used to say that if you can't find the solution to your prob-lem, it's because you're seeing the wrong problem. I turn over the urn to see how much glue they used on the base. Aha! The bottom is held together with six screws. I retrieve a Phillips head and quickly begin to unscrew. Two minutes later, I have the base off. Success.

But when I open it, it's just a bag. Nothing special. Ashes stuffed into a bag, by a guy who does this every day. And the ashes aren't gray. I always thought people's ashes would be gray—like cigar ashes. But Dad's are white. They look like the white sand at a beach in Hawaii my parents took me to before they divorced and everything got messy.

Suddenly weak, I slide down to the kitchen floor and begin crying in the corner. Nat is out cold on Vicodin, so I'm by myself, wondering how I'm ever going to get through this. When does losing a parent quit hurting?

There's this person who's supposed to be around no matter what. No matter what! How can I continue to live without the person I can't live without?

Ironically, the guy I most want to call right now is Dad. He'd make me feel better. He'd say the perfect thing. Something to let me know that this gut-wrenching feeling is temporary. That I will get through it. That I love and am loved by lots of people, and how lucky I am that I have at least ten people I could call right now who'd be here in a heartbeat.

Or something like that. The truth is, I know that's what I'm saying to myself. And it's not making me feel better. I have no idea what my dad would say.

My phone beeps a text. I wipe my tears from my face and walk into the living room to pick it up.

None of this is getting decided today.
You've already done way beyond what

I could have expected from you this soon.
Take the rest of the day off.
Inspiration for how to get through this will come
to you.

What the . . .
That's exactly what Dad would say.
Except the text is from Joe. How would Joe know what's going on with me?
I text back:

> Truer words were never spoken. But I have a
> feeling your text was not meant for me.

Crap. I'm so sorry. That was for my director of
photography, Holly. The lighting on this next
commercial is very tricky because it's all
supposed to be one shot. I'm so sorry.

> You have a woman DP?

Um . . . yeah.

> That's very cool. I don't know a lot of men who
> think to hire women for that job.

Joe doesn't write back for a minute or so, and I wonder if my text came off as critical. But finally he comes back to say:

I have a woman editor too. As I told you before,
I'm really not as much of a dick as I was to you that
day.

And suddenly, I hear my father, as though he's whispering in my ear, say, "Ask for help."

Something I remember my dad saying one night, sitting in his favorite chair, wearing his favorite tattered white bathrobe: "The greatest gift we can give other people is to accept their help. People love feeling needed."

I pick up the phone and dial. Joe answers on the first ring. "Hey," he says. "How's my favorite shark diver?"

I sniff, trying to steady my voice so I don't sound like I've been crying. "Ummmm . . . Okay, I guess. Do you have time for lunch?"

"Are you crying?" Joe asks, his voice soft.

"Yes and no. I . . . Actually, more yes. I'm having a bad day."

"I'll be right over."

Soon after, I hear my doorbell chime. I open the door to see Joe. He takes one look at my tear-stained face, juts out his bottom lip to make a sad face, and puts out his arms. I walk in for a hug. "I'm an idiot," I tell him sadly.

"No, you're not."

"You haven't seen what I've done to his ashes."

"Did you accidentally drop them onto your carpet?" he asks quietly.

"No."

"Well, then, you're ahead of my mom," he says.

I pull away from him. "Can I show you something?"

"Yeah."

"I'll warn you. This is the worst kind of freak flag to have waving. If you want to just leave after this, I totally understand."

"Please. Where would I go?"

I take him by the hand and walk him over to Dad's now upside-down urn in the middle of the floor, a sealed, clear plastic bag of ashes resting next to it. "It's awful, right?"

"Your dad dying suddenly was awful. This . . . this is normal."

I can't breathe and almost start crying again. To show someone the worst possible side of me, the crazy, and have him not flinch? To just accept it? What do you say to that kind of acceptance? "I'm not normal," I tell him.

"No, in many ways, you're not. You're gorgeous, you're smart, and you could pass for twenty-five, which for those of us with receding hairlines and crow's-feet borders on annoying. But let me turn this around. If you were at my house, and you saw this in the middle of my floor, would you think I was an idiot?"

"No, of course not," I answer.

"Would you secretly be planning your escape?" he continues.

I shake my head vigorously from side to side . . .

"You said 'freak flag,'" he continues. "So I guess you'd think I was a real loser for still caring so much about—"

"No."

"Then why won't you treat yourself as well as you'd treat me?" he asks.

I smile, then shrug. "Habit?"

Joe gives me another hug, then kisses my forehead. He looks me in the eyes and assures me, "You're right on track. You're exactly where you're supposed to be in the process. Healing is messy. It's not only okay to be a mess, I'd think you were a freak if you weren't. So, are you more in a salad or a burger mood?"

"Actually, I could really go for nachos," I tell him honestly. "Is that weird?"

"Wouldn't it be fantastic if that was the weirdest thing about you?" He takes my hand and says, "Come on. I know the best place in town for nachos. It's a little hole-in-wall Mexican place in East Hollywood."

I stop suddenly. "Oh, God. I totally forgot. East Hollywood reminds me of West Hollywood, which reminds me . . . Today's Monday. Do you have any interest in going to drag queen bingo with me tonight? It's really fun, and it's for charity, and I told my friend I'd go."

Joe smiles. "That sounds like a blast. I'd love to."

"Really?" I say, suddenly feeling . . . better. Not perfect, but better. "Okay, let me grab my purse."

And he took me for nachos, and he bought me a really big hot fudge sundae for dessert, and he talked to me about everything and nothing for three hours. Which was exactly what I needed.

Chapter Forty-six

JESSIE

I spent all day Monday shopping, hitting twelve stores, and finally recklessly splurging on a sexy, super-tight, purple velvet evening gown. It's sleeveless. It has a slit that goes so far up the leg that I needed an above-the-knee wax. It's so tight I needed to buy a bustier just to cinch my waist enough to fit into it. It's made for a Bond Girl. It's so not me.

I fucking love it.

I had texted Giovanni my address and am not surprised when he arrives at my door promptly at five. I open the door to a dream. He looks fantastic. Dark tuxedo, black tie, perfectly polished shoes—you know the drill.

He walks in, clearly troubled, and not noticing me in the least.

"Can I ask you a question?" he says as he turns around. Then his jaw drops. "Wow. You look stunning."

Suddenly, I'm nauseous. Oh, my God, he's hot. I forgot how hot he is. What am I doing? I can't breathe. "So do you," I manage to stammer out without throwing up on him.

He stares at me for a minute, and all I can think about is straddling him. "So what happened?" I ask.

"I got the strangest text from Natasha, and I think she might be breaking up with me."

Inside, I'm bursting with hope: *Really? Yaaaayyyyy!!!! Now nothing will be my fault.* While the outside of me assures Giovanni, "Noooo, that's impossible. She would never do that."

"She left me these weird messages in the middle of the night last night, when I was asleep. I have played them at least five times each, and for the life of me, I don't know what she meant." He puts out his hand. "Look at me. I'm shaking a little."

I take his hand, which feels warm and soft, albeit a little jittery. I love these hands. I want these hands all over my . . .

"You're shaking too," Giovanni says, confused.

"Me? Oh, no. That's just . . . ummm . . . I haven't eaten today because I . . . wanted to fit into this dress. I figured I'd eat at the event."

"Oh, of course. I'm so sorry. We should go. Get some food into you."

"You know what? I actually have some cheese and crackers here. And wine. And you look like you could use a glass of wine. So why don't I take your jacket . . ." I say, slowly removing his tuxedo jacket, careful to brush my hands against his perfect chest, then up over his shoulders, then down his exquisite arms. "And we'll hang out for a bit, and you can play me the messages."

Our lips are inches from each other. He stares at me, clearly knowing my game. I am hitting on him, and even the densest of men couldn't miss it.

Giovanni seems to snap out of the brief trance I put him in. "Okay. That's not a bad idea. What can I help with?"

Aaannnddd . . . maybe he's not perfect. Maybe he actually is the densest man on the planet.

"Nothing," I tell him, trying to hide my disappointment as I make my way into my kitchen. "I have pretty much everything you sell. What wine would you like?"

"Let's do the Super Tuscan." He pulls out his phone. "Can I play you her messages?"

"Sure," I say, getting out two glasses and a corkscrew.

As I open and pour the wine, I hear Nat sounding . . . well, high, actually.

"Hey, it's me," Nat slurs. "This Vicodin has made me really woozy. That's why I don't like to take it. Where are my consonants? Can you understand me? I feel like my *s*'s sound weird. Sssssssss . . . yeah, okay, that's good. Anyway I just woke up and I've been thinking about you and . . . I don't know. So many women at the bar talk about how cute you are. Jessie thinks you're cute. I think you're cute too. You should be with someone like Jessie, though."

Wait, what's that? I want to ask him to hit Repeat.

"She has her shit together," Nat prattles on. "I don't have my shit together. I mean, I am a total mess. You don't see me picking out rings and houses. She even has a 401(k) that she SET UP HERSELF!" Then Nat's yelling voice comes back down to a normal range. "I have a shoe box of receipts I give to her every year at tax time called 'receipts of all sorts.' I think I'm better in bed, though. Well, I guess you don't know that yet."

Wait—she hasn't slept with him? I should not be immediately gleeful. But, boy, "gleeful" is a good word. I finish pouring the wine and turn to my refrigerator to get cheese.

Nat continues. "But trust me, I am. Although not on Vicodin . . . I think I told you, this stuff's weird, but Chris made me take it, and now I'm awake and I have to tell you . . . You know if you told someone your deepest darkest secret, or maybe just like this terrible thing you did, you're sure they'd go away. Well, I guess the good guys, they figure it out anyway, even though you think you're being clever, but you're not. And then they stay. Which is weird! Although I don't know why they stay, I wouldn't stay. 'Cuz you could do so much better than me. I mean, you know how people say it's not you, it's me. But it really is me. You deserve so much better than me."

His machine cuts her off. He looks over to me. "So you've known her a lot longer than me. Did she just break up with me?"

"Well . . ." I hedge. I unwrap the Brie, careful to avoid eye contact. "You should probably ask her."

He nods. "Okay. You're right." As I put the cheese on a plate and pull out some water crackers, he asks, "Can I play her other message?"

"Sure."

He hits Play, and we're back to Nat. "Seriously, if someone I wanted wanted someone else, why would I stay? Wish is what I'm thinking."

I think she meant "which" there.

"Oh, but you're so cute, though. And NICE. So nice. Men who look like you don't have to be so nice. I mean, granted I think I'm smarter, but you're so much nicer. Oh, it's late. I need to go back to bed. Alone. And I think I need crackers. Or In-N-Out. So, you know, love, peace, and all that. We're in agreement, right? I wouldn't want to text. That would be rude."

And she hangs up.

Giovanni puts out his hands. "Well?"

"Well," I begin cautiously, handing him his glass of wine, then taking my glass and the plate of cheese and crackers out to my living room. "I'll admit, if I were to guess, it sounds like maybe it's a breakup."

"You think?" Giovanni asks, taking both of our wineglasses and following me to my couch. We sit down.

I take a nervous glug of wine. "I can't tell you for sure. But I've know Nat a really long time and . . . if it's not a breakup, it's a hint that one is coming."

Giovanni nods. Also takes a rather large swallow of his wine. "Can I confess something to you?"

"You're horribly uncomfortable in that tie. You feel like you're choking."

"Well, yes, but . . ."

"Oh, feel free to loosen it, then. We don't have to be anywhere for a few hours."

He does the ever so slightest double take, then says, "Thank you." He loosens his tie and undoes his top button.

I wonder if Nat's Chris is right, the trick to getting a man to strip really is just asking.

"This is a horrible thing to say," Giovanni tells me, "but if she were breaking up with me, I think it would actually be a relief."

"Oh. Wow. Okay."

"I mean Nat is great. I adore her. She's beautiful and smart and funny and well read and an amazing—"

"Okay!" I interrupt loudly. "Nat's perfect. Got it."

"She is. She's awesome. But I just don't see myself ever taking her to Santa Barbara for dinner."

"Really?" I ask, my voice getting a little too breathy and high.

"Really," he confirms. Giovanni moves his face close to me. "I probably shouldn't . . . kiss anyone before I know, for sure, that she's broken up with me, though."

Kiss me, kiss me, kiss me. "Probably not," I agree.

"Are you getting warm?" he asks.

"Ummm. A little."

"Feel free to loosen this," he says, putting his arm behind me and slowly unzipping the back of my dress. "Because we don't have to be anywhere for a few hours."

He zips down to the small of my back, and the top of my dress falls to reveal my dark purple bustier. Giovanni begins slowly licking my neck.

"I'm pretty sure you're just making things even hotter in here," I tell him.

And that's all I say for quite a while.

Many hours later, we are both naked in my bed, sitting with the plate of Brie between us, finally eating. I'm starving. But I cannot remember the last time I felt so satiated and happy. "We need more crackers," I tell Giovanni.

"Yeah, and maybe some Thai food," he suggests.

"Oohhh, some shrimp fried rice and some pad Thai sounds perfect. Let me go get the delivery menu."

Giovanni follows me to the kitchen, grabbing me twice to kiss me before we make it to my menu drawer. I open the drawer to grab menus while he grabs his cell phone to order.

"Okay, the better place takes forty-five minutes to an hour to deliver. The faster place . . ."

I look up to see Giovanni staring at his phone, looking worried.

"What's wrong?" I ask.

"Nat left me a message around seven forty-five. Obviously, we were in there"—he motions with his head toward my bedroom—"so I didn't hear it."

I take a deep breath, then ask, "Okay, do you want to play it?"

He presses Play, then puts his phone on speaker. "Hey, it's me. I'm sorry for the rambling message last night, I was totally whacked out on painkillers, and I must not have made much sense. Listen, I miss you, and I really want to talk to you. Are you free for lunch tomorrow? I know you and Jessie have that thing tonight, and you're probably exhausted from your wine and food weekend, but just, you know, whenever works for you is cool."

She pauses, and I hope maybe the last sentence will be something straightforward like, "Sorry we broke up" or "You know I was serious about how you should date Jessie."

Instead, she says, "I just want you to know, I adore you. You're amazing. Truly." Another pause. "Okay, so I'm gonna go. Call me whenever. Lots of love. Bye."

The message ends. Giovanni looks at me, his face saying, *What do you think?*

"Ffffuuuuccccckkkkkk," I say, falling halfway down. "OhmyGod! OhmyGod! OhmyGod!"

"Okay, calm down."

"I just slept with my best friend's boyfriend."

"Now we don't know that," Giovanni says calmly.

"What?"

"I meant the boyfriend part. Remember how we thought she broke up with me?"

"Of course I thought that! I wanted to have sex with you!" I cover my face with my hands and race toward my living room. "This is bad. She's going to kill me. No. Worse. She's never going to talk to me again."

Giovanni follows me to the living room. "Okay, this is not as bad as it seems."

"It's worse! I slept with you. Twice! She hasn't even slept with you once. And to think I judged her for dating a married man . . . I'm an awful person."

"Nat is sleeping with a married man?" Giovanni asks.

"No. She used to. And now I'm a fink besides. Perfect."

"Calm down," he says, pulling my naked body to his. He rubs my back and says, "Sssshhhh."

And I melt again. Why does he feel this good?

"Okay," Giovanni says soothingly. "Let's order some food. I'll text her that I'm going to bed early. Then tomorrow, together, we'll tell her what happened."

I start to speak, but he says, "It's all going to work out. Trust me. She's going to be fine. She's just going to be mad for a little while, and she has the right to be. But then it's all going to be okay."

"You're sure?" I ask/whine.

"I'm positive," Giovanni reassures me. "I haven't known Nat long, but I know she has a good heart and would only wish us well. She won't hold a grudge."

He hugs me again, and I mutter, "You don't know her at all. That woman's still mad at Shelley Long for leaving *Cheers*."

Chapter Forty-seven

HOLLY

"I-18!" Roxy yells out to us, looking fierce in her black-and-white blinged-out minidress and platform heels.

"That's what she said!" the crowd (including Joe and me) yells back to her.

Ahhh . . . drag queen bingo. Very few things make me so happy to live in Los Angeles.

Where else can you donate twenty dollars to a charity (tonight the charity of choice is the cat shelter Santé D'Or, and you know the pussy jokes are going to go all night) and in exchange get ten bingo cards and a drag queen with a black strap for spanking people who call false bingo. And drinks. Goblets and goblets of drinks. There is no fine wine here. I just finished off some concoction that as far as I can tell was made with hard liquor and Sprite. And it is fantastic.

Plus some nights, if you're lucky, you get to sit next to the wall showcasing a bazillion stiletto heels. "Personally, I like the purple paisley pump," Joe decides.

"No," I disagree. "If you're going to go that ridiculously high, you gotta go animal print: the zebra or the leopard."

"You're a good influence. That's the second time I've been near something called zebra in two days. Another round?" Joe asks, signaling to our waiter.

"Yeah, but this time I want a Strawberry Tease Me," I tell the waiter.

"I'll switch to Coke," Joe tells him.

"I-29," Roxy calls.

"Yes I am . . . and holding!" we all yell back.

"Bingo!" someone yells out and races up to the stage, decorated with a disco ball, tons of red velvet, and a pole (because why not?).

"Okay, baby, let me check your numbers," Roxy says. The player insists he has them, but she mocks, "I don't know you from Adam. I gotta check your numbers." Then she waves and yells at someone across the room. "Oh, hey, Adam!"

"This is really fun," Joe tells me. "How come I never knew about his place?"

"Neglected youth, I presume."

"All right, ladies, we have bingo," Roxy announces. She hands the winner a gift basket filled with board games, then says, "Now run all the way across the bar, then back to the wall of shoes, so the losers can pelt you."

As the winner runs around the room and back, we all crumple up our losing bingo cards and throw them at him.

He runs past, and Joe quickly crumples and throws.

"Okay, bingo whores," Roxy calls out. "Now for this next game we're going to pole-dance!" Her assistant slowly swings around the pole onstage. "This means you have to have your bingos going vertically."

Joe looks up. "Huh?"

I explain. "Oh, it's not like regular bingo, where you just have to get five in a row. There are specific patterns they play all night. Each board is different."

"For our first number, everyone sing with me: Will you still need me . . ."

And the audience sings, "Will you still feed me, when I'm O-64?!"

"And next: Ladies, what's the Bo Derek B?"

"B-10!" I yell out.

"Seriously, how do you know all these?" Joe asks.

I hand Joe a yellow sheet of paper that explains all of the bingo games and the callbacks. Soon Joe can answer Roxy when she says, "Not malignant but . . ."

". . . B-9!"

And G-54? "The disco G!"

And some more indiscreet answers I won't mention. Let's just say there is an O-69, and it does have a callback.

After the first five games, neither of us has even come close to bingo. But it doesn't matter, because I don't remember the last time I was having so much fun. I cannot stop laughing as Roxy flirts with Joe as she walks around the room, mingling.

Joe actually wins game six, Around the World, and the prize is pretty good: two bottles of wine and a gift card to a sushi place.

"Oh. Jealous," I tell him. "I've been dying to go there."

"Well, what are you doing next Monday?" he asks.

I don't know why, but somehow him asking me out for a week from now makes me . . . unsettled. "No, you should take a date. It's supposed to be super romantic there."

"Our next card is the ten in one box!" Roxy begins.

Joe looks around. "More romantic than this?"

"The first number's B-11. Arms to heaven!"

As everyone in the audience puts up their arms, I say, "You know what I mean. You want kids. A boy and a girl. You should be dating, and I'm only a distraction."

Joe puts down his arms. "I thought neither of us were dating right now."

"I'm not, because I have nothing to offer at the moment. But you should. You're hot, and really funny . . ."

"I'm hot?" he repeats almost jokingly.

"Yes. And you're smart and interesting to listen to and you're going to make someone a really good boyfriend, and I shouldn't get in the way of that."

"Sure, you should."

"G-50," Roxy calls out. "The Sally O Malley G!"

I take a big gulp of . . . "What the hell is in this?" I ask. "Seriously? I feel like I should be at a fraternity house drinking out of a red Solo cup."

Joe looks at the menu. "Vodka, peach schnapps, Strawberry Pucker, and Sprite."

"I can't believe there is still such a thing as Strawberry Pucker."

Roxy calls out a bunch of numbers, and the two of us focus on our game boards again.

But after someone at the end of game eight yells out "Bingo!" I return to the dating discussion. "I mean, I'll admit, sure, I have thought about kissing you," I tell Joe.

Joe makes a show of resting his chin on his left palm and imitating a gossipy housewife. "Go on."

"Come on. Do you mean to tell me kissing me has not even crossed your mind?"

"Nope," he says.

"Oh," I say, not able to hide my disappointment.

"Wow. You can't tell when men are lying to you," Joe says, smiling. "No wonder you're still single."

"That is a false bingo!" Roxy calls out. She points to the table the girl walked over from. "Did your friends tell you you have bingo? These are not your friends."

Everyone laughs at the way Roxy says that. Roxy tells us to uncrumple our cards so we can continue to play. She then gives the girl a spanking and sends her back to her table.

I'm too shy to continue the conversation, so I make a point of staring at my bingo card, acting immersed in the drama of the numbers.

We play the last few games and then it's on to the "championship" cards, which are for the grand prize of the night. You have to fill out every space of every card, so it takes a while.

And damn if Joe doesn't win the big prize of the night: an expensive gift card to a Beverly Hills restaurant and another two bottles of wine.

"So what'll it be?" he asks. "Dinner at an amazing restaurant, or back to my place for wine?"

"I ate way too many mac and cheese balls to appreciate the Beverly Hills place tonight," I tell Joe as he signs his credit card receipt (I let him pay. Gracious of me, no?), and we each take a gift basket and slowly walk out with the crowd.

"My place it is," he says cheerfully. "I have nothing there to eat other than a couple of bags of Cheetos."

"Crunchy or puffs?" I ask in all seriousness.

"Crunchy."

"Dinner is served," I tell him happily.

We walk to his car in silence. I think (okay, I hope) we're both thinking about that kissing conversation we never finished earlier tonight.

"So, next Monday: sushi or California French steakhouse, whatever the hell that means."

I don't answer for a while. He should be taking some totally together woman who would be thrilled to have him and could actually contribute something to the relationship. "Sushi," I finally answer.

We stop at his car. He beeps the alarm but then leans against the passenger's side. "So, you've thought about kissing me."

I sigh and look away from him. "Well, I'm not dead. Sure, I've thought about it. And that stupid Arctic Monkeys song you played for me . . ."

"Oh, good. I was hoping that would make you think of me . . ."

"I even put it on our women-singers-only playlist at work," I admit. "You know that 'constantly on the cusp of trying to kiss you' line kind of wasn't fair, because I swear I thought you were singing that to me. Which of course I'm sure you were just singing along . . ."

As I talk, Joe puts down his basket, puts his arms around my waist, pulls me into him, and kisses me. I drop my basket lightly onto the grass below, freeing up my arms to put around his neck.

But after a minute, I pull away. "I am just no good to anyone right now."

He makes a show of a mock-serious face and nodding before pulling me in to kiss again.

Oh, my God, he's a good kisser. I decide maybe just a few minutes of this will get it out of my system.

About five or ten minutes in, I'm thinking maybe not.

I finally force myself to unstick and breathe. But I don't pull away so much that his arms don't stay around my waist. "See, if you keep that up, we can't be friends. Because now I'm not just thinking about sticking my tongue in your mouth. I've moved on to your ears. And maybe licking your neck. And climbing on top of you like a kitten on a scratching post."

He grins and leans back in. "I like your thinking . . ."

I pull my head back so he can't swirl my brain with his kisses again. "But it can't work. Seriously, I have played out every scenario in my head, and they all end badly. I'm a basket case. I don't know how to be in a relationship. I have this series of dating failures I can point to, and eventually I'll let you down and we'll break up and I'll be heartbroken. And I just can't do it again. I just can't."

Joe puts down his arms, and I can tell he's suppressing a sigh. "Okay, how about this? We keep doing this . . ." he says, alternating his index fingers back and forth at me. "And when you start to freak out, you talk to me about it, and we deal with it. And if I start to freak out, I'll talk to you about it, and we'll deal with it."

That does sound reasonable. "While I think about your plan, can we kiss for a little bit longer?"

He smiles, wraps his arms back around my waist, and brings me in again.

I'll admit I'm mostly thinking about the kissing. At some point we sort of naturally break. So I decide to use that moment to warn him, "When we have our first fight, I'm going to assume you're breaking up with me."

"Okay. I'll make sure I don't."

"And our second fight," I admit grudgingly. "And our third . . . Actually, all of our fights. I'm the child of divorce, I always jump to 'the guy's leaving.'"

Joe does seem a bit surprised. "Wow."

"But that's probably my biggest freak flag," I tell him quickly. "You know, that and the . . . well, the ashes were not my finest moment."

Joe gives me a quick kiss. "Let's get you home."

Damn it! I blew it! I just talked this great guy out of dating me. What is wrong with me? I watch him pick up one of the baskets and walk around to his side of the car. "So what now?" I ask him. "You take me home and we go back to being friends? Or is this just it?"

"Not your home. My home," Joe says. "I totally want to see that kitten thing."

And that, ladies and gentlemen, is the friend-of-a-friend story of the girl who absolutely stopped dating and found a great boyfriend anyway.

Chapter Forty-eight

NAT

Getting ready for my dinner with Marc was . . . let's just say tricky. Holly was with Joe, and so I had no one to help me with my red lace bra. Which was probably fine, because I didn't want anyone to know where I was going anyway, and who shows up to a Writers Guild function in a sparkly red minidress and FM pumps, much less a matching red lace bra and underwear?

I woke up in the middle of the night, still high on Vicodin, from a very disturbing dream. Okay, it was a sex dream, but it was disturbing because when I woke up, I knew I needed to call Giovanni and break up with him. But he didn't pick up (it was kind of late), so I left him a message. If my drugged-up memory is correct, I might not have been completely clear about my intentions. But I'm not supposed to see him until tomorrow, and I'll just have to deal with him then. I have too much on my plate.

Chris must have texted at least ten times today, leaving everything from . . .

I'm texting instead of calling because I'm hoping you're resting and I don't want to wake you. But

let me know if you need anything. I can be at
your house with a double-double in 20 minutes.

Thanks. I'm good.

And . . .

Take your damn pills! All of them!

I told you, they make me woozy.

So does wine, and I've seen you drink that.
Don't be a hero.

But the one that messed up my head the most came at six o'clock,
just as I was getting ready to go out with Marc.

Sure you don't want to go to the Lakers game
with me?

I can't.

I'll leave your ticket at Will Call if you
change your mind.

I don't take a Vicodin, instead opting for some ibuprofen and the
ability to have fabulous wine with Marc. He chooses the newest hot
spot in downtown. I tell him I want to meet him there rather than
have him pick me up, which isn't unusual. I never wanted him to
run into Holly at the apartment if I could avoid it. But I have another reason to want to meet him there: instinct. Not sure why, but

my Spidey senses are up. Chris knows who I am with tonight, and although 99 percent of me is sure he wouldn't suddenly show up to check up on me, there's this 1 percent which isn't sure . . . Or maybe there's this 1 percent that hopes he shows up.

I don't know. I'm such a mess.

I take an Uber and walk in at seven twenty to the most breathtaking restaurant: shiny white marble floors interspersed with cobalt and silver tiles, luscious red tablecloths and booths, sparkly crystal chandeliers. The kind of place that screams seduction. Or maybe whispers it.

As I crane my head toward the bar, looking for Marc, I hear behind me. "You look exquisite."

I turn around, and there is Marc, wearing his best navy blue Turnbull & Asser suit and looking like the devil would appear if he wanted you to do something really wicked.

"Thank you," I say, holding up my bandaged left hand. "Hard to get ready in this thing."

"Well, you're perfect," he tells me, giving me an innocent kiss on the cheek. Then he leans in close, whispers, "Truly stunning," and blows into my ear.

My body quivers, my knees shake . . .

And I think of Chris.

Wait—what?

Marc gives the hostess his name, and she leads us to a secluded booth in the back. I slide into the booth, and Marc slides in close next to me. The hostess hands us large menus and a wine list, and disappears.

Marc takes a moment to peruse the wine list while I look at the food menu. Everything looks amazing, from the wagyu filets to oysters flown in from New England to a chateaubriand for two. *Almost as good as In-N-Out.*

Stop it, Natasha.

"What do you think of Bollinger to begin our evening?" Marc asks. "Just for old time's sake."

"It sounds perfect," I say. And it does. The waiter appears and Marc orders us a bottle and some oysters to start.

After the waiter leaves, Marc says, "I miss oysters. The ones in London—"

I interrupt. "I just have to get this out of the way. Did you break up with Elizabeth?"

Marc seems startled but quickly catches himself. "That's fair. You've waited long enough. The truth is, I have started the conversation, and we're halfway there. She was very upset, and we talked all night before I left. I have sown the seeds. When I get back to London, I'll finish what I started. By the time you land at Heathrow, I'll be a free man."

He didn't really do it, my brain blasts at me. *Something feels wrong.*

Before I can ask more questions, the waiter arrives with the bottle of Bollinger and two glasses. "Champagne!" he announces cheerfully.

"Perfect timing," Marc tells him.

The waiter begins opening the champagne's cage as he asks, "So are we celebrating anything special tonight?"

"I have just asked my girlfriend to move to London with me. I'm hoping a little of your ambrosia will help me persuade her."

Ambrosia? Has he always talked like that? And girlfriend. Wow. That's the first time he's ever called me that. I check his left hand and notice he's not wearing his ring.

The waiter puts a red cloth over the cork and gently pops it. "Excellent. Would you like to taste?"

"No. Have the lady do it."

The waiter pours me a small taste in my flute. I quickly take the sip, not bothering to put my nose into the glass or savor the bubbly. I want to get back to our conversation. "It's great. Thanks."

The water pours for both of us, places the bottle in a silver bucket next to the table, then asks if we'd like to order. I tell him I need a few minutes. The moment he leaves, Marc says, "So, will you take the job now?'

I sigh, "Marc . . ."

"I know. I'm not totally done with Elizabeth, but by the time you land in London I will be."

"It's not just that. I switched careers. I own a bar now," I remind him.

"I've been giving that a lot of thought. What if I give you the money you invested in the place, and you just give it to your friends?"

"I'm not having you buy out my share of the bar."

"I wouldn't buy it out. This is an outright gift. Consider it a signing bonus for your new job. That way, your friends won't be punished in any way because you're leaving, and you can come to England with no guilts."

Again, I have no words. I take a sip of the champagne. All I can come up with is, "That's a really generous offer. I'll have to think about that."

"Take all the time you need. Talk to your friends. I'm here until Friday."

He has a sip of his champagne, then says, "Although maybe this can persuade you." And he leans in and kisses me.

He is still the quintessentially perfect kisser. Perfect form. Would definitely get a ten from the judges in the technicals. I kiss him back, but my brain has too many thoughts racing around to really enjoy the kiss.

Marc doesn't seem to notice. He smiles after the kiss ends, then segues into a casual, "So what happened to your hand?"

I can't do this now. I begin sliding out of the booth. "You know what? I totally screwed up. I have a Lakers game tonight, and I'm going to be late."

"Natasha . . ."

I stand up. "No. It's my fault. I double booked. And it's with the girls . . ."

"You're lying," Marc states unequivocally.

He always did know me pretty well. I take a deep breath, then admit, "You're right. I am lying. But it's not with Giovanni either."

I give him my best pleading look to say, *Please let me go. Don't chase after me. Just let me go.*

Marc's jaw tightens. "I'm confused. I'm giving you everything you asked for."

"I know," I answer immediately. "You are, and that's amazing. I just need to think about everything. And I need space to do that. With a friend who's not going to judge me because I'm confused."

Marc, angry but covering, shrugs. "Go. My offer's good until Friday."

"Thank you," I say, leaning over to give him a quick peck on the cheek. "I'll let you know by Friday."

He turns to kiss me on the lips, but I back away too quickly, which throws him. But he quickly recovers. "You'll talk to your friends?" he asks.

"Yes, I promise. I just . . . I really need to go."

I quickly walk out of the restaurant, trying not to run. Both because running out would cause a scene and also . . . what was I thinking wearing these shoes? It's even worse as I race down Figueroa, clip-clopping as quickly as possible without falling.

Fifteen minutes later, I am in Staples Center, walking down to the second row behind courtside.

Chris is sitting near center court. I think I surprise him when I sit down. He turns slightly but says nothing at first. No hug or kiss. We both just sit there.

I look at the scoreboard. "Ooohhh, that doesn't look good."

"Yeah. Lakers had two guys go down with injuries in the first six minutes." He shrugs. "Guess it's a chance for the rookies to show what they really got."

I nod. A moment later I confess, "You do know I have no idea who any of these guys are."

"I know." He gives me a wink. "But hey, two days ago I had no idea what a hydrangea looked like. Maybe we can teach each other a few things." He motions for the waitress. I guess when you sit this close to the court, you get a waitress. "You didn't take your Vicodin, did you?"

"I'm telling you—"

"I can't have this argument one more time," he interrupts. Then he says to the waitress, "When you get a chance, can you bring the lady your favorite red?"

"Actually," I tell her, pointing to his big plastic cup filled with beer, "I'll have what he's having."

She smiles, says, "Right away." And leaves.

We watch some tall guy throw the ball to another tall guy, who passes it to a third tall guy, who throws and makes a three-pointer. The crowd cheers.

"So, if I kiss you by halftime, would I retroactively pass the kissing test?" Chris asks.

I think I'm blushing. I'm definitely smiling. "No. Because this isn't a date."

He nods. "That's a shame. Because I told the tech guys if you showed up they should put us on the kiss cam."

I try not to stop grinning, but it's a losing battle.

"You met me at a very strange time in my life," I admit.

He turns to me, an impressed smile creeping onto his face. "*Fight Club*?"

"Indeed."

"Book or movie?"

"Both."

"You never fail to surprise and delight me, Miss Osorio."

"You as well, Mr. Washington."

The waitress brings me my beer and asks if I want anything to eat. I order some french fries, then settle in to watch a different tall guy race past me.

I turn to Chris and ask, very nonjudgmentally, "Why didn't you want to have sex with me?"

Chris looks perplexed. "What? When?"

"The night we got together after finals were over. Right before Christmas. I showed up on Thursday night, and I kissed you . . . . and you didn't want to have sex with me." I look up and nervously wait for the answer I've always/never wanted to know: "What was so bad about me that you didn't want me? Was I that hideous? Too fat? Did I talk too much? I know we used to spar, but I put myself out there, and you didn't want me. Why?"

Chris gently takes my good hand and gives it a light kiss. "I didn't sleep with you that night because you were wasted, you were slurring, and believe it or not there are men out there who don't want a woman who won't remember anything the next morning. Plus I thought we should have a better first time than doing it on unwashed sheets in a rickety old bunk bed with Green Day and Eminem blaring downstairs."

Well, now I feel about two inches tall. "And my reward for you being a good guy was to leave in the middle of the night."

He forces a smile. "Yeah. That was a fun morning. And believe me, it was one of a long list of times that made me realize women may say they want a nice guy, but when they get one, they throw him away."

"Huh. Maybe . . ." I agree. "So maybe I wasn't ugly or unlovable or unfuckable. Maybe I was just neurotic and a little mean?"

Chris attempts a joke. "Was?"

I smile and lightly kiss his hand. "You do know we're gonna sleep together, right?" I say, referring to his first comment to me four days ago.

"You do know I'm gonna propose to you, right?" he returns.

The Lakers won that night. And while no one slept together or proposed that night, I will say I definitely liked overtime.

Chapter Forty-nine

I am feeling beyond guilty for what I've done to Nat.

But there is a solution to every problem. I just have to figure out . . . how she's not going to kill us in our sleep.

Giovanni and I ordered Thai to be delivered, and over chicken satay, shrimp pad Thai, and crispy wontons, we decided on a plan of attack. Giovanni would come into the bar tomorrow, after we closed, and we would tell Nat together. She only has one good hand—how bad could it go?

We celebrated our plan after dinner and, I have to say, celebrating with Giovanni is my favorite new activity.

And, also, I'm going to hell.

Around two A.M., just as Giovanni is drifting off to sleep, I ask him if I can hear Nat's messages one more time.

He hands me his phone, tells me his code, and falls asleep.

I tiptoe into my living room and play back the messages. Twenty-seven times. Well, the first one twenty-seven times. The second one maybe only twenty-two. Mostly, I was trying to find anything I could use for evidence that she had already broken up with him.

The problem is, I don't think she did break up with him.

And I think I just lost one my best friends in the world.

And possibly my bar. Because there's no way she will stay and work with me, and Holly and I can't afford to keep the place open by ourselves.

Okay. Think it through, Jessie. Options. Everyone has choices.

Option #1: Tell Giovanni this was great, but it can never happen again. Hope Nat and he eventually break up. Find him five years after the breakup, when the statute of limitations on exes expires.

Who am I kidding? Nat doesn't believe exes have statutes of limitations. One of her exes once kissed Holly good-bye on the cheek, and Holly had to hear about it for two months.

Option #2: Tell Nat the truth, preferably in a public place where she can't let her half-Latin tempter get too out of control. Throw myself at the mercy of her court.

Get myself killed—option #2 is totally out.

Option #3: Leave town with Giovanni, change my identity, and write her a heartfelt note of apology on Crane stationery, careful to mail it from a town nowhere near where I will be living, so the postmark doesn't give me away.

Hawaii is supposed to be nice. I'll keep option #3 in my pocket for now.

Chapter Fifty

NAT

When I get to work Tuesday afternoon, Jessie takes one look at my hand and yelps as though it's her hand in bandages, "Jesus! Look at you! You should go home."

"I'm fine."

"But look at what I did to you!" she exclaims. "If I hadn't dropped my phone, and you hadn't tried to catch it, your hand would be fine. Seriously, you should go home. No one would be mad at you if you needed a few more days' rest."

I glance over at Holly, to silently check if it's just me noticing Jess's jumpy behavior. Holly gives a shrug—meaning she sees it but has no idea what's causing it.

I assure Jessie, "I'm good. It was an accident. Don't give it another thought."

I think we'll get back to normal, but fifteen minutes later, she charges out of the office looking like a cheetah who has just escaped confinement. "Did you want to order two cases of the Ice Wine you liked from upstate New York?" she asks, while nearing hyperventilation. "Because I will order *whatever* you want."

"I think half a case should be more than adequate," I tell her as

I take down wineglasses, one by one, with my good hand. "It's a dessert wine. I don't see us having a huge call for it, but we should have some on hand."

"Okay," she says. Then she puts a hand on each of my arms and faces me, telling me in all kinds of seriousness, "But you promise me you'll let me know if you want to order anything else. I am just the paper pusher. You are the brains behind this whole shebang."

I furrow my brow and ask, "Thank you?"

Then she hugs me so hard, I look past her to Holly, who openly throws up her arms as if to say, *No fucking clue. She's mental.*

At five fifteen, the bar has a few customers indulging in happy hour. Holly's friend Joe sits at one corner of the bar hanging out while Chris sits at his usual Norm seat in the other corner, working on his laptop, a pint of beer by his side. Joe seems to have clawed his way out of the friend zone, judging by the postcoital glow he and Holly both have every time they make eye contact.

A thin, blonde woman wearing large Tom Ford sunglasses nervously walks in. She takes off her glasses and quickly scans the room. Not seeing a familiar face, she takes a seat at the bar two seats away from Chris. "May I have a Chardonnay, please?" she asks me in a quiet British accent.

"Sure thing," I say happily. "Do you have a preference in terms of region? We have one from California, of course, but also . . ."

"Anything that's not from California will be fine," she tells me in a clipped voice.

Chris and I exchange a look. *Who is this broad?* As I pour her a glass, I say, "This is a very good one from the Willamette Valley in Oregon. It has won several gold medals, and—"

She shuts me down with, "Thank you."

I decide not to push. "Would you like to start a tab?"

The woman looks around the bar again and debates. "No . . . Yes. I'm sorry. Yes." She pulls out a black AmEx card and hands it to me. I smile and take it.

As I head to the cash register, I read the card and see the name: Elizabeth Winslow.

Marc's wife.

Holy crap.

Jessie walks up to me, still as energized as a puppy right out of the Christmas box. "Would you like me to order you a pizza? You need food with your antibiotics, and I'd be happy to—"

I hold up the AmEx card for Jessie to read. Her eyes bug out. She leans in and whispers, "Should I ask her to leave?"

"Don't do anything. Act normal."

"No, but I will take her," Jessie whispers threateningly. "I love you. And if anyone tries to hurt you . . ."

"Seriously, what is wrong with you today?" I whisper back. "You're as nervous as a virgin on prom night. Chill."

Chris eyes Jessie and me, and decides something's up. He closes his laptop and smiles pleasantly at Elizabeth. "So, not a big fan of California wines, huh?"

"Not a big fan of California in general. No," she tells him.

I stand at the register, frozen. I can't move. Jessie slowly pours some wine, and we both watch Elizabeth.

"So what brings you to our fair city, then?" Chris asks. No, Chris. Please, no. Don't engage.

Elizabeth looks right at me when she answers. "I'm here with my husband."

I try not to give away any reaction. But inside I'm thinking, *Did she follow him to the restaurant last night? Does he know she's here now? Did she bring a butcher knife?*

"Really. What does he do?" Chris asks her pleasantly.

Elizabeth turns to Chris, gives him an enigmatic look (or at least one I can't read), then says, "He's a game show producer."

Jessie freezes midpour.

Chris, on the other hand, doesn't miss a beat. "What a coincidence. My fiancée used to write for game shows. Which show?"

His face is open, happy, curious.

Elizabeth, on the other hand, might throw up on him. "*Genius!*" she answers.

And at that point I realize she's here to find me, but she has no idea who I am. I'll rephrase—she doesn't know what I look like. She knows exactly who I am.

"Wow. Nat. Honey . . ." Chris says, projecting his voice as though to get my attention. "I just met the wife of someone you used to work for."

"Really?" I say, walking back over to them and pretending not to have listened in. "I know everyone there," I tell her brightly. "Who's your husband?"

Clearly, Elizabeth doesn't know what to make of this. She came here for a fight. Granted, a mousy fight, but a fight nonetheless. "Marc Winslow."

"Love Marc," I tell her. "You know, he offered me a job in London with his next show, but obviously I couldn't do it. What with the bar opening and my wedding coming up and everything."

"Wedding?" She repeats. "When are you getting married?"

I spout out, "Valentine's Day. We're having an intimate ceremony on Coronado Island . . ."

"We were going to elope," Chris continues, "but both sets of parents insisted on coming . . ."

"His mother threatened to show up with a machete and a flashlight looking for us if we didn't tell her when and where it was . . ."

"So now we're doing it on the beach at the Hotel del Coronado. It'll be a small luncheon, just twenty people . . ."

"It's where I always dreamed of getting married . . ."

"And I agreed. Because, seriously, I'm a dude, why do I care where we get married? And then we're throwing a party here the following Saturday night."

"You and Marc should totally come," I tell her. "I'll send you an invitation. How is Marc, by the way?"

"He's fine," Elizabeth begins. Then she reconsiders. "Actually, he's not fine. He's cheating on me." She turns to Chris, then back to me. "And I think I know with who. Where were you last night, Natasha?"

Crap, she knows my name. Well, of course she does—I was sleeping with her husband for God's sake.

I try to appear confused. "I was with Chris at a Lakers game. Why?"

"My husband went out to dinner last night, with a dark-haired woman. I tried to spy on them. And you are the only woman from America he ever talks about."

Okay, so now I'm going to throw up.

Chris saves me. "Well, I'm sorry to hear that. But it can't be Nat. We were at a Lakers game."

Clearly, he's thrown her for a loop. "But that's . . . no, you couldn't have been."

"Second row center," Chris elucidates. "We were on TV and everything."

I hold up my bandaged left hand. "Can't miss me."

Out of the corner of my eye I see Jess carry her tray of wines to table four, making a detour to lean in and whisper to Holly, who's staring at us from table seven. Great, why don't I just sell tickets to this show?

"I'm sorry to bother you," Elizabeth says, quickly standing up. "Can I get my check, please?"

I quickly grab her AmEx card, thankful for the save. "No charge," I say, handing her back her card. "And tell Marc I say hi."

She eyes the card in my right hand, and hesitates. Finally, she plucks it out of my hand. "Thank you. I'm sorry to have troubled you."

As she makes her way to our front door, Chris and I share a look that can only be described as *Yikes!*

But then . . . . I can't help myself.

"Wait," I call out to Elizabeth.

She turns around.

"I . . . I can't have you feeling like you can't trust your instincts. And if my husband were cheating on me, I'd want to know." I look down at the shiny wood floor beneath me, beyond ashamed, then take a deep breath and admit, "I did sleep with your husband. Not in a while. But I did."

She stares at me, eyes twitching. I don't know if she's going to throw a glass at me, or pull a gun out her purse, or what.

She slowly walks back over to me and doesn't stop until her face is inches from mine. "How long?"

I swallow hard and answer, "Almost two years."

She nods, almost to herself.

I brace, waiting for whatever explosion is justifiably coming my way.

But all I get is a very dignified, "Thank you for your honesty."

Wow. She is so much more elegant than I am.

"No problem," I tell her quietly.

More silence.

Elizabeth shakes her head slowly. "I utterly loathe you right now."

"You should." Then I ask, "Is there anything I can do to make it up to you in any way?"

Elizabeth looks at me, an idea percolating in her mind. "As a matter of fact, there is." She pulls her phone from her purse and presses speed dial. "Marc, darling, I'm here with an old friend of yours. Natasha, say 'Hello.'" She hands me the phone.

I slowly take it. "Hey, Marc."

I hear a sigh on his end, followed by "Christ."

"So I'm going to guess you didn't really ask her for a divorce," I say.

"I can explain . . ."

I hand Elizabeth back her phone. "He's all yours."

Elizabeth walks out of the bar, saying into her phone, "So you told her you were getting divorced? Well, I should think that won't be a problem . . ."

We all stare in silence to see the front door close and Elizabeth step into a waiting black limousine.

I finally let out a breath, grab my stomach, and nearly fall over. Holly quickly walks up to me and rubs my back. "You did the right thing."

"Yeah. Finally," I say, still ready to pass out from nerves. "For a moment there, I really thought she'd come after me. I'd've come after me. I'd've punched me dead in the face."

"No . . ." Jessie says. "You wouldn't have done that."

"If some woman slept with my man? Are you kidding me?"

"No. You're so sweet, though," Jessie tells me, and she walks up to me and starts stroking my hair (!). "You of all people would understand that sometimes people make mistakes. And they would do anything they could to make up for their mistakes. I mean, you're such a loving, good, forgiving person . . ."

I swat her hand away from my hair. "Okay, seriously, what is with you today? How many Diet Red Bulls have you had?"

Jess backs away from me very quickly, then heads behind the bar. "I slept with Giovanni," she admits.

"What?" I exclaim.

Jessie puts up her hands in prayer. "I'm sorry. I'm sorry. Please don't kill me. I did a horrible thing, and I want to fix it. How can I fix it?"

Somewhere near me I can hear Joe whisper to Holly, "Let me get this straight . . . you're the one with the freak flag?"

Holly shushes him.

I begin pacing. "Are you? . . ." I can't finish the sentence. I pace again, then stop. "How could . . ." Still at a loss. More pacing. "I can't . . ."

Jessie begins vomiting words. "I thought you broke up with him. You left this really rambling message on his voice mail . . ."

"You listened to my messages on his voice mail?!"

"Not intentionally. Well, I mean, yes, intentionally. But only because he asked me to when he picked me up for the fund-raiser. And yes, I did listen to them again afterward, but only once he was asleep, because . . ."

"Oh! My! God!" I yell.

Jessie stutters a bit, "I swear it sounded like you were breaking up with him."

"So even if I was, you're supposed to be my friend. Couldn't you at least wait for the body get cold?"

She winces. "Apparently not?" Then she tries to crack a joke. "You know, the whole warm body thing is kind of funny in this case because . . . I'm shutting up now."

I take a deep breath to calm myself. "I need a minute," I say, then point to Jessie. "I can't even look at you right now. Holly, can you cover for me? I'm gonna go to the back room and take five."

I storm over to the storage area, open the door, and slam it behind me.

I hear the door open and turn to see Chris's hand in the doorway, waving a white cloth napkin as a flag of surrender.

I roll my eyes. "You can only come in if you don't take her side."

He pops his head in. "I would never." Then he walks in and shuts the door. "Although, can you imagine the points you'll get for the rest of your life if you just admit this wasn't the guy you wanted anyway and let her have him? I mean, seriously, change-your-diaper-in-the-nursing-home kind of points."

"You cheat on boyfriends. You don't cheat on your girlfriends."

"Yeah, we're going to be circling back to that at some point," he tells me. "But for now . . ."

"Hos before bros."

"That will never catch on."

"She . . ."

"Did you try to break up with Giovanni over voice mail?"

I cross my arms. "That's not the point."

"Have you been kissing me for the last forty-eight hours?"

"Wait. So now I'm the bad guy?"

"Of course not. But did you ever sleep with him? Or meet his parents? Or go away for the weekend together?"

Chris could go on, but he doesn't need to. We stand face-to-face, neither of us moving. "Jessie's still out there," Chris says.

I sigh. Loudly. "But I don't want to do the right thing twice in the same day."

Chris gives me a kiss on the lips. "I promise to make it worth your while later."

We hear a very quiet knock on the door. "Come in," I tell Jessie.

She opens the door. "I swear I will find a way to make this up to you."

I still want to tell her I feel betrayed. But I'm not exactly one to throw stones. "I know."

She stands awkwardly in the doorway. "What can I do?"

Argh . . . I don't want to be the grown-up. I have every reason in the world to feel betrayed and wronged right now. But I tell her, "You can go to Santa Barbara with him and have that twelve-course meal."

Her face relaxes and she brightens. "Really?"

"Yeah," I continue. "I'm not eating braised blood sausage, I don't care what sauce it's served with it. Food should be like men: Don't eat it unless you really want it."

Jess breaks out into a huge grin and she runs up to me, "Awwww . . ."

"Don't . . ."

Too late. She hugs me so hard I yelp, "My hand!"

"Sorry." And then she continues to hug, but not quite so hard. I hug back, but less enthusiastically.

"That's another thing we'll be circling back to," Chris jokes.

"Shut up."

I suppose if the worst thing your girlfriend ever does is date your ex, you should consider yourself lucky.

And at least I never have to go to the opera ever again.

Two years later . . .

Epilogue

On the morning of my dad's birthday, Joe and I wake up very early, load Dad's old kayak onto the roof of Joe's car, and head down to Newport Harbor.

We launch the kayak as the sun begins to rise.

Neither of us says anything as we row out past the rocks of the jetty and over to the buoy. There is almost no wind, which I have already learned is an important part of the process. (As Joe's mom pointed out to me from scattering her husband's ashes, there is nothing more confusing than what to do when a few ashes lightly blow back onto you and cake your lipstick.)

I take a deep breath, then open Dad's urn. I pull out the bag of ashes and rest the bag on the side of the boat.

"Okay, Dad. It took me awhile, but I'm finally doing it."

I open the bag and look at the ashes. This is harder than I thought it was going to be. I look up at the sky. "You know, I'd really like a sign that I'm doing the right thing, though. I mean, I know you said you wanted an ocean burial. But maybe in your afterlife you changed your mind. Maybe you want me to get you a nice drawer at the

Hollywood Cemetery where I could visit you. Or that place in Westwood where Marilyn Monroe is buried. You liked her."

I take a small plastic shovel I bought just for this occasion and begin to spread the ashes out over the water. Some of the ashes become airborne and form a whitish-gray cloud over the water. Others, particularly the teeny shards of pulverized bone, sink immediately. I continue to talk to my dad. "Now, I'm sure you'll think this is morbid, but I took a few of your ashes and turned them into a diamond. And I also sent some ashes to your sister. But, like, a tablespoon's worth. You won't even miss them. I hope it wasn't your penis ashes or anything. That would be weird."

About half the ashes are already gone, sinking to the bottom of the sea where I can never get to them again. Did I do the right thing? I turn to Joe, who smiles at me supportively.

Then I continue my one-sided conversation with Dad. "So maybe I'll keep this other half, just for a little while. Until I know for sure you really want an ocean—"

Suddenly a seal bursts out of the water and tries to jump into our kayak. A very heavy seal.

I scream. Joe tries to gently push it off with his oar. The seal (I just remembered, she's a sea lion—I learned that at the aquarium) starts chatting with us like we're old friends, "Uhr, uhr, uhr!"

"Go away! Get out of here!" I yell to the seal. "Not the time!" Then I look at Joe and yell in panic, "Oh, God! Don't sharks hunt sea lions?!"

"You've swum with sharks," Joe points out.

"Not the ones who hunt sea lions! Oh, now I'm hearing *Jaws* in my head!"

The sea lion dives into the water and disappears.

And all is quiet again.

Joe and I sit in the kayak for a while, looking deep into the water to search for the sea lion and trying to get our bearings. Celia (I've decided to call her Celia) pops her head up out of the water but this time just nuzzles the front of the boat.

And I start laughing.

"Are you okay?" Joe asks sympathetically from behind me, rubbing my shoulder. I think he thinks I'm crying.

"I'm fine," I say, now starting to laugh so hard tears are glistening in my eyes. I yell into the air, "I get it, Dad! I get it!"

I take the bag, put it over the water, and turn it over, dumping the rest of Dad's ashes into the sea. I pull a few roses out of my bag, give each one a kiss, place them on top of the water, and watch them float. Finally, I blow a kiss into the air. "Thank you for being an amazing person, and an amazing parent, and giving me a great life. I love you more than you will ever know."

Joe and I spend the next few minutes in silence as I watch the small ash cloud dissipate and the flowers float away. We watch our sea lion dive deep into the water, then pop up with a fish. Celia looks at me, and her eyes look the eyes of the Dalmatian I had as a kid.

I turn to Joe. "Can we keep her?"

"Not sure my pool is big enough."

I laugh a little—more smiling than laughing. "Okay, let's head back. We've got a lot to do today."

And we slowly row back into the harbor, Celia following us the whole way. She swims with us all the way to the dock, and as we disembark, I'm sure she's trying to figure out a way to climb on the dock and go home with us.

There really is a part of me that wants to keep her.

I drop Joe off at home and make it to the bar around noon, having promised Nat that I'd come in early to help decorate for the party tonight.

Three weeks ago, Nat and Chris got married in a small ceremony at the Hotel del Coronado, with just family and friends. Her colors were red and white, and we made many jokes about how she'd be serving wine at the reception in those colors.

They went on a lavish honeymoon, touring much of Europe and hitting all the great museums—and not one vineyard.

Tonight, Jessie and I are throwing a big party for them at the bar, with the help of the staff we've been slowly hiring over the last couple years.

That staff has become crucial, because a lot has changed in two years. For one thing, we now own two wine bars: Wine for All and our newest endeavor, Love the Wine You're With, out in Highland Park. We also have a third place, Hollywood and Wine, opening in Hollywood later this month. So business is booming.

Despite our success, Jessie has not been putting in nearly the amount of hours she used to. And what hours she does work seem to be at home with the business paperwork and marketing plans—she only tends bar two nights a week these days.

I park in my designated spot in the back and walk in to see Nat in jeans, a baby on her hip, pointing to a corner of the bar as she instructs one of our guys, "Just string the lights sparsely. We want twinkling, not glaring."

"Hey, Mrs. Washington," I call to her.

Nat turns, smiles brightly at me, and walks over with the baby. "Hey. You're early."

"Well, I was up early running errands," I tell her, then make a silly face for the baby as I ask her in baby talk, "Hello, Isabella, you beautiful girl. Where's your momma?"

"Jessie went to pick up the cake," Nat answers. "I said I needed a little snuggle time with my goddaughter." She gives Isabella a light kiss. "Do I have you for the whole afternoon?" she asks me.

"You do indeed."

"Awesome. There shouldn't be too much to do, though. Caterers come at five, and we're not having seating charts or anything, so it's mostly decorating."

"Behind!" I hear Jessie yell from our back door. "And a little help here!"

I trot over to see Jessie trying to balance and lug a two-tiered wedding cake inside by herself. I quickly grab one of the sides, and the two of us sidestep into the great room.

"Wow, that looks amazing!" Nat says, looking at the white buttercream-frosted confection swimming in dark red and white roses. "Do you think we'll have enough cake, though?"

"The groom's cake is in the car," Jessie tells Nat as we practically toss the cake onto a large wooden table. "It's a dark chocolate cake with raspberry filling, shaped like a giant beer bottle."

"That's the one," Nat says. "Did I mention how many breweries we toured when we were in Germany?" She hands Jessie the baby, then runs out to get the groom's cake. A minute later, she places the large one-tiered cake on the table next to the wedding cake.

"Well, what do you think?"

"It's perfect," Jessie says. "A little tradition, a little whimsy."

"Sooo . . . Basically nothing like us," Nat says.

I furrow my brow. "Did you really just use the word 'whimsy'?"

As Jessie shrugs, Nat claps her hands once. "Okay, now that you're both here, I have a surprise." She makes her way to the bar and walks behind it. "We picked up the most amazing bottle when we were in Champagne." Nat disappears behind the bar, pulling the bottle from our small wine fridge below, then pops back up. "I dragged it from train to train and flight to flight just so the three of us could toast before the party."

Nat takes off the cage, puts a cloth over the bottle, and . . . *pop!*

"I can only have a glass," Jessie says. "Still breast-feeding."

"No problem," Nat says, pulling down some flutes from the wooden overhang. She yells out to a few of our employees working on lights, "Alejandro, Kate, a little bubbly?"

They both say yes, so Nat pulls down two more flutes.

When she gets to pouring the fifth flute, I instinctively throw my hand over the glass. "Just water for me."

Nat's jaw drops and Jessie screams in delight.

I clarify. "It's nothing. I'm just on some antibiotics."

Nat mock-chastises, "You are such a liar." While Jessie simultaneously asks, "Can I throw your baby shower?"

"Wait," Nat says. "But didn't you drink at my wedding?"

I smile and shake my head. "Nope. I was pretty stealthy about it. I drank orange juice and soda water."

Jessie's face lights up. "Why, you little sneak. So how far along are you?"

I pull out a small black-and-white picture to show two little babies swimming happily. "This far along."

"Twins?!" Jessie and Nat scream simultaneously while jumping up and down.

And to paraphrase the ending of a story I had to read in an AP English class (though apparently Jessie didn't):

And they lived happily ever after.

The End